Praise for *The Curse of King Midas:*

"Colleen M. Story has woven a spellbinding tale of revenge, magic, and redemption. I was captivated by the characters, the mythology, and the thrilling rollercoaster of the plot. This first book in Story's mythological fantasy series will stay with you long after you turn the final page."

~ Beth Castrodale, award-winning author of *Marion Hatley, In This Ground,* and *I Mean You No Harm*

"Filled with unexpected twists and heartrending sacrifices, *The Curse of King Midas* spins an expertly woven tale with a rich cast of characters that had me laughing one minute and crying the next. I've been in a horrible book slump for months, but I breezed through this with ease. It tugged at my heart and made me look forward to reading every night before bed (I stayed up way too late more than once). It's the sort of story that lingers long after it's finished."

~ Jinx Moreland, creator of "Oregon Family Adventures"

"Colleen M. Story's epic, *The Curse of King Midas*—the first in The Midas Legacy—offers a tapestry of legend and myth intertwined with plenty of action, Greek tragedy-like drama, and blood-thirsty revenge. This tale of a wish gone horribly awry is imaginatively rich in characterization and setting, and will captivate readers of all ages."

~ Sharon Ledwith, author of *The Last Timekeepers* time travel adventure series

"This book kept me glued to my laptop screen! The desires of each character are tightly woven into a spidery web of intrigue, twisting and turning at every angle, spun so masterfully, that I felt like prey advancing along each silky strand of plot, unable to breathe, wondering what predatory twist would jump out at me next."

~ Janet Wagner, Independent Academic tutor

"Intrigue, mystery, suspense and revenge—this story has it all. It grabs you and does not let go. The plot and characters pull you in until you are fully immersed in the saga of King Midas and his battle against his mortal enemy King Sargon. Every character has a story to tell and their stories are so intertwined, they come head to head in battle and you find yourself holding your breath waiting to see who emerges on top. Ms. Story's style of writing brings each character to life and you will find yourself fully invested in to what happens to each one of them and how each wages their own personal battle. There is so much more to this story and I personally can not wait to see what happens next."
~ Taffy L. Homyak, Pre-K Teacher

"Not many people are fortunate enough to have a last name that echoes their calling, but in the case of Colleen M. Story, it's a perfect match—she can create an extraordinary story! I consider myself a vivacious reader, and few authors I have seen can craft a tapestry of plot and narrative as skillfully as Colleen can. I was enthralled by this story from start to finish. Do yourself a favor and immerse yourself in the world of *The Curse of King Midas*."
~ Andrew G. Hansen, Creative Writing Instructor

"Embark on an exhilarating journey into a meticulously crafted world by Colleen M. Story, where the captivating themes of King Midas' mythology, revenge, and redemption converge in a mesmerizing narrative. Prepare to be riveted by a story that transcends the ordinary, leaving an everlasting impact on your imagination. Your next epic fantasy awaits."
~ R. J. Jeffries, award-winning poet, writer, editor at Tiferet Journal and Co-Host/Producer Author2Author Interviews

"In "The Curse of King Midas," Colleen Story crafts her own mythos around the historical King Midas, remaining faithful to both historical accounts and the Greek myth that immortalized him. The story is expertly weaved together from multiple viewpoints, including Midas himself, his adversary King Sargon, the prince and princess, his three comical advisors, a vengeful goddess and a host of other vibrant characters. The book unfolds at a deliberate pace, drawing the reader into the worlds of each character—revealing their motives, fears and desires—building towards the culmination of the king's wish . . . . Just when readers believe they have a firm grasp on what happens next, another layer of detail in a character's story emerges, upending all expectations. However, even as the main dilemma reaches a satisfying conclusion, Story entices readers with lingering questions and unresolved mysteries, perpetuating the legend of King Midas and leaving them eagerly anticipating the next installment in the series."

~ Cloie Sandlin, award-winning editor and journalist

"Everyone has heard about the plight of King Midas, but Story brings it to life in a unique and refreshing way. 'The Curse of King Midas' humanizes the myth in a way that made my heart ache for the unfortunate situations that Midas found himself in, but also allowed me to see the dangerous sides of his greed and selfishness. A great read for lovers of Greek mythology, ancient history, and those that love a good tale of revenge."

~ The Book Nerd's Corner, Reader and Book Reviewer

"Story excels in creating action-packed scenarios that are thoroughly engrossing . . .This will prove attractive to a wide range of readers, from those interested in stories built from new historical discoveries to others who just want a rollicking good read replete with myth, magic, and entwined lives, that exhibits rich and satisfying twists and turns of experience and intention. "

~ D. Donovan, Senior Reviewer, Midwest Book Review

THE CURSE OF KING MIDAS

Also by Colleen M. Story

FICTION

Rise of the Sidenah

Loreena's Gift

The Beached Ones

NONFICTION

Overwhelmed Writer Rescue

Writer Get Noticed!

Your Writing Matters

For more information, please see:

colleenmstory.com

writingandwellness.com

COLLEEN M. STORY

THE CURSE *of* KING MIDAS

THE MIDAS LEGACY BOOK 1

MIDCHANNEL PRESS

This book is a work of fiction. References to real people, events, establishments, or locales are intended only to provide a sense of authenticity, and are used fictitiously. All other characters, and all other incidents and dialogue, are drawn from the author's imagination and are not to be construed as real.

Books may be ordered through booksellers or by contacting the publisher at:

Midchannel Press
P.O. Box 131
Iona, ID 83427 www.midchannelpress.com
Email: publisher@midchannelpress.com

To receive Colleen M. Story's email newsletter, register directly at www.colleenmstory.com. Writers may prefer her writing newsletter at www.writingandwellness.com/newsletter.

Cover Design: Damonza.com

Map by: BMR Williams

Ebook ISBN 978-0-9990991-6-2
Hardcover ISBN 978-0-9990991-7-9
Audiobook ISBN 978-0-9990991-8-6
Paperback ISBN 978-0-9990991-9-3

Library-of-Congress Control Number: 2023924534

Originally published in hardcover in the United States by Midchannel Press in 2024.

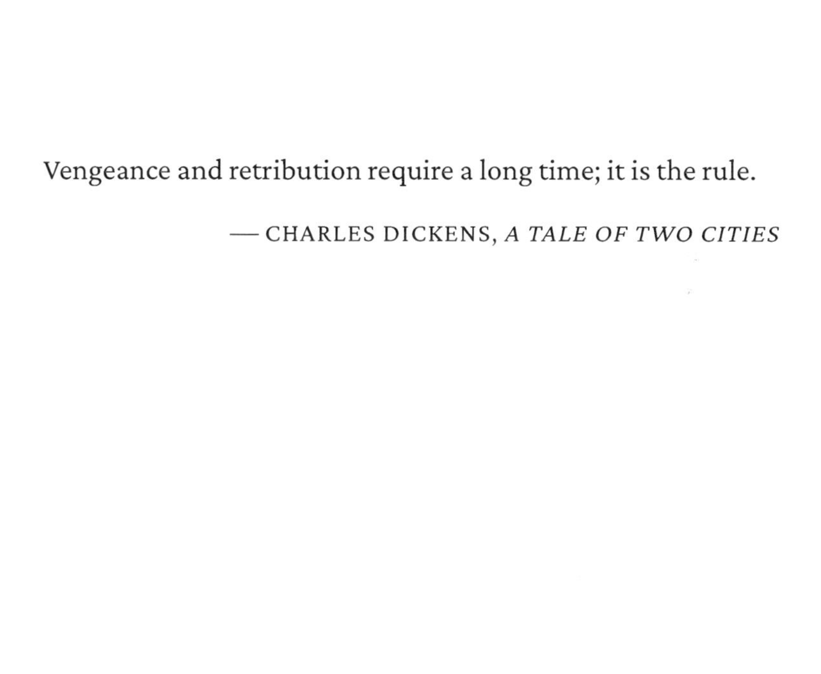

Vengeance and retribution require a long time; it is the rule.

— CHARLES DICKENS, *A TALE OF TWO CITIES*

Note from the Author

Originally recorded and dramatized by the Greeks, the tale of King Midas and his golden touch has entertained audiences for centuries. But many remain unaware that the real King Midas ruled the kingdom of Phrygia—what is now part of Turkey—in the eighth century B.C.

Until fairly recently, we knew little about Midas beyond the myths. Some Assyrian texts and Greek records mentioned him, but it seems any Phrygian writings perished. Then, in 1893, German classical philologist Alfred Körte visited a location on the Sangarius (today's Sakarya) River where engineers working on the Berlin-Baghdad railroad had discovered an ancient settlement. He identified it as the city of Gordium (Gordion on current maps), the capital and largest city of Phrygia.

Seven years later, Alfred and his brother Gustav returned and spent three months excavating the site. No further exploration occurred until the 1950s, when excavations resumed under the sponsorship of the University of Pennsylvania. Archaeologists now believe that King Midas ruled Gordium at the height of Phrygian power in the eighth century. Research at the site is ongoing at the time of this writing.

Did history impact the King Midas myth? From my research, I couldn't find a definite answer. *The Curse of King Midas* is an imagining of what King Midas' life might have been like were myth and archeological evidence combined.

THE BLACK SEA
SCYTHIANS
THRACE
URARTU
CIMMERIANS
SANGARIUS R.
Gordium
Ancyra
THE AEGEAN SEA
LYDIA
Sardis
Athens
PHRYGIA
Karama
Durukin
ASSYRIA
GREEK CITY STATES
THE MEDITERRANEAN SEA
N
W
E
S
716 BC

PROLOGUE

750 BC—in the hills far north of the Assyrian Empire

Karem strolled into camp, proudly carrying a dead rabbit by its back feet. His hunt had been successful, and he couldn't wait to show Mama. He found her stirring stew in a large ceramic pot. It swayed from a spit outside their tent, the food filling the camp with its savory scents. He got a curt nod of approval as he walked by and smiled. He'd done well. He made quick work of skinning and hanging the meat and returned to watch the pale parsnips, pungent onions, and savory meat roil in the bubbles. The morsels appeared and disappeared in the broth with each stroke of Mama's wooden spoon, steam rising to dampen his chin. He wished she'd offer him a taste, but she pressed her thin lips together, too focused on her task. A drop of perspiration hung precariously from her nose before she brushed it away with the back of her hand.

Little Elanur played with her doll on a blanket nearby, her tanned legs stretched straight out, bare heels extending into the dirt.

She was like sunshine, Mama always said, so using safflower petals, she'd dyed the blanket the same yellow color. Elanur had adopted the word as her doll's name, mispronouncing it "Sunsine" in her baby talk.

"Mama, Sunsine go da-dah eee!" she said as she made the doll dance.

"Yes, my sweetheart, I see." Mama concentrated on the stew.

Elanur called out again, and Karem turned. She smiled at him. Then she laughed, and he laughed with her.

Yes. Like sunshine.

THE END of it all began with a distant shout.

Karem didn't pay it much attention at first—the stew was too tempting. Then came another shout, followed by another. A woman called for her children, her voice high and tight. From somewhere off to the east came the rumble of horses' hooves.

Mama paused her stirring and turned to look behind her, her gaze surveying the camp. The broth boiled faster, the bubbles popping and snapping. Elanur stopped her chatter and held her doll to her chest. More shouts. Anxious voices. Black tendrils of smoke ribboned into the southern sky. Yellow-orange tongues of flame licked the tops of two distant tents, more consuming the roof of the goat shelter.

"The gods have left us," Mama whispered. She dropped the spoon, leaving it to sink into the broth. One of the few men who hadn't gone on the hunt ran past, warning everyone to gather weapons. Mama darted inside the tent. Karem followed. Crouching low, Mama dug into his father's chest, the one Karem and Elanur were forbidden to touch. She tossed aside folded clothing, a bow and arrow, and a belt before whipping out Father's old iron dagger. The blade was long and threatening, the wooden handle darkened from use. It had been many seasons since Karem had seen it—since he'd seen his father.

"Take your sister to the trees and hide." Mama grabbed Karem's shoulder, her thick fingers digging into his skin. "Don't come out until the attackers are gone."

The crackle of flames snapped in his ears. Someone screamed outside.

"Ride Halime."

The donkey?

"Are you listening?" Mama wrapped his cloak around him. "You must go quickly."

Elanur appeared at the tent's opening with her doll clasped in her arms. Mama pulled her in and prepared her for the journey, her fingers flying over sleeves and ties. She retrieved some dried meat and cheese from the storage bin, stuffed them into a leather satchel, and hung it over Karem's shoulder.

Another scream tore through the air, followed by approaching hoofbeats. Mama gave them both a brief hug. Then she gripped the dagger and ushered them out. "Go."

Karem grasped Elanur's hand in his and headed out back where the donkey waited in a small corral. He kept his head craned around with his gaze on Mama. She remained in front of the tent, holding the dagger aloft.

"Mama?" Elanur reached back, fingers outstretched.

"Go!" Mama said.

Other villagers blurred past them, women and children scattering into the flatlands while a handful of men took up posts at the perimeter. Karem untied Halime. The donkey pulled the rope taut, her head up and eyes wild. Karem boosted Elanur onto the animal's back.

"Hold on!" he said. He leapt up behind Elanur and, with the rope in his hand, scanned for Mama. She was coming toward them, a bag over her shoulder. He urged Halime forward and then jerked back, pulling the animal to a halt. A soldier dressed all in black trotted up beside Karem's tent. He paused and looked in their direction. A lion's head decorated the apex of his helmet, his bronze armor gleaming on his chest, long dark hair flowing over his shoulders. He hesitated a moment, as if deciding what to do next, then with a slight flick of his wrist, directed the horse toward them.

"Mama!" Karem pointed.

Mama turned. Spotting the soldier, she glanced at Karem in alarm. "Hurry! To the trees. Protect your sister!" She dropped the bag and, with the dagger aloft, stood directly in the soldier's path. "Go, Karem!" she screamed. "Do not fail me!"

Karem hesitated as the soldier lifted his gaze. Dark eyes bore into Karem's, sending a jolt of adrenaline through his limbs.

"Now!" Mama barked.

Karem released the tension on the rope, and the donkey launched into a bouncing gallop. Karem clenched his knees to the animal's shoulders and his arms around Elanur to keep her steady as Halime hurried away from camp. Behind him, the soldier stopped in front of Mama and pointed his sword at her chest. Karem yelled for her to run, but Mama bent forward at the waist and let loose a screech Karem had never expected could come from her throat.

"Mama!" Karem yelled.

He pulled back, but Halime would not be swayed. Panicked, the animal ran flat out toward the trees, the smoke and tents soon concealing any sight of Mama. Up the hill they went, the sure-footed donkey maneuvering easily between the rocks. When they reached the forest's edge, Karem pulled on the rope again, but it wasn't until the pines had surrounded them that the animal began to tire and slow. Finally, she plunked to a stop, nearly sending the children tumbling over her head.

Karem slid off. Elanur reached out. "Stay on Halime," Karem said. The donkey's muscles were trembling, her breath blowing fast through her nostrils. Karem patted her sweaty neck and spoke soothing words. Then he started walking back the way they had come, the rope clenched in his fist.

"Mama!" Elanur cried.

Karem kept his gaze down, navigating the ferns and fallen trunks until he neared the edge of the forest. There, he hovered behind an evergreen, peering between its long branches. He could see the smoke-filled camp. Gray plumes rose high into the sky like ghostly warnings. Five soldiers remained around the perimeter. A sixth carried a blue flag that fluttered behind him as he galloped past the burning tents with his voice raised in a battle cry. At least ten more had gathered in a group on the east side, surrounding and imprisoning a cluster of children who cried for their mothers. Other soldiers gathered the villagers' horses or herded the remaining goats away.

Elanur whined behind him, murmuring "Mama" over and over again. Karem wanted to get closer to find out if Mother had escaped, but he dared not. He had to keep his sister safe. He tied Halime to the tree, lifted Elanur off, and huddled with her at the base of the trunk.

"It will be all right. We'll see Mama soon."

WHEN THE SUN came up the next morning, Karem observed the camp once more. He could see no trace of the enemy, so he put Elanur on Halime's back and left the safety of the trees behind. A cloud of smoke hovered over the massacre, but the fires had mostly burned out. A few tents stood like skeletons, their hide coverings reduced to ash. Karem whispered to Elanur to keep quiet, but even at her young age, she didn't need the warning. She watched Karem as she clutched her doll close.

At the sight of the first dead body in the distance, Karem searched for somewhere to secure the donkey. An old post remained upright near an outlying shelter. He tied the rope around it and pulled his sister off Halime's back.

"You stay here."

"Mama?"

"I'm going to look for her. Hold on to Halime, all right?"

Elanur clenched Halime's rope in her little hand.

"That's right. I'll be back." He turned away.

"Karem."

Karem whirled. She'd never said his name before. She waved at him, her dark hair playing about her head in wispy ribbons, her lips red and chapped. "Karem," she said again and wiggled the doll's arm.

"Yes. And you . . ." He pointed. "You are Elanur."

She pointed to herself and then to the doll.

"Yes. That's Sunshine."

Elanur studied the doll's face made of lamb's hide with shiny black beads for eyes. "Sunsine."

"Stay there. I'll be right back." He crouched low and began jogging toward the camp.

"Sunsine. Karem."

At nine years old, he had helped prepare slaughtered animals for food. He'd seen prisoners die, enemies his father had slain before he'd left for battle and never returned. But he hadn't encountered carnage like this—humans cut up and left to spoil in the sun. The first was the man who had stayed home from the hunt because of a leg injury. He now lay face down, his wrapped leg the only thing identifying him. The second was the younger man charged with protecting the camp, the one who had warned everyone to get weapons. They had left him face up, his vacant eyes focused on the sky. A third, smaller figure, near one of the burnt tents, appeared crumpled and broken as if they had thrown it there. Karem cautiously lifted the cloak. A mean cut sliced open her flesh from the cheek to the neck. His stomach roiled, and he retched onto the ground beside her.

He threw up twice more while checking bodies before there was nothing left in his stomach to expel. By the time he neared the area where their shelter had been, his legs were shaky, sweaty skin sticky under his clothes.

Where was Mama? He had almost convinced himself she had gotten away when a piece of yellow fabric caught his eye. Elanur's blanket. A plaything in the morning breeze, it lay half trapped under a body lying on its side, the rest blowing over the top of the torso and head. Familiar brown sandals protected the feet.

Tears fell down his cheeks. He needed to go closer, but dreaded what he would find. A lone goat bleated behind him. He spotted it not far from what had been Halime's shelter. A young doe, she bleated again but dared not venture out to find her herd mates. He wiped his face with his sleeve and approached the figure under the blanket.

"Mama?"

A breeze ruffled the folds in Mama's skirt. He walked around the sandals and knelt down. With a trembling hand, he pulled the yellow blanket down.

"Mama!"

Her eyes were closed, her cheeks pale. He combed her hair back before tucking it behind her ear the way she always did. Her skin felt cold and stiff.

"Mama, wake up. I have Elanur. We're all right. Mama!"

He shook her shoulder, and everything else moved, even her hip and foot. He withdrew his hand and cried until his eyes stung. He might have stayed forever if it weren't for the thought of Elanur waiting for him. Mama had told him to take care of her.

What if the soldiers returned?

Folding back the blanket, he found Mama still held the dagger. Dried blood covered the blade. She had wounded whoever had killed her. The vision of the young soldier flashed through his mind. *Brave Mama.* Crying again, he slipped the wooden handle out of her stiff fingers, smoothed her hair once more, and got to his feet.

He didn't know how long he stood there. He didn't want to leave Mama by herself. But Elanur was alone too. Mama would want him to check on her. He forced himself to explore what remained of their tent. Inside, a few things had survived—some bowls and utensils, the stone his mother used to grind grain into flour, his father's trunk, and some tools. The food, though, which he had hoped for, was only ash and dust. They'd have to get by on what Mama had packed inside the satchel.

He exited the tent and cast one last look at Mama. New tears spilled down his cheeks. He gripped the dagger tightly and walked away to get Elanur. They would ride to the next village. They would find shelter. It was all up to him now.

He moved with his head down, sniffling. As he passed the last burnt tent, he tried to summon his courage. He had to be like Father, he told himself. Strong. And brave, like Mama. The wind whipped past him, drying his cheeks.

"Karem!"

He jerked his head up. Halime remained where he'd left her, the donkey's short body dwarfed by a strapping sorrel stallion standing beside her. The beast was impressive, with muscles glistening in the morning sun and mighty hindquarters set to spring. The young soldier on his back wore a helmet with a lion carved into the apex. It was the one who had attacked Karem's mother. He'd placed Elanur on the saddle in front of him, where her little legs stretched to either side, her arms resting helplessly on the soldier's sleeves.

"Karem!" she called, pointing to the doll on the ground below. "Sunsine!"

The soldier nudged his horse forward. As the mighty beast approached, Karem had a powerful urge to run, but he couldn't leave Elanur. He slipped his father's dagger into his belt at the small of his back, dropped his shirt over it, and readied himself for what was to come.

The soldier stopped and drew his sword. "So, you've returned, donkey boy." He smirked. "Join us or die."

Elanur's lower lip protruded, her dark eyes fixed alternately on her brother and the ground where the doll lay.

"What say you?" The soldier pushed the sword toward Karem's chest.

Be brave. Karem looked up into the soldier's eyes. "Who are you?"

"I am the one who conquered your village. One day, I will be a great king. They will call me King Sargon II, after the legendary leader of the Akkadian Empire. Like him, I will rule over all these lands." He stretched his hand out, gesturing to the wide horizon. "I have defeated you and your people. Since you are a boy—a stupid coward of a boy who ran away—but a boy, I offer you one last chance for your life. Follow me or die here like the rest of your pitiful camp."

Sargon. Karem repeated the name in his mind. He imagined rushing the soldier and rescuing Elanur, but he knew he'd be sliced in two before he got there. "Why did you attack us?"

Sargon sat up straight and then winced, favoring his right side. Karem noticed a small tear in his tunic and dried blood underneath. *Had Mama given him that wound?*

"We are conquerors," Sargon said. "I will see you surrender."

Elanur reached for the doll. "Karem," she said.

Karem felt his own features crumble. He looked down, made his face stony, and lifted his gaze to the soldier.

"You killed my mother."

"And, it seems, I have your sister." Sargon patted Elanur's head.

Ice ran through Karem's veins. He stared at his ash-stained sandals. Everything was gone now. Everything and everyone. Worse, this soldier had been the one to take his mother from him. He trudged forward, shifting his arms behind his back and assuming the pose of surrender.

"You have decided well," the soldier said.

The mighty stallion's thick front legs ended in black hooves planted firmly in the dirt. Karem walked past them, stopping when he came near the rider's boot. This close, the soldier appeared younger than before, the bronze armor too big for his shoulders. Karem whisked the dagger out and stabbed it hard into Sargon's thigh.

Sargon howled in pain. Karem reached for Elanur, but Sargon struck out clumsily with his sword. The blade caught Karem's neck and sliced over his chest. He stumbled back. Sargon transferred the sword to his other hand and pulled the dagger out of his leg with a shout. It dripped with his blood. Karem turned and ran. The stallion came thundering after him.

There were no trees to climb, no areas of low ground where he could hide. Ahead lay only a broad stretch of hilly land covered in wild grasses. Blood soaked his shirt, but Karem stayed on his feet. "Elanur," he said, but his voice had little energy and his dagger was gone. Sargon was gaining on him. Karem wasn't going fast enough. The enemy would soon be upon him, and he had no ideas left.

He would be like Mother, face down in the dirt.

A FULL MOON gleamed brightly overhead, casting the stars into shadow. Karem shivered, his fingers stiff with cold. He raised his hand to his chest and touched dried blood. The horror returned in a rush. The soldier. Mama. Elanur. He pressed his hands into the dirt and sat up.

"There you are."

A shadowed figure lingered nearby. Perched on a high stool, she had her back to him, her blue gown sparkling as if it had captured the stars themselves within its seams.

"I wondered if you had the strength." She peered over her shoulder at him.

Never had he seen such a woman. Her fair skin was flawless. Dark eyes framed by lovely arched brows lingered on him, her silky black hair cascading in waves past her bare shoulders. Even more of a marvel was the white light emanating from her body, as if she were made of the moon itself.

"The soldiers are long gone." She rotated toward him, her dress clinging to her breasts as if it were part of them. "The last one took the little girl, too."

"You saw her?"

The woman stroked an animal he hadn't noticed before. It stood at her side, tall enough that its head rose above the seat of her stool, its haunting blue eyes focused on him. A wolf, it looked like, though it was taller, its coat as black as the night. Its ears were longer too, like a horse's ears, pointed and thin.

"I thought you might want this." The woman held up Elanur's doll. Karem's chest tightened. *Sunshine.* The woman slid off the stool and approached, her body rolling like waves in a river. She came until she was so close that her light was almost blinding. Her scent wafted toward him, sweet like evergreen leaves in the rain.

"What is your name?" she asked.

"Karem."

"I am Katiah." She straightened a clump of hair that remained on the doll's head. "Some call me by different names, but your people prefer Katiah. Truthfully, it's my favorite." She smiled at him, then pointed. "I found you over there."

Karem looked behind him. A figure his size lay on the cold ground.

"Tell me, Karem. Have you been told of the underworld?"

He nodded.

"So, you know. That's where some people go when they die."

A thought occurred to him. "Mama?"

"She is on her journey. It's possible you could join her."

Karem's heart leapt in his chest. See Mama again! But then his gaze fell on the doll. "Elanur?"

"She lives, in the possession of the young soldier."

Karem grimaced, closing his eyes. *Sargon.*

"Tell me something, Karem. Do you want to rescue her?"

He didn't have to think about it. He nodded.

"And does your heart long for revenge against this soldier who killed your mother and stole your sister?"

He nodded again, clenching his fist.

She cocked her head, studying him. "If you really want it, you must be willing to sacrifice for it."

"He killed Mother. For no reason." Karem blinked, his eyes stinging. "He took Elanur. She was my responsibility."

Katiah extended her hand to him, the strange wolf-like creature observing from a few steps back. "Beg me for your life, Karem, that you may have your revenge. Promise to worship your goddess Katiah for all your life, to honor her in every way, to share her name with all you meet." She raised her other hand toward the sky. "Beg the goddess Katiah for a chance to save your sister, and I will grant it."

She gestured once more to the figure on the ground. Karem walked toward it, sweat breaking out over the back of his neck. He peered down at the boy. A long wound stretched from the neck to the chest where blood stained the shirt and pooled underneath. When he glanced back, the goddess was there, waiting.

Karem rushed toward her and dropped to his knees. "Please, beautiful goddess. I must save Elanur. Mother told me to keep her safe. I failed." His voice caught. "I left her alone, and he took her. It was my fault. Please, Goddess Katiah. Give me my life so that I may have another chance."

"You will worship me always?"

"Always."

"Remember your promise, little king."

Karem frowned, puzzled. King? When he looked up, the goddess had lifted her arms. Bright streaks of moonlight rained down from the sky. She spoke words he didn't understand, the light expanding around her. His instinct was to flee, but he resisted, letting the glow encircle him. Its beams warmed his limbs as Katiah's words filled his ears. Gradually, he rose into the air, floated over the boy's body, and then dropped back down into it. He felt a mighty crash, a rumbling of the earth, and then a searing pain in his neck and chest. He cried out for what seemed like forever until everything went quiet.

When he opened his eyes, the sun had returned. The goddess was gone, and so was the pain. He touched his chest, but his shirt had been repaired. The skin underneath held only a long, thin scar. By his side rested Elanur's doll, discarded in a crumpled heap. Clutching it to him, he stood up and scanned the area. He was alone. Beyond, the camp lay deathly still, the smoke dissipating into the new day. At its edge, Halime stood tied to the post.

"Goddess Katiah?" he called, but there was no answer. He looked to the sky. "Thank you. I will remember my promise." After a few more moments in reverent silence, he retrieved Halime. He would find a nearby village and gather some supplies. Then he would go after Sargon. He would save Elanur. He would have his revenge, in the name of Katiah.

CHAPTER ONE

716 BC (thirty-four years later) on the flatlands between the ancient kingdom of Phrygia and the Assyrian Empire

Prince Anchurus sat atop his muscular blood bay stallion, sword in hand. A vast swath of grassy flatlands surrounded him, a strong breeze blowing his hair back from his face. He was in the thick of battle with no cover in sight. All around him, soldiers fought, the raucous sounds of combat relentless in his ears. Swords clanged, arrows hissed, and axes whumped, their discordant rhythms accompanied by the pained groans and triumphant shouts of men. The prince squinted dust out of his eyes as he surveyed the area, the iron-like scent of blood in his nostrils. He wasn't one to choose battle, but after years of leading men to victory without a single serious injury to himself, he had grown confident in his ability to win.

This time, they'd been at it since sunrise, King Midas seeking to deal King Sargon II a final defeat after vanquishing him several times before. The fighting began on a wide stretch of plain halfway between the kingdom of Phrygia and the Assyrian Empire. There, neither side could find a hiding place or vantage point. All had to rely on raw skill, grit, and the speed of their horses. Anchurus had thought the circumstances would tip the scales in his favor, but King Sargon II had surprised him with more horses and men than before. What Anchurus had thought would be a quick, decisive encounter had dragged on for much of the day.

Recently, however, his men had gained some ground. Sargon's troops were falling back. The surrounding energy intensified, his commanders urging their men to rally. King Midas' army would have their victory.

And then the fog descended upon them.

It was thick and heavy, a mist like one might encounter at sea. Anchurus pushed on at first, certain it would pass. Yet within moments it grew so dense it forced him and his men to a standstill.

"Baran!" Anchurus called to his first commander.

"Over here!" The man's voice came from somewhere on the right. Anchurus could see nothing but gray.

"This way!" Selim, his second commander, called from the left.

Swords clashed up ahead. Anchurus released Ambrose's reins and wiped the sweat off his eyelids. The horse did not leap ahead as usual but stepped gingerly, blowing anxious snorts. An enemy soldier thundered toward them out of the soup, his sword swinging. The prince defended himself with the clash of iron ringing in his ears. He turned as the soldier passed and struck a sound blow to the enemy's back. The man cried out and disappeared into the fog.

"It's too thick, sire!" Baran called.

"Press on!" Anchurus shouted. "Fight!"

Another soldier came out of the gray. At the sight of the prince, he jerked in the saddle and brought his sword around. Anchurus stabbed swiftly before the enemy could strike, pulled his sword free, and moved on. A taller soldier came from the left. Anchurus had just dispatched him when a third, thicker man appeared right behind him. It was fighting unlike the prince had ever experienced. Soldiers faded in and out like spirits. Enemy commanders shouted orders, but the fog ate their words, making it impossible to predict their movements. Over it all hung a strange, sickly sweet scent, the accursed fog persisting. The more Anchurus pressed forward, the more of the enemy's troops he encountered.

He twisted in his saddle. A thickly built soldier emerged from the haze, his sword slashing Ambrose's flesh. The horse squealed as blood oozed onto his shoulder. Anchurus stabbed in retaliation, but the attacker had already disappeared. More came in his wake, leaving the prince no time to check the wound. He fought harder, slicing through torsos and ribs, puncturing faces and legs while praying to the gods his mount would stay strong.

"For Gordium!" he shouted. His men echoed the cry, the clang of swords steady in his ears.

Finally, the fog dissipated, revealing a sight that filled him with dread. Despite the strange weather phenomenon, Sargon's men had organized their offense. By the time the sky turned blue once more, they had nearly surrounded King Midas' army.

Baran and Selim appeared on either side of him. "Sire, we must flee!" Baran shouted.

"This way!" Selim called. "Hurry!"

Anchurus set his jaw and kept pushing forward.

"Sire!" Baran stayed with him. "They have surrounded us. We must go, or Sargon will have a royal prisoner."

Anchurus searched his commander's face. A gifted fighter, Baran was experienced, his forehead sporting deep wrinkles, his black beard thick over a square chin. Beyond, the men faltered around the perimeter as Sargon's soldiers closed in. Anchurus warred with himself. Gordium's glorious army, defeated by Sargon? Everything in him rebelled at the idea of retreat. But with another sweep of his gaze, he knew that if he did not, they would all perish.

Baran was right. Sargon would have the Prince of Gordium as his prize.

"Fall back!" He raised his sword and turned Ambrose around. "Men, with me. Fall back!"

The men glanced his way. Some hesitated, clearly unused to such an order, but as the prince repeated it, they began to respond. Soon, all of them had turned to fight their way back, seeking to lose the ground they had worked so hard to gain. Anchurus rode alongside them, shouting encouragements. Many of his valiant men fell, Sargon's hated soldiers stomping them underfoot. He saved one man by swooping in to unseat his attacker while others struggled to clear a path. They had to reach the road ahead if they wanted a chance to outrun the enemy. He paused to look back, calling again to his men.

"Sire!" Baran shouted.

Pain whitewashed his vision as the sword entered just below his left ribcage. The enemy pulled the blade free as he rode past. Anchurus folded, his grip loosening on Ambrose's reins. The panicked horse plunged back into the fray, running toward the enemy. Anchurus pulled him around just as two more soldiers came at him. He lifted his sword in defense. His breath came fast, blood staining his shirt. He blocked one blow but remained helpless against the other. He might have taken his last breath then had not Baran shown up to block. The commander cut off the enemy soldier's head in a swift counter move, then grabbed Ambrose's reins and ran back the other way, pulling the prince behind him. Anchurus clung to his sword, his eyesight blurring. The wound sizzled in his flesh, like fire in his flank. His legs trembled against the saddle. He wobbled and tipped before barely catching himself on Ambrose's bleeding neck.

He could not fall. He had to get his men to safety.

CHAPTER TWO

The city of Gordium never looked so beautiful as it did that fine spring day when Princess Zoe turned nineteen. The sun beamed down brightly from a dazzling blue sky, its rays blanketing the valley in yellow gold and winking mischievously over the Sangarius River as it weaved its way past the east gates and on north. Already, the surrounding fields showed the promise of budding crops, the young green shoots like forest moss when viewed from the high castle window.

Carried along with the morning breeze was the scent of freshly baked bread, hazelnut pudding, and pancakes. Zoe inhaled with pleasure, then felt a pang of guilt. Most citizens of Gordium would understand the privileges given a king and his family. But it made her uncomfortable that they wouldn't share in them. At least she had succeeded in convincing her father to approve a lottery. One hundred people had been invited to take part in the festivities later that day. An abundance of food would be shared with them all for the first time in the city's history.

It was a start.

Beyond her perch in the castle turret, the sounds of merriment danced on the air. Someone played a happy tune on what sounded like an oud—a pear-shaped stringed instrument. Zoe recognized the song and started humming along, her feet twitching with the driving rhythm. She searched for the musician, but because the citizens were on the other side of the castle gates, she couldn't see where the merrymakers were. It wasn't Anchurus playing, that much she could decipher. Her older brother wouldn't play so roughly. His long fingers would bring forth the dance as if the instrument had the music stored within its wooden fibers and needed only to be coaxed to let it out. But this crude player still had his charms. As Zoe listened, she couldn't help but feel the uplifting tune was fitting on this day. She pointed her face toward the sun and closed her eyes, letting the warmth soak into her skin. She might have stayed for some time, but her brother was home from battle and she wanted to see him. Wounded though he was, he was alive and would recover. She took in the brilliant view once more, then turned and descended the stairs.

She skipped along, her feet a blur over the stone steps. When she reached the last flight, she slowed, senses alert. Pilar, the head cook, would not welcome the princess' appearance in the middle of her efforts to create the perfect birthday feast. Zoe crept quietly, holding her skirts tightly to her legs. She arrived at the first level, pushed her shoulders back, and, assuming her princess posture, walked regally down the hall. No one would question her presence here. Nearing the dining room, she peered around the corner.

Anchurus was already there, sitting in his usual chair at the right hand of the king. Rumor had it the battle had not gone well. The medicine woman had been sent to treat his injuries the night before. Zoe wondered how badly he'd been hurt. His pride was probably worse off than his body, this being his first defeat against King Sargon.

"Surrounded?" King Midas said. He sat at the head of the table with his hands laced in front of him. A simple cream-colored tunic flattered his fit form, his hickory-brown hair tamed by a morning wash. Brown eyes looked out from under a noble brow, his long, slim nose accentuating his somber expression. "Nonsense. We had men from Ancyra with us. There's no way we could have been surrounded."

"We were gaining the upper hand." Anchurus' voice was gravelly from too much shouting. "But then a strange fog descended over us. We couldn't see anything."

Midas nodded stiffly. "You were on the grasslands?"

"It makes no sense. But it was there. We were blinded."

"As were they?"

"One would think. But they managed to surround us. I can't explain it."

Zoe hovered near the double doors, ignoring the two guards, and watched as her father absentmindedly rubbed a familiar spot on the left side of his chest. An old wound, her mother had told her.

"You rode out to win our final victory," Midas said. "You've returned, having capitulated to Sargon and this . . . fog."

Zoe sighed and leaned back against the wall. Another birthday full of family turmoil. She didn't know why she kept expecting it to be different. Perhaps it was the idea of defeating Sargon for good that had raised her expectations. But the rumors were true—for the first time, Gordium had lost to the king of the Assyrian Empire.

She took a second glance at her brother. Broad-shouldered with sandy hair and a finely trimmed mustache and beard, he held his body awkwardly in the chair, his skin pale. She wondered how many wounds raged under his shirt.

King Midas served himself some cooked eggs and cheese. "You allowed Sargon a victory." He took a bite and chewed like it was a task he must complete. "We'll have to double our efforts to regain what's been lost."

"The men speak of gods."

"I fail to see how—"

"The fog was unnatural," Anchurus interrupted. "As if conjured by magic."

"Men will say anything to avoid responsibility for their defeat."

"We have prisoners. They describe a glow that surrounds the king. As if the moon itself has chosen him."

Zoe frowned. Superstitious nonsense, her mother would have said. Surely her brother didn't believe it?

"The fog was like that," Anchurus continued. "Dense, but with a light within it. A light that made it harder to see."

Midas took a drink of water. A servant woman came from behind him to refill it.

"I know how you feel about such things," Anchurus said. "How Mother felt—"

"You must deal with this," Midas said.

"How should I do that, sire?"

"They're your men."

"I trust them."

"Perhaps you need to reevaluate that." Midas spoke in clipped tones, his eating motions taking on a nervous quality.

Anchurus pushed his plate forward. It hit his cup, upsetting the water. The servant woman sopped up the mess. "I've fought with these men for years," he said. "You might trust me to know them."

"This was to be our victory." Midas thumped his fist on the table. "You want to blame it on the gods?"

Zoe's shoulders stiffened. If Mother were here, she would put a stop to this bickering. At least until breakfast was over. Without her, Zoe could listen to no more. She stepped away and headed for her room, her mind so troubled that she nearly ran straight into Pilar. The old woman yelped, barely keeping her serving tray from tipping over and dumping its contents all over the floor. Zoe held out her hand to assist, but Pilar managed to keep it level.

"My apologies," Zoe said. "I didn't see you!"

The old woman bowed her head. "Good morning, Your Highness.

And happy birthday." She looked up with fierce gray eyes. "Don't you be thinking about sneaking a glance into the kitchen. It's supposed to be a surprise."

"Of course not." Zoe gestured for the woman to carry on. Pilar walked into the dining room, holding the platter high. Zoe watched her go and then resumed her retreat.

"Zoe?" her father called. "Is that you?"

She'd been caught. With a heavy sigh, she turned around and entered the hall.

"Good morning, Father." Casting her gaze right, she nodded at her brother. "Welcome home, Anchurus."

Both men rose at her entrance, a custom that always made her feel like she needed to hurry to avoid inconveniencing them. This time, it was even worse as Anchurus grimaced with the movement, his left arm pinned to his body. Zoe hurried to her chair, one of the servants holding it out for her. Once settled, she focused on her brother. "I'm glad you're back safely."

He slipped his hand inside his pocket and emerged with a small leather pouch. "Happy birthday." He pushed it across the table.

She smiled. He remembered. He always remembered. She set the pouch in front of her and pulled the tie free. The folds dropped open, revealing a delicate wooden horse figurine stained a bright yellow and made shiny with glaze. "It's beautiful! Where did you get it?"

"A merchant was selling them in one of the settlements we passed through. He had a little girl with yellow hair, like yours."

Zoe ran her finger down the horse's nose and over its slender ears. The eyes had been painted black, the mouth upturned so that it appeared to be smiling. "You kept it safe all the way home."

"Had to," Anchurus said. "You wouldn't want it broken, would you?"

"Did you see it, Father?"

"A nice trinket," Midas said.

"I shall treasure it." Zoe wrapped it back and pulled the string tight.

"Come. Eat." Midas shifted impatiently. "The food is getting cold."

Zoe tucked the pouch in her lap and tried again to smile at her brother, but the moment was gone. His stern expression had returned, his gaze flat. She helped herself to the meat, eggs, and pancakes before one of the servants dished her up a dollop of pudding. "Will we not be celebrating Anchurus' return, then?"

"There's little to celebrate," Midas said.

"He made it home alive."

"If we celebrate such things as that, the kingdom will not long survive."

"What is worthy of celebration, then? Nothing but conquest?"

Midas gave her a condescending look. "You don't need to understand a king's matters, my girl. When it's time to celebrate, we will celebrate. As we shall do today for your birthday." He lifted his cup. "Happy birthday."

Zoe stuffed eggs into her mouth.

"Come." Midas opened one hand. "Let's have breakfast together without arguing."

"You were arguing before I came."

"If you wouldn't eavesdrop, you wouldn't upset yourself."

"You wouldn't have said that to Mother."

"Your mother was the queen."

"And I am the princess. Today, I am nineteen. Old enough to be more than an ornament at royal gatherings."

Midas gestured to the servants for wine. When they brought it, he took a long drink.

"We have things to discuss," Zoe continued. "Improving our access to fresh water, for one."

"Your canal system."

"I need assistance to build it."

"Canal system?" Anchurus asked.

Zoe turned to him, pleased by his interest. "We must expand what we've started. It could save us all should the drought return."

She became more animated, explaining to her brother the way the storage tanks and additional canals might work to preserve water throughout the city.

Midas appeared to be listening, but then suddenly blurted out, "Slaughtering innocents to acquire additional horses and soldiers. That's what he did. It's been his way from the start."

His children stopped and stared at him.

"Now he assumes he's gained the upper hand. We must not let him keep it." He turned to his son. "He had more horses this time?"

Anchurus nodded. "As many as we did, or more."

Midas grumbled. "I will not burn and pillage to get them as he does."

"We are handicapped without them."

"Do they truly think he's a god?"

"From what I've heard, they believe the gods—"

"From whom?"

"The prisoners."

"They're lying."

"They're hungry. Exhausted. But still, they tell the story."

Midas pushed his plate away and got up from his chair. He began to pace, his fingers stroking his neatly trimmed beard. He walked with a certain grace, one hand behind his back. His spine was straight, though a veil of anxiety shadowed his features. "Who would do such magic for him?"

Anchurus turned up an empty hand.

"If he has some sort of witch working a spell over his subjects, we must find her and dispense with her."

"One needs magic to discover magic."

"A god. Hmph." Midas threw up his hand. "He killed his own brother to assume the throne!"

"We never found proof—" Anchurus began.

"I need no proof! I know who he is." Midas glared at his son with a sudden ferocity. "He will do anything to advance himself, including murder, and they believe he is a god?" When Anchurus said nothing, Midas glanced toward the main entrance doors. "Timon. Timon!"

The king's minstrel emerged from the servant's door in the back. He wore a blue vest and baggy pants. A little man with short dark hair and a fat nose, he stood about two-thirds the height of the king.

"Yes, sire?"

"I need FAX immediately," King Midas said.

"Yes, sire." Timon bowed and hurried out as quickly as he had come in.

"We will get to the bottom of this." Midas returned to the table. "Next time, we shall defeat him, then we shall have a celebration worthy of a true victory." He winked at Zoe, gripped Anchurus' shoulder, and sat back down. "Now, my girl, let's talk about this water-preserving system of yours."

FOTIS, Aster, and Xander, the king's advisors, had lived in the castle since before Zoe was born. Their arrival at the dining hall should have engendered an air of sobriety, but instead Zoe caught her brother's eye and was thrilled to see the mischief in his gaze. Many times growing up, they had mocked the three men, joking about their strange ways. Now was their chance to have a little fun at the advisors' expense once more.

"There are rumors Sargon may be using magic to strengthen his army," Midas said to the trio lined up on his right. "What do you know of this?"

The men stood silent, appearing to carefully consider the king's question. Then, one by one, they began to answer.

"We know nothing," Aster, the middle man, said. Lean and muscular, he had thick almond-brown hair and a medium-length beard, his jaw firm and his gaze fixed on the back wall as if his true desire was to be somewhere else entirely. Zoe glanced at him and blushed. Long had she secretly considered him handsome.

"So, you do know something!" Midas said, for it was understood within the castle that Aster almost always spoke the *opposite* of the truth. Not to deceive, of course, for no king's advisor would dare to deceive, but because of an unusual speech defect that had plagued him since birth. A curse of the gods, some said, as Aster often struggled when sharing his thoughts. But he was more perceptive than most, his frequently astute observations highly prized within the castle, where everyone had learned to correctly interpret his speech.

"We don't know anything for certain, Your Majesty," Fotis said in a thin, nasally voice. The leader of the group, he was the eldest and wore a long snow-white beard, always freshly combed. His head was nearly bald save for a few gray wisps that splayed about on his crown. He pointed his nose a little too steeply toward the ceiling for a man standing in the presence of the king, but it couldn't be helped. A wooden eye filled the empty socket on the right side, a wound left over from a horse-riding accident. Maintaining a slight tilt was the best way to keep from losing the prosthetic, which was a truly embarrassing experience for everyone.

Anchurus glanced at Zoe. How many times as children had they tried to trick the old man into dropping his gaze just to watch the wooden eye roll across the floor?

"We know nothing," Aster repeated in his opposite way of speaking.

"We suspected something," Fotis said, "but we did not have enough information to report."

"Ooooooh, but the pretty light!"

They all turned to the third man, Xander, the youngest and broadest of the three. He had a baby face that made him look even younger than his twenty years, and when he spoke, it was always a startling experience because his voice was so childlike, as if a boy had just drawn everyone's attention to his wonder.

"Light?" the king asked.

Xander gazed at something above him that only he could see. "When he speaks to the people, he glows. Like the moon."

Midas and Anchurus exchanged glances.

"King Sargon does not glow, sire," Aster said.

"There are rumors that he does," Fotis said. "But they are only rumors."

"Why haven't you told me about this?"

"We should not have told you, sire," Aster said.

"Yes, we should have told him," Xander squeaked.

"We didn't, Your Majesty," Fotis said, "because so far we have only rumors and,"—he cast Xander a disapproving look—"conjecture. We didn't want to give you misleading information."

Midas stood up and thrust his chair to the side. The three men took a simultaneous step back, two lowering their heads in respect, while Fotis kept his gaze on the ceiling. "I send my son into battle," Midas said, "and you don't see fit to warn me that the man he goes to defeat may be protected by magic?"

"We knew at that time, sire," Aster said.

"We didn't know before Prince Anchurus left, Your Majesty," Fotis clarified. "We still know very little. All we have is Xander's vision. And as you are aware, sire, he is young, and his visions are yet untested. In truth, nonsensical."

"The light!" Xander pointed up. "Like the moon all around." He drew a circle in front of him and stared into it as if it held a fascinating spectacle.

Midas glanced at Fotis, an exasperated expression on his face. "Have I not commanded you to alert me to any news of Sargon and his armies?"

"As I said, Your Highness," Fotis added, "pure conjecture. The odds of King Sargon possessing some sort of magic—"

"Tell him about the glow," Xander said.

"Yes," Midas said. "Tell me."

"We can't be certain if there even *is* such a glow, Your Highness," Fotis said. "Most likely, they are rumors meant to frighten Sargon's enemies."

"She uses the moonlight," Xander said, "and Sargon glows."

"She?" Midas turned a sharp gaze on Xander. "Who is she?"

"We don't know who she is, sire," Aster said.

Fotis shook his head. "He is off on a wild fancy."

"I'll be the judge of that," Midas said.

Fotis stooped at the waist in deference, holding his head up to prevent his eye from falling out. "Very well. Tell him about your vision, Xander. Keep in mind, sire, that we can confirm none of this."

"She likes those wolf creatures," Xander said. "She has one black one with sharp teeth." He shuddered.

"The wolves are friendly looking," Aster said.

"*Who* likes the wolves?" Midas bellowed.

"Xander seems to think she is a goddess," Fotis said.

"She's pretty." Xander grinned, his full lips pulling back to reveal gleaming white teeth.

"She's what?" Midas moved his gaze to Xander, who drew a woman's full figure in the air, then lowered his head and giggled.

"Xander believes she has some charms about her, Your Majesty," Fotis said. "If we are to trust his opinion."

"It matters much how charming she is," Aster said.

"From the dark world she comes." Xander hugged himself. "Cold, dark places. Where the dead live."

"A highly sought-after destination," Aster said.

"The dark goddess," Fotis said. "He means to say it is the goddess of the underworld, sire. Again, pure fantasy."

Zoe exchanged perplexed glances with her brother. Midas stared at Xander, then turned his back on him and walked toward the other side of the room.

"It is not she," Aster said. "Underworld, overworld."

"Yes, yes, he got it!" Xander said, pointing at Aster.

"It is very clear," Aster said.

"That's not what you said before," Xander mumbled.

Midas turned to Fotis. "You don't expect there is any truth to this?"

The old man drew his head back. "As I mentioned, Your Majesty, we have no information outside of Xander's . . . vision. And as you know, it isn't wise to trust visions alone. We were looking into the rumors. It is only now that we hear from you that even Sargon's soldiers are telling these stories."

"*I* was the one who told you first," Xander said. "You wouldn't have even considered it."

"He enjoys considering gods and goddesses," Aster said.

"Our apologies, Your Majesty," Fotis said. "We simply did not want to give you incorrect information. We know the seriousness of the matter."

"It is not alarming," Aster said.

"Indeed," Fotis said.

"I will tell you again," Midas said. "You *must* alert me to *any* news that affects our battles with Sargon, including *any* visions or rumors, understood? I will decide whether to be alarmed."

"Of course, sire," Fotis said. "Our apologies."

"I *told* you to tell him," Xander mumbled.

"He didn't tell you to tell him," Aster said.

"Now it's gotten worse," Xander said.

"It has not," Aster agreed.

"Enough!" Midas said.

The advisors fell silent. The king paced back and forth, his hands behind his back. "Katiah of the underworld," he said in a low voice.

"But Father," Zoe said, "Mother forbade—"

"Yes. Your mother forbade any talk of the dark goddess."

"We know how the queen felt about her," Fotis said. "It's another reason why we hesitated to bring such news."

"The dark goddess is highly respected here," Aster said.

"He glows." Xander started dancing about, holding his robe away from his legs like a lady might hold out her skirts. "The people stare. Where does the light come from?"

"Katiah." Midas pursed his lips together, his eyes unseeing.

"Father?" Zoe said. "Surely you do not believe—"

"I must have answers," Midas turned to his advisors. "*Clear* answers, Fotis. Yesterday. Understood?"

“Of course, Your Majesty.” Fotis contorted himself into his best bow.

“It is not understood,” Aster said.

“Will you listen to me now?” Xander asked, turning to Fotis.

Midas exited the dining hall, leaving the rest staring after him.

CHAPTER THREE

The goddess Katiah walked alone through King Sargon II's animal sanctuary. She wore a short-sleeved gown made of an airy material with tiny crystals embedded into the neckline. Her hair hung loose about her shoulders, a black headband keeping it away from her face. The animals stirred as she passed, yellow gazes following her under the glow of the oil lamps. At the tiger pen, she stopped and watched the male rise to study her. He and his female had a large space that had been fashioned to include a cave in the back, but she pitied them nonetheless, robbed of their right to roam the lands.

"One of these nights, I will open your cage," she said, "when I'm feeling adventurous."

She found the king where she expected she would—at the lion pen. She observed undetected as he gazed over the wall into the largest enclosure in the animal sanctuary. The moon's glow illuminated the male lounging on a nearby rise, his shoulder braced against a block-shaped boulder. The female was nowhere in sight, which meant she had to be in the cave below.

It was late. What the king had planned now, Katiah couldn't

guess. Sargon was his most attractive when he was deep in thought, his long oval face drawn down into his cleft chin, lips slightly pursed under the powerful nose. No other king had such a nose, like the side of a mountain, sloped and bold. It was the king's nose that made his face worthy of being sculpted into stone. She had told him so one night while looking into his brown eyes.

He'd raised his finger to stroke the bridge. "I thought it was my brow," he'd said.

The cage doors squeaked open. They were on the right and down the sloped path, near the farthest edge of the enclosure. The lion waited, ears perked, tail twitching. Katiah couldn't see the servant from where she stood, but imagined a young man having been roused from his sleep to face one of nature's fiercest predators. She felt a moment's concern for him, followed by a mild curiosity at what Sargon had ordered him to do. Suddenly, a little lamb appeared, stumbling over its own legs as it was pushed from behind. The gate closed, the servant safe for another day. The lamb, on the other hand, stood clearly at risk, its white wool picking up the moon's light so that it was plainly visible even in the night.

"Not hungry, Tai?" Sargon asked in a smooth voice. "I must be feeding you too well." He waited, but Tai only regarded the lamb with mild curiosity. The lamb, for its part, was smart enough not to go fleeing across the enclosure and, instead, picked its way carefully about its new home, nose down and then up, eyes alert.

Katiah watched for a little longer and, when it seemed there would be no drama worthy of her attention, walked toward the king. He noticed her presence almost immediately, as if she had dropped a veil from around her body.

"I'm afraid if anyone is going to be doing the hunting, it will be Zehra," he said.

"The female is the more cunning of the two," Katiah agreed, "and the more efficient."

They stood together at the wall, both of them leaning on their forearms. Katiah inhaled his scent, a pleasant mix of musky sweat and laurel leaf oil. He wore a heavy cloak, for the night was chilly, his head bare so his black hair moved with the breeze. A few gray strands played about his temples, though they dared not disturb his forehead, which seemed, as the rest of his face, built like a barricade against all who would challenge him.

"I assume you know my son has disappeared," he said.

Katiah's heartbeat quickened. Surprising that he would bring that up so soon. She kept her expression neutral. "Which son, Your Majesty?"

His features stiffened. He pulled away from the wall. "I'm not in the mood for games. If that's what you came for, I bid you be gone." He turned his back on her and started walking down the stone path toward the exit.

Anger flared in Katiah's breast. Who did he think he was, talking to the goddess of the underworld in such a way? With a flick of her hand, she could send him into spasms of pain. But he was right. She knew more than she was saying, and part of her admired him for sensing it. "Come, Your Majesty. I've only just arrived. If something has displeased you, perhaps I can help." She followed him with light footsteps. "Even a goddess can be . . . distracted. You know how hard I've been working on your behalf. I hear your army recently experienced an unexpected victory."

Sargon walked on.

"The last battle against King Midas' forces. Word is that a strange fog descended, blinding them all against your attack. A serendipitous occurrence, no doubt."

Sargon slowed at the far edge of the lion enclosure, his gaze on the lamb, which had remained near the entrance. "Aw," he said and clucked his tongue. "You understand what awaits you, don't you? It's only a matter of time."

"As it is for you, Your Majesty." Katiah came up beside him once more. "Soon your lands will spread all the way to the western seas, your kingdom so vast and boundless few will find where it ends."

He waited, his jaw working back and forth. He was deciding

whether to go along with her feigned ignorance. "It is Emir," he said finally.

Katiah smiled to herself. "And this concerns you?"

"He is my son."

"You have many sons. Emir Alkan is hardly one who matters. He's not an heir. And you've had him tucked away in your army for years. He could have been killed anytime. Why would it disturb you now if he were gone?"

"No one leaves my kingdom!" Sargon turned an angry glare on her. "Not one of my soldiers, and particularly not my son."

Katiah averted her gaze to see Tai watching them, his golden eyes piercing even at a distance.

"I want to know how he slipped away," King Sargon said.

"He's lived here his whole life," Katiah said sweetly. "He probably figured a way out." *With a little help from an interested party.*

"He must be found." The king turned back to the lions. "Have you seen him?"

It was time for her best performance. "Me?" She laughed her most tinkling laugh. "Why would I have seen that mutt of a boy? I was far from here, toiling for your benefit. Now I'm beginning to feel a bit unappreciated. Do you honestly think I have nothing to do but babysit your progeny?"

Sargon didn't believe her, it was plain, but he had no evidence with which to contradict her. He would have to swallow his suspicions for the time being. She watched with amusement as he worked at it, the veins taut in his neck. "You came with news," he said finally.

"I'm not sure I want to share it now that I've received such an impolite reception."

He cast her a wry sideways glance, then heaved a mighty sigh, his broad chest rising and falling. Finally, he turned toward her with a chivalrous bow. "Great Katiah, my apologies. I have been rude." When he stood, the anger was gone from his face, replaced by his charming smile. He took her hand in his. "Perhaps you might retire with me to my chamber. We could have some fresh fruit and wine and discuss what it is you came to discuss."

How quickly he changed his demeanor! Here now was the engaging man she enjoyed with the deep-set eyes and tender lips. With one sweep of his arm, he could make her body wilt. It wasn't hard at all to smile back, to forgive him his single-mindedness, to take his hand and walk with him alongside the lions' enclosure toward the castle, where she would share his bed once more and what bits of her plan she wanted him to know.

She would enjoy the evening. Sargon was a powerful and often considerate lover, particularly when he was getting something in return, something more than bodily pleasure. She felt her heart racing, her desire rising despite herself. "I think you will be pleased," she said. "It won't be long before Gordium will be yours."

He acknowledged her with a hum in his throat, but his gaze was directed at the space in front of him. She checked his expression and found he was holding himself in more than usual, his jaw set even as he appeared at ease. He was truly bothered by Emir's escape, more than she had imagined he would be.

"Will we attack again soon?" he asked.

"Soon," she said. "I will bid you ride west for your ultimate victory."

"I see," he said.

"I am foreseeing riches beyond your wildest dreams, and they will be laid out before you for easy picking." She stood up on her toes and kissed him. He was hesitant at first, but then his lips warmed, and he kissed her back the way he always did, the passion in him irresistible. She was lost in it for a moment, and then his grip on her arm tightened. She opened her eyes to find him looking at her with an intense gaze.

"My beautiful goddess," he murmured, "you wouldn't betray me, would you?"

Katiah felt a flash of anger. Betray *him*! It was men who did the betraying, men who neglected their promises and took her gifts for granted. She cocked her head by reflex while she imagined the punishments she would visit upon him, but then he leaned down and kissed her again. She resisted at first, but her body relented even as her mind sought to come up with a suitable punishment.

Suddenly, the lamb bleated. Katiah paused, her lips still against Sargon's as the bleating became more urgent and then more sporadic and, finally, dropped off with one last pitiful utterance before the night returned to its quiet rest.

"You were right." Sargon lifted his head to examine the kill. "The female is more efficient." He listened to the sounds of fangs ripping flesh, his grip loosening on her arm. As the lioness ate her fill, Sargon released Katiah, turning back to draw one finger softly down the side of her face. "Come. Tell me more about this ultimate victory." He looped her arm in his and started walking.

Katiah walked alongside him, smiling to herself. Yes. The female was more efficient, for she knew how to wait for just the right moment to get what she wanted.

EMIR ALKAN HEARD the thud and creak of the wooden gates opening and then closing again. A member of King Midas' royal guard strode toward him. Emir kept strumming his oud, head down over the instrument as if he were lost in the music. It wasn't hard to pretend. He was playing one of his mother's favorite tunes, a song about a little girl skipping happily alongside the creek. She sang to the birds and the trees and even the insects, her skirt swaying as she traveled down the hills to the wildlands where the horses ran. Emir remembered his mother singing it in her smooth alto voice. He could imagine her then, before she was a slave woman, as that girl running free under a bright yellow sun.

Thick leather boots appeared next to him. "The king desires your presence at the music contest this evening." The guard spoke in a measured, clipped voice.

Emir's heart leapt in his chest. He had made it! A smile creased his lips, but he focused on the strings until he ended the song. Then he stood up, holding the oud by its neck. "A music contest?" he asked innocently.

"The king supports talent among the citizens of Gordium. When he wishes, he holds a contest. Any musician may enter. The victor wins the king's favor and may be granted land and stock with which to make his fortune. He may even gain a position in the castle if the king wishes it."

"I have no need for sheep and cattle," Emir said in his most respectful tone. "I am a musician. I play for my meals." He gestured behind him to his open case, where some grateful listeners had left bread and dried fruit.

"The princess heard you playing this morning, and thus, the king offers you the opportunity."

The princess? Emir raised an eyebrow.

"Should you accept, you are to report to the castle immediately, where you will be prepared to perform this evening."

Emir studied the man's face. He was young and clean shaven, his skin unscarred. This was a man who had yet to see battle. "What if the king doesn't like my performance?" Rumor had it that a loser could be separated from his hand, so he might never play again.

"You may go free, unharmed."

"I get to keep my hand?"

"By the princess' grace."

Princess Zoe again. He'd heard reports of her kindness.

"Your decision?" the guard asked.

Emir cast his gaze around. The orphan boy was supposed to meet him here. "I need a moment to gather my things."

"Your name?"

"Emir Alkan."

"Come to the gates and speak your name. You shall be allowed entrance." The soldier walked away.

Emir crouched down and stuffed the food in his pockets. Once the case was empty again, he tucked the instrument inside and paused to look at it. The wood was scratched in various places, its surface worn and aged, but his heart warmed when he gazed upon it. Since he was a child, it had been with him, a friend when he had none, a savior when he needed one. Best of all, when he played it, he made his mother smile. Now, it had gained him entrance into King Midas' castle—where he might improve his fortune. Or at least escape imminent death at the hands of King Sargon's hunters for a time.

Two bare feet appeared at his side, and Emir breathed a sigh of relief. A stray boy like that. They were stolen for slaves every day. One who was mute, such as this boy, could be taken easily. Emir had tried to impress upon him the danger, but the boy didn't listen to warnings very well and often disappeared on his own.

"It worked," Emir said to him, latching the case closed. "They're letting me in."

With dark brown eyes, the boy stood only as high as Emir's hip, seven or eight years old, maybe, though Emir had never asked. He was a fair-faced boy, one that might almost be mistaken for a girl but for his short brown hair and firm chin. It was because of this boy that Emir had escaped Sargon's capital city of Durukin. The orphan had shown him the secret tunnel out, and for that, Emir would be eternally grateful. Without the boy, he might have never had a chance at freedom. The tunnel escape had also given them a head start, which so far had saved him from Sargon's hunters. Though Emir wasn't resting easy. The dreaded Olgun brothers were known for finding every deserter, no matter how cunning, and returning him to the king for disembowelment.

"I need you to follow me," he said. "Sneak inside."

The boy observed the castle up on the hill. Fear flashed across his small features.

"This is a kind king. Not like the other one."

The boy continued to stare.

Emir hoisted the strap over his shoulder. "It is the princess' birthday today. There will be much food and fresh bread." He paused. "But if you're too frightened, you may stay here." Taking a large refreshing inhale, he started toward the castle gates.

Fast footsteps soon padded after him. When the boy caught up, Emir gave him one of his pieces of dried fruit. The boy stuffed it into his mouth. "Up there, you'll eat like a king," Emir said. "They discard food that is better than anything you've ever set your eyes upon. But you must be the little mouse you are. I want to know everything that goes on in there."

The boy gazed up at Emir and made a series of gestures with his hands.

"Slow down," Emir said. He'd grown to understand most of the boy's strange language, but still got lost when he moved too quickly.

The boy repeated the gestures, more slowly this time. *What if they catch me?* he signed.

"Don't worry," Emir said. "This will be fun." When the boy didn't seem convinced, Emir dug out another piece of fruit and handed it over. His own stomach was growling, but he had a feeling the king would feed his musicians. At least, he would the winner, and Emir planned to win.

CHAPTER FOUR

The fireplace on the south side of the strategy room lay bare and cold. Midas stood next to it, staring into the darkness. "Defeated by Sargon." He shook his head. "He says a fog descended upon them?"

Rastus Volkan, the commander of the king's guard, sat at the pinewood table on the other side of the room, his long legs stretched in front of him. "A strange occurrence on the flatlands, sire."

Midas turned to a second table at his left, a heavyset mahogany piece on which a rudimentary map of Lydia, Phrygia, and Assyria had been painted. The three kingdoms formed a mighty expanse between the Aegean, Marmara, and Black Seas. Tiny wooden figures symbolizing Midas' and Sargon's armies lay clumped at one end, having been swept aside after the disappointing defeat. "Anchurus has never been caught off guard."

Rastus rubbed his chin. With wavy blond hair, he was clean shaven and dressed in a guard's uniform of pants, boots, and a long dark tunic that left his tanned neck bare. "There are rumors it was the gods, sire."

"Yes, so Anchurus said. And FAX seems to agree." Midas started across the room, pausing by the cabinet against the outside wall. On its upper shelves were displayed numerous trinkets and gifts from other lands, most collected by his adopted father, King Gordius, when he'd ruled. An intricately painted flower vase. A miniature marble sculpture of a sheep. A leather satchel. His gaze passed over all of these and came to rest on the very bottom shelf. It was one of two that had a door, its contents hidden from view. "We must find out what happened."

"Yes, sire. I will do some more checking." Rastus left the room.

Midas returned to his map and glared at the line that divided his kingdom from Sargon's. He had expanded his lands to the north and west, but the east remained stubbornly the same as it had since he'd been crowned king over twenty years before. Despite his best efforts, he'd failed to defeat Sargon and recover his sister, Elanur. Instead, it had been a series of frustrating advances that never culminated in a final victory. Now, Sargon had won an important battle, enough to tip the balance.

On the other side of the room, the queen's blanket lay draped over her chair. She'd often used it on chilly mornings. He caressed it, sensing his wife's slim shoulders underneath. "I haven't spoken of the goddess, as you asked," he said to the empty air. "Since your decree five years ago, no one has spoken of her." He could see Demodica, his Greek princess, sitting there with her hands demurely folded in her lap. Her sandy hair—the same color as Anchurus'—was done up high on her head, her gaze focused on a small sculpture of the dark goddess on the table in front of her.

"She is evil, Karem," she had told him, eyeing the likeness with clear revulsion. "You can no longer encourage evil in this kingdom."

"Without her, I wouldn't be king," he'd said.

"Being king was your destiny."

Midas let his fingers trail over the blanket as he left it behind. His wife had been wise. He felt her absence keenly. It had been over two years now since she'd passed away.

A knock came at the door. "The princess, Your Majesty," the guard said.

"Come."

Zoe entered, holding something in her hands. Midas groaned inwardly. It was another of her inventions, and he wasn't in the mood.

"This will only take a moment." She hurried to the pinewood table and placed the device in the middle of it. Midas gazed at the two sticks of wood that formed an inverted triangle. A third crossed the two near the bottom, a wheel attached to one end to facilitate turning. The whole device was held upright by two pieces of twine tied to the top junction and stretched back so that each wound around a small stake. Zoe held these in her fingers. Suspended from the top of the contraption was a pulley with a hook on the end. A third piece of twine extended down and around the turning wheel below.

"Your napkin," Zoe said.

Midas pulled the square piece of cloth from his pocket.

"Now hold these." She indicated the two stakes. Midas obeyed. With the gadget stable, Zoe turned the little crank, which lowered the hook to the surface of the table. She laid the corner of the napkin over the sharp end, then turned the crank in the opposite direction. The machine lifted the cloth until it dangled between the sticks, swinging slightly.

"Ah," the king said, though he remained confused.

"You don't know what it is, do you?" Zoe asked.

"It's a . . . well, it lifts things."

"Exactly!" She smiled at him. "Now imagine if this whole mechanism was much larger. Suppose it rests outside of the castle, the triangular section here three times as tall as you are. This part,"—she pointed to the pulley—"would dangle over your head."

It took a moment, but then King Midas brightened. "Oh, I see! How much could it lift?"

"I'm not sure yet. I'll need to make a few more calculations."

"More than a man?"

"Many times what a man could lift. I believe, Father, that if we could build this much bigger, it would make it easier and safer for the workers to erect the buildings of the city. Perhaps those in Ancyra, as well."

Midas studied the gadget. This wasn't the first time she'd asked for more men to bring her designs to life. At the edge of the castle yard lay remnants of other projects completed and discarded because they'd proven to be of little practical use. There was the large piped instrument that played sounds no one wanted to hear, the pedal-powered wagon that was so heavy it fatigued the occupant within a short distance, the broad wooden wings that were supposed to allow one to fly but had only resulted in a servant breaking a leg. Some had been more successful, though. There was Zoe's double blade with the handles that made it easier for the servant women to cut their sewing materials. And the teetering board and boulder that had become one of the children's favorite riding toys in the city square.

This contraption, however. Now that Midas could envision it, he grew excited at its prospects, imagining how it might speed up the work on most any structure. If they could build their sister castle in recently conquered Ancyra more quickly than expected, the people would flock there. He would have more men to fight for him. "What will you call it?"

"I haven't thought of that yet." Zoe folded and returned his napkin, allowing him to let go of the stakes. The gadget crumpled gently onto the table. "It's a lifting mechanism, as you said. But that's not really a name."

Midas studied it. "It looks a little like a crane."

Zoe followed his gaze. "The bird?"

"Look here. The long neck, the beak pointing down."

She nodded. "Very well. It's a crane." She lifted it up into her hands.

"Was there something else?" Midas asked.

Zoe fingered the device. "The dark goddess." She looked up at him. "I remember you and Mother arguing. And then Mother said all representations of the goddess were to be removed." She paused, watching him. "Is that why—"

"You are the princess," Midas interrupted, holding up his hand. "Today is your birthday. The townspeople will come—the ones you convinced me to invite. Let's put these worries aside for now, all right?"

Zoe gazed at him with that anxious expression she had, the one where her eyes got wider than usual and her mouth puckered. It reminded him of when she was a toddler about to cry. "Is it possible she's helping Sargon?"

He glanced at Queen Demodica's blanket. Zoe was no longer a child. Still, he wanted to protect her from any talk of danger. "It's possible," was all he managed to say.

She adjusted the gadget in her hands. "I know you'll do what's best," she said finally.

Midas felt his gaze drifting to the bottom shelf with the door. "Sometimes, you must take risks to set things right."

"What is it you must set right?"

Elanur's face flashed in front of him, her small hand outstretched toward him.

"Father?"

"Let's not speak of it now," Midas said. "Today is for celebration. I must go prepare." He escorted her out and followed her down the stairs. As she returned to her quarters on the second level, he continued down to the first and made his way out the castle doors.

"Will you quiet down?" Fotis sat at a small table on the north side of the advisors' quarters, a long scroll partially unrolled in front of him. Shelves stacked with tablets, more scrolls, and sheets of parchment lined the north wall, a few extending onto the east and west walls so that the eldest advisor was surrounded by historical volumes. "A person can't hear himself think."

"He's listening to you." Aster lay on his bed in the middle of the room, his hands behind his head.

"Well, make him listen!" Fotis said.

"Right away, Your Highness," Aster said.

Fotis grumbled and unrolled more of the scroll, using one finger to plug his ear against the noise that came from the south side of the room. There, Xander stood at another table, tossing bits of herbs and spices and who knew what else into a large wooden bowl. Like Fotis' area, Xander's was surrounded by shelves. But instead of books, they held a collection of vases, bowls, jars, and satchels, each with something in it that only Xander could identify, for none of the containers were labeled. He lifted and lowered them one after the other, checking for which he might need. Each time he added an ingredient to the mixture, he made an accompanying sound, a yelp or guffaw or groan, meanwhile maintaining a cheery melody over it all.

"You're not supposed to summon her!" Fotis turned toward the young advisor. "The king asked only for information. He didn't say to bring her here."

"He always proceeds with the utmost caution," Aster said.

"Then why don't you do something?" Fotis asked. "You lie there as if there's nothing to worry about."

"There is nothing to worry about," Aster said.

"Summon her, and we get the information," Xander said.

"You think she's going to answer your questions?" Fotis asked.

"Only one way to find out." Xander wrinkled his nose.

"You will not find out," Fotis said. "All you're doing is making it stink in here!"

Aster sneezed. "Most appealing."

"What *is* that anyway?" Fotis asked.

"A little crushed stink beetle." Xander hummed. "Makes it more potent, they say, though it's not a mixture I'd like to make every day!" He laughed at his own rhyme as the putrid smell filled the room.

Aster got up and opened the shutter to the one window they had, but it was warm outside and no breeze relieved them of their discomfort.

"I don't understand why the king can't give you your own room," Fotis said.

"There are many rooms to spare," Aster said.

"He gives one to his musician winner!" Fotis complained.

"He does not award the dank storage space underground, which is quite cozy," Aster said.

"Even so," Fotis said, "that we must all be cramped in here together is an infernal injustice."

"Working together is a joy," Aster said.

"The pretty one is coming," Xander crooned. "Soon she will be here."

"She'd better *not* be here!" Fotis said.

"But the king told us—" Xander began.

"You bring her here now, and you'll be lucky if she doesn't turn you into a stink bug yourself," Fotis said. "Should you escape her wrath, the king will likely behead you once he finds out what you've done!"

"The king is fond of beheadings," Aster said with a smirk.

But Xander had stopped to stare at his colleague. "He said we must help."

"By gathering information!" Fotis said.

"I can't do that without talking to her," Xander said.

Aster sighed. "It wouldn't be best to let him be," he said. "He doesn't know what he's doing."

"Of course, it wouldn't be best—" Fotis spouted and then paused, realizing the true meaning of Aster's words. "Very well. If you think he knows what he's doing, you can clean up the mess when he's done it."

"I'm being very neat." Xander resumed his mixing. "Nothing on the floor. See?" He gestured at his feet, then perused the wall of shelves for another ingredient. "Wolfsbane, wolfsbane," he mumbled under his breath. "The pretty one likes wolves. Keeps them as pets, they say."

"Charming," Aster said. "I do hope we get to meet her."

"You're such a help." Fotis glared at the middle advisor. "Just because you've caught the princess' eye doesn't mean you can lie about like a loafer."

"The princess is ugly," Aster said.

Xander burst out laughing. "The princess is ugly! The princess is ugly!" He danced about with a new satchel in his hand and then whirled and dumped it all into the bowl. Dust exploded above it, making him sneeze. "Imagine if the king heard that!"

"He *will* hear it if you don't pipe down," Fotis warned. "He was down the hall in his strategy room."

"The king would be happy to hear of his daughter's ugliness," Aster said.

Xander sneezed again and kept giggling as he picked up his wooden spoon and stirred. "The princess is ugly, sooooo ugly," he sang.

Fotis set the scroll aside and cast his gaze about his shelves. After a moment, he stood up, pulled a wide box down, and set it on his desk to study the stack of parchments inside. "For years, the city worshipped the goddess of the underworld at the direction of our king. Then Queen Demodica demanded a stop to all of it. The 'pretty one,' as someone calls her,"—he glared at Xander—"was dark and dangerous, the queen believed. I'm inclined to agree with her assessment."

"You would know," Aster said. "You have personal experience with her."

"I have no personal—" Fotis caught himself. He pointed to the pile of parchments in front of him. "You could help by reading some of these."

"I'm not busy," Aster said.

"No other princess was ever so ugly," Xander sang as he stirred. "It needs something else."

"Busy doing what?" Fotis asked.

"I'm not thinking," Aster said.

"I'm sure you're not. You're—" Fotis stopped. "Oh, to the underworld with both of you. If we're going to be saved from the executioner's sword, I guess it's up to me as usual."

"You are truly the best of us all," Aster said.

"I so appreciate the compliment," Fotis said sarcastically.

"Oh!" Xander whirled around to stare at the west stack of shelves. "I forgot the quartz. A sprinkle of quartz is what we need. She sparkles and shines with the moon's light. Shimmery and bright. We need something sparkling."

Fotis grumbled and started lifting the parchments page by page, holding them up in front of his face. Xander continued going up and down the step stool and mixing his potion while Aster went on "thinking" or whatever he was supposedly doing. Fotis had just finished another page when Xander began to chant a series of unrecognizable words.

"Oh, for crying out loud," Fotis said. "I can't read with all that—"

The howl stopped him. Fotis froze, the parchment still held in front of him. Aster sat up. The sound rose eerily into the air and wormed down Fotis' spine, encircling the vertebrae one by one.

"Well, three men at once," the goddess said. "I'm flattered, but this is a rather inconvenient time."

Aster leapt to his feet. Fotis dropped the parchment onto the floor. Xander stood wide-eyed and trembling at the sight of the goddess Katiah. She had appeared in the center of the room, bathed in what looked like moonlight, though it was early afternoon. Her blue and silver dress sparkled in her self-made glow, her long dark hair cascading over bare pearlescent shoulders, hands covered in stark white gloves that reached up to her elbows. Xander squelched a squeal. "She's here!" he whispered to the others. "We can ask her!"

Fotis steadied himself with one hand on the back of his chair.

Aster grasped the hilt of the dagger at his belt, ready for a fight. Xander gaped at the goddess, a silly smile on his face. "Are you Katiah?"

The corner of her lush red lips curled. "And you are King Midas' famed advisors." She looked them over, her black eyes studying them up and down as if they were wares in the marketplace. In the end, she chose Aster, tucking her chin and walking toward him, hips swaying. "Come now. No need to be so uptight."

Aster bristled, his jaw clenched as the goddess took a tour around him, at one point trailing her fingers along his broad shoulders.

"You look more like a soldier than an advisor. I imagine you feel a bit cooped up with these two?" She cocked her head as she came around to face him again, then turned to Fotis. Her smile faded at the sight of him, so she cast her gaze back to Xander.

"I can't believe you came!" he said.

She looked at him as one might a child. "Unusual to find such power in one so young."

Xander shivered with delight, his hands pumping involuntarily in front of him.

"You summoned me with this?" She gestured toward his mixing bowl.

"They didn't know how to do it." He pointed to the other two.

"Watch your tongue," Fotis said.

"She is your friend," Aster warned.

Katiah smiled at the handsome advisor. "I can be, under the right circumstances." She tickled Xander under the chin, sending him into spasms. "So, I'm here. What did you want?"

"He said we had to . . . to . . . well, the king said . . ." Xander babbled.

"You will hold your tongue!" Fotis growled.

Xander ducked his head, then asked, "Are you helping King Sargon II?"

"You asked me here at King Midas' request?" Katiah said.

"Xander, *that's enough*!" Fotis barked.

Xander wilted like a guilty dog. Katiah turned her dark eyes toward the eldest advisor. "What's the matter, old man?" Fotis lifted his head even higher as she glided over to him. "Worried about your king?"

"You're working for his enemy." Fotis' voice caught. He cleared his throat. "We'd like you to stop."

"Because you asked nicely?"

Fotis peered at her over the top of his long nose.

Katiah turned around, her gaze falling on Aster again. "And how about you?" She walked over to him. "What is it you want?"

Aster's expression remained calm. For some time, he looked directly into her eyes. So long, in fact, that Katiah seemed to grow uncomfortable. He leaned toward her and, holding her gaze, said, "This is a game, and in the end, you will be victorious. You will ride back into the underworld the elevated being you are, your eyes red with joyful weeping, your heart soaring in pieces."

Katiah's cheeks flushed. "One would think you aim to flatter." She pulled her glove up her arm, then brushed both hands down her dress. All the while she flicked her gaze from one advisor to the other, ending on Aster's face. Suddenly she lifted her hand, and Aster's arm burst into flames.

"Oh!" Xander ran to his colleague. "You're burning!"

Aster grabbed a blanket off his bed and quickly doused the fire.

"In case you were being mean," Katiah said with a light toss of her head.

"Your Highness." Xander bowed. "Or, Your Darkness? Please, don't set us all on fire. We must follow the king's orders. If we don't, we could be executed."

"It *is* your king you wish me to punish, then?"

"No!" Xander held up his hands. "No punishing. We did not mean to offend the shiny one!" He turned to the elder advisor. "Tell her, Fotis."

Fotis stepped out from behind his desk. "I'm afraid, great

goddess, that we have summoned you by mistake." His disapproving gaze shifted briefly to Xander. "Now that you're here, we wish only to ask why you're helping King Sargon II in his war against our king. You see, we have heard rumors you may be assisting him."

"Not that it's any of our business," Xander added.

"We live only to respect the dark goddess," Aster growled, dropping the blackened blanket onto the floor.

"Of course," Xander said. "We give you only respect. You will win, of course. You will win the game!" He spread his hands wide and smiled, but his eyes were rimmed with little lines.

"We beg the goddess' pardon," Fotis said. "We would be grateful for any information you may be willing to share."

Katiah gazed at them all. "To ask something of a goddess, you must have something to offer in return. I'm sure such wise men as you understand this." She paused. "Tell me, what are you willing to grant me in exchange for this information?"

The three advisors cast nervous glances at one another.

"Come, come. I do not have all day. What will you offer me?"

Fotis' gaze darted about the room.

"You are supposed to be wise," Katiah said. "Surely you know that to make a bargain with the goddess of the underworld, it is common to offer one's soul?"

The room fell silent. Katiah waited. When no one said anything, she turned as if to leave.

"You may not have mine," Aster blurted.

Katiah paused.

"No!" Xander said. "Dear goddess, sparkling goddess. I . . . I can be useful sometimes, as you can see. I summoned you! I did that."

Katiah turned to the young advisor. "Very well. Your soul I will take." She cocked her head to the side. "When it's time."

Xander beamed as if triumphant. Then, quickly realizing what she had said, he gulped.

"I am not the superior advisor," Aster said.

Katiah gave him a seductive look. "He is young and gifted. That will suit my purposes better in the long run." She glanced at Xander. "In return for your gift, I will tell you this: I brought the fog that confused your army, and I will continue to tip the odds in Sargon's favor."

"But why?" Fotis managed to ask. "Why would you help him?"

Katiah cocked her head. "That is more information than your young advisor's soul is worth." She turned her gaze back to Fotis. "For that, you will have to ask your king. He knows the answer. He also knows the solution, but I doubt he will do what needs to be done. He has already waited much too long." She gazed out the window. "I do enjoy imagining he might come around, eventually." She clasped her hands in front of her. "But men are as they are. If I were you, I would keep your heads down. I imagine it won't be long before you'll be serving a new king." She lifted one finger in emphasis. "Be smart, and you may live to one day advise him."

With that, she raised her palm, blew on it, and then watched as a ball of light floated toward Xander. Startled, he backed up a little, but it reached him nonetheless and dissolved into his chest. Before their eyes, he began to glow, a little of Katiah's moonlight emanating from his skin. When he looked up again, the goddess was gone.

"I'm like the moon," he said, gazing down at himself. "She made me like the moon!" He chuckled a little, but it was halfhearted. Fotis stared at the new source of light and grimaced, a sour taste in the back of his throat.

Zoe bustled about her workshop. She moved from one shelf to another, lifting and shifting parts and pieces. "There has to be something," she said to her maidservant. Elif, a slip of a girl not yet sixteen years old, stood near the longest table holding a child's hand. He had short, mussed brown hair and was wearing pants, but his skin was smooth and his features feminine. "If he can't speak, maybe he can draw."

"Your Highness." Elif's dark eyes darted back to the dress she'd left hanging on the hook by the door. "Time is running out. We must prepare you."

"Where did you say you found him again?" Zoe asked.

"At the food tables, Your Highness. He was taking the figs."

"Yes, well. He's probably hungry." Zoe glanced back at the child, noting the dirt smudges on his cheeks and the tatters on his sleeves. "There will be plenty of food for everyone tonight."

"But he was trespassing, Your Highness."

"Or perhaps he slipped in with some of those who were invited," Zoe said. "He is very quiet."

Elif looked down with a suspicious gaze at the boy.

"This might work." Zoe grabbed a thin slate from a low shelf, dusted it off, and set it on the long table. "Now to find a drawing tool."

"Your Highness." Elif bowed her small head. "If you please, the ceremonies begin soon."

"I know, I know." Zoe was on the hunt again, this time on the other side of the room. She opened and closed drawers in her cabinets, then rose on her tiptoes to check the higher shelves. "Bring me the step stool."

Elif dropped the boy's hand and hurried to obey. The princess stepped up three rungs, leaning precariously forward while Elif held the stool steady. The boy watched from the middle of the room.

"A-ha!" Zoe held up a slim, sharp rock. "I knew I had one!" She jumped to the floor and went back to the table while Elif folded and stored the stool in its place against the wall. When she returned, Zoe was scratching the rock against the slim slate. "See?" The princess showed the boy the face she had drawn. "Now," she said, handing the tools over to him, "your name?"

The boy started drawing. When he finished, he lifted the slate to show her.

"That's a bird, and that's a nest." Zoe rubbed her lip. "You're named after some sort of bird?"

"Or perhaps Nestor, Your Highness," Elif said.

Zoe looked into the boy's eyes. "Are you Nestor?"

The boy shook his head.

Zoe frowned. "But there are so many birds. Hawk? Sparrow? Are you Sparrow?"

Again, the boy shook his head.

"Robin? Crow?" Zoe continued to guess while the boy repeatedly shook his head.

"Your Highness," Elif urged, "we must—"

"Yes." Zoe handed the slate back to the boy. "Fine. You will be Little Bird. Will that suit you?"

The boy smiled and nodded.

"Very well. Elif, take Little Bird and clean him up for the party tonight."

"But I must help you—"

"I can get dressed on my own. He needs a bath. Go now, so you won't be late."

Elif gazed at the princess' dress once more.

"Go with her," Zoe said to the boy. "She will make you look nice, so you can meet the king."

The boy seemed nervous, but he tucked the slate and rock together into one fist and then followed Elif out the door.

A heaviness settled over Zoe's shoulders. If she had her way about it, she'd stay here with her work. The thought of putting a broad smile on her face while floating among the people in the dress that now hung near the door made her feel like a new lamb about to be marketed for slaughter. She crossed into her bedroom and over to the bath Elif had prepared for her. After shedding her clothes, she sank into the tepid water and rested her head on the edge of the tub, closing her eyes. At least she would have a chance to hear Anchurus play. That was something to look forward to. And she had to admit she was curious whether the stray musician had accepted the king's invitation, and if so, how he might perform. That her father would be at the height of his charm was certain. There was no king so handsome or charismatic as Midas. The people loved seeing him at events like these, as his graciousness always came shining through. Once she got herself into the right frame of mind, it would be a fun evening.

She opened her eyes and focused on the painting hanging on the wall opposite her. It was of her mother, made shortly after Zoe had been born. Queen Demodica had a glow about her cheeks, her lips slightly upturned, which was unusual. In most of her likenesses, she looked serious, thoughtful, and regal. This was Zoe's favorite, as it showed a little of the warmth Zoe remembered.

"He's not going to give it up," she said to the picture. "He's going to keep going until something terrible happens." She waited, as if expecting the painting to talk back. She could almost hear what her mother might say.

Trust him, darling. He's a good king.

Zoe rubbed soap over her skin. "The army is depleted, exhausted. If you were here, you could get him to let up."

Not for long.

Zoe paused, her hands under water. "If it's true that the dark goddess is helping them . . . ." She was tempted to dunk her head under, but there wasn't time for her hair to dry before the festivities. "Why did you demand all representations of her be hidden?"

She didn't know what her mother might say to that. She finished bathing, wrapped herself in the towel Elif had laid on the chair nearby, and padded across the room. With a sigh, she sat down on her bed. Clean underclothes rested beside her, but she didn't feel like putting them on. She lay back and stared at the ceiling. "I don't want to do this. Go down and act like everything is great when it's not."

It's your birthday. Go have a little fun.

"And what happens tomorrow? Father sends Anchurus back out with a depleted and tired army to fight Sargon and whatever magic he has with him." She threw up her hands. "Why is he so obsessed about this?"

She couldn't imagine an answer to that either. She rested, her skin drying under the towel. Suddenly, she narrowed her eyes and sat up. Her gaze jerked back across the room to the painting. “You knew, didn’t you?” She crossed over to the wall. “You knew why.”

Her mother’s hazel eyes stared back at her. It had been two years since she’d passed, but already it seemed so long. Staring at the likeness, Zoe felt a swell of energy, her heartbeat quickening. The longer the thought rested in her mind, the more power it gained. Her father was keeping a secret, and her mother had known what it was. Perhaps that had been her reason for banishing the goddess from the city?

When Elif returned, she seemed surprised to find the princess ready to go. Elif hurried to help Zoe with her green and gold jeweled necklace, the boy trailing by the door. He looked transformed in a little maroon jacket, breeches, and moccasins, his hair freshly washed and combed and his cheeks ruddy from all the scrubbing.

“My, don’t you look handsome!” Zoe said.

“He insisted I leave while he bathed,” Elif said. “A peculiar boy.”

“He seemed to have done well on his own,” Zoe said.

The boy smiled at her, showing pearly white teeth. The sight of his dancing eyes lifted Zoe’s spirits.

Elif finished fastening the necklace and stood back. “You look beautiful, Your Highness.”

Zoe smiled, glanced down at the boy, and set her hand on her hip. “You will follow me,” she said to him, “and you will conduct yourself like a young man, understood?”

The boy nodded, clutching his slate and rock in one hand.

Turning to Elif, Zoe said, “Take your time getting ready. Then join us. You deserve a night of fun.”

“But, Your Highness—”

Zoe cast her a look that made it clear there would be no more discussion. Elif bowed her head and dashed off down the hall to her room.

. . .

THE CASTLE HALLS teemed with servants rushing back and forth, some of them carrying food, others running about with costumes in their arms, preparing for the evening theater. The advisors walked in a line toward the south room, their heads down, their shoulders hunched with the weight of the news they carried. As they approached the four columns that spanned the entrance by the great double doors, they turned to see Haluk walking in.

They all stopped and stared. It was a rare occurrence for the king's garden guard to enter the castle. A slight, older man, he'd served for over forty years—first for King Gordius, Midas' father, and then for King Midas. A devoted guard, Haluk never left his post at the Rose Field except when he retired to his quarters, which were behind the castle grounds in the servants' barracks. But now, here he was inside the castle, escorting a heavyset old man with a full white beard and bald head. Strangely, the man was wearing no pants, only white underclothes and a blue cloak, his feet bare. He gawked at the entrance as they passed through the doors, at one point stopping to look down at the stone floor. Standing on its cold surface, he pointed. "Now that's mighty fine work there."

Haluk touched the man's upper arm. "This way." He pointed to the left. The man started walking again, but slowly, his gaze still on the detailed artwork at his feet. Xander looked down to see what was so interesting. It was the same swirling design he had walked on for years, the geometric shapes in yellow gold and scarlet, the gold particularly attractive under the gleam of the fading sun's rays. Fotis, impatient, moved on with Aster on his heels, but Xander waited until Haluk and the old man came abreast of him.

"Hello," Xander said to the newcomer. Bright blue eyes gazed into his own. The old stranger was about the same height as Xander, which was refreshing, considering most other men were taller. "Did you forget your pants?"

Haluk eyed the advisor with a warning glance. "We must meet with the king immediately."

"Oh, me too," Xander said. "We can go together!" He smiled at the stone-faced guard, then returned his attention to his companion. "I have some that might fit you. Pants, I mean."

The old man took Xander's arm and leaned heavily on it, as if the walk had already tired him. "I don't know how I left without them. I never used to forget such things." He chuckled, and Xander laughed with him. Ahead, Fotis gestured emphatically for Xander to return to his place in line. Xander ignored him.

"Tell me, son." The man's breath smelled like wine and cheese, his soft beard long enough to brush Xander's wrist. "Are my eyes going, or do you have a bit of the moon in you?"

Xander smiled sheepishly. "I'm the lucky one today, I guess you could say. The dark goddess blessed me, and now I am glowing!" He did a sort of half skip and hop, but the old man didn't smile.

"The dark goddess? You don't mean Katiah?"

"I summoned her. She glows. You should see her. And such long dark hair." He gestured at his neck, demonstrating.

The old man stopped, forcing Haluk to stop. "You summoned the dark goddess?"

Xander puffed up. "At the king's order, of course."

"The king wanted you to summon the dark goddess?" the old man exclaimed.

"Well . . ." Xander looked for Fotis, but the lead advisor had already disappeared around the corner. "He wanted more information about her. It was the only way."

The old man frowned, his expression troubled. Haluk steered him left and then right into the narrow passageway that would take them toward the back of the castle where the king waited in the south room. It was where he frequently met with merchants and traders and where he passed judgment on those who'd been captured.

"You must have traded something for it?" the old man said.

Xander looked down at himself. "I didn't really mean to."

"I am sorry for you," the old man said.

Xander's expression sobered. He glanced down the hall to where the other two advisors waited by the south room door.

"We have information for the king," Fotis said to the guard.

"And I have a trespasser," Haluk called.

"A trespasser?" Xander stared at him.

"A little stiff, this one is," the old man said, gesturing toward Haluk.

"Why do you say he is a trespasser?" Xander asked.

"Haluk is perfectly capable of handling it," Fotis said.

"Thank the gods he's protecting us from such danger," Aster said.

"We must speak to the king!" Fotis demanded.

The guard knocked on the door. "Your advisors, Your Majesty," he called, "and Haluk."

The door opened, and Rastus poked his head out. His gaze darted to the garden guard.

"A trespasser, sir," Haluk said.

Rastus observed the old man, then turned to Fotis.

"Very important news," Fotis said.

"I get to tell him," Xander said.

"Since the rest of us are so eager to," Aster added.

Rastus' gaze settled on Xander. "What happened to you?"

"Let them in," King Midas called.

Rastus opened the door. Fotis gestured for Haluk to go first. The guard guided the old man through, and the advisors followed. The room was about half the size of the king's strategy room. The king stood behind a tall oak chair in the center. Prince Anchurus lingered nearby, his arms crossed over his chest. "We could send scouts," he said to his father.

"That didn't work last time," Midas said. "Perhaps if we come from the north."

"It will take longer."

"Summon Commander Baran," Midas said to Rastus. "He may have another idea."

Anchurus, duly chastened, stepped back and was silent. Rastus bowed and left the room. The trespasser, still holding on to Xander's arm, slowly lowered himself onto one knee.

"King Midas. I am Silenus. It is a great pleasure to meet you."

"A trespasser, Your Majesty," Haluk said, "in the gardens."

"Silenus." Midas mused over the name. "How did you get past the wall?"

"The wall around your gardens?" Silenus frowned. "I'm afraid I can't remember. I was walking on the road toward your fine city. I got tired and stopped to rest. When I woke up, I was surrounded by multi-colored blooms." He rubbed his forehead. "I do have a bit of a headache."

Midas turned his gaze to Haluk.

"We don't know yet, sire," Haluk said. "We are searching the perimeter and inspecting the walls."

Midas addressed Silenus. "Do you know the penalty for trespassing in the king's gardens?"

"I assure you that wasn't my intention," Silenus said.

"Get him up," Midas ordered.

Haluk grabbed Silenus' arm and tried to jerk him up, but the man was too heavy. Xander reached under his other arm, and together, they managed to get the trespasser back on his feet.

"Thank you, my boy." Silenus tapped the back of Xander's hand.

Midas glanced at Xander, then at Silenus, then jerked his gaze back to Xander. A troubled expression came over his face as he studied his youngest advisor. Xander wilted and stepped back.

"It's gracious of you, Your Majesty," Silenus said, "to take time out of your day."

Midas glared a moment more at Xander before pulling his attention back to the old man.

"It's understandable you don't remember me," Silenus continued. "You were just a boy when I was here many years ago. You hadn't yet seen battle, but you were good with the sword. Your father, King Gordius, was so proud." He raised his chin, as if he himself were the proud one. "He took me to see you spar with the blond guard. I can't remember his name . . ."

"Volkan?" Midas said. "Otar Volkan?"

"Volkan. Was that it?" Silenus rubbed his beard.

"He was the captain of the king's guard for my father. His son, Rastus, holds the position now."

"Ah, yes," Silenus said, nodding, though it didn't seem clear he remembered.

Midas took in the old man's expression, appearance, and bare white legs. "Where was it you found him?" he asked Haluk.

"In the perennial plot, Your Majesty. I'm afraid he squashed one of the tulips."

"My apologies." Silenus bowed his head. "I tend to be a bit clumsy."

"Silenus?" Midas said.

The old man smiled. "Yes. I am Silenus of Mount Nysa, Your Majesty." He bowed his head again.

"You have traveled far?"

"It is a good journey from there to here. But there's no better city for a party, at least not when your father ruled. And I hear there is to be a party? Gordium always has the best wine in all the kingdom."

The three advisors exchanged glances. A trespasser, assuming an invitation to the princess' birthday party!

Midas rested his hands on his belt. "I remember a story about a rodent, one that kept me listening far into the night. I believe you were the one who told it?"

Silenus laughed. "That was Alp, the kangaroo rat, who could hop as high as a man's shoulder!"

"Yes! That was it." Midas' eyes took on a faraway look.

Silenus pulled his shoulders back. "You have before you, Your Majesty, one of the finest entertainers in the land. Grant me a cup of your best wine, and I shall regale you with music and dance, after which I shall keep you entranced with stories such as you've never heard."

Midas watched him another moment, then turned to Haluk. "Take him to Timon."

Haluk blinked. "Your Majesty?"

"Have Timon prepare him for the party," Midas said, "then return to your post and find out where he got in."

Haluk looked from the king to Silenus and back as if he couldn't quite grasp what he'd been told.

"Haluk?" Midas said.

"Yes, Your Highness." Haluk bowed and gestured for Silenus to lead the way out.

Silenus stepped toward the king. "If you'd like to hear the end of Alp's story?" He wiggled his eyebrows up and down and smiled.

Midas chuckled. "Later, perhaps."

Silenus' smile faded. When Haluk took his arm, he followed the guard out.

"Oh, and Haluk," Midas said. "Tell Timon. A jug of my best wine for my father's friend."

Silenus uttered a loud guffaw and clapped his hands together. "Aha! You do take after your father."

Midas bowed his head in acknowledgement. Haluk, still looking puzzled, took Silenus' arm, and the two left. The advisors exchanged glances but said nothing.

Midas went back to his chair and sat down. "You have news?"

Xander glanced at Aster, but the middle advisor stood by the door, his gaze on some unknown spot on the wall. Fotis gestured for Xander to proceed.

"Well?" Midas said.

Xander laced his fingers together, cleared his throat, shifted his weight, then cleared his throat again.

Fotis sighed. "We have information."

"We did it," Xander blurted.

"We did not," Aster said.

"Did what?" Midas said.

"What you wanted us to do." Xander glanced nervously at Fotis.

"We must clarify, Your Majesty," Fotis said.

"Good communication is not important," Aster said.

"I did what you told us to do!" Xander opened his hands in front of him.

"Your Majesty," Fotis said, "Xander sometimes has . . . difficulty following directions."

"I do not!" Xander said.

"He does not," Aster said.

"I'm afraid he does," Fotis said. "He is still young, and he can get a bit too enthusiastic."

"Enthusiasm is bad," Aster said.

"I made it work. I did it!"

"His intentions were good, Your Majesty," Fotis said, "but a bit too enthusiastic—"

"Well, *you* weren't going to do it!" Xander said. "You never would have figured out anything from those old dusty parchments and tablets."

"That is not true," Aster said.

"If you had lent some assistance instead of 'thinking,'" Fotis growled at Aster.

"I was the one who did it." Xander turned back to the king. "It was me."

"He did not," Aster said.

"I'm afraid he did, Your Majesty," Fotis agreed.

Midas turned a tired gaze to Xander. "Out with it."

"I summoned her."

Midas' expression remained flat.

"I summoned her, Your Majesty. I got her to come!"

No response. Only Anchurus moved, taking a step closer to the group.

"The one you wanted to talk to," Xander continued. "You wanted to find out if she was helping you-know-who, remember?"

The king frowned and turned to Fotis in alarm.

"As I said, Your Majesty," Fotis said. "A bit too enthusiastic."

"If only he had less enthusiasm," Aster said.

"She came. She came!" Xander clapped his hands.

"She didn't come," Aster said.

"I warned him, Your Majesty, several times," Fotis said.

"Which worked exceptionally well," Aster said.

Midas leapt to his feet. "She's been here?" He glared at Xander. "In *my* castle? This is why you're . . . you're *glowing?*"

The three advisors fell mute. Xander stopped clapping. "But you wanted to know," he said meekly.

"She is gone now, Your Majesty," Fotis said. "I assure you there was no damage done. Well . . ." He glanced at Xander, who now stood wringing his hands.

"No damage at all," Aster said sadly.

"I got her to tell us, Your Majesty," Xander said. "About you-know-who."

"And?"

"She said she was. Helping him."

"She did not say that," Aster said.

"She did indeed," Fotis said.

"She did," Midas said.

"Yes, Your Majesty," Xander said.

"She admitted it freely," Aster said, "requiring nothing in return."

"It seems you were right about her," Fotis said. "She did confirm it. Directly."

Anchurus came closer, his attention now fully focused on the conversation.

"So what?" Midas gazed at each of his advisors in turn. "You had a nice little chat with her?"

"Yes!" Xander brightened. "She was nice, Your Majesty. Well, most of the time. You'd be surprised." He glanced at his colleague. "She did set Aster's arm on fire."

"It was nothing, sire," Aster said. "A pleasant exchange."

"He put it right out," Xander said. "The blanket is ruined, I'm afraid. But she is very powerful. And beautiful. You should have seen her. She was wearing a blue dress that glimmered like the stars. Her hair was as soft as violets and fell in waves past her shoulders, and her skin—" He glanced up to see the king glowering at him. "Well, it sort of glowed."

"Like you seem to be doing right now?" Midas said.

Xander looked down at himself.

"Your Majesty," Fotis said. "The point is that you were correct. She is assisting your enemy."

"I got the information you needed." Xander gazed hopefully at his king.

"At the expense of your soul, it seems," Midas said.

Xander appeared surprised, then nervous. He shifted his weight and rubbed his palms on his robe.

"It was a well-thought-out encounter," Aster said.

The king walked around to the back of his chair. Gripping the top of it, he stewed, dropping his gaze to the cushion. "So. You are hers."

"We had to give her something," Xander said meekly, "in return for the information."

"She didn't insist," Aster said.

"Aster was going to do it," Xander said, "but I didn't want him to."

"It was regrettable, Your Majesty," Fotis said.

"She has you now, too." Midas cast his gaze to the painting of the queen that hung on the opposite wall. The others looked confused.

"So Sargon's army has the assistance of the dark goddess." Anchurus spoke for the first time. "She brought the fog."

"Yes," Fotis said. "She admitted that too."

Anchurus stood a little taller.

"All right," Midas said. "You've relayed the information. Go now. I must think it over."

Fotis and Aster were quick to obey, but Xander stared at the king. Aster returned, spun him around, and with a hand on the small of his back, pushed him forward.

"But I did what he wanted," Xander said.

“You didn’t think it through,” Fotis hissed as he opened the door.

“Thinking is one of his strengths,” Aster said.

“Is he going to execute us?” Xander asked.

“You should be more concerned about what the dark goddess will do to you,” Fotis said.

“Scare him some more,” Aster said. “It is very helpful.”

“He should be scared!” Fotis snarled. “He never thinks before he acts.”

“Thinking is always best,” Aster said with an exaggerated nod of his head.

Xander turned back to the king. “I got the information for you, Your Majesty,” he said.

Aster bundled Xander out and closed the door.

CHAPTER FIVE

The goddess Denisia of Mount Nysa patted her face with the edge of her wrap. The sun blazed hot in the afternoon sky, and there was no shade to be found. After four days' travel, they were finally nearing the city of Gordium, the great wooden gates looming up ahead. With its imposing columns and tall lookout towers, she knew that she and her faithful servant, Chetin, were already under surveillance. This didn't concern her. Chetin would tell the guards that they were here on trade business. With his calm brown eyes and direct way of speaking, he'd easily convince them. Besides, Gordium was a friendly city—a likely place to find her missing grandfather.

Denisia thought back to his stories. If there was one location Silenus loved almost as much as Mount Nysa, it was Gordium. He'd often told of its bustling marketplace and well-groomed streets, fondly recalling its bountiful food and talented musicians. He'd spent his days there sleeping in rented rooms and his nights singing and dancing with whatever musical troupe would have him. There had been many, for he had a beautiful baritone voice and a whimsical way with the flute. He could spin a yarn fascinating enough to keep people entranced for hours, after which they'd inevitably shower him with gifts of food and drink that he'd devour with glee.

Two days into their journey, Denisia and Chetin had come upon a group of minstrels who'd reported having seen a portly old man with a long white beard and friendly manner entertaining crowds in the city. One young woman with a silk scarf covering her luscious black hair mentioned hearing him sing in the streets at night. Her delighted smile when speaking of him was proof enough to Denisia that she'd find her gregarious grandfather here.

They paused at the top of the last rise. Below, the beautiful Sangarius river wound lazily toward them, its path forming a wide hook in front of Gordium's eastern gates and then snaking northwest, the water winking happily under the warm rays of the sun. A broad wood and iron bridge offered the only easy crossing, King Midas thus controlling much of the trade between kingdoms. His castle was an eye-catching architectural wonder elevated on the west side of the city, a cluster of rolling hills at its back. The natural gray and white of the marble and limestone took on a two-toned creamy sheen, with three levels rising high above the grounds, one watchtower for each of the north and south sides. Denisia had been here several times before, at least once with her grandfather. The last time had been about five years ago. She'd gathered goods from the market—spices, herbs, clothing, and jewelry. But she'd found something else she hadn't expected.

She'd been out walking late at night, imagining how she might lure some of Gordium's most virile young men to her next harvest festival when she'd come upon the young prince in the auditorium. She'd recognized him instantly, having seen him on her previous visits. He sat alone in the center of the stage, a handsome but unassuming young man with sandy hair that fell softly on his forehead, his royal maroon cloak resting over his shoulders. Under the watchful eye of the empty benches, he played his instrument, the stars his only audience.

Drawn by the music, she walked closer and peered around the stone wall that served as the backdrop. She'd never seen an instrument like the one he held. Made of light-colored wood, it had a triangular body with an elegant curved top line. Delicate carvings adorned its surface, the strings placed close together and stretched from top to bottom, their ends disappearing into the frame. When he played, he had to reach a full arm's length to pluck the lowest note, yet he did so with gentle grace, the way a tender man might handle a woman. Multiple tones sounded, creating the melody and the accompaniment at once, as if many people, rather than one, were manipulating the music. She became so entranced that she forgot herself, dizzied by the young man who brought forth such feeling from his fingers, a depth of emotion that normally would have taken decades to develop.

It wasn't until the moon drifted into the western half of the sky that he ended his last song and stood up to leave. She made her presence known then, walking up behind him as he placed the instrument into a wagon.

"What is this instrument you play?" she asked.

"A harp." He secured it with ropes, readying it for transport back to the castle.

"I've heard of these. They're like lyres, but this one is so much grander!"

"My sister made it."

"Made it!" Denisia stood back to take another look. Princess Zoe. She knew of the golden haired girl, the jewel of the kingdom. "She must be very gifted."

The prince bowed his head and started to leave, pulling the wagon behind him.

"Wait," she said.

He paused, out of politeness she was sure, for he clearly didn't know who she was. She had no followers with her that night, no entourage to announce her presence. To him, she was just another citizen of Gordium, perhaps one of the wealthier residents, judging by the forest green gown she wore.

"Will you come back and play again?"

"There will not be much time for playing now." He looked longingly at the harp. "Tomorrow we are off to battle."

She imagined his youthful body sliced through with a sword, his smooth forehead pierced with an arrow. Such a waste! He should play his music to inspire the people, not fight wars in the king's name.

"When you come back," she said, "you must delight us with your songs once again. To have such talent and not use it is an affront to the gods."

He'd cocked an eyebrow then and held her gaze. Denisia wondered if he sensed something about her, but he only nodded and walked on as the wagon wheels rattled over the stones. Watching him go, she whispered a protective spell, one that would bend nature's gifts toward him. A stray tree branch to block an oncoming blow. A spinning dust devil to obscure the enemy's vision. A fast-growing vine to delay an attacking soldier. She hoped these would be enough to keep him safe so that one day he would return to her.

Fortunately, he had. As she crossed the mighty bridge and approached the city of Gordium, she knew the prince was likely having breakfast in the castle. News of a royal homecoming did not go unnoticed. Nearly every commoner had something to say about the prince's return. He hadn't garnered a hero's welcome. Whispered rumors painted a dark picture of King Sargon II riding forth from a strange fog to achieve a surprising victory. Denisia didn't care. She would see the prince again, and that was all that mattered. This time, she would not be some stranger in the night. She would reveal her true nature, for what prince could deny a beautiful goddess?

But first, she had to find her grandfather. Or at least, the man she called her grandfather. She'd learned the truth when she'd reached the age of ten. Silenus had told her that her mother was a mortal maiden and her father, Zeus, the king of the gods. They were no actual relation to Silenus. Instead, Zeus had appointed the forest god as guardian after Denisia's mother died during childbirth. The story had unnerved Denisia, but Mount Nysa was such a magical, peaceful place to live, and Silenus so warm and kind, it wasn't long before she'd forgotten all about it. Silenus was immortal and wise, but far more than that, he was the only family she had.

She fluffed her wrap around her and scanned the city again. He'd been gone for many days, longer than ever before. She was worried. She'd been doing her best to keep his illness quiet—to protect his dignity, she told herself—but now he was lost, and it was her fault.

They trotted into a shallow draw and approached the stone walls that framed Gordium Road. Twice the height of a man, they appeared a pale yellow in the sunlight, painted with colorful pictorials that revealed the story of King Midas' conquests. Hearty evergreen bushes threatened to hide the paintings, the taller leafy trees sporting trimmed branches. Denisia reached out to one as they passed, squeezed a leaf, and felt it swell in response. When she looked back, the branch had sprouted three new purple flowers, each as big as her palm. If only her powers could help her find Silenus, but alas, her influence seemed limited to the natural elements, the plants, trees, rocks, and earth. Those and the bottomless bag of wine she kept at her belt, which often proved the most effective power of all.

Traffic slowed as the road narrowed, the walls closing in on either side, funneling the travelers toward the city gates. The people crowded together, some on horseback and some with ox pulled wagons, but most on foot. The wait seemed interminable, but finally, Denisia and Chetin came to the grand archway. Chetin talked confidently to the guards, explaining they had arrived to trade. A big guard with a stout belly looked them over and then permitted them to enter.

Denisia took the lead as they rode under the archway and on toward the market. A few merchants remained, some men displaying tools, hunting gear, and weapons, while women showed fabrics, clothing, and food. One woman had a small boy no more than five years old sitting next to her. He looked up as Denisia passed, and his eyes widened a little. She smiled to herself. Unlike the adults, the children could always sense the power that emanated from her. She might have given him the gift of a goddess' blessing then, but time was of the essence.

They reached the end of the marketplace, where the main road forked. One branch took the traveler north toward the heart of the city and the castle beyond, while the other angled south where the inns could be found and later, the poorer citizens living in tents. Denisia pulled her horse to a stop and dismounted. "Search the city," she told Chetin, handing him the reins. "I'll meet you near the castle gates tomorrow morning."

He bowed and left her, walking away with her horse in tow. She turned and followed the castle road. Wide enough to accommodate two horse-drawn wagons, it was sparsely populated this evening, with only a few fellow travelers passing her by. Narrow alleyways formed offshoots in both directions, the stone and wood dwellings clumped together in cozy communities. She had started up the hill when something caught her eye: a modest mud dwelling on the right. It sat back from the road, dark and forgotten. She didn't know why this one had drawn her attention and was about to move on when something moved. A small animal?

Curious, she approached. Stray dogs were common in the city, but she sensed a vague memory stirring as if she had seen this animal before. She spotted it again, or at least thought she did. But it wasn't real—only a clay sculpture sitting at the corner of the dwelling, nearly hidden under a bush. She pulled it out and ran her hands over it. It had been molded into the shape of a cat. Strange that she had imagined it moving. She set it back in place, walked to the wooden door, and raised her hand to knock. Paused. She needed to get to the castle. She glanced down at the bush and, on impulse, squeezed one of the branches. It swelled, lifted, and filled with slender green leaves, two blooms appearing with teardrop petals of white and pink. A stray dog trotted past. She exhaled and knocked three times.

There was no answer. As she thought. Abandoned. She was about to leave when she heard a click. Two small eyes underneath a scraggly nest of gray hair peered out from behind a candle flame. *Lady Verna*. The name echoed in her mind.

"You're too early," the old woman said. Her voice was thin and frail, the words trembling in her throat. "It's not yet time."

"I apologize." Denisia studied her face. "Do I know you?"

"Come back when it's time." Lady Verna started to shut the door.

"Wait." Denisia put her foot out. "The cat?"

"Is Talu there?" The woman leaned out to look. Denisia noted the thinness of her neck, the bones sharp in her shoulders. "I haven't seen her for days."

"Talu is the cat?"

"I'm not surprised you remember her. She liked you."

Denisia recalled a gray cat rubbing against her leg. "I was here before?"

Pale blue eyes searched her own. "You're still plain, but older. That is what he wanted."

"What who wanted?"

"It's not time."

"But—"

"Talu, I'll have meat tomorrow," Lady Verna called. "You'll have to find your own tonight." She pushed the door shut.

Denisia remained with her palm on the wood, her heart racing. Memories flooded her mind. She was lying on a cold table, a fiery pain in her chest that made it hard to breathe. Silenus stood over her with his white brows knitted together in concern. He held onto her hand and told her it would be all right.

She lingered, gazing at the bush's new blooms. Had Silenus left something out of his story about her past? She backed away, her mind swirling with questions. If she found him, she would ask him.

In a lucid moment, perhaps he could tell her when they had visited Lady Verna. And just who Lady Verna was.

She returned to the narrow alleyway and headed for the castle road. A few steps later, she stopped dead when a gray cat passed in front of her. It watched her with jewel-blue eyes and then dashed off in the opposite direction.

"Talu?" she whispered.

To enter the king's grand hall on the evening of the princess' birthday celebration was to enter a magical world. Tables lined the perimeter filled with food of every kind, delicacies the like as would not be seen any other time of year. The hunters had worked for weeks to stock the underground pits with venison, rabbit, duck, goose, boar, and pheasant, while the farmers had pitched in extra beef, lamb, and chicken. From the king's stock and gardens came more beef, fruits and vegetables, dried tomatoes, shelled hazelnuts, cooked corn, baked parsnips, raisins, and dried pears. The figs filled a pyramid centerpiece against the far wall that, despite being depleted early on, stood powerfully stout on its wooden feet. Against the other wall, the kitchen servants kept tables of tempting desserts consistently replenished, cookies and cakes and pies and custards and puddings and creams and pastries and more appearing and disappearing and reappearing again.

Set within the hall's vast interior were six performance squares —sections of the room where the king's entertainers were already dazzling the guests. Artists painted and danced and sang and made people laugh. One square featured a puppet show where the performers hid behind a small wooden stage. The king's guests drifted about, some of them sitting on the rugs to watch the shows in their entirety, others lingering farther back for a time before moving on. The grand stage at the front of the hall remained empty, reserved for the play that would take place later that evening.

Having generously shared her wine bag while wafting a magical mix of herbs and extracts under two of the guards' noses, Denisia had slipped into the party unhindered. Suitably camouflaged in her plain sage-green gown, her hair done up and covered in a pale linen scarf, she began her search for Silenus. She tried to hurry, but everyone else was ambling and gawking, and she didn't want to bring attention to herself. At one station, a crowd had gathered to watch a painter craft a busy castle scene. She paused for a moment to join them, then quickly moved on, observing with awe all the king's grandeur until she returned to the double doors, disappointed.

Her grandfather wasn't there.

Gliding over to the left, she gave the room one last sweep of her gaze. Nowhere could she see Silenus' bald head. The worry that had been hovering over her like a cloud expanded, shortening her breath. She steeled herself against it and stepped out into the hallway. Here, people gathered to admire the murals on the walls interspersed with life-sized bronze statues of wild animals, maidens, warriors, and nymphs. Colorful vases full of fresh flowers adorned small tables while above them, paintings of the royal family members decorated the walls. Many guards stood watch, but Denisia had to give the king credit for allowing the citizens such leeway inside his magnificent castle. It wasn't something most kings would do.

At the end of the hall, she spotted the opening to the stairwell. There were extra guards posted there. No citizen would get beyond the first level. She turned around, intending to continue her search in the other direction.

And ran straight into a man.

At first, all she saw was a cream-colored linen shirt over a broad chest. She murmured her apologies, then stepped back and looked up into his face.

The prince!

"Pardon me." He started to step past her and then met her gaze. "Have we met?"

How he had grown! Gone was the boyish softness about his cheeks, replaced with a trimmed growth of sandy brown beard, his neck thick between broad shoulders. His defined brow shaded hazel eyes that had darkened under the weight of command.

"Many years ago," she said. "You were playing your beautiful harp."

His eyes narrowed. "That was you? My only audience?"

He remembered! "I was fortunate," she said.

"I don't know about that." He chuckled, some of the tightness leaving his shoulders. "I was no master. It's why I went to play somewhere quiet, where I believed I would be alone." He arched an eyebrow at her. "You're a citizen?"

"I'm a . . . traveler. Searching for someone."

He glanced around. "Maybe I can help."

Denisia tried not to let her excitement show. He remembered her. And despite clearly having something important on his mind, he wanted to help her. "He's an old man. Portly. Mostly bald, with a long white beard. He loves to tell stories. He may seem a little . . . confused."

The prince's expression darkened. "Do you mean Silenus?"

"Yes!" She reached toward him. "Have you seen him?"

The prince glanced away. "What is your business with him?"

"He is my grandfather. He left a couple of days ago and didn't tell anyone where he was going."

"Left where, may I ask?"

"We live on the Isle of Mount Nysa."

He nodded. "And you thought to look for him here."

"My grandfather loves Gordium. He's visited many times before. And some minstrels on the road said they had seen him in the city."

The prince gestured down the hall. "This way."

She tried to find his eyes, but the soldier in him had taken over, so she walked toward the guarded stairwell she had left only moments before. They had to navigate through the crowd, but eventually, the path cleared. She hung back to let him come forward. "Do we keep going?"

He pointed to the next door on the right. Had he been anyone else, she would have refused to go in with him, but this was Prince Anchurus. Stepping past him, she scanned the room. "He's not here."

"He was caught. Trespassing." Anchurus closed the door.

Denisia's heart fell. Trespassing was a serious enough offense to land a man in the dungeon. She made her way toward the three couches beyond. "He is awaiting judgment?"

"The king was merciful."

She folded her hands and faced him.

"Who are you?" he asked.

"A simple traveler. Please. I'd like to see my grandfather." When he didn't respond, she was tempted to leave. She need not be held hostage. Yet, he stood like a bull in front of the door. She pulled her scarf off her head and drew herself up to her full height. "I am Denisia of Mount Nysa. I demand you let me see my grandfather."

He did a double-take. Her name was well known in the Kingdom of Phrygia. She felt a moment's satisfaction. But then he took a step toward her.

"Prove it."

"I need prove nothing. I told you who I am. Now where is he?"

"Prove it, and I shall show you."

Denisia gritted her teeth. So many ways she could think of to punish such insolence! But this was Anchurus. She inhaled and looked around. A stone vase sat on the low table by the couch. Inside rested three fading blooms, two blue and one white. Holding it up so he could see, she touched the petals. The blooms expanded to twice their previous size, their scents exploding into the air.

The prince observed it all, seemingly unaffected.

She returned the vase to its table.

"Very well," he said, bowing his head. "I will take you to your grandfather."

She brightened, but he didn't move. Instead, he seemed to struggle with something.

"Once you've seen him . . ." he began, then cleared his throat.

"After you've seen him, might you . . ." He paused again and dropped his gaze. "I need your help, Goddess Denisia."

She almost agreed immediately, but stopped herself. "If my grandfather is well, I will consider a favor."

He nodded and gestured toward the door. "This way, please."

CHAPTER SIX

Zoe had planned to go straight to the grand hall, but halfway down the stairs, she paused. The boy looked up with a questioning glance. She ignored him, thinking over her "conversation" with her mother. This would be a good time. Her father was likely preparing for the festivities.

She tapped her fingers against her thigh. She'd never snooped into her father's things before. But if there were any clues to be found, they would be in his strategy room. No one was allowed in the room when the king wasn't there. Not even the princess.

"I forgot something," she said, dropping the boy's hand. "Let's go back."

They climbed to the second level, hurried down the hall, and ascended the third flight of stairs on the other side. Zoe paused to make sure they were alone, then, holding her skirts aloft, strode to the second door on the left. The guards stood stiffly on either side, so she put on her friendliest smile. "The king asked me to retrieve something for him."

The two men exchanged glances.

"He is preparing for the party. Must I go get him?" She kept the smile on her face. The guards didn't budge. "You know I wouldn't ask if the king didn't wish it." Still nothing. She turned to the one on the right, a muscled man with fat cheeks. "You are a loyal guard. But the king asked me. I promise I will be in and out quickly."

The guard looked straight ahead.

"Very well," she said. "I shall go get him, but he will be irritated at the interruption." She started walking away, but then the muscled guard relented and opened the door. She paused, turned back, and lightly touched him on the arm as she slipped inside, the boy tight to her heels.

"Don't touch anything, all right?" She drifted away from him, allowing her gaze to take in her surroundings. Her enthusiasm waned. She'd been in this room many times. What made her think she'd find something new? There were the table and chairs where her father took counsel, the weapons displayed on the wall to her right, the battle strategy table beyond, and the fireplace after that. She moseyed along, trying to imagine where her father might hide a secret. On the battle map rested the small figures he used to plan his tactics. She paused to look at the black one that represented King Sargon. Her father had handled it so many times that the tops of the horse's ears were smoothed, the folds of its mane beginning to fade.

Drifting across the stone floor, she observed the shelves against the wall. Up high, she could see the wooden bridge she'd made for him. A stepstool was required, but this room didn't have one. With the boy's help, she pulled one chair over and stepped up onto that. A spinning top rested near the bridge. She twirled it, remembering when she'd made it. She'd been seven or eight? A knife lay in the corner, the blade adorned with a wooden handle she'd carved with the image of a horse. He'd kept that, too. She smiled to herself. Toward the back, there was the miniature wind-maker she had designed. Its blades still turned. And the glove she had tried to sew, but that had proven too small for her father's hand.

A creak sounded near the door. Zoe whirled around, holding her breath, but no one came in. She explored the middle shelf with more urgency. It held gifts the king had received from other kingdoms, precious stones and miniature sculptures and beaded jewelry. On the lower shelf were several parchments with writing on them. Zoe glanced at a few, but they were old messages to King Gordius, some of them decrees he had signed. Nothing to reveal what her father might be hiding.

She stepped off the chair and sighed. Foolish to believe she could figure everything out with a quick search of her father's favorite room. She had begun to think the idea of him holding a secret was silly too when she decided to check the cabinet, just in case.

It sat against the wall, a tall, thick, and heavy piece of furniture made of maple wood with three open shelves on the top and two closed on the bottom. She checked the top ones but found only trinkets, vases, and parchments, along with a few miniature sculptures, a painted clay pot, two small animal hides, and a leather satchel with colored rocks inside. She hesitated before opening the first closed shelf, but found only daggers, pokers, and several arrowheads. This, too, was proving useless. Then she opened the bottom door.

It was empty save a ragged thing dropped in the corner. A child's toy. She pulled it out. Its stitches were torn and the clothes stained. One beaded eye stared back at her, but there was only a bare spot where the nose must have been. A tuft of hair remained intact, the head floppy on the neck.

Zoe frowned. This was not her doll. It made no sense for her father to have it in his strategy room. She gently squeezed the toy, her mind spinning with questions. Whom did it belong to? Another daughter? One her father kept secret? But she couldn't imagine him loving anyone but her mother. Unless it was an older relationship, someone who came long before the queen? She knew little of her father's younger days.

She pursed her lips. The doll felt fragile in her hands but softly worn, as if it had been treasured once. She placed it back in the corner and closed the door. She would find no more answers here. With the boy's help, she restored the chair to its place under the conference table. She swept the room with one last gaze, then, taking the boy's hand, walked out with a parting smile at the guards.

THE ENDING scene of Timon's play brought the audience to their feet. They applauded and shouted for some time, calling the actors out for repeated bows, which they performed with suitable flare, the dancers returning to frame the leads in waves of colorful ribbons. When they left the stage for the last time, the crowd dispersed for more food. Excitement buzzed throughout the room, as everyone knew that the last event of the evening was about to begin: the king's music contest.

Timon needed a short period to prepare, so the servants refreshed the offerings, bringing more dishes and treats from the castle kitchen to fill up vacant spaces on the tables. Denisia cast a quick glance at Anchurus and then started meandering through the room, serving the wine she always carried in the magical bag at her belt to anyone with an empty glass. She put on her best smile and most gracious manner, and they all received her contributions with effusive gratitude, but inside, she was in turmoil. The play was over, the contest about to begin, and still she hadn't seen her grandfather. She had just decided to sneak out of the grand hall and start searching again when she felt a familiar presence at her shoulder. She turned to offer the prince some wine.

"This is the only thing that makes all this tolerable," he said after draining the cup.

"Come, come," she said, filling it once more. "The play was quite intriguing."

"I would have preferred a battle story."

"It's a small stage." Denisia walked again, pleased when he fell into step beside her. "Not much room on which to set a battle scene."

"It would have made things more exciting," Anchurus said. "I had a hard time not falling asleep."

Denisia laughed. "I thought it was fun. Helped me forget about everything for a while." She turned to him. "You promised to reunite me with my grandfather."

"I expected to find him here." He paused as they neared the double doors, casting his gaze about. "The king invited him to the party."

Denisia looked around, alarmed. The king was on the other side of the room, conversing with some of the wealthier citizens, judging by their richly decorated clothing. The princess floated through the crowd, her maidservant and a small boy tagging along behind her. "You mean he's lost?"

Anchurus shook his head. "The king assigned chaperones. They will keep him safe."

"But where is he?"

Anchurus beckoned the nearest guard standing at the entrance and spoke quietly to him. The guard turned and hurried out. "I will have him recovered," Anchurus said. "Wait here." He gently touched her elbow, then started to walk away.

"Where are you going?"

He paused, his expression pained. "The contest. It begins shortly."

When she looked puzzled, he went on.

"They will demand an encore."

"You will play?" she asked. When he nodded, she smiled happily. "How wonderful!"

"It's been many moons since I've strummed the harp."

"It will be magical," she said. "Please. Go and prepare. I look forward to it."

He glanced at the entrance, then back into her eyes. "Perhaps we can share another cup of wine? After it's over?"

"I will wait for you."

He held her gaze long enough for the heat to rise to her cheeks, then turned and disappeared into the crowd.

. . .

TIMON ARRIVED on stage dressed in his best outfit, his face cleaned of the makeup he'd been wearing earlier for the theatrical performance. Donning a jeweled hat and a blue and cream-colored cloak, he called the audience to assemble. Once they had gathered in front of him, he relayed the rules of the contest. To begin, pairs of musicians would play, one after the other. The crowd would choose a winner from each pair. Then those winners would battle two at a time until there were only two left, after which the king would select the final victor.

Denisia glanced at the double doors, but the guard had not yet returned with her grandfather. As Anchurus had set the young man on the task, there was nothing for her to do now but wait. She drifted toward the stage, curious to hear the musicians.

With the crowd settled and listening, Timon introduced the first pair. A small woman played breathlessly on a wooden flute, after which an equally small man stumbled through a series of halting rhythms on a slightly larger version of the same instrument. The audience chose the woman, who returned backstage while the guards escorted the small man out through the double doors.

The next pairing placed a stocky, middle-aged man on a thin reed instrument with a wiry younger man on a dulcimer. The man on the dulcimer remained while the reed player hurried out, the crowd threatening to break his instrument in half before he escaped.

And so it went, pair after pair playing their pieces, the audience delighting in choosing the winner and shaming the loser. At the final pairing of the first round, a young man with matted hair played a tanbur, a long-necked stringed instrument with a pear-shaped body. He created a rounded sound, but within moments, the audience members were shifting restlessly, grateful when Timon announced the challenger: "Emir Alkan."

He came like a shadow, dark and silent. He was built like a warrior, which was unusual for his profession. Denisia couldn't help but compare him to Prince Anchurus, as there was a certain similarity in the broad shoulders and sharp gaze, his muscles tight under his worn tunic and black cloak. All the other musicians had taken their seats immediately upon reaching the stage. This competitor stopped in front of his chair and gazed out at the audience, his gray eyes seeming to challenge them. Eventually, he flipped his cloak behind him and sat down, drawing his oud into his lap.

The crowd whispered among themselves. The instrument was clearly aged, the wood scarred and stained and the edges rough. Denisia wandered closer, wondering how anyone could produce a winning tune out of something so worn. The musician sat for longer than the audience would have normally tolerated, but they were held spellbound, his movements alone enough to entrance them. As they waited, the small boy who had been tagging along behind the princess crept forward until he was sitting almost at the musician's feet.

Finally, Emir began.

The other contestants had performed solo pieces, but when Emir played, it was as if he had a group with him. He used his boot against the floor to set the walking rhythm, the toe and heel percussive accompaniments to the wistful melody he lured from the strings, a song so full of movement and memory that Denisia felt herself sailing across the sea, the moon beckoning over the waves. She closed her eyes, letting it take her where it would, but then had to open them again to watch, for the musician had added more percussion to his performance. He thudded the heel of his hand against the wooden body of the instrument, the drum-like beat complementing his boot thumps as his fingers fused harmonies with the melody.

Just when she thought he had done all he could, he added his voice, a low baritone hum. It blended sonorously with the sound of the strings, transporting her to a world she'd never before imagined. The crowd listened, mesmerized, until ultimately the rhythm slowed and the song faded into a gentle conclusion.

No one moved. The musician remained where he was, draped over the instrument, while the audience recovered. When they eventually did, they leapt to their feet, roaring and shouting and whistling.

"More!" they cried. "Emir Alkan! More!" The small boy jumped up and down with a child's enthusiasm, repeatedly thrusting his hands toward the stage, though no sounds came from his throat. The noise from the rest of the crowd was so great, however, that Timon had to come out to control it. It took him some time, but finally he gained their attention enough to ask for a winner. The audience roared again in response, and the young tanbur player hurried out of the room as fast as he could. Emir retreated to prepare for his next performance.

Denisia was surprised to find herself almost at the front of the crowd. Never had music transported her like that, except for when Anchurus played. Yet, this had been different. The prince's song had made her feel light, joyful, and full of warmth. But this song had brought tears to her eyes and, like the rest of the crowd, she wanted to hear more. It was a relished kind of sadness, and she longed for it as one might long for that lonely sail on the sea under the moon.

"He's very good, isn't he?"

Startled, Denisia looked left. A young woman stood next to her. Strikingly beautiful, she wore a common cream-colored scarf and a simple dress lacking any embellishments. Her silky dark hair caressed her pale neck, her eyes large and bewitching under smooth eyebrows. Denisia thought she looked familiar. "Do you know him?" she managed to ask.

The woman glanced back at the stage. "I've seen him around. But I've never heard him play like that."

Denisia waited, but the woman revealed nothing further. At the entrance, the guard had yet to appear with Silenus. Denisia searched for Anchurus, but it seemed he had gone backstage. She returned her gaze to the woman, who was now watching as Timon announced the next phase of the contest where the winners would compete against the winners. Everyone sat back down, so Denisia followed suit, taking a spot on a nearby rug.

"Do you mind?" Without waiting for her answer, the beautiful woman sat down beside her.

Denisia felt a strange tingling up her spine, but she didn't protest. The winners came on, pair by pair, and performed as was determined by the rules, but it was all rather pointless. The audience kept shouting for the oud player to return. "Emir Alkan!" they cried. It was so disruptive that finally Timon glanced at the king with his hands raised in surrender. Midas nodded his permission to allow the final contest to begin.

The first flute player was chosen to challenge the favorite. She emerged to a polite applause and performed another difficult piece that required great dexterity, her fingers flying over the instrument. The crowd cheered for her briefly but then began chanting for the oud. Soon, Emir came forth and took his seat. This time, he chose a cheerful, fast-paced tune that had everyone tapping their feet along with his strong boot. The small boy got up and danced, moving his lithe arms overhead like saplings in the wind. Denisia caught the beautiful woman watching him with a soft smile on her face and had to smile herself. The child's joy was infectious.

When Emir finished, the crowd cheered all the louder, Princess Zoe and the king happily joining them. As the applause continued, King Midas came forward. The final decision was his. He milked the moment, walking around the flute player first with one finger placed thoughtfully against his chin, then directing his attention to the oud player. At last, he gestured toward the oud, signifying Emir as the victor. The crowd roared, the great hall filling to deafening levels. They clapped and shouted for a long time. Gradually, their shouting changed as they began to call for the prince.

"Encore Prince Anchurus! Encore Prince Anchurus!"

The beautiful woman sitting next to Denisia joined in the chorus. Denisia checked the doors behind her. The guard had returned to his post, but she couldn't see Silenus. Timon and two servants emerged with the prince's royal harp. They carried it cautiously between them and then set it on the stage. The audience quieted at the sight of it. Taller than a man, it was decorated with jewels, its smooth, curved wood polished to a sheen, its strings so long it seemed near impossible they could be so straight. When all was ready, Prince Anchurus came forward and took his seat. The crowd hushed.

Denisia checked the back of the room once more. She wanted to hear Anchurus play, but her grandfather's continued absence concerned her. Perhaps she could slip quietly through the crowd to ask the guard what had happened. She had just started to get up when a new sound reached her ears.

A familiar baritone voice.

Denisia whirled to see her grandfather on the far side of the performance area opposite Anchurus. He began to dance for the crowd, his arms high in the air as he twirled around, his big belly protruding over his thighs.

"Call the men to arms," he sang, "the proud king riding on ahead. We shall not fail to win the day . . . once more, we ride into the fray." He paused, his gaze darting about.

Denisia's cheeks warmed with embarrassment. All eyes were on her grandfather, Silenus' antics interrupting the grandest moment in the contest. The prince hovered near his harp, staring like everyone else. Silenus laughed, as if something had suddenly struck him as funny. He sobered just as quickly and started his song over again.

"Call the men to arms, the proud king . . . the battle awaits, and no soldier shall waver . . . to arms, my men . . ." After another few painful attempts, he stopped to stare at the people. They gaped back with confused expressions.

"Oh, dear," the beautiful woman next to Denisia said. "How embarrassing."

That was where she had seen her! The image flashed in Denisia's mind. On the road to Gordium. The minstrel who had told her she'd find her grandfather here. This was the same woman. Denisia opened her mouth to question her, but then Silenus started singing again.

"Call the men to arms, the proud king riding on ahead. Call the men . . . uh . . . we ride into the fray . . ."

Denisia walked toward him, uncertain how she was going to handle this, but she couldn't allow it to continue.

"Ah, Silenus, you were right!" King Midas said suddenly. "Such an entertainer I have never seen!"

Everyone turned. The king had risen from his royal chair and was now approaching the old man while applauding him, his big hands whapping exuberantly together. Silenus looked around, confused. Once he spotted the king's joyful face, he responded with a wide grin and started his dancing anew.

"Do you like it, great king?" he asked. "It was a song I used to sing for your father. Reminds you of the glory days out on the battlefield, does it not?" He clenched his fist and held it tightly in the air. "You can smell it in the dirt and blood, hear it in the clash of iron. The day shall burn and the night freeze and the men forget the tales . . ." He raised his hands high and sang a long sonorous note, then stopped suddenly and looked around, his expression changing from triumphant to distressed.

"Yes, yes, I remember." Midas stopped clapping, but continued to walk toward Silenus with a pleased smile on his face. "It is a grand tune, that one." At the twitch of the king's hand, two guards approached Silenus from behind. Denisia strode forward, determined to save her grandfather from the humiliation of being seized. Midas placed a hand on Silenus' shoulder and turned to the audience. "The great Silenus of Mount Nysa!" he announced. "A gracious entertainer."

Taking the king's cue, the audience clapped. The guards came near and started talking to Silenus, nodding and gesturing for him to walk across the front of the stage where the crowd could see him. Silenus took the bait, waving to the people as they continued to clap at the king's behest. Midas watched patiently. When Silenus reached the other side of the stage, Midas gestured once more in his direction. "Again, my friends, the great Silenus!" The audience responded more enthusiastically this time.

Silenus waved and smiled and, to Denisia's relief, went quietly with the guards to the backstage room, where the door closed behind him.

Without another word, Midas returned to his royal chair and, once seated, gestured for the encore to continue. Anchurus leaned close to his instrument and began to play. As his music filled the grand hall, Denisia observed Midas, gratitude filling her heart. Never before had she seen a king do something so generous and kind. As she turned her gaze back to the prince, she knew she must find a way to thank this royal leader of Gordium—a gift that would be truly equal to the one he had just given her.

"Such a king is a rarity, is he not?"

The young woman had appeared near her shoulder once again. Denisia stepped back to get a better look at her. "Didn't we meet?" she asked. "On the road?"

"Please." The woman raised one hand to her chest. "Accept my apologies. I meant no intrusion."

"You knew he would be here."

The woman appeared sympathetic. "You must long for a solution to his illness. Perhaps we could discuss it?" When Denisia only stared at her, the stranger placed a soft hand on her arm. She held Denisia's gaze before retreating down the side of the hall.

Denisia glanced back at the prince. She had looked forward to his performance, but the woman was leaving. No one had a solution to Silenus' illness. Denisia had searched for years. But if there was a chance?

The woman nodded graciously to the guards and slipped out.

Denisia picked up her skirts and went after her, Anchurus' beautiful music beckoning her to come back, come back.

CHAPTER SEVEN

King Sargon II looked out the window on the south side of the high tower. From this vantage point, he could see the wide expanse of castle grounds all the way across to the wall that surrounded them. Beyond rested his city of Durukin, still under construction but looking more like a city than it had only the season before. The main roads were nearly complete, his dual monuments at either side of the entrance gates taking shape. There was work to be done on the castle garden, the central canal, and the stables beyond, and most of his soldiers were living in tents, but it wouldn't be long now. He would be king where there never was a king before, his city a lasting reminder of his reign long after his death.

It had been another hot day, but the air was cooling with the approach of evening. The men would work until the sunlight was gone, his commanders and overseers supervising the building of the new army quarters and horse shelters. Beyond, the rest of the city was quieting down, a sense of peace coming over the valley, the shallow southern hills showing a little green with the beginning of the warmer season. Typically, this sight would restore him, remind him of all he had accomplished so far, but today, it failed to improve his mood. He turned from the window and directed his attention inside.

It was about twenty paces across and fifteen wide, built originally to observe those who entered and exited the castle grounds. The king soon made it his own private sculpting room with his stones, tools, and water basins stacked on the north side. One unfinished piece drew his eye, a hunk of limestone about four feet high that was beginning to resemble a woman's head and torso. The face was turned toward the wall, the graceful neck the only part sanded smooth.

Sargon studied the sculpture and his muse, a slave woman who stood just inside the door. She looked like she hadn't bathed in weeks, her dark hair matted and her linen dress stained with mud. But her neck had the same graceful curve as the one in the sculpture, her dress baring one exquisite sloping shoulder.

"Where is he?" he asked in a tightly controlled voice. "Or would you have more men killed?"

"I told you, Your Majesty," the woman said. "I don't know." She didn't look at him, her gaze cast down.

The air was so warm. He was already sweating. He removed his jacket. An adolescent slave boy ran across the room and took it from his hand, hanging it on a hook nearby. Sargon remained in a short-sleeved linen shirt, his hands on his hips. "Do you remember when you first came to my father's city of Kalhu?"

"I was too young," the woman said.

"You were a frightened little lamb." Sargon glanced out the window again to see the road that wound into the city. "You trembled as we rode through my father's gates. You were right to fear. Most captured children faced dismal lives under his rule. But now here you are. Well fed. Clothed. Alive. Do you want to know why?"

"You've told me many times," she said.

"You need reminding. You forget where your loyalties should lie."

"I haven't forgotten."

He turned to her then and folded his hands in front of his waist. It still pleased him to look upon her. Despite everything, it pleased him, and this made him even angrier. He walked over to the long table and scooped up his chisel.

"You learned sculpture as part of your education. What did your instructor tell you about determining the stone's eventual form?"

"To pray for inspiration," she said.

He caught the small movement of her toes on the dusty rock, but forced his attention to the carving. The shoulders were coming along, though he liked the idea of one being uncovered. On the other should rest the sleeve of a torn gown. "And to whom do you pray?"

"To the gods, Your Majesty."

"I doubt you pray to all of them."

"To those who listen."

Sargon chipped a little at the spot where the hair would fall on the covered shoulder. "Were you not also instructed to look at someone when you're talking to them?"

She lifted her head then, her full lips relaxed, her brown eyes flat. This, too, angered him. It was her way of punishing him, making herself as absent as possible. "Leave us," he said to the guards. The two men who had been standing behind her left the room, their boots heavy on the stone floor.

The woman stared out the window. Her dress hung loosely tied at the waist, the fabric so worn as to appear veil-like, revealing a shadow of her body. She had lost weight, her collarbones more prominent than he remembered, her elbows knobs near her ribs. He had a sudden thought that she might be starving herself in an attempt to get away from him.

"You expect me to believe that you have no idea where your son is?" he asked.

"Ten years ago, you took him to serve in your army," she said. "I haven't seen him since then."

A logical response. Though likely a lie. "He deserted. I assume you are aware of the punishment for that." Sargon watched her carefully. Her mouth opened a little, but then her gaze flicked to the floor.

"I would beg you for mercy," she said. "But I've tried that."

He remembered her pleas as his men pulled the boy away that day ten years ago. "He's a soldier. He has a duty."

"He served diligently for a long time."

"A soldier's duty is for life."

He chipped a small piece of stone away. A breeze wafted in through the window, accompanied by the faint sound of men's wailing. Criminals, deserters, or others the king deemed unsuitable suffered their punishments near the city gates, their broken bodies left on display as warnings. Necessary but distasteful. Sargon longed for the cool shade in the animal sanctuary.

"When we capture him," he said, "you understand the consequences. It would be better if you told me where he was."

"If I knew, Your Majesty, I would tell you. It would be unbearable to see him tortured."

The sculpture mocked him. Why was he making it like her? The curves already echoed her small waist and thin neck, though the swell of the breasts had yet to be coaxed forth. He turned to his model and observed her without shame.

"If there's anything I can do, Your Majesty," she said.

He set the chisel on the table, crossed the room, and took hold of her shoulders. "You think you can escape me, Elanur? You think you can get away from me? I will have them force-feed you if I must. You *will* remember your place."

But she wasn't looking at him. It had always worked before, frightening her. He gripped her tighter, but she wouldn't meet his gaze.

"Look at me, woman!" he shouted.

She raised her almond eyes. The slope of her neck. Her breasts against his chest. His desire for her rose inside him, his blood hot. He pressed his lips hard against hers, seeking a response. She gave him none. He pulled her close. She didn't fight, but neither did she surrender. She was a doll in his hands, placid and lifeless. He shoved her away from him. She stumbled, wiping his kiss off her lips with the back of her hand.

"I saved your life," he said. "I gave you a son. I allowed you to live near the castle where you would be protected. You are ungrateful. I should have you killed!"

"If you wish." She recovered to stand with her hands clasped in front of her.

He could take her now, have his way with her, but the thought of that lifeless rag underneath him cooled his ardor. She was winning, and he didn't know how to regain the upper hand. He gestured to the slave boy. The waif emerged from the corner with a cup of water. Sargon drank it all, then motioned toward the woman. The boy retrieved another cupful and offered it to her. Elanur took a small sip.

"Tell me," Sargon said, waving the boy away. "After all this time. What is it you want?"

Elanur remained silent.

"I suppose you wish to be set free."

She started at the statement, her hands lifting and then lowering again in front of her.

The motion reminded him of the day he'd taken her from her home. She'd reached for her doll in the same way, grasping at the air. There had been a boy there.

"If I released you," he said, "you could search for your long-lost brother."

Her gaze darted to his.

"Do you remember him? You were, as you say, very young." He took a few steps toward her. "It's likely he did not survive, but . . ." He paused.

"Do you know where he is?" she squeaked.

He dropped his head and brushed the dust off his thumb. Without looking at her again, he returned to the sculpture, picked up the chisel, and prepared to smooth out a rise in the stone.

"I might be able to find him. I have many resources."

A long period of silence passed between them. Sargon pretended to focus on his work.

"You say this only to bait me," she said finally. "What do you want?"

"I already asked you. Help me find our son, and I will search for your brother. Determine whether he still lives."

"You might break such a promise."

He stooped over, pretending to examine the neck more closely. "Whatever else you may think of me, you know I am a man of my word."

Her feet shifted on the dusty stones.

"I will not help you torture him," she said.

"So, you know where he has gone."

She shook her head, her hands clenched.

"It is near impossible for a soldier to escape the city," he said. "He must have had help."

"I don't know where he is," she said again.

He set the chisel down and crossed the room toward her, more restrained this time. "There's something you're not telling me."

She backed up. He pursued. Cat and mouse, they played across the room until the wall stopped her from retreating any farther. She glanced up at him, her brown eyes sharp with fear, then recovered her courage and, with her palms pressed against the stone behind her, stood up straight.

"You want to know who I prayed to for inspiration, Your Majesty? Who I prayed to before sleeping? Before eating? Before lying in bed with you when you came to me? I prayed to the one goddess who would have the power to defeat you. The one goddess I know you fear. I've heard you say her name in your sleep. I've heard you utter it with fear in your throat."

He felt his own features go slack, the hairs rising on the back of his neck.

She forced a smile, her lips parting to reveal strong white teeth. "I heard you speak her name. More than once I heard you, your voice trembling. And because of your kind efforts to educate me, I learned who she was. I prayed to her. For years, I prayed to her." She closed her mouth, her eyes mocking him. "And now you say my son has escaped. It seems the dark goddess has answered my prayers."

He hit her hard across the cheek with the back of his hand. She yelped and went down. "Guards!" he bellowed. The two men rushed in. "Get her out of here. To the dungeon. Now!"

They grabbed the woman, one on either side. Sargon turned away, but her laughter made him pause. It started out small, but then grew as the three retreated down the hall. He pushed the door closed against it.

It was a lie. She was lying. He paced the room. Noticing the slave boy cowering in the corner, he barked at him to get out, too. The waif obeyed, sprinting away. Sargon grabbed the bucket against the far wall and threw it. Water splashed across the stone floor, then ran toward the other side as if it too wanted to escape the king's wrath.

DENISIA HURRIED through the castle doors and down the steps, but when she reached the courtyard, there was no trace of the mysterious woman. Panic seized her. Had she let a once-in-a-lifetime opportunity escape? But then she spotted movement out of the corner of her eye. A slight figure walking down the path toward the king's garden.

Denisia started after her, her quick steps betraying her eagerness. *Be careful*, she warned herself. It was too much of a coincidence that a woman she had met on the road had appeared at the king's contest just as Silenus embarrassed himself. Denisia had to proceed carefully. The woman wanted something. That was clear. But there were a lot of things Denisia would trade if it meant her grandfather might be well again.

Even the thought of it made her catch her breath. She remembered Silenus leading her around the forest when she was a child, helping her memorize the names of all the plants and trees. So many nights he had sat with her by the creek and told her stories of the gods and goddesses, acting out Zeus' adventures and showing her how some of her father's magic had been passed on to her. He was wise and patient and kind before the illness had made him confused and irrational. If only he might be well again!

She rounded the curve and spotted the woman up ahead. An unusual glow surrounded her as she lingered near a solitary old maple tree, its uppermost branches invisible against the darkening sky, its lowest, thickest branch supporting a wooden swing designed for a child. Princess Zoe, perhaps. Denisia slowed as she approached. In the dark, the woman seemed taller, her form somehow more intimidating.

"Hello, Denisia," she said in a smooth voice. "My name is Katiah." She removed her scarf, revealing a lustrous mane of black locks that twirled like ribbons down to her shoulders.

Denisia stopped, her sandals sinking into the new spring grass. She'd learned of the dark goddess of the underground, the one who seized souls and walked in the land of the dead. She cast spells on men for her own amusement. This slender, alabaster-skinned woman didn't seem to fit the reputation.

"We are sisters," Katiah said. "Half-sisters, anyway."

"Sisters," was all Denisia could think of to say.

"I had a hard time believing it, too." Katiah said it congenially, but it sounded like an insult. "On our father's side. Amazing, really, that we haven't met before. I guess you've been sequestered away on that island all this time."

And you dwell with wolves in the bowels of the Earth, Denisia wanted to say, but bit her tongue.

Katiah caressed the rope tied to the wooden swing. "You're wondering why I'm here. Why I sought you out."

"It was you who told me I would find Silenus in the city. You wanted me to come."

"Don't you think it was time we met? We are family, after all."

Denisia felt her expression harden. The only family she had was

Silenus. "If you wanted to meet, why didn't you come to Mount Nysa long ago?"

"I've been busy. And you were young. Besides, there's a pesky magic about the island that can be . . . difficult to penetrate." She glanced up at the castle. "But now the timing seems perfect."

Denisia studied her, trying to determine if she was telling the truth. It was true the Isle of Mount Nysa was protected by magic. She'd never considered it might be strong enough to keep a powerful goddess away. "You need help with something?"

"Not only me." Katiah came closer, her skin a radiant ivory under the moon's glow—definitely not something one would see on a normal human female. "You seek a solution for your grandfather's condition."

Denisia didn't want to feel the lift in her heart. When it came to seeking cures for her grandfather's illness, she'd endured enough disappointment. But she couldn't help it. If this was the goddess of the underworld standing in front of her, she was powerful enough to provide a solution.

"Surely you've heard of my magic?" Katiah asked.

"What I've heard has little to do with magic," Denisia said.

Katiah cast her a long-suffering look. "So, you've heard *those* stories. Ushering souls to the underworld. Walking among the dead. Making deals to capture innocents for eternity. Something like that?"

Denisia didn't say anything.

Katiah rested her hands on her hips. "It really does get tiring, trying to live down these rumors. As if one could be satisfied spending one's entire existence among the dead. Can you imagine?" Katiah shook her head and walked back to the tree. "You have a reputation for doing the opposite. Reveling in the living. Particularly with the mortal men. Stories of your harvest celebrations have spread far and wide." She cast a mischievous grin over her shoulder. "Do you find it satisfying, this relationship you have with the prince?"

Denisia was caught off guard. "Relationship?"

"Please, my dear. It was only obvious from the looks you two were exchanging. You are a goddess. He would not refuse you."

Denisia frowned. She had never thought of the prince that way, as something to take.

"You haven't acted on your feelings?" Katiah said.

"What feelings?" Denisia asked.

Katiah pressed her hand against her heart. "Oh dear. You're in love with him, aren't you?"

Denisia looked away, heat rushing to her cheeks. Behind her rested a wooden bench, one that allowed the perfect view of a child on the swing. "Have you ever been in love?"

Katiah gazed up into the tree as if searching for something among the branches. "Love is such a tedious thing. Requires all your energy and, in the end, delivers few rewards. But let's not talk about that now. We don't have a lot of time."

Denisia sat down on the bench. All of this was making her a little lightheaded.

"I'm sure you agree that the king made a kind gesture tonight." Katiah walked toward her. "One that deserves gratitude."

"Yes," Denisia said.

"Offer him what he desires most in this world." Katiah's voice seemed suddenly lower. "Do it tonight."

Denisia shifted, struggling with a sudden wish to flee. "Why would you care what the king desires most?"

"All you have to do is discover his deepest desire and fulfill it." Katiah stopped a few steps away, holding Denisia in her gaze.

"You seem to know a lot about me," Denisia said. "If that's true, you know that I have not the power to grant the king whatever he wishes."

"I have a feeling he will wish for something you can grant him."

Behind the bench rested a row of evergreen bushes. They formed a partial perimeter on the castle side of the area around the swing, sequestering it from the path and adding to the impression that this was a child's peaceful sanctuary.

"If he doesn't?" Denisia asked.

"Then our deal is off."

"What deal?"

"Come, Sister. Surely I have been clear?"

Denisia's mouth was dry. She grasped a corner of the bush and, briefly closing her eyes, drew in some of its moisture through her skin. "Why not grant the wish yourself?"

"I have my reasons."

"Why me?"

"Sisters should help each other. Besides. You need something I can give you."

The evergreen branch dried and crumbled in her grasp. Denisia felt a moment's regret, but its power had replenished her. She stood up, her back to Katiah. "If you heal my grandfather, how will you benefit?"

"The king and I. We knew each other long ago. You could say that I owe him a debt."

"You don't want to pay it yourself?"

Katiah paused. "It is not yet time."

The light seemed to shift, the sky darkening.

"So," Katiah said, "do we have a deal?"

Denisia walked around the row of bushes, putting them between her and the dark goddess. "You say we are sisters, but I don't know you."

"You doubt I am the goddess Katiah." Without waiting for an answer, Katiah looked upward. A rumble of thunder greeted her. "Might this convince you?"

Denisia yelped. Anchurus had appeared beside the dark goddess, looking bewildered.

"Prince Anchurus, you played so beautifully tonight." Katiah took his left arm and sidled up next to him, batting her eyelashes. "It's such a shame you ride out to battle tomorrow, wounded as you are." She pressed her elbow into his ribs. The prince winced.

"Stop it," Denisia said.

"Need more proof?" Katiah flicked her hand and Anchurus' arm burst into flames. Denisia raced over to him. He slapped at the fire but it raged wild, eating through his royal jacket. Denisia grabbed his arm and closed her eyes, expelling the moisture she'd just gathered from the bush through her palms. A swell of fatigue flowed through her, but when she opened her eyes again, the fire was out, the royal jacket ashes in her hands.

Anchurus stared at her, his breath coming fast.

She released his arm.

"Aw, isn't that sweet," Katiah said.

The prince bristled. "You are Katiah." He turned to address her. "The one who has been playing with us."

"He's quick," Katiah said to her sister. "No wonder you love him."

Denisia's cheeks flamed hot.

Anchurus glanced at Denisia, his expression momentarily confused. "You know her?"

"She is . . . my half-sister," Denisia said.

"Sister?" The prince considered that, then once again addressed Katiah. "You are helping King Sargon in his quest to defeat my father."

Denisia's brows furrowed. *Helping Sargon?*

"No matter," Anchurus said. "We will crush him, nonetheless."

Katiah laughed. "I remember when you were a boy. You used to pray to me. You wanted so badly to be stronger, faster, better with the sword so that your father would be pleased." She shifted her hips. "And here you are, fully grown now, still ready to sacrifice everything for him. I'm not so sure he deserves it." She drew her finger along his jawline, then descended on Denisia. "Do it," she said. "Tonight. There are worse things than a mental illness." Then she smiled. "And just imagine. Silenus, cured, and the object of your affection, *safe*." She walked away, her form dissipating into a gray fog.

Denisia stood frozen, the woman's words fresh in her ears. Then

Anchurus approached, bringing her attention back to him. "Are you all right?" she asked, checking his arm.

He brushed off the ashes. "Are you helping Sargon too?"

She looked up into his hazel eyes. What must he think of her, out here chatting with the goddess who had caused his defeat? "I didn't know her," she said, "until tonight." When he gave her a doubtful look, she went on. "I've never met any others like me. I've lived with my grandfather on the Isle of Mount Nysa." She glanced toward the space where Katiah had stood. "She says she's my half-sister. Grandfather told me stories. But . . ." She shook her head.

"What did she want?"

Denisia hesitated. Whatever plan Katiah had, she'd just made it very clear what would happen to Anchurus if Denisia didn't go along. "She wanted to meet me."

"Now?"

"We've never met before."

"Why now?" He crossed his arms over his chest.

"She was talking about family and my grandfather's illness. Then poof, she brings you here." She turned away, avoiding his gaze. "I had no idea she was helping Sargon until you said so. No wonder your last battle ended in defeat." She could almost feel him cringe. "No army can fight against her magic."

Beside them, the tree hovered like a kindly matron, its leaves fluttering in the slight breeze. Denisia gazed on the stout trunk and sensed the breath of the roots under her feet. "Your father was kind to my grandfather." She turned once again to face him. "Back in the castle. You said you needed my help. Now I understand why. And I mean to show the king my gratitude. Perhaps that will even the odds for you on the battlefield."

He tipped his head, studying her. "You *will* assist us?"

"I have my limits. But whatever I can grant the king that he may wish, I will do so."

"And Katiah?"

"My grandfather tells stories of her treachery."

"As did my mother. She had all representations of the dark goddess banished from the castle three years before she died."

Denisia fought to hide the surprise on her face. King Midas had worshipped Katiah? She sat down again. After a moment's hesitation, the prince sat next to her. Her heartbeat quickened. He was so near, his presence so alive beside her.

"You didn't know she'd be here?" he asked again.

She heard the struggle in his voice. He wanted to trust her, but wasn't sure he should. "You remember the night I listened to you play in the auditorium?" she asked.

He nodded.

"You went off on your first battle after that. Since then, you've fought many battles. And you've never been hurt. Until now."

He said nothing, but he was listening.

"Despite the men around you falling," she continued. "Others being wounded. Savage, bloody fighting. You have escaped unscathed. Until this last time."

It took another few moments. Finally, he turned to her. "You?" he said quietly.

"A spell. That night. It's protected you until now."

He stared at his hands. "Katiah was with Sargon in this last battle."

"Her powers, at least," Denisia said. "My magic against hers. It apparently left you vulnerable."

He tucked his arm close to his ribs, favoring his wound.

"I would never harm you or your father. I hope you can believe me."

He studied her with his intense gaze, the war inside him evident in the firm set of his jaw. His hard body emanated strength, his shoulders and arms natural weapons. But in his eyes, she saw the thoughtful boy he had once been. She longed to touch his cheek, reassure him with a kiss, but she waited, wanting him to decide for himself.

"We cannot defeat Sargon's army without help," he said.

"If I can, I will give your father what he most desires. I'm guessing that would be something with which to defeat his enemy."

Anchurus moved his arm to the back of the bench and looked out on the path that weaved its way down and across to the king's gardens. "Father never said why Mother ordered all Katiah's statues and paintings removed from the castle. They were building a monument too, but it was abandoned."

"Perhaps she learned about the goddess' reputation." Denisia expected a quick agreement, but Anchurus sat quietly thinking. He leaned forward and rested his forearms on his knees. She worried he was about to dismiss her, but then he stood up and offered her his hand. "We would be grateful for your help."

She slid her hand inside his and got up. "I will be glad to give it."

Anchurus bowed his head, but didn't let go of her hand. She waited, holding her breath. When he lifted his gaze, his eyes had changed. The expression shot fire through her. His grip tightened. Her weight shifted to her toes. He moved closer, then seemed to think better of it and tucked her hand into his arm.

"We shall go, then," he said, heading toward the path. "Talk to the king tonight."

"One moment." She grasped the evergreen bush once again. Absorbing its life force, she restored her energy. Then she fell into step beside him.

Anchurus meandered along as if they had all the time in the world. He remarked on a bright star twinkling in the east, then on the clean, fresh night air. She nodded, letting the silence surround them. When they reached the stairs, he covered her hand with his one more time, then released her, gesturing for her to lead the way. Denisia looked down at her sandals as she climbed one stair and then another. If only the journey back had been a little longer. She would have enjoyed a few more moments with the gallant prince.

. . .

THE THREE ADVISORS waited until all was quiet. When it was clear they had remained undetected, they heaved a collective sigh and crept out of their hiding place. They'd been crouched behind another row of bushes on the north side of the child's play area, close enough to hear everything but far enough away that no one had noticed them. Fotis groaned as he straightened and walked directly to the bench where Denisia and the prince had been sitting.

"So, that is her plan." He eased himself down on one side and rubbed his left knee.

Xander plopped on the other side, the bench reverberating with his weight. "She's going to grant the king's wish. That should be good."

"The goddess Katiah would promote only good things." Aster took the space between them and crossed his arms over his chest.

"It doesn't matter," Xander said. "The king will choose wisely."

The other two rolled their eyes.

"He will! He is the king."

"Who is not obsessed with defeating Sargon," Aster said.

"And who has already exhausted his army and plans to send them back out tomorrow," Fotis added.

"Well, what do you think he'll ask for?" Xander said.

"Whatever it is," Fotis said, "you can bet it will be something to help him ride to victory."

Xander shrugged. "He defeats Sargon. We have peace. What's wrong with that?"

"When one is dealing with the dark goddess," Aster said, "one has nothing to worry about."

"She's weaving her web," Fotis agreed. "You can be sure of that."

Xander sauntered over to the swing. "Should we do something?"

"We should warn the king," Fotis said. "Try to get to him before Denisia does."

"That will accomplish stunning results," Aster said.

"What do *you* propose, then?" Fotis said.

Aster got up and paced. "It is not Katiah we should focus on. She is not the problem."

"We already know that," Fotis said.

"She's too powerful." Xander took hold of the rope.

"Don't tell me you're going to try to sit on that," Fotis warned.

Xander ignored him.

Aster tucked his chin into his neck. He was a bull, restlessly pacing the fence. "It is a blessing, what has happened to Silenus."

"What's wrong with him, anyway?" Xander asked.

"A disease of the mind," Fotis said. "One that attacks older people."

"But the parchments say he's a deity of the forest," Xander said. "Immortal. He's not supposed to be like normal people."

"The one that didn't make you glow," Aster said, glaring at Xander, "surely didn't have anything to do with that."

Xander's eyes widened. "You think Katiah cursed his mind?"

"A fascinating theory," Fotis said.

"To trap Denisia in her web!" Xander said. "Clever."

"What would be her motive?" Fotis asked. "She has enough power herself."

"The king would surely accept a gift from the goddess Katiah," Aster said, "after the queen banished her likeness from the land."

"Good point." Fotis stroked his beard. "She gets Denisia to grant the king's wish. And thus, he will be cursed."

Xander laughed. "She's not going to curse him, silly! She's going to fulfill his deepest desire." He said the words with a grandiose flare.

Aster turned to Fotis, and they both heaved tired sighs.

"What?" Xander asked. He was on the swing now, the wood creaking under his bottom as he moved his legs to and fro.

"How many kings have you known who would make wise choices, given the chance to have anything they desired?" Fotis said.

"But King Midas isn't like other kings," Xander said.

"One must not remember what most kings want," Aster said.

"You mean, what any king wants most is something bad?" Xander asked.

"They want power, you nitwit," Fotis said. "Power! That's what any king wants. Power to defeat his enemies, conquer more lands, and expand his kingdom."

"Katiah fixes Silenus." Xander held up one finger. "He and Denisia are happy." He held up two fingers. "Denisia grants the king's dearest wish while continuing to protect the prince." Three fingers. "King Midas defeats Sargon and everyone is happy." Four fingers. "What's the problem?"

"Four points so well made," Fotis said mockingly.

"Truly the outcome Katiah longs for," Aster said.

Xander thought about that. "Maybe she wants peace?" he squeaked, but when the other two only glared, he rested his head against the rope. "You think she's counting on this turning out badly."

"She doesn't own your soul," Aster said.

"That's just one soul. And I did offer it to her."

"She took it out of the goodness of her heart," Fotis said.

"I just can't imagine the king making a bad choice!" Xander said.

"He will do it intentionally," Aster said.

"He will not intend for it to turn out badly," Fotis agreed. "But it will."

"How can you be so sure?" Xander asked.

"Because Katiah is involved!" Fotis said. "The dark goddess! How long will it take to get that through your thick head?"

Xander frowned. He looked like a child pouting in the swing.

"Come." Fotis pushed himself to his feet. "We must warn the king now."

"It will do much good," Aster said.

"We must try."

A soft crack arrested their attention. They looked back to see Xander on the ground. "I told you not to sit on that!" Fotis said.

Xander used the rope to pull himself up, then dusted off his robe. He glanced at the swing with a guilty expression. “They can fix it.”

“You didn’t break the princess’ swing,” Aster said. “The king will be ecstatic.”

“Come,” Fotis said. “You can tell the king about that later. We have to go if we’re going to reach him in time.” He found the path and, holding tightly to his walking stick, started toward the castle, Aster on his heels. Xander hurried to catch up. They had just approached the curve in the path when a wave of energy sent Fotis sprawling to the ground. The other two stopped to stare at him.

“Very clever, king’s advisors.” Katiah emerged from a cloud of fog to pose in front of them, her gaze amused as she looked down on Fotis. “But you shall not be disturbing my plans tonight.” She made a flourishing gesture, and a strange film surrounded them, dropping like a sheet of rain. “Don’t worry. You’ll be free to go once Denisia has completed her task. Enjoy your evening.”

The three advisors tried to break through, but the film was like a wall. They could do nothing but watch Katiah shimmer out of sight.

CHAPTER EIGHT

Denisia stepped back inside the grand hall with some trepidation. With the contest over and the entertainers gone, the crowd had thinned. A few people still milled about, engaged in lingering conversations. She'd told Anchurus she needed to check on her grandfather before seeing the king. He had left her just outside the double doors, instructing a guard to bring her to the king's strategy room when she was ready.

She scanned about but didn't see Silenus. She didn't expect to see Katiah, but looked for her anyway, relieved when she couldn't find her. Touching the back of her hand where Anchurus' warmth still lingered, she walked along the perimeter, searching. She'd nearly reached the stage area when the side door opened.

"Who are you looking for, my dear?" Silenus peered out at her.

"Grandfather!" She ran over and embraced him, then remembered he wasn't always comfortable with such displays these days and stepped back. "I was looking for you." His kind smile softened the wrinkles under his eyes, his white beard extra fluffy, as if he'd just washed and combed it. "Are you all right?" she asked.

"This party has done me a world of good." He downed the rest of a cup of wine he was holding, set it on a small stand, then stepped out and closed the door behind him. "I'm so glad I came. Things look a little brighter now."

"Brighter?"

"Sometimes all you need is a celebration. And the young people are so nice. Intelligent, most of them." He cocked his head. "A few dullards. But the rest seem to have at least a basic understanding of the ways of the world. And this king. They love him!"

Denisia studied her grandfather's face. He was calm. Speaking intelligently. "Who were the young people you were talking to? A woman, perhaps, with long dark hair?"

Silenus cast his gaze upward. "A few of those," he said. "Many very attractive." He smiled at her. "Though none as fair as you. I dare say the prince noticed."

"He did?"

"Didn't you see him watching you? Many times throughout the evening."

His words covered her like warm water. She looped her arm through his. "Would you like to go for a walk?"

"A short one, perhaps. I'm afraid my old legs are weary."

"Very well."

Outside, the grounds were peaceful, the food tables cleaned and put away. The musicians had gone home. Clumps of people meandered toward the gates, heading back to their lives in the city or among the farms beyond.

"Grandfather," she said, "do you remember when you used to tell me stories of the dark goddess?"

"Tricky, that one. But beautiful."

She looked up at him, surprised he'd remembered so quickly. A bench sat at the top of the stairs on the left. She led him over to it.

"Very jealous." Silenus eased himself down with a grunt. "It's why I kept her away from you."

"You did?"

"Your father tasked me with protecting you, so I set a spell over our island around Mount Nysa."

Denisia nodded. *A pesky magic,* Katiah had called it.

"I thought at one time of inviting her," Silenus continued, "introducing the two of you. Allowing you to know your family." He paused. "But I couldn't risk your safety."

"You believe she might have harmed me?"

"She would have longed for whatever you had. It's in her nature."

"But what could she have wanted?"

Silenus' gaze took on a faraway look. "A peaceful home. People who care about her. These things are not so readily available to goddesses."

Denisia thought about that. Might Katiah be lonely? But it didn't trouble her for long, as a new joy was bubbling up inside her. Her grandfather was chatting away like he had never been ill or confused or angry. With every moment that passed, she grew more convinced that Katiah had held to her part of their bargain.

A group of four people stumbled out the doors and down the steps, laughing and sharing a last drink. "I met her," Denisia said. "Tonight."

"Katiah?" His wiry eyebrows shot up. "She was here?"

Denisia nodded.

Silenus' expression turned thoughtful. "The young advisor was glowing."

"What do you mean?"

He paused, then said, "What did she want?"

Denisia met his gaze. At that moment, she knew. He was no longer ill. Those were the words of someone whose first concern was her welfare. No longer was she a person to be wary of. She was the one he protected. "She wanted . . ." She hesitated. "A bargain."

She expected him to ask what the bargain was for. Instead, he looked out into the night, breathing audibly through his big nostrils, the sound rhythmic and soothing, his belly rising and falling in time. "And you are considering it?"

She rested her cheek against his broad shoulder. "She asked me to show my gratitude to the king for his kindness to you and me."

He sat the mountain he was, his hands laced in front of him, his legs relaxed and splayed at the knees. After a few beats, he started humming a tune Denisia had often heard when she was a child. It frightened her at first. She looked up into his face, but the confused expression had not returned. Instead, he appeared as he often had—pensive. She rested her head on his shoulder once more.

"The bargain would be good for me," she said. "And at the moment, I can see no harm in it."

"My dear, you are past the age of needing an old man's advice."

"You aren't just an old man. You are Silenus the wise. Your followers come from far away to hear what you have to say. I, too, value your opinion."

He shifted his weight, the movement enough that Denisia had to sit up. When she did, he extended his palm to her. She unhooked her bag of wine from her belt. He enjoyed several swallows before he spoke again. "You already know what I think."

"That I should avoid any bargain with the dark goddess."

He licked his lips, then took another swig. "Since you're asking me anyway, I must believe whatever she is offering is something you dearly desire."

She thrilled at the insight of his answer. He was back! She had to restrain herself from leaping off the bench to shout it to the world. Katiah had given her what she most wanted, what she had long since given up on believing she could ever have. "Yes," she said simply.

"Since it seems you are determined to go forward with this bargain," he said, tapping the back of the hand she had wrapped around his arm, "understand this. Katiah will honor her part of the deal as long as you honor yours. She is a goddess of her word. But the second you show any hesitation, she will withdraw, and whatever she gave you will be lost."

This Denisia already knew.

"Likely the consequences will be greater than that," Silenus said. "The dark goddess does not like to be disappointed."

Denisia remembered Anchurus' burning arm and stifled a shudder.

Silenus looked at her then, his eyes full of concern. "Whatever you desire, surely you can get it on your own?"

She dropped her gaze. *No. Not this time.* So many green concoctions, every plant and herb combination, petals and leaves and stems and roots mashed and ground and mixed and pummeled with water and oil and sometimes even powdered rock, but none had touched the illness stealing Silenus' mind. Some had made him sick. Most had passed through him without effect. Whatever powers she possessed had been useless in the face of his worsening condition.

She glanced up at the castle towering above them. Silenus was well, and Anchurus was safe. She must call the guard and go to the king before it was too late.

Silenus gently took her chin. "What is it?" he asked.

"Nothing." She smiled at him. "Thank you for your advice." She glanced around. "It's getting late. I will ask if the king might be gracious enough to put us up for the night." She kissed him on the cheek. "I'll be right back."

Emir explored the room again, impressed with what the king had granted him for the night. He'd expected to land in the barracks with the soldiers, perhaps, or even with the servants. Instead, he was in the undercroft, a spacious storage room that smelled of root vegetables, wine, and clean earth. A single straw mattress sat in the corner, flanked by a lamp and nightstand. He would sleep well tonight.

He set the oud at the foot of the bed, washed his hands and face in the water basin, and dried off with the towel that had been left for him. The boy should be here, but he'd been tagging along behind the princess, dressed in his royal garb, stuffing his face with all the king's bounty. Likely, he would see even nicer quarters than Emir this night. But Emir paced restlessly. Strange to be worried about the child. He was used to worrying about no one but himself.

He rested his hands on his hips, perusing the storage containers around him. He could steal a drink from a wine barrel, but he thought better of it. His plan was going well, and he needed to proceed carefully. His thoughts drifted to the hunters. King Sargon always sent them after deserters. Emir was sure he would be no exception. There were many at the king's disposal, but the Olgun brothers were the ones every deserter feared. Baris and Bain were their names, one quick and smart, the other an oversized brute of a man who could crush a soldier's skull with his fist. Even they wouldn't be able to penetrate King Midas' castle, however. For this night, at least, Emir had nothing to worry about.

Not even the boy.

He lowered himself to sit on the mattress, bouncing a little to test the cushion. It wasn't bad, especially considering he usually slept on the hard ground. Exhaling a long sigh, he laid down, wondering if his mother was also preparing for rest. He could hear the song she always sang to him when he was growing up. Even now, the memory of it calmed his nerves. It played in his mind until a familiar anger rose in his chest. A slave. That's what she was to Sargon. A slave to be used and mistreated. Emir stared at the wooden beams above him. Soon that would change. His plan was working.

"I will come back," he said to the empty room. "One day, you will be his slave no more."

The dim glow of the lamp cast nebulous shadows on the stone walls. It was quiet here. Peaceful. He had just about drifted off to sleep when he heard the door latch click. He sat up, one hand dropping to the dagger at his belt. When the boy came into view, he relaxed, warm relief flooding his chest. "Where have you been?"

The boy sat down beside him. He still wore his maroon jacket and tan britches, strapped sandals on his freshly cleaned feet. He dug into his pocket and pulled out a handful of figs. With a broad smile, he handed two to Emir, who popped them in his mouth.

"Getting a little fancy, are you?" he said.

The boy smiled, showing his teeth covered in fig pieces.

"Don't get used to it. We aren't staying here. One day, we'll go home." He settled back against the wall. "We will rescue my mother and give her the life she deserves." He glanced at the boy. "You'll like her. She's warm and kind. Has a lovely voice. She always sang to me. Plus, she makes the best sweet pudding you've ever tasted."

The boy licked his fingers and then offered Emir his last fig.

Emir shook his head. "You have it. I'm full. Wash your hands after."

The boy did as he was told. While he was washing, Emir relaxed on the mattress once more. Now he could sleep. He said nothing when the boy snuggled up beside him. Normally he'd have ordered him to find another corner, but he was growing used to him being around. Rising on one elbow, he blew out the lamp and settled back down, his left ribs warm from the heat of the little body next to him.

KING MIDAS STOOD by the inside wall of the strategy room, his royal cloak still over his shoulders. "We cannot afford to wait. He will only grow stronger."

Rastus sat at the conference table, one ankle propped on the other knee, his sharp features drawn into a thoughtful expression. "But is it wise to send the army back out, depleted as it is?"

"We will recruit more men."

"The fighting will be fierce. We need our strongest, most loyal soldiers, and many of them are injured."

The king shook his head. "You wish for me to let them sleep in their beds, but that is what *he* will expect. Our only chance is to strike now."

"The dark goddess is with him."

Midas grabbed a short wooden vase from an open shelf and threw it. It collided with the opposite wall and fell to the floor, still intact. "She *will not win this!* She must not."

Rastus fell silent. He breathed calmly, accustomed to such outbursts. Midas hovered by the wall a moment more before coming over to sink into his chair. "We must do something."

"He will not be victorious," Rastus said. "You *will* find assistance."

"I asked them. The advisors. They've come up with nothing."

"I can't imagine it a simple task."

Midas leaned his forearms on the table and heaved a heavy sigh. "Nineteen. It doesn't seem that long ago she was still running about the castle, shouting for her mother."

Rastus smiled. "You can be proud. Of *both* children."

A knock at the door. "The prince, Your Majesty," the guard said.

Midas cocked an eyebrow at Rastus. "Enter."

Anchurus still wore his evening dress robe, the rich maroon color setting off his sandy hair. He bowed to his father and then took the chair to Rastus' left.

"Nice playing tonight," Rastus said.

Anchurus nodded his acknowledgment and turned to the king. "I have found the help you are seeking."

Midas looked at him nonchalantly.

"Denisia of Mount Nysa. She was here tonight."

"The goddess?" Rastus asked.

Anchurus nodded.

"And she has offered her assistance?"

"She has." Anchurus addressed his father. "The old man. Silenus. He is her grandfather. She is grateful for the kindness you showed him. She wishes to repay you."

Midas laced his fingers together on the table. "Are not her powers limited to wine and merrymaking?"

"She brought dead flowers back to life in front of my eyes," the prince said.

"Flowers." Midas gave him a stony look.

"And she . . ." Anchurus hesitated. "She can draw moisture from the plants and redistribute it."

"A watering source," Midas said wryly.

"She must be capable of more," Anchurus said. "She didn't deny it."

"Deny what?" Rastus asked.

"That she is the goddess Denisia of Mount Nysa."

"She will be no match for Katiah," Midas said.

"But she can help," his son countered.

"How?"

"She can control the natural world," Anchurus said. "There are many possibilities."

"Such as?" Midas opened his hands.

"I have heard tales," Anchurus said. "They say she can make vines strangle a man. Direct trees to fall."

"You're suggesting what?" Midas asked. "We have trees fall on Sargon?"

Anchurus pursed his lips and sat back. "She's the only goddess I could find on such short notice. Do you have another option?"

Midas walked to the strategy table and laid his fingers on its edge. "What do you know about Denisia of Mount Nysa, Rastus?"

"Nothing more than what the prince has already said, Your Majesty." Rastus glanced apologetically at Anchurus.

"Why hasn't FAX come to me with this information?" Midas asked.

"I don't know if they saw her," Anchurus said.

"They should be here," Midas said.

"I will summon them." Rastus got up to leave.

"I will accompany you," Anchurus said, following suit.

"Son, wait," the king ordered.

Anchurus cast Rastus a resigned look and sat back down. Rastus opened the door only to run into Zoe.

"There you are!" she said, looking past him toward her father.

"The happiest of birthdays, Your Highness." Rastus bowed and ducked out.

Zoe entered the room and closed the door behind her. "I was afraid you'd be back at it already," she said to her father.

"I'm surprised you're still on your feet after all the excitement," Midas said.

Zoe laid a hand on her brother's shoulder. "I wanted to say good night," she said. "It was a grand party. Thank you."

"You're very welcome," Midas said.

Zoe walked over to him, perusing the strategy table. "Are you talking battles already?"

"Considering our next move." Midas took her hand. "You need not worry. Anchurus will still be here tomorrow."

The prince raised an eyebrow.

"I will hold you to that," Zoe said. "If I awake and he is gone, I won't forgive you." She glanced around the room. "I was thinking of Mother tonight, of what she might have said to us. She always had so much faith in you, Father."

"She was an amazing woman," Midas said.

Zoe glanced at the bottom cabinet of the shelf against the wall. "The boy. The small one at the party tonight. Would you mind if he stayed a little longer?"

Midas let go of her hand and returned his attention to his strategy table. "We can't take in every poor waif."

"A few more days is all," Zoe said. "I need time to find him a proper home."

Midas picked up a black horseman and turned him around in his fingers.

"Is it all right?"

"Of course."

"Thank you." Zoe paused as if waiting for her father to say something more, but he was lost in his own thoughts. "Well, good night."

"Good night, my girl."

"Good night," Anchurus said.

Zoe walked out, closing the door quietly behind her. An awkward silence filled the room.

"If he's so into secret attacks," Midas said finally, "then we must surprise him next time."

Dutifully, the prince got up and joined his father at the table. "We will need the right location."

"Somewhere we would have the advantage," Midas agreed.

They both studied the replica of the terrain around Gordium. Anchurus made one suggestion, then Midas another. They continued to debate until a light knock came at the door.

"The goddess Denisia," the guard announced from the other side.

Father and son exchanged glances. "Enter," Midas said.

CHAPTER NINE

Sargon stormed up the stairs to his quarters, his boots scuffing the stones. He wore only his shirt and pants, his brow furrowed heavily over his eyes. The evening had been dismally disappointing. After the time he'd wasted with Elanur, he'd spoken to his commanders only to find that they were behind schedule and wouldn't be ready to attack Gordium the following morning. The wounded were still recovering. The numbers were down, and the lost horses were not yet replaced. He'd nearly sent several of them to the dungeon, but for the knowledge that he had no one ready to replace them.

After that, his dinner consisted of dry meat and undercooked vegetables. He'd ordered the cook lashed for punishment, but that hadn't helped his stomach. To top it all off, Tai was limping. The result of another quarrel with Zehra, no doubt. In his youth, the lion would have recovered quickly, but now he was nine years old and any injury took longer to heal. It was unclear how serious the wound was. Sargon had visited hoping to assess the damage, but the beast would not get up for him. He'd only lain listlessly outside of the den.

Sargon was wondering how he might replace Zehra with a more

submissive female when he threw open his door and found Katiah standing by his bed. He stopped, his breath caught in his throat. She was completely naked, her skin glistening with the light of several candles she'd placed about. Her dark hair hung loose over her shoulders, a few long curls brushing softly against her breasts. She held on to the headboard with one hand, the other dangling loosely at her belly.

"My darling," she said. "I've been waiting for you."

The sight of her stirred his passions and his anger at the same time. He was desperate to know if what Elanur had told him was true: that Katiah had assisted Emir in his escape. He would demand answers, he thought, but when she started toward him, his body decided he would hold his tongue.

She paused at the end of the bed and shifted her weight, allowing him a glimpse of her luscious backside while she gazed at him over her shoulder. Sargon groaned, and then he was pulling off his shirt and, in the next moment, wrapping her up in his arms. With fierce energy, he kissed her lips, neck, and breasts, gradually surrendering to the moment and allowing himself to consume her.

He would demand answers in the morning.

DENISIA WALKED INTO KING MIDAS' strategy room to find Prince Anchurus standing opposite his father over a stout mahogany table. The two pored over a set of small figurines resembling mounted soldiers, a map painted on the surface. As she drew closer, she gleaned all she needed to know. King Midas was planning another attack on Sargon. No doubt he would send Anchurus to lead it. The fighting would be difficult, particularly with tired, battle-weary men and a dark goddess in the mix. Worse, Denisia couldn't protect the prince—not if Katiah was involved.

Midas welcomed her to sit down at a second table. This one was long and skinny and surrounded by chairs. She glanced at the prince before taking the chair closest to her. The king sat across from her, Anchurus lingering nearby.

"Your Majesty," she said. "Thank you for seeing me."

"I have heard tales of the goddess Denisia and her bottomless bag of wine," Midas said, his charm on full display.

Denisia graciously handed it over.

Midas took a long drink. "Delicious."

"I'm glad you approve." She offered the bag to the prince, but he declined.

"You have come a long way, then?" the king said.

"I was seeking my grandfather, Silenus. I apologize for any inconvenience he may have caused. As you noticed, he has been unwell. I've been searching for him for days—"

Midas raised his hand to stop her. "No need for apologies. Silenus was a friend of my father's. I remember him visiting when I was young. He was always an entertaining guest."

Denisia bowed her head. "I understand he was caught trespassing. A considerable offense in most kingdoms."

"It was clear your grandfather was not a threat," Midas said.

"Be that as it may," she continued, "I am deeply grateful to you for keeping him safe. Which is why I asked to see you. We are without lodging for the night. I was hoping—"

"Say no more," Midas interrupted. "We have many guest rooms in the castle. You are more than welcome."

Denisia smiled. The immediate concerns were addressed. If only that were all she had to worry about. King Midas watched her, his brown eyes kind but curious. She clasped her hands together in her lap. "Your Majesty. I have come for one other purpose. To express my gratitude for your kindness."

"There is no need," he said.

She gave a demure turn of her head. "My grandfather has suffered for many years. Never has he encountered the graciousness he was given here, in your castle, and from you personally. Having witnessed his struggle, I was greatly moved by how you managed the difficulty during the contest. The rumors about you are true. You are a kind and caring king. Gordium is fortunate to have you as ruler."

"Some citizens may disagree with you."

"Few, I am certain. I wish to thank you for your kindness. And to offer you something in return."

"You owe me nothing," the king said.

"Perhaps not, but I'd like to help. And I have the sense,"—she glanced at Anchurus—"that you may need it."

The king waited, watching her with a gentle but curious gaze.

Denisia smoothed her dress and tucked a few hair strands behind her ear. "Perhaps you'll allow me to ask you a question?"

The king laced his hands in front of him.

"If I were to grant you anything, what might it be?"

Midas cocked an eyebrow. "I've learned it is not wise to accept gifts from the gods."

"You have never accepted a gift from me. I simply wish to show my gratitude."

He watched her, considering, then glanced at his son. Anchurus nodded slightly, an almost imperceptible move. Midas' gaze fell to his strategy table and shifted to the bottom shelf of the tall cabinet against the wall. "If I were to ask a great goddess for something," he said finally, "it would be for the means to defeat my enemy. A mountain of riches with which I might fortify my army. A way to grow my forces to such a level as to win a final, deciding victory." He looked up at her with a flat expression. "I might wish that everything I touched would turn to gold."

Denisia studied her hands. As Katiah had predicted, this was within her power. As she was to the plants and trees, she was to the dirt and stones, a goddess who could give and receive the earth's treasures. If he wanted the touch of gold, she could give it to him. She took a drink of her wine and then handed the bag to the king. He swallowed twice and handed it back. She offered it once more to Anchurus and this time, he too took a few swallows. When they had all finished, she secured it to her belt and raised her gaze to the king.

"You are certain. That is your wish?"

"If I had the touch of gold," he said slowly, "nothing would stop me from achieving my aims. I would bring peace to the kingdom. I would right the wrongs and start anew."

"There may be risks," she warned. "No power is without its pitfalls."

He rubbed his mustache with his finger. "You're sincerely offering?"

She nodded.

He looked down, considering, and heaved a great sigh. Then he raised his gaze once more. "I would wish for the touch of gold."

Perspiration pricked at her palms. What would be the consequences? There was no way to know for certain. But it was what he wanted, and what Anchurus wanted. To hesitate now would put her grandfather and the prince in danger of Katiah's wrath.

"Very well." She stood up. "If you will allow me, we shall proceed."

Midas centered himself in his chair. Denisia walked around behind him, placed her hands on his shoulders, and closed her eyes. She sent her thoughts to the floor, then to the land supporting the castle, then deeper still into the rocks below. Her mind traveled to the mountain ranges, her blood pulsing through the soles of her feet. Her being filled with a heaviness that weighed her down. With every moment, it took more strength and energy to stay upright, the earth desiring to suck her into its depths, to force her to surrender rather than yield its riches. She gripped the king's shoulders, in the end fiercely clasping, her knuckles prominent under the skin. Gradually, the power surrendered, flowing from the bowels of the earth into her belly, through her arms, and out of her palms. She opened her eyes and released the king. Perspiration wetting her collar, she returned to her chair.

The king awakened as if from a trance.

"Father?" Anchurus asked.

Midas glanced at Denisia and then pressed his hand flat on the table. Nothing happened.

"It will take some time," Denisia said.

"How long?"

"It depends. A little while." She stood up. "Might the guard show me to our room?"

King Midas rose with her. "Of course." He turned to Anchurus.

The prince responded, escorting her to the door.

"I wish you and your grandfather a good night," Midas said.

"Good night, gracious king." Denisia took the prince's arm and walked out.

XANDER SAT SLUMPED on the ground, picking at a piece of grass. "The night is nearly over. We're too late."

"She has cursed the king by now," Aster said.

"She did say that we'd be released when Denisia 'finished her task,'" Fotis said. He lay on his back, gazing up at the stars. "I assume that means once she has granted the king his wish. But we are still trapped."

"Hey, over here!" Xander waved at a guard passing by in the distance.

"He can't hear you," Fotis said.

Xander waved vigorously, but the guard disappeared up the path. "We're going to be here forever."

Aster paced the small space in which they had to move. "We should not have done something," he said.

"What on earth could we have done?" Fotis said. "We've been trapped here."

"Hey!" Xander waved again.

"Now who?" Fotis asked.

"I thought I saw someone." Xander stopped waving.

"Of course you did," Fotis groaned.

Aster's pacing grew more frantic. Suddenly, he punched against the invisible wall. Nothing happened. He moved a little closer, shifted his left shoulder, and leaned into the space as one might lean against a door. There was no resistance. He took another step forward. Nothing. With his hand extended in front of him, he took several more steps until he was standing beyond where the barrier had been.

"He's out!" Xander leapt to his feet.

"Who's out?" Fotis asked wearily.

"Aster! He got out. How did you do that?"

Aster rested his hands on his hips. "We were not trapped until Denisia completed her task." His shoulders slumped, he walked toward the castle.

"Come on, Fotis," Xander said. "We're free."

Fotis sat up, blinking. "What happened?"

"The pretty one has removed the barrier. We can warn the king now." He hurried through the nonexistent wall, trying to catch up to Aster. "Fotis, come on!"

"There is no need to hurry," Fotis said.

"But we can warn the king!" Xander called.

"We're too late. What's to warn him about now?"

THE ROOM KING Midas granted Denisia was small but comfortable, positioned on the east side of the second level. There were two straw mattresses, two basins of water, and a privacy stand in the corner for dressing. Silenus had been slow on the stairs, but he hadn't complained, and now hummed as he washed his face and prepared for bed. Listening to him, Denisia felt a lightness in her heart. Despite her misgivings, it seemed everything was going to be all right. Silenus was well, and Anchurus would be safe. As for Katiah's plans, Denisia couldn't be sure, but Silenus had said she would keep her word. Midas would have what he wanted, and it was up to him what he did with it. Besides, he and the dark goddess apparently had a history—which was none of Denisia's concern.

She was getting Silenus settled when she heard a knock at the door.

"Prince Anchurus," the guard said.

The prince! Denisia froze, blankets in her hands. When the guard announced the prince again, she said, "Just a moment!"

Silenus grinned at her.

"Oh, hush!" she said.

"I said nothing!"

She wagged her finger at him and spread the blankets over the mattress.

"That's good," he said, shooing her away. "Go!"

She turned to the door, checking her hair before opening it. There stood the prince, still looking so handsome, though the lines were heavy around his tired eyes.

"I apologize," he said, glancing inside the room. "If you have a moment?"

"Of course." Denisia reached for her shawl, threw it over her shoulders, and closed the door behind her. The prince gestured down the hall to their right. They walked almost to the opposite stairwell before turning into a room on the left. It was larger than hers, dimly lit by two oil lamps hanging from hooks on the walls. Sparsely furnished, it had only a thick bear rug on the floor by the far window, a small wooden cabinet near the bed, and a backless bench sitting underneath a wall full of weapons.

Anchurus closed the door behind him. "I apologize for the intrusion," he said. "I only wished to thank you."

She turned to face him. "I am the one who is grateful. The king is so kind. Our accommodations are comfortable."

Anchurus bowed his head in acknowledgment. He stood silent then, looking at the floor.

"There is something else?" Denisia asked.

"The wish." Anchurus raised his gaze. "It will happen soon?"

"By tomorrow, I'd guess." She shrugged. "To be honest, it's a wish I haven't granted before."

"But it's within your powers?"

"Yes." She gazed into his hazel eyes. "Do not worry. Your father will be pleased."

He forced a smile, but his discomfort was plain.

"You are a loyal son," she said. "I'm sure he appreciates that."

"To defeat Sargon," he said. "It is something he has long desired."

"Something you have worked hard for." She took a step toward him.

"If we achieved it," he said, locking eyes with her, "it would mean much to the kingdom."

"And to your family," she said, a little softer now.

"We will be grateful for your help." He paused. "Is there anything else he must do?"

She shook her head. "Sometimes the magic takes time to adhere itself." She touched his arm. "You were not wrong to have faith in me."

"Very well." He nodded and gave her a brief smile. "My apologies again for the interruption. I will leave you to your rest." He stepped back to allow her to pass.

Denisia glanced at the doorway. She wouldn't get another chance like this. Surely, he had brought her to his room for a reason? Katiah's words echoed in her ears. *He would not refuse you.* She turned her head and found his hazel eyes on her, an intense gaze sizzling with fire. Her heartbeat raced. She could hear his breath, sense his broad shoulders there, so close. She took a step toward him and placed her arm on his chest. He smelled like leather and musk.

"Goddess Denisia," he said in a near whisper.

It was all she needed. She moved into him, her lips meeting his in a warm kiss. He enveloped her in his arms, his mouth drinking hers as one hand came up behind her head. She felt her desire rise, and soon they were lost in one another, moving as one to the bear rug,

Denisia's clothes melting off her body. She had been with men before, often during the harvest celebrations in the forest, young and virile men who never seemed to tire, but this was different. Her mind dizzy with passion, she loved Anchurus again and again that night, every time finding him there in step with her, as if the two were no longer separate beings but born of the same spirit, rejoined in some other world where barriers no longer existed and reality was only a dream that paled in the presence of one another.

Anchurus.

CHAPTER TEN

Sargon woke in the middle of the night to see the dark goddess staring down at him. Her hair hung loosely on either side of her face, the strands tickling his bare chest, her black eyes studying him. She began to pull away. Like a viper, he snatched her arm. "My dear Katiah, couldn't sleep?"

She tried to reclaim her arm, but he held fast, so she relented. "I'm restless," she said. "Perhaps anticipating things to come."

"Anticipation only hastens the passing of time, and we have so little." He released her. "Of course, I forget you are immortal."

A candle flickered on the nightstand, casting her face in a yellow glow. "Do you believe you have little time?"

"A king's reign comes and goes." He snapped his finger. "In a blink, you are an old man surrounded by enemies trying to seize your power." He lay back a little, bracing himself on his elbows. "I sense some of those enemies nibbling about the edges of my realm even now."

"A dark thought to have when you were sleeping so peacefully," she said.

He let his gaze roam over her body, her curves visible under her sheer nightgown. She was too tempting. He sat up and kissed her shoulder. She lowered her head in response. He continued up and over the nape of her neck. There was a distinct quality about the way her skin tasted, like snow. His desire began to rise, so he pulled away from her and moved to the other side of the bed.

"Something else troubles you?" she asked.

He drew his robe over his shoulders and poured himself a cup of water from the basin.

"You don't have to keep secrets from me," she said.

Who is keeping secrets? he wanted to ask. Instead, he said, "I had a disturbing encounter with a slave woman today."

He walked over to where his many weapons hung on the wall: several swords, a bow and arrow, a couple of axes, and a scythe. The last reminded him of his childhood, when his father had made him work among the commoners in the fields. To understand what it was like, he'd said. Sargon had torn up his hands day after day, his mother bandaging them at night.

"She infuriates me," he said, "yet she is . . . enticing."

"You are attracted to her?" Katiah said, a slight edge to her voice.

Was she jealous? "Attracted may not be the right word. You, I am attracted to." He turned to see her lingering by the bed. "This woman . . ." He pictured Elanur standing in the tower room, her dark hair unwashed and sloppily tied with a leather band. He could still hear her laughing as the guards hauled her away. "Since I was very young, she has been . . . important."

"And you don't like anyone having power over you."

Sargon perused the cabinet that rested beneath his weapons. On top rested three of his favorite blades. He picked up the longest one, which stretched the length of his forearm. "She said something disturbing."

Katiah came up behind him, reached past his robe, and began caressing his stomach, sending shivers through his ribs. "She clearly has you preoccupied."

He stared at the wall, tightening his grip on the dagger. "It was Emir's mother."

"Oh, darling." She paused, then pulled away. "Are you still upset about that wayward boy?"

"He is my son."

"One of many. And as I recall, you tossed him to your armies to be killed on the battlefield. I don't understand this obsession you have with him now."

"He escaped. And has yet to be found."

She glided toward the wall of weapons. "Surely you've had other deserters?"

"He was under watch," Sargon said. "He should not have been able to escape unnoticed."

"A king's guards sometimes shirk their duties."

Sargon replaced the dagger. "I put my sons in the army to test them. It weeds out the weak ones. Emir was strong. He became a powerful warrior."

Katiah passed her hand over the scythe. "Why do you keep this thing? Surely you never use it in battle."

"She despises me for taking him away at such a young age. She said she prayed to the gods for her son's safety."

"So do they all."

"She specifically mentioned you."

"They all know about me. I am the goddess of the underworld, or have you forgotten?" She turned to face him.

"But she is a common woman. A servant."

"Even those who understand little about the gods know Katiah."

Sargon ambled toward the door. He had to choose his words carefully. "When this woman prayed to you, did it please you to answer her?"

"Prayers and my responses to them are none of your concern," she said.

He shot her a look across the room, angry words on the tip of his tongue. "I'm curious. This woman prayed for her son's—my son's—safety."

Katiah heaved a heavy sigh. "Must you continue this morose mood?" She placed her hands on her hips and walked toward him.

Sargon's heartbeat quickened. As she approached, her face seemed to grow in his perception, triggering a distant memory. He saw himself on the flatlands, his sword aloft, riding down on the wounded brown-haired boy while balancing little Elanur on the saddle in front of him. He had nearly struck the boy a second blow when the weather changed. A powerful blast of wind pushed dust into his eyes. His horse swerved, frightened. He pulled back on the reins, clutching Elanur to his chest. Through his blurry vision, a face appeared, black eyes boring into him.

"Leave him," the apparition ordered.

The dust cleared, and a path opened to the east, away from the village his soldiers had plundered. He had eagerly taken it, urging his mount to flee the deathly spirit.

Now here was that same face staring at him. *Elanur was right.* "It was you," he whispered, stumbling back against the door. "You stopped me." How had he not recognized her before?

"My king," she said sweetly, "do you wish me to continue helping you?"

Those eyes! They emanated the same darkness they had that day so long ago, as if she'd finally dropped her veil.

"Where is my son?" he managed to ask.

She shook her head. "You are so close to having everything you've dreamed about. Would you destroy that now?"

"Did you help him escape?" he asked.

She placed her fingers at the hollow of his throat and pulled down through his coarse chest hair. "A goddess need not reveal her plans to a mere mortal. But since you're so uptight, I will tell you this. Emir is special. I may have use for him. He did not matter to you, so let that be that. It would be unwise to allow your pride to interfere with your coming triumph." She moved her hand down farther still, his skin twitching under her touch.

"Did you help him?" he asked in a breathless voice.

She flattened her palm against his stomach. "A king's pride might lead to his downfall."

A stabbing sensation seized his gut. He groaned, bending inward. She lifted her hand, and the pain stopped.

"There now," she said, touching his cheek, "I've answered you. Since you have bored me, I'm leaving. Should you want my assistance in your final battle against Midas, let me know." She stepped back and then moved toward the door. "Perhaps Elanur can advise you on how to contact me. She's become quite practiced at it." She winked at him and walked out.

IT WAS near dawn when King Midas approached Rose Field. He nodded to Haluk, who bowed and opened the short wooden gate into the large fenced enclosure. Inside, Midas meandered past multiple rows of bushes. It was too early in the season for blooms. He searched for them anyway, as it always pleased him to find the first one. In the process, he spotted a few young weeds and pulled them up. Thanks to Bastian's fine gardening skills, there weren't many. Occasionally, Midas wondered if the cunning old man left some behind just to make the king feel useful.

He arrived at the bench in back and turned around to take in the view. From here, he could see much of the gardens, the fig orchard on his right, the hazelnut trees down the hill to the northwest, and, beyond, the man-made creek. It all appeared quiet and peaceful this early in the morning, not a soul but Haluk nearby. Midas exhaled a long, heavy sigh and sat down.

Shortly after the goddess had left his strategy room, he'd tried touching things. His chair. His tunic. Even the battle table. But nothing had changed. Not that he'd really expected it would. It made no sense that a goddess of flowers would have the power to grant the touch of gold. Anchurus had believed in her, and Midas had to admit she was convincing, but in the end, she didn't deliver. Perhaps she'd wanted to. Gods were known to overestimate themselves.

"She said it would take time," his son had said. But here it was the next morning, and there was no sign of any magic. He rested his forearms on his knees and gazed out at the landscape. He always did his best thinking here, where he could take in the beauty of his kingdom and no one would bother him. No one except the queen. Sometimes she would join him on the bench and they would talk. Those were some of his most treasured memories. How he wished she were here now to help him with the situation he faced.

As he saw it, he had only two options: risk his son's life sending him back out to battle against a powerful king with a goddess' magic on his side, or give up the fight for the time being and allow Sargon to gain even more strength. Queen Demodica would have told him that the last option was best. Midas imagined the conversation, his heart aching at the thought of her sitting beside him. Yet, the idea chafed like sand on his skin. More waiting. More time gone. Less hope he'd ever find Elanur alive.

He cast his gaze north where the Sangarius River flowed toward the Black Sea, its life-giving waters shallower this year than last. Zoe's water storage system would be needed if the gods chose to be stingy with the rains once again. Today would be dry, the sun already warm in the east.

It hit him suddenly: There was one more option.

You promised me.

He envisioned his wife's sweet face, the paleness of it, her soft fingers relaxed in her lap the way she always held them. His longing for her had eased some, changing from a breath-seizing stab to a dull ache. But even now, the memory of her was enough to bring tears to his eyes. He rubbed them dry, got up, and walked.

Haluk opened the gate, allowing the king to exit Rose Field. Midas turned right and headed deeper into the garden toward the fig orchard. He and the queen had passed many a morning together picking figs when they were in season. Demodica's fingers had become sticky with their sweetness, her lips tasting of their flavor. When he'd taken her behind a tree, she had looked at him in that mischievous way she had and said, "Oh my, is this behavior becoming of a king?"

He chuckled at the memory, then quickly sobered, letting his feet take their time on the path. The other option. It would require sacrifice from only one person: himself.

No, Demodica would have said.

"What choice do I have?" he said aloud to the morning air.

A bluebird flitted past on its way to the orchard. He marveled at the rich color of its feathers, remembering how the queen always picked them up when she found them, saving them to use as decorations for a variety of her creative projects.

You promised to be done with her, she had told him once.

Guilt blackened Midas' heart as he relived the moment. They'd been arguing in their room. He couldn't forget how she'd looked at him, the disappointment in her face. It was shortly after that when she had ordered all representations of Katiah banned from the castle and the city at large. She hadn't consulted him, but he didn't contradict the order. It had been his own fault. He'd succumbed to temptation—a goddess' powerful temptation, but his failing nevertheless. It was his own weakness that had started all of this.

A shadow overhead alerted him to the fact that he'd entered the orchard. He inhaled the fresh scent of the new leaves. There were no figs yet; only a few buds beginning to form. He let his fingers caress the branches as he passed, eventually gripping one firmly in his hand. The action stopped his progress. He waited, fully intending to walk on, but then folded inward toward the trunk. He pressed his forehead against it, the bark biting his skin.

"It was a mistake, taking everything down," he said out loud.

I will not have your children worshipping that . . . that woman! the queen would have said.

"We replace the sculptures," he said. "Rebuild the monument. We lived with them before."

He could imagine how angry she would be, almost hear what she would say to him. *Don't you remember Zoe dressing up like her? Anchurus praying to her over breakfast? They would have been her servants, Karem.*

"They're adults now," he said. "They know better."

And your grandchildren? The rest of the kingdom? Will you have them enslaved by the dark goddess?

"It may be the only way to stop her," he said.

"Father?"

Midas turned to see Zoe standing at the edge of the orchard.

"Are you all right?" she asked.

He stepped away from the tree and straightened his tunic. "You're up early."

Zoe started toward him. "It sounded like you were talking to someone."

"Only your mother." He smiled.

"Oh. What did she have to say?"

He embraced her, inhaling the sweet scent of her hair. "That I need to watch out for you and your brother." He took hold of her hands. "You have her eyes."

"So you've told me many times."

Midas held her gaze. "You are nineteen. If you were queen, what would your counsel be?"

Zoe blinked, clearly surprised. "About what?" When her father said nothing, she let go and walked toward the tree that he had embraced. "So it's him again." She lifted her hair off her neck. "What is it about King Sargon that goads you so? And don't tell me you wish to keep him from becoming too powerful."

"That's not enough?" He started after her.

"If you pursue him now, you'll be risking Anchurus' life. The odds are against you. You might suffer another defeat. A worse defeat."

She stopped by the same tree and turned toward him. "Does this have something to do with the doll?"

Midas paused, startled.

"Mother knew about her, didn't she?"

"Your mother didn't approve of intruding upon another's private matters."

"If you'd ever talk to me, I wouldn't have to," Zoe said. When her father looked pained, she relented. "I would counsel you to be patient. Give your army a half moon's cycle at least to rest and regroup while FAX finds a way to fight Katiah. Sargon is not eager to attack Gordium. He will want to prepare." She started back toward the path, lightly touching his arm as she passed.

Midas glanced toward the distant wall enclosing the gardens. Observing its height, he wondered how Silenus had gotten past it. The old man must have charmed one of the soldiers guarding the entrance. Midas would ask Rastus to find out which.

A light breeze stirred, and he swore he could smell the queen's rose perfume. He inhaled until it was gone, then followed his daughter, reaching for her hand as he came up behind her. She took it, and they walked back together.

"Why were you out here so early this morning?" he asked.

"Looking for you," she said.

"Oh?"

"I wanted to tell you to keep an eye on the musician."

"Why?"

"I ran into him after the festivities were over. He was wandering the hallways, out of his quarters. He is ambitious."

"Ambition can be a good thing."

"Perhaps." Zoe cocked her head. "But he's not just a simple musician."

Midas smiled to himself. She was as astute as her mother. "I shall remain alert."

They kept talking as they walked, gradually falling into the comfortable rapport they had always had, conversing about topics that were easier to discuss, like the building of the new crane device and the possibilities of storing water in large underground rooms, pumping it out when needed. When they reached the Rose Field, Midas paused and kissed Zoe on the cheek. "You go ahead to breakfast. I'll be there soon."

She searched his face, her mouth set in a serious line.

"It's all right," he said. "We'll talk more."

She reluctantly obeyed, nodding to Haluk as she passed. After she'd gone, Midas meandered through the field once again, thinking over what his daughter had said. He reached the last row of bushes, planning to retake his seat at the bench, when something caught his eye. Could it be? He stepped into the row on his right. Sure enough, there was a single bud that had started to open. He knelt down before it, marveling at the brilliant yellow color brightened by the sun's rays. He'd never had a yellow rose before. Red ones. White. But this one was a bright yellow. He looked up, thinking he might call Zoe back, but she was long gone. She was never much for flowers, anyway. Demodica would have appreciated it. He leaned forward and inhaled, allowing the subtle scent to fill his sinuses. It was like honey-butter, so sweet as to make one want to taste it. His shoulders relaxed as the fragrance filled his head. Zoe was right. He would wait a little longer. Keep Anchurus safe. Care for his kingdom. The time to rescue Elanur—if she was still alive—would come.

He started to get up, then hesitated, wanting to experience the sweet aroma once more. He cupped the flower in his palm, closed his eyes, and inhaled. The bloom shifted against his skin. He couldn't detect the scent. Frowning, he opened his eyes.

The rose had changed. A darker hue covered the petals—more gold than yellow. He rubbed his thumb against one of them. It felt hard, the edge sharp. He inhaled again, but the scent had gone.

There was no doubt. The rose had turned to gold.

CHAPTER ELEVEN

The knock sounded distant in Xander's ears. He was still in bed, his eyes closed. He heard the door open, then a messenger spoke, but he couldn't make out the words.

"The king doesn't order us immediately to the dining hall," Aster said, closing the door.

Xander groaned. "Now he wants to see us?" He glanced over at Fotis' area. The old man was already dressed in his long white robe, but he was lying on his mattress, staring up at the ceiling.

Aster returned to his space, folded his nightclothes, and then washed his hands at the water basin. "No need to hurry," he said. "It's only the king's order."

"I don't want to know," Xander said.

Fotis didn't move.

"The king does not call us!" Aster said.

"Very well!" Xander threw the blankets off. "I don't understand the big hurry now. We tried to see him last night. He refused us."

"Unlikely that he was contemplating the wish he made," Aster said.

Xander reached into the trunk by his bed and emerged with a

clean tunic. "Now he probably wants to announce our execution, 'Good people of Gordium, I'm happy to announce that today, I will execute my advisors.'" He lifted his hands into the air and mimicked the applause of a crowd.

Aster turned an expectant gaze on Fotis, who gestured toward Xander. "He's not ready yet."

"But you are not ready," Aster snapped.

"So glad you two are so eager to have your heads removed." Xander found his advisor's robe and slipped it over his head.

Aster paced between the door and his bed, his arms crossed.

"Why are you so agitated?" Fotis asked, sitting up.

"The king is not in danger."

Fotis huffed. "There's nothing we can do about it. We tried to warn him."

"Now he's just going to blame us for whatever goes wrong." Fully dressed, Xander sat back down on his bed.

"Because you can predict what the king is going to say," Aster said.

"Shall we wager?" Xander said. "He's going to say, 'I asked you to come up with a solution, and now look what has happened! Off with your heads!'"

Aster looked at Fotis and got nothing but a raised eyebrow. Exhaling loudly, he walked to the door.

"Where are you going?" Fotis asked.

"The king has not called us," Aster said. "I will not obey, as that is not my duty."

"I will not obey, as that is not my duty," Xander mumbled under his breath.

Aster paused at the door. "You are not children pouting because things went your way. So we could warn the king last night. We must not warn him now about Katiah's influence. The fate of the kingdom does not hang in the balance. A soul,"—he gestured toward Xander—"does not hang in the balance." He opened the door and strode out.

Xander sighed and looked at the floor. He and Fotis stood up at about the same time, then followed their colleague like two condemned criminals on the way to the burning post.

"You think she gave him the gift?" Xander said as they trudged down the hall.

"I'm certain of it," Fotis said. "Katiah wouldn't have released us otherwise."

"So we're going back to war," Xander said.

"It is to be expected."

"But we haven't found a way to defeat the shiny one."

"That is correct."

"We will lose."

"Most likely."

"Unless the gift was really good." Xander tapped his hand along the wall as they descended the stairs. "What do you think she gave him? We should wager on it. I'd bet on thousands of strong steeds to carry the men into battle."

Fotis said nothing.

"Come on. Guess." Still nothing. They reached the first level and strode into the hall. Ahead, Aster walked alone.

"Aster," Fotis called.

The middle advisor waited for them to catch up. Fotis moved into his usual place in front, Xander in the back. When they started walking again, Xander tapped Aster on the shoulder. "What do you think she gave him? I say thousands of horses."

"Power," Aster said. "She did not give him power."

"But what *kind* of power?" Xander asked.

"The kind that, with intervention, will not be the end of our king," Aster said.

Denisia came away from the window, lit the candle on the nightstand, and settled into the chair next to it. Silenus was still sleeping on the other side of the room, his breathing gentle and even. She envied his rest, wishing she had been able to do the same, but her thoughts were troubled. She'd left Anchurus in the middle of the night, sneaking out while he slept. Silenus had been on her mind, and she'd wanted to be certain he was all right. She found him in sound slumber and had considered then returning to the prince, but it wouldn't do for her grandfather to find her gone in the morning. Besides, she couldn't deny feeling anxious about her deal with Katiah. Anchurus would be safe and her grandfather well, but what about the king? And what about Gordium? These things were not her concern, but they would affect Anchurus, something she had to admit she hadn't thoroughly considered.

As morning approached, she got up and peered out the window again. The king would soon find that his wish had come true. She wanted to believe he and the prince would be happy about it, but doubt gnawed at the corners of her mind. It would be best to leave now. She longed to see the prince again, but feared how the events of this day might unfold. The touch of gold could make Midas' dream of victory a reality. But it could also come with complications. She could control certain things about her powers, but a spell had its quirks, unpredictable and sometimes surprising. It would be better for everyone, she told herself, if she got out of the way.

She turned back to her grandfather. He was still sleeping, his belly rising and falling underneath the blankets. She longed to wake him, but couldn't bear to disturb him. He looked so peaceful.

A gentle knock came at the door. She threw on her cloak. "Yes?" she whispered, peering out.

A guard stood in the hall. "The king requests your presence at breakfast at your earliest convenience."

Denisia nodded. "Very well. Thank you." She closed the door. The king was up already? Her first thought was that she would see Anchurus. Her second was that something had happened. Perhaps something bad. The king might have questions she couldn't answer.

"Is everything all right?" Silenus eyed her from his bed, his white hair disheveled.

Denisia hurried over to him. "Of course. Are you all right?"

He rubbed his eyes. "The bed is a little lumpy, but it's been a while since I slept that well."

"A little too much wine last night, perhaps," Denisia said.

"Never too much wine." He smoothed the wispy hairs back. "Why are you up so early?"

"It's a beautiful day." She handed him his shirt. "If we go now, we can hasten our journey home."

Her grandfather sat up slowly, grunting as he did so. "There is no handsome prince at home."

Denisia chuckled and glanced nervously at the door. "I can see him again another time."

"You're dragging me back to my cage, then?" he asked.

"Home is not a cage, Grandfather. I was worried about you."

"You found me," he said. "I'm well. And I don't need a chaperone."

"Yes, you do." It fell out of her mouth too quickly. She held her breath, staring at him.

Silenus sighed and swung his legs over the side of the bed. "I was taking care of myself long before you came along." He reached for the shirt she had left on the nightstand. "You are a penned-up doe pacing the fence line. Frankly, you're making me nervous."

Denisia looked down at her hands. The king's guard would be watching for her exit, planning to escort her to breakfast. When Silenus reached for his pants, she scooped up her own clothes and moved behind the dressing screen. "You don't want to go home?" she asked.

"I enjoy traveling," he said. "There is much great country to behold."

"You wish to continue seeing it?"

"Send your man with me if you must. I can't remember his name."

"Chetin?" Denisia asked.

"He seems capable enough," Silenus said. "I could stand his company if he's willing."

Denisia emerged from the screen to see Silenus sliding his feet into his sandals. He'd always fought against having a chaperone before. It was comforting, his agreement, proof that his mind remained clear. The thought filled her with joy and worry at the same time. She washed her face in the water basin, patted her cheeks dry, and glanced at him. "I would be happy to grant you Chetin's services, on one condition."

He cocked an ear her way.

"We leave immediately."

"Without breakfast?"

"Please, Grandfather." She gathered up her nightclothes and put them into the linen sack. "The king has been kind. I don't want to stay past our welcome." When she looked at him again, his expression had changed to one of concern. She tied the small rope around the sack and moved to the door. "We can get breakfast in the city."

He watched her for another moment. "Very well. I will go. *After* you tell me what's bothering you."

"It would be better if I told you on the way—"

Silenus shook his head.

Denisia had her hand on the door handle. They didn't have time for this. But she knew her grandfather well enough to know how stubborn he could be. She dropped the sack in exasperation. Resting her hands on her hips, she stared at the stone wall. "What do you do when you're worried you've made a mistake, but you can't take it back?"

He didn't appear to have heard her at first. She was about to repeat the question when he said, "You find a way to correct it."

Cancel the spell. But that would mean Silenus would succumb once more to his illness. Worse, Anchurus would be vulnerable to Katiah's wrath. "What if things are already in motion and there is no stopping them?"

He pulled at his beard, gazing toward the window. "Imagine

you're traveling across the top of a hill," he said in his singsong storytelling voice, "and you come to an enormous boulder that has fallen in the middle of your path."

Denisia clamped her teeth together. She shouldn't have said anything. This would take too long.

"You have to get around it somehow," Silenus said. "Go up the hill or down the hill. Imagine you're carrying something heavy or, worse, trying to drive a herd of goats. You're suddenly quite stuck, or at least in a fairly difficult pickle." He turned to be sure she was listening.

"Please," she said. "We must hurry."

He rubbed his nose and continued. "You decide to clear the pathway. You get behind the boulder and push as hard as you might. Eventually, you dislodge it and send it careening down the hill. At first, you are pleased that you've solved your problem. But then you realize that the enormous boulder is headed straight for a small cabin down below. You failed to notice it before. And in front of that cabin is a little boy playing in the mud."

Denisia pictured it in her mind. Her grip loosened on the door handle.

"If that boy doesn't move," Silenus said, "the boulder will crush him and anyone else in the cabin. 'Things are in motion,' as you said, and there is no stopping it." He laced his fingers together. "What do you do?"

Denisia rested her back against the door. "You call to the boy. You warn him."

Silenus nodded his agreement.

Denisia realized what he was telling her: She should warn the king. Tell him of her deal with Katiah. Let him decide what to do from there. But she couldn't do it. Couldn't admit she had granted the king his gift out of selfishness. What would the prince think of that? "What if you can't?"

"Then once the boulder has come to rest beyond the cabin," Silenus said somberly, "you go down the hill."

"And do what?" Denisia asked.

"Go down the hill," her grandfather said. "What you encounter there will tell you what to do next." Slowly, he stood up, pushing against the bed for support. Upright, he gazed at her with worry in his eyes.

She went over then and embraced him, holding him close. "Everything is all right. As long as you are."

"I'm perfectly well," he said.

She nodded, pressing her cheek against his shoulder. "Yes," she said and smiled, because no matter what else had happened or might yet happen, he was, indeed, perfectly well.

King Midas cast a sweeping glance over the dining hall. The servants had set up the table with nine chairs around it, as he had asked. His daughter and son were already there, Rastus standing next to Anchurus. His advisors were in their places as well, but the goddess and her grandfather were missing. He checked behind him. He'd wanted to express his gratitude. That they might not come had never occurred to him. But the hallway was empty and there was no sound of footsteps on the stairwell. After waiting another moment, he entered the room.

Eleven eyes turned to watch him, awaiting his instructions. He nodded to them as he walked across to stand behind his chair. Clasping his hands in front of him, he looked upon each one in turn. They all looked back with questions on their faces. He paused when he came to Zoe. Her skin appeared radiant in the morning light, worry etched in the lines around her eyes. No more worry after today, he would tell her. No need for her to worry ever again. He turned to his son, and his breast swelled with pride. Anchurus might have failed on the battlefield, but he had brought the goddess to him. Now they had their ultimate victory within reach. He shifted his gaze to his advisors and opened his hands. "Everyone, please, sit."

They all obeyed. But when he didn't sit with them, they turned toward him, waiting.

"This is to be a glorious day," he said, "and I wanted to share it with all of you. To thank you. You are all so important to me." He rested his gaze on Anchurus, then Zoe.

"Your Majesty, we—" Xander began.

Midas held up his hand. "Not now." He gestured to Rastus. "My loyal friend. You deserve so much, and now you shall finally have it." Rastus frowned and opened his mouth to speak, but again Midas held up his hand and turned to the prince. He wanted to say something to him too, but standing so near, staring down at the top of his son's head, he couldn't think of the right words. He glanced at the food spread out on the table. "My girl," he said, addressing Zoe, "you will no longer have to worry about the townspeople. There will be plenty of food for everyone. We will plant more crops and purchase more livestock. We will build the water storage system you designed and find craftsmen to create the new lighter armor you've suggested. Work will begin on more secure dwellings at the south side of the city immediately, and we'll build a new road between here and the north river. Gordium will be the envy of all the lands."

"Father?" Zoe asked.

He wanted to extend the moment a little longer, enjoy the anticipation. But Demodica's sweet voice echoed in his ear.

Come, darling. No one's enjoying this but you.

He extended his hand, looked around the table, and lowered his fingers to the top of his chair. Like water over rocks, a golden syrup covered the wood from the back of the chair to the seat and down over the legs. Midas watched their eyes widen, their spines straightening as they sat taller in their chairs. Smiling, he dropped his hand, his chair now solid gold.

Emir awoke when he heard the loud knock on the door.

"Emir Alkan, the king summons you."

The boy sat up bleary-eyed at the edge of the mattress.

"Go," Emir whispered. "Hide."

The boy ducked behind the nearest barrel and waited while Emir opened the door.

"You are to report to the soldiers' barracks immediately." The man addressing him was shorter than Emir by a hand or so, but thickly built. He wore a cream-colored shirt and pants with his sword hanging on his belt.

"The barracks?" Emir frowned. "I am a musician. I won the king's contest last night."

"I know very well who you are," the stranger said. "Count yourself fortunate that you have found a position in the king's army. You will be in Commander Baran's unit. Should you perform well, you may be allowed to stay."

"Commander Baran."

"Second-in-command after the prince."

"Are you in this unit?"

The man cocked his thick head. "I was the unlucky one assigned to get your ass moving. If you want breakfast, follow me now."

Emir cast his gaze back. The boy remained out of sight. "Do you eat in the barracks?"

"You are the winner of the contest, as you so politely reminded me." The man smirked. "A prize breakfast awaits you in the kitchen. It will be the last of the special treatment you will receive."

"In the kitchen," Emir repeated loudly enough for the boy to hear. "Very well. We leave now?"

"Unless you need to pretty up your face?"

Emir followed the soldier down the hall, his thoughts troubled. Once he was firmly ensconced in the king's army, his chances of getting Midas' attention would be lost in the wind. "How long do I have for breakfast?" he asked.

"You may eat at your leisure, but report to the first barracks by midday, or you will find yourself escorted off the castle grounds for good." The soldier paused at the doorway, the smell of cooked lamb and pudding emanating from within. With a last disparaging glance back, he walked away.

Emir watched him disappear up the stairs, then checked back down the hallway. The boy peered out from behind the doorframe. Emir scanned the kitchen. It was empty. He made a few hand motions. The boy ducked back inside the undercroft. Emir sat down at the table to wait. He drummed his fingers on the wood surface. Perhaps the king wasn't even awake yet. His leg bouncing up and down, he considered his options. Go upstairs now and ask to speak to the king, or wait for breakfast. The boy would need to eat. He waited.

Back in the dining hall, everyone at the king's table sat speechless. Fotis looked on with an expression of doom. Aster appeared more disgruntled than usual. Anchurus stared at the chair as if he couldn't believe what he was seeing. Zoe looked from the chair to her father to her brother and back. Rastus seemed ready to jump at the king's first command.

"Pretty!" Xander said, breaking the silence.

Fotis scowled at him.

"Well, it is!" he protested.

"Its aesthetics are the primary factor to observe," Aster said.

Xander's smile faded.

The king addressed Anchurus. "Do you know what this means? We can finally do it, Son." He gestured between the two of them. "We can defeat him. An end to the tyranny, the suffering. An end to the threat."

Anchurus looked at the chair, then his father's face, a dawning of understanding taking over his features. "Denisia's gift?" he said.

"Watch." Midas picked up his son's knife and held it in his palm. It quickly changed. "That's gold," Midas said. "We can exchange this for supplies, horses, armor, men. We finish it, once and for all." He set the knife down and lifted the plate. That, too, changed before their eyes. "Everywhere I go, pure gold. Do you see? Do you understand?"

Anchurus pushed his chair back and stood up. He was hesitant at first to touch the gold items. Curiosity won out, and he took up the knife and brought it close to his face, examining it.

When his son set the knife back down, King Midas placed both hands on the table. Ripples of gold flowed down the length of the wood. Everyone sat back, their hands raised. Soon they were all standing, the golden table gleaming in front of them. Midas absorbed the looks on their faces and then dropped to his haunches and touched the floor. It took a little longer, but gradually it began to change under their feet. They moved instinctively, but the gold surged toward them like a river, then passed harmlessly underneath their sandals.

Xander broke out laughing. "It's a golden lake!"

"That's how it shall be from now on," Midas said. "There will be splendor like you have never seen before. This will be known far and wide as the Golden Castle of Gordium." He spun around, taking in the imagined grandeur. "People will come from the far ends of the Earth to see it. They will clamber to be a part of the city of gold! This candelabra. Tarnished already." He reached across the table and changed it. "And this sculpture. Boring bronze. Yes, that's it! And this vase." He crossed over to the wall. "I have grown tired of it. Ha ha! And look, even the flowers have turned!" He gestured to show the others, who stood stupefied. "How about this painting?"

"Er, it's your great-great-grandfather, Your Majesty," Fotis said, holding up one finger.

Midas paused. "You're right. I don't imagine that would be appropriate. Would take all the color out of his cheeks, wouldn't it?" He chuckled, then touched the royal flag of Gordium hanging above him. When it changed, he stepped back to examine it. "It doesn't flutter very well that way." He clapped his hands twice, and a young servant man came running in. "Remove this," Midas said to him. "Place it in the storeroom of things to be sold."

"Sold, Your Majesty?"

"You heard me. Tell Timon I wish a new storage area to be set aside immediately. Then put this into it."

The servant bowed and ran out. By the time he returned, Midas had drifted to the back corner of the room. He touched more chairs and tables, a rug on the floor, more vases and sculptures, and the serving platters that had been set on the side table for future use. He bade the servant to take them too, this one and that one. The man had to get help, as many of the items were heavy. Soon, four servants were carrying items out, clearing the corner of everything that had been there only moments before.

"Do you see the possibilities?" Midas asked.

"Of course, Father," Anchurus said. "This is what you've been waiting for."

"What *we've* been waiting for!" Midas said.

"How did this happen?" Zoe spoke for the first time.

"The prince!" Midas gestured toward Anchurus. "He brought me the goddess Denisia last night, and she granted me a wish." Midas beamed at Anchurus, who glanced hopefully at his sister. "Now we must move quickly while we have the chance. I don't know how long this gift will last." He opened his hands in front of his face and studied them, as if by memorizing the lines in his palms, he might glean some information about this new power. "I asked her to come to breakfast. Do you know where she is?"

"I haven't seen her this morning." Anchurus cast a fleeting glance toward the double doors.

"I believe she may have left, Your Majesty," Rastus said.

"Left?" Anchurus said. "So early?"

"Perhaps to get her grandfather home?" Rastus said.

Anchurus frowned, but King Midas seemed not to notice. "I must change everything I can," he said. "Then we will send it off to the royal kingdoms out west, exchange it for the supplies we need. Swift horses, weapons, armor."

"Will you change everything?" Zoe asked.

Midas looked at her. “You’re right, my girl. I can’t very well clean out the castle. I must go into the city.”

“The people’s things, Father?” Zoe said.

“Anything we claim, we will pay for,” he said. “Imagine how the citizens will react to having their own gold pieces! A golden bowl or mug. A golden cloak.” When Zoe didn’t appear convinced, he went on, “We will only change things that they readily surrender or trade. Or things that no one owns. Rocks. Trees. Animals. I will have the hunters bring them to me. Imagine the magnificence. A golden stag!” He turned his attention back to Anchurus. “Assign your trustworthy soldiers to deliver the gold to the neighboring kingdoms in trade for strong men and horses. Rastus, you’re in charge of securing the new items.”

“Yes, Your Majesty.” Rastus bowed his head.

“Praise the wonderful Goddess Denisia.” Midas laughed. “We will be victorious at last!”

Anchurus glanced again at the double doors, craning his neck to see into the hall.

“Your Majesty.” Fotis stood stiffly in front of his chair. “There’s something you should know.”

“Now?” Xander whispered.

“Now would not be prudent,” Aster said.

“We wanted to tell you last night,” Fotis said, “but—”

“We will act now,” Midas interrupted, demanding his son’s attention. “Before Sargon gets wind of what has happened.”

“Yes,” Anchurus said, looking distracted. “As quickly as we can.”

“Your Majesty, we must tell you,” Fotis said a little louder.

“It is not of the utmost importance,” Aster said.

“We have much to do,” Midas said. “Timon! Timon, where are you?” The servant man ran back in, breathless. “Summon Timon, immediately!” the king ordered. The man bowed and ran back out.

“Your Majesty,” Fotis tried again, “there really is something you should know.”

“It is not critically important,” Aster said.

"We really must—"

"The horses." Midas raised one finger to the side of his mouth. "A golden horse! Yes! Anchurus, just one horse we can spare. Have it brought to me immediately. And the sheep. Five golden sheep." He smiled and clenched his fist.

"Your Majesty, it was Katiah!" Xander shouted.

Midas turned to him, his smile frozen on his face. Everyone else stopped to look at the young advisor.

"It was not Katiah's idea," Aster said.

"I'm afraid they're right, Your Majesty," Fotis said. "Denisia may have granted the gift, but she did so at Katiah's request."

Anchurus stared at them as if his stomach had just soured. Midas' smile faded.

"We heard them last night," Xander said. "That's what we've been trying to tell you."

"They did not make a deal," Aster said.

"The pretty one with the other goddess," Xander said. "They're sisters. Half-sisters."

"They do seem to be related," Fotis said.

"But they don't look alike," Xander said.

"Which of course is critical information," Aster said, glaring at the younger advisor.

"Katiah manipulated Denisia into agreeing to the deal, Your Majesty," Fotis said.

"It had nothing to do with her ill grandfather," Aster said.

"It seems she did it for his sake, not for yours," Fotis said and then, with a guilty glance at Anchurus, "or for anyone . . . else in the castle."

Anchurus caught Fotis' look, then turned his back on the table.

The advisors continued with their story, the details tumbling out of their mouths. At first, Midas simply stood, listening. As they went on, his jaw tightened, and then the tendons showed in his neck. While Anchurus paced back and forth behind his chair, Midas took up the golden knife, his knuckles rising on the back of his hand.

"We wanted to tell you," Xander said. "We tried."

"The old man was ill, as you know," Fotis said. "Katiah promised to cure him in return for Denisia granting you the gift."

"It wasn't her fault," Xander said. "He was her grandfather, after all."

"But the gift is not tainted," Aster said. "It is unlikely that Katiah has some other purpose in mind."

"Denisia wasn't sure about doing it at first," Xander said. "But then Katiah threatened the—"

Aster elbowed Xander in the ribs.

"Hey!" Xander complained, but then he followed Aster's gaze to the prince. Anchurus had stopped pacing and now stood in the middle of the room, his expression filled with dread.

Midas dropped the knife. It clattered noisily on his golden plate. His back to them all, he crossed his arms, his shoulders hunched. For a long while, no one said anything.

Then the prince spoke. "It does not matter."

Everyone turned to him.

"It doesn't matter," he said again, turning toward his father. "We can exchange these things for what we need. Bolster our army. Take Sargon once and for all. Put an end to the war."

"But she is evil," Zoe said.

"It doesn't matter where he got the gift," Anchurus said. "He is the king."

"Association with the dark goddess will bring darkness," Zoe said, quoting the queen.

"Why didn't you warn me last night?" Midas barked at his advisors.

"As we noted, Your Majesty," Fotis said, "we were trapped."

"The dark goddess did not trap us," Aster said.

"She put up an invisible wall," Xander said. "You couldn't see it, but when you tried to walk through, *wham*!" He slammed his palm against his nose.

"We know how you appreciate the details, Your Majesty," Aster said with a wry glance at Xander.

"She knew you were there," Midas said, "that you were spying on her."

"We were quiet!" Xander said.

"We were stealth, Your Majesty," Fotis said, "but she is a goddess, after all."

Midas stewed, fingers pulling at his short beard.

"What matters is what we do now," Anchurus said.

"The dark goddess' influence," Zoe said. "Father, please."

Midas looked at both his children, then at the chair on his left where the queen had always sat. For a long while, he seemed to fight a battle in his mind. Finally, he said, "Anchurus is right. We take advantage of this opportunity. We bring Sargon to justice now."

Zoe shook her head and turned away. The prince came back toward the table, as if eager to begin.

"But if Katiah continues to help him?" Fotis asked.

"Let her come!" Midas threw up his hands. "We have our own power now."

"Father, give it time," Zoe said. "You're not thinking clearly."

"I'm thinking very clearly, my girl. Clearer than I ever have. Don't worry." He gave her a reassuring glance. "We will be victorious. There is no doubt of that now. But there is much to do, and we can't do it on empty stomachs. We're here for breakfast and to celebrate. Let's eat!"

CHAPTER TWELVE

The dungeon closed in around King Sargon II, the air rank with human sweat and waste. Oil lamps lit the way, the daylight fading behind him. He paused by the second cell and barked at the guard to open it. The man jumped to obey, his hands shaking as he released the bolt. Sargon ground his teeth. A coward. He would speak to his overseer about having this one removed to cleaning detail.

"Leave us."

The guard closed the heavy door and hurried away.

Elanur stood in the far corner, her face smudged with dirt.

"I want to know," Sargon said, "what you asked of Katiah?"

Elanur pressed her lips together, her eyes blazing at him. After hours spent down here, she was still going to be difficult. Nevertheless, it was she who had enlightened him to the fact that he was being played by a goddess. He rested his back against the wall.

"When I took you from your home," he said, "your brother tried to protect you. Do you remember?"

"Karem," she whispered. She turned toward the wall and ran one finger down its hard surface.

"He wanted me to let you go." Sargon thought back to that day. The entire village flattened, the air filled with suffocating smoke. Over thirty-five prisoners, most of them children. Half that many horses. He'd known that his king would be pleased. "He wounded me. But he had only a crude dagger. I struck him a return blow with my sword. He ran, and I rode after him."

Elanur's finger stopped moving down the rock.

"I didn't catch him. Because of . . . Katiah."

She turned to him, a question in her eyes. "The dark goddess?"

He fingered the sheath at his belt. It encased the same crude dagger the boy had used to stab his leg. He'd kept it all this time as a reminder never to underestimate anyone.

"You were right," he told Elanur. "For years, I have been haunted by the image of a demon woman. She was there the day I captured you." He squinted, the memory terrifying. "The goddess Katiah. She appeared before I could be sure that your brother was dead. I never did discover whether he survived."

Her glare hardened. It seemed this news made her hate him even more.

"She is the one you've been praying to, the same one who is assisting me in my conquest of the west. It was partly because of her magic that we claimed victory over King Midas' army only days ago. We have the city of Gordium in our sights. But now I know something I didn't know before: she helped Emir to escape. She admitted as much to me this morning."

Hope sparked in Elanur's eyes. It angered Sargon. He clenched his teeth, keeping a tight hold on his temper. "She is interested in our son. Why?"

Elanur walked over to the opposite wall and leaned her shoulder against it. "If what you say is true, Katiah saved my brother from your wicked sword. And now she has helped my son escape. From what I see, she is on my side."

Sargon forced a smile to his lips. "My dear, if she were on your side, why did she allow me to capture you? Why did she allow you to be enslaved?"

Her shoulders stiffened.

"And why does she return now to help Emir escape? Why didn't she come before, to help *you* escape?"

Someone groaned in a nearby cell. "Perhaps she meant to use me against you," Elanur said, pulling away from the wall.

"Did you hear me? She is *helping* me. My army is victorious. My kingdom is growing."

"Your son is gone," she said.

He peered through the small window in the door. "Answer this. Is it more likely she allowed him to escape to wound me or because she means to use *our* son as a pawn in some larger plan?" He let the question linger. "I have sent my best hunters after him. They will find him. What happens to him next will be up to you."

"I asked you before what you want me to do," she said.

Sargon turned around. "Tell me what you know. Did you summon the dark goddess?"

"If I tell you, what guarantee do I have that you will show mercy?"

Sargon considered it. Could he promise her now that when he captured the wayward deserter, he wouldn't string him up and separate him from his bowels? "Guard!" he shouted. The cowardly man rushed in and, with a trembling hand, opened the door. Sargon stood back and gestured toward it.

Elanur stared at him like a wild animal in a trap. Finally, she took a couple of tentative steps and rushed through. Sargon followed her, the guard closing the door behind them. Soon they emerged into the fresh air. The king paused for a moment to breathe. Elanur stopped too, her gaze on the horizon, her profile soft against the golden-blue sky.

"What now?" she asked him.

In the light, she was beautiful again, her dark eyes entrancing. He took her arm roughly and headed for the horse stables. "You are going to show me," he said, "exactly how and where you summoned the goddess."

Back in the Gordium castle dining hall, Midas continued to talk about his plans over breakfast. He rested his elbows on the golden table while the servants replenished the food. Many of them hesitated upon entering the room, as if unsure whether they could believe their eyes, but then they proceeded with their tasks, trained as they were to attend to the king no matter what else might occur. They brought freshly cooked eggs and apricots, pancakes, roasted lamb, and small individual bowls of yogurt. The last of them poured cups of wine before they all left.

"The food is getting cold," Midas said. "Please." As his children, the advisors, and Rastus began filling their plates, he took hold of his golden cup. Without attempting to drink, he set it back down. Next, he pulled a plate full of eggs toward him. Before he had a chance to serve himself, it all turned to gold.

Rastus handed the princess the second plate of eggs. She gave some to her father. Midas started to pick up his spoon, but then put his hand back in his lap. "How long do you think we need to gather our supplies?" he asked Anchurus.

"Ten days at least?" the prince said, biting into a piece of lamb.

"That's too long."

"We will have to travel. Even Ancyra is a day away. Lydia is three out and three back."

"That will not do," the king said. "We must borrow from the nearby outposts. We will promise the citizens payment." He eyed the eggs on his plate. In one quick movement, he put a bite into his mouth.

"Sargon was victorious this last time out," Anchurus said, "but we still killed many of his men. He, too, will need time to recover."

The king worked his jaw back and forth. He could sense Zoe's concerned gaze on him. Something hard formed under his tongue.

He winced and tried chewing some more, but then spit the food out. Little pieces of golden egg dropped onto his plate, clattering like stones.

Everyone stared. Midas scowled, grabbed a pancake, and quickly bit off a piece. Surely a goddess' spell wouldn't leave him unable to eat? He simply had to figure out a new technique. He chewed as rapidly as possible, but it was futile. The pancake landed a golden shard on his plate.

Zoe covered her mouth with her hand.

"Pilar!" Midas shouted.

The side door opened, and the stout cook waddled in. "Your Majesty?"

"I can't taste your delicious food this morning. Send someone in to help me, would you?"

"But, Father, I—" Zoe began.

Midas held up his hand. "Someone you don't need at the moment," he said to Pilar.

The cook bowed and waddled back out. Midas looked around the table. "Go on. Eat!" He gave them a halfhearted smile. "A king deserves to be fed from time to time, doesn't he?"

The familiar sound of spoons against plates resumed, though more reserved now. It wasn't long before Pilar sent the wayward boy scurrying across the golden floor.

"You!" Zoe exclaimed upon seeing him. "You were supposed to stay in your room."

"He's the only one we can spare, Your Majesty," the cook said. "With your permission?"

Midas stared at the boy as if Pilar had brought in a wet, muddy dog.

"Very well." Zoe turned her attention to the child. "You will tend to the king, then go back to your room. Understood?"

The boy nodded. Pilar whispered something into his ear before leaving once again. The boy scooped a small piece of egg into the spoon and held it up to the king's face. The others pretended they were eating, but they all anxiously watched. Midas took the bite. For a moment, he simply held it in his mouth, refraining from chewing. It didn't help. He spit out another hard nugget.

"No," Zoe whispered.

"Father?" Anchurus said.

"Mind your own breakfast," Midas said. "I'll figure it out. Go on with the plan. How many horses do we need?"

Anchurus answered while Little Bird lifted a piece of pancake to Midas' lips. The king gestured to the water instead, and the boy obeyed. Midas took a small sip and swallowed quickly, trying the opposite tactic. He waited, hoping, but it hardened and stuck in his throat. He coughed, unsuccessfully. When he inhaled, it lodged itself more securely in his windpipe. He scooted back in his chair.

"Father!" Zoe jumped up and moved to his side. He backed away from her, waving her off as he tried to breathe. It wasn't working. He stumbled over the chair legs. Zoe came toward him again, but he glared at her, his skin turning hot.

"He's choking!" Zoe searched their faces. "Someone!"

Rastus ran to the king, but again Midas put out his hand, stopping his commander from getting too close. Anchurus took a few steps forward, but abruptly halted, as if unsure what to do. The advisors stared, perplexed.

"Do something!" Zoe shouted at them.

Midas' chest tightened, pressure pushing against his face.

"He's choking, Your Highness," Fotis said.

"He knows what to do," Aster said.

"We don't know!" Xander said.

Midas swayed, his knees buckling. Zoe called for help a third time and, when no one responded, screamed, "Help! The king!"

Timon appeared from the side door.

"The medicine woman!" Zoe said. "Now!"

Timon disappeared. Midas dropped to one knee. Zoe ran toward him. "Father!" She turned toward the double doors. "Someone, please help!"

Footsteps sounded at the entrance to the hall. Midas looked up to see the musician standing there. Emir surveyed the room and immediately ran toward the princess.

"The king!" she said, pointing.

Emir shifted his gaze to Midas.

"He's choking. Can you help?"

Midas wanted to protest, but he couldn't speak. Emir came up behind him. Midas felt a heavy blow to the middle of his back. He braced himself with one hand on the floor, the other clutching at his throat.

"Stop right there!" Rastus confronted the musician, his hand on his dagger. Anchurus joined him, both preparing to remove the intruder.

"Wait!" Zoe commanded.

Emir hit Midas again. The blow echoed through Midas' chest, but he hardly noticed it. His eyes were popping out of his skull, his vision blurring. Emir grabbed him under the arms and placed him back on his feet.

"I apologize, Your Majesty." Emir wrapped his arms around Midas' middle and thrust both his fists up under the king's breastbone.

"Your Highness?" Rastus asked the princess.

Emir thrust twice more. A hard nugget rose through Midas' esophagus and flew out of his mouth to land on the golden table. There, it clattered back and forth before coming to a stop.

Midas inhaled a long, raspy breath, coughed, and inhaled again. Relief flooded his body. He could breathe! Emir let him go, stepping back while Zoe rushed forward.

"Father?"

Midas swayed and, still gasping for air, reached out to steady himself. One hand found Zoe's shoulder. He snatched it back, regained his balance, and took in another breath. Gradually, his burning chest cooled, though his heartbeat still raced, his hair mussed with sweat. His breath dragged over the back of his throat with every inhale. "I'm all right." He acknowledged Emir. "Thank you."

Anchurus glared at the stranger. Rastus seemed ready to arrest him. At the tab∂le, Xander plopped down into his chair. Fotis and Aster remained standing. Everyone appeared relieved except Emir, who was staring at something in shock. Midas turned to see what it was. On his right stood a golden sculpture that hadn't been there before.

He blinked, his breath still ragged, and took a step back. The figure was motionless, the hands held out to him, the body stooped to assist. Long hair fell over the shoulders, but it was no longer hair, the mouth open but no longer a warm mouth. Midas checked behind him, certain his eyes were playing tricks on him. "Zoe?" he whispered. He glanced at her chair, but it was empty. "Zoe?"

"Oh," Xander said, his hand on his heart.

"Princess?" Aster asked.

Fotis stood speechless.

Midas looked at Anchurus. "Where did she go?"

His son stared at the statue. "She . . . she . . ." was all he managed to say.

"Your Majesty," Rastus whispered.

"She is not right there," Aster said, his face stricken.

"Where?" Midas asked.

Xander started crying. "The princess!"

Midas took hold of the back of his chair, his balance unsteady. He grasped the water pitcher, but it changed to gold before he could pour. Little Bird hovered nearby with a forlorn look on his face.

"Where is my daughter?" the king asked.

Anchurus pressed the heels of his hands into his eyes. Aster stared at the sculpture, murmuring *yes yes yes* under his breath while gripping the sides of his head. Rastus approached the golden figure, his hands alternately reaching out and then dropping in front of him. Emir looked from the princess to the king and back again.

"Zoe?" The king was more frantic now, his gaze darting about.

Anchurus, red-faced, glared at his father. "That's her," he said, pointing.

"No," Midas said. "No."

"Your Majesty." Fotis came forward. "It is the work of the goddess."

Midas looked at him, bewildered. Slowly, he turned once more to the golden figure. "Zoe? My Zoe?" He squinted in anguish, his hands open in front of him. "Can you get her back?" he asked Fotis.

"We must find the goddess."

Midas regarded the other two advisors in turn. "Where is she?"

They only stared in shock.

"Denisia!" Midas bellowed. "Denisia!"

Everyone gaped at the entrance. Within moments, footsteps answered the king's call. Timon entered the room and bowed, the medicine woman by his side.

"She's gone, Your Majesty," he said. "Denisia has left the castle."

Midas' face burned with fury. "Find her. Bring her back here. Now!"

CHAPTER THIRTEEN

Anchurus marched up the stairs to the second level and slipped into his room. He shoved the door closed. Fury heated his blood. He wiped sweat off his brow and tossed his royal cloak onto the bench. Quickly, he changed into his riding gear and was reaching for his armor when he stopped. This wasn't a battle. He was going to search for a goddess.

Against the far wall lay the bear's hide where he and Denisia had made love the night before. Anchurus drifted toward it. He couldn't reconcile the tender woman he'd held in his arms with the events that had occurred this morning. She'd done what he'd asked her to do. What his father had asked her to do. But Anchurus felt betrayed. Surely, she must have known what would happen.

A row of weapons hung on the south wall. He took a compact sword, tested its weight, and tried another. Eventually, he settled on the longer, thinner one, slashing it a few times through the air. He wished mightily for an enemy he could fight. But this was Denisia, the one who had protected him for years. He returned the sword, took a dagger instead, and then sat down on the bench underneath.

His thoughts went immediately to Zoe. His dear sister. Was she still in there somewhere? Denisia would know. She lived on the Isle of Mount Nysa, she had said, but had she gone back home or somewhere else? He mentally kicked himself. He knew nearly nothing about this goddess he had enlisted to help his father. This woman he had lain with. The one he had trusted.

He exited the room and flew down the stairs, wanting nothing more than to go straight out to the stables, saddle up Ambrose, and ride out on his mission. But it would be a fool's effort. He would only ride away time, and that was one thing his family didn't have.

When he reached the first level, he paused. His father, unable to eat. A swell of anger passed over him. How could she? She'd seemed genuinely grateful to Midas, and the way she had looked at Anchurus, the softness in her gaze. Had it all been a distraction?

Footsteps sounded from the lower stairway. Princess Zoe's little waif emerged, holding a cup of broth. Seeing the prince, he ducked his head and ran on, turning to enter the dining hall. Anchurus followed him.

He found the king still sitting at the table. The musician was gone, as were the advisors. Only the boy with the broth, the king, and that . . . *thing* behind him remained. Anchurus couldn't bear to look at it.

"Are you going?" Midas asked.

"I must speak with FAX."

"They've gone to their quarters. To concoct something, I imagine."

"Can they cure this?"

Midas shrugged a shoulder. "Perhaps? With enough time."

Anchurus glanced at the boy, whose gaze was fixed on the king's face. Where was Rastus? He checked around the room.

"I sent them away," Midas said. "They were all hovering like hens."

"You shouldn't be alone," the prince said.

"I'm fine as long as I don't eat." Midas cast a glance at the broth.

"It appears they have something else for you to try," Anchurus said.

The boy lifted a spoon to the king's lips. Midas took only the smallest sip, but had to spit it out. It clattered onto the table. "Away with it," he said, shooing the child out of the room.

Anchurus was at his side in a blink. "Don't worry, Father. I'll find out how to reverse this . . . this curse."

Midas sat back in his chair. "The goddess Denisia. What do you know of her?"

"Not as much as I should." Anchurus dropped his gaze. "This is my fault."

"I made the wish," Midas said.

"She fooled us all." Anchurus turned away. "I will find her, and I will get her to fix this."

"She's a goddess, Son. You can't go tearing after her like you do Sargon's armies."

"She must pay for what she has done!"

"You're going to have to be smarter than that," Midas said. "*We* are going to have to be smarter if we're going to save your sister's life." He paused, his gaze darting over the table. "And, Son?" He reached out, forgetting himself.

Anchurus stepped back. He immediately regretted the move, for Midas looked stricken.

"Timon," the king shouted. "Timon!"

The little minstrel came running. He looked even more haggard than he had the night before. "Your Majesty," he said, bowing low.

"Coverings, Timon." Midas held up his hands. "Get me something to cover these infernal things!"

Timon bowed twice more and ran out.

"I will consult with FAX," the prince said. "Find out where Denisia is hiding. Meanwhile, Father . . ." He waited until Midas looked at him. "You must continue with your plan. Like you said, we cannot lose this opportunity."

The lines softened around Midas' eyes. "You're going to be a good king, my son."

Anchurus blinked. “Not for many years, Father.” He bowed and walked away. He had almost reached the doors when FAX came in.

“Your Highness.” Fotis bent his knees in deference as he passed, both hands clinging to a golden candelabra. The other two followed, Aster with an armful of pouches and jars, and Xander with an elaborately painted Darbuka drum, which he hugged close like a beloved doll. They hurried to the table and began setting up their equipment. Anchurus glanced back at his father, who raised his eyebrows in a bemused expression.

“Denisia,” the prince said.

The three advisors turned their heads.

“Where is she?”

“The realm of the gods is ever changing,” Fotis said.

“It is clear where she is, Your Highness.” Aster measured herbs and other ingredients in a large bowl.

“She’s on the Isle of Mount Nysa,” Xander said. The other two looked at him. “Well, that’s where legend says she lives.”

“But where did she go this morning?” Anchurus asked.

Fotis set the candelabra down. “We don’t know, Your Highness.”

“You must find out,” the prince said.

“But the spell.” Fotis gestured toward the king.

“It may allow him to eat,” Xander explained.

“It’s an old water purifying spell.” Fotis adjusted the candelabra to a central position. “From the days when disease spread rampant over the lands. I thought perhaps more purified water would make it past the goddess Denisia’s—”

“How can I find her?” Anchurus interrupted.

“He does not need an answer,” Aster said.

Fotis looked pointedly at Xander.

“I thought you wanted me to play the drum,” the youngest advisor said.

“He’s very good on the drum,” Aster said.

“Answer the prince’s question!” Fotis said.

“The summoning spell just came to me,” Xander said. “It brought the pretty one. But I don't know how to call the wine goddess."

"Think about it," the prince said.

"But we're trying to help the king."

"You can't do more than one thing at a time?"

"He is a master multiple task-doer," Aster said.

"Our apologies, Your Highness," Fotis said.

Aster added something else to the bowl, causing it to emit a cloud of smoke. They all leaned back. When it dispersed, Aster started mixing again.

"Xander," Anchurus said, his voice louder now, "how do I find Denisia?"

Xander tapped his fingers on the drum, his gaze on Aster's mixing hand.

"Well?" Fotis said.

"He thinks quickly," Aster said.

"You're not going to like it." Xander glanced up at the prince.

"Like what?" Anchurus asked.

"She seemed to . . ." Xander began. "Well, I noticed that she . . ."

"Be certain you draw it out as long as possible," Aster said.

"She what?" Anchurus and Midas said at the same time.

Xander looked at them all, then focused on the prince. "Liked you."

"Yes?" the prince said.

"It may work to your advantage," Xander said. "Give you a more direct way to communicate with her, so to speak. Try going somewhere, alone. By the river, perhaps? Ask her to come."

"Ask her?" Anchurus said.

"Nicely," Xander said.

The prince glared at him.

"A goddess like her," Xander said. "She would sense it with . . . someone she likes."

Anchurus thought back to the moments of closeness with Denisia. When he looked up again, he found his father watching him.

"Go," Midas said quietly. "It's the best we've got."

Anchurus bowed and walked out of the hall.

Emir paced the undercroft, back and forth over the dirt floor, his boots leaving renewed prints each time. Step, step, step, turn, step, step, step, turn. One wall, another wall, past the barrels, past the shelves filled with clay storage pots, to the mattress, and back to the door. *Think!* But it was difficult, considering all he had witnessed. The king's new power, the princess' transformation, and now the very real possibility that the king was in danger of losing his life. How long could one survive without eating and drinking? Emir had gone over a week without food himself, but water . . . that was a different matter. There had to be a way to get the king some water. Otherwise, he'd be dead before Emir had a chance persuade him of his worth. Then all of Emir's hopes would vanish, his mother relegated to a lifetime of slavery.

He needed some air. He threw open the door and started out, nearly running over the boy.

"There you are!" He grabbed his arm and pulled him in, shutting the door behind him. "What have you found out?"

The boy's face was pale, his brown eyes dull. He looked as if he was about to cry. Emir wrapped his arm around his shoulders, pulling him close. "Don't worry; it will be all right." He felt the boy's small hands around his back, his cheek pressed near Emir's belt. "Are you all right?"

The boy wiped his nose on the back of his arm. *FAX's potion didn't work,* he signed. *King almost choked again.*

"They haven't figured it out yet?"

The boy shook his head.

Emir glanced around the room. Something needed to be done, and quickly. If he was the one to do it, the king would be grateful. Again.

The boy tapped his arm. *Prince went to find goddess.*

"Where?"

The boy shrugged. *King asked cover for his hands.*

"Good," Emir said. "They're dangerous."

Will king die?

Emir squeezed his shoulder. "Don't worry. Everyone is working to save the king. Meanwhile, keep your eyes sharp. Now that the princess is . . . gone, she can no longer protect you. The king is too distracted to worry about a little boy. You must stay charming and make that lady servant who's taking care of you like you."

The boy pointed to his outfit. He wore a smart pair of black breeches and a long cream-colored tunic. *Like a prince,* he signed.

"Don't get used to it," Emir said.

The boy puffed up his chest and strutted back and forth.

"Is that how a prince walks?" Emir asked.

The boy pointed his nose up and cast one arm out in a grand gesture.

"Your kingdom. Yes, I see."

The boy smiled.

"Very good. Remember, this servant lady will probably keep you around if that was the princess' wish. Be extra nice to her."

The boy nodded again and waited, looking at Emir expectantly.

"Was there anything else?" Emir asked.

The boy shook his head.

Footsteps sounded outside of the door as the servants ran up and down the stairs. Pots and pans clattered in the kitchen on the other side of the wall. The head cook shouted orders. It was all muffled inside the undercroft. "We have a plan, right?" Emir said.

Make Elif like me, the boy signed. *Listen.*

"You've got it," Emir said. "I'm not sure where I'll be. I'm supposed to report to the barracks, but I'm going to help the king first. I may not be here if you need me, so watch out for yourself." He moved to the door, the boy at his heels. "We'll see each other around. But be careful. Do as you're told." He lifted the latch.

The boy grabbed Emir's hand, pressed it against his cheek, and darted out.

Emir watched after him, resisting the tug at his heart. He was just a mongrel. Emir remembered trying to shoo him off when he'd first come around, but the boy had been persistent, urging him to follow. Emir had finally relented, and the boy had led him across the city and into a goat pen. It had been inside the animal shelter that they'd found the opening to the tunnel. By sunset, they were out of Durukin and away from King Sargon, free. Emir owed the boy now. He owed him everything.

MIDAS LONGED FOR WATER. Something to get this infernal metal taste out of his mouth. He walked down the hall and slipped into the stairwell. There, he paused to catch his breath. The stone walls were comforting in their rigid closeness. He waited until he heard footsteps, then hurried up two flights to the third level. He pushed on until he reached the last room on the right. At the door, he rested his hand on the handle and watched it change. He'd planned to barge in, but the door was a reminder.

It wouldn't be the same.

It had been over two years since he'd visited the room he'd shared with his wife. After her death, he'd moved to a smaller room adjacent to his strategy room. Now he ached for her presence. He turned the golden handle and pushed. It took him another moment to walk inside.

The scent of her perfume flooded his sinuses, transporting him to the rose garden when it was in full bloom. He felt the urge to retreat. But it was too late now. He pushed the door shut. Alone, he dropped to his knees. Covering his face, he wept, his tears wetting his palms and then turning into little gold flecks that dusted the air.

"Demodica, what have I done?"

It made him angry, the crying. When the first flush of it had passed, he slapped his cheeks hard until they stung. One of her dresses hung off the corner of their bed, the pastel blue one she'd worn so often. Half-burned candles sat on the nightstands. Her hairbrush rested on top of the storage chest along with the green beaded necklace she'd often worn. The window against the far wall illuminated it all, the rectangular hole covered in the thinnest of animal hides. Underneath rested their sofa, the blanket she'd so often wrapped herself up in crumpled in the corner. He crawled over to it and almost pulled the blanket toward him when he remembered. He didn't want to alter it. His wife had always sat there, across from him, her hands clasped together. He reached out, almost certain he could touch her, but then withdrew as if bitten.

If she'd been there, she'd have been turned into a sculpture too.

His hands. His infernal hands! They didn't appear any different from the day before. But they'd taken his daughter away from him. He folded in half, resting his head on the cushion. "I'm sorry," he said. "I'm so sorry." He longed for his wife's voice. Longed for her to yell at him, to tell him she'd warned him and he hadn't listened. But the room was deathly quiet.

"Katiah!" he called, pushing himself to his feet. "Katiaaah! I demand you come. Face me now!" It was wrong, calling her from this room. But he couldn't care about that now. He called and called again, pointing his voice first at the ceiling and then at the window. He was almost hoarse when a sudden chill gripped his body. Slowly, he turned around.

There she was, just inside the door. Her beauty struck him as it always did, her skin fair and flawless in a white gown that left her shoulders bare. The gown itself glowed like moonlight, her black hair hanging in lustrous waves around her face.

"Such noise from the king's bedroom," she said. "The guards are sure to be whispering."

Her words broke the spell. Midas stormed toward her with such fury that she took a step back. When he didn't stop, she held up her hand. An invisible wall arrested his progress. He slammed into it and stumbled back. "What have you done?" he said, regaining his balance. "How could you?"

"Whatever are you talking about?" Katiah said. "I've done nothing."

"My daughter! I thought that even you . . ."

"What about your daughter?" Katiah looked genuinely curious. "What has happened to Zoe?"

"You cursed me knowing this would happen," Midas said. "Why can't you just leave me alone?"

"As you wish." Katiah began to shimmer away.

"No!" Midas shouted, his hand out. "Wait." He paused. "Please." His voice broke over the word.

She solidified again, her features softened.

"What do you want from me?" Midas said. "I'll do it. Please. Bring her back."

With a flick of her hand, Katiah dropped the wall between them. She walked past him toward the window. "You know what I want. You chose to ignore my bidding."

"I did as you asked for years," Midas said, weariness in his voice. "Statues, idols, paintings, all of the great Katiah. I even built a stone monument at the edge of the city."

"Which is now covered in weeds and mud," Katiah said. "And all your statues and idols and paintings are buried in some storage room."

"The queen didn't approve," Midas said.

"What do I care what your wife thought? I didn't want you to marry her in the first place."

"I needed a queen."

"I was your queen!" Katiah pointed to her chest. "I put you on that throne. Did you so easily forget?"

"You were supposed to help me rescue my sister!" Midas walked back to the center of the room. "Revenge against Sargon, remember? You said nothing about a throne. I didn't care about a throne." He threw his hands in the air. "We made a deal. I held up my end of the bargain. You did nothing. Sargon has remained out of my reach all this time. You lied to me!"

They glared at one another. Katiah lingered near the sofa, the sun beaming in behind her. Midas stood opposite her, the bed in between them. She glanced at it, then at him, and her anger dissipated.

"He's been . . . very possessive of her," she said.

"She's still alive?" Midas searched Katiah's face. "You've seen her?"

Katiah turned her back to him, her gaze out the window.

"Answer me!" Midas said.

"I saved you. I gave you a better life. That should be enough."

"Enough?" Midas huffed. "Enough? You promised a chance to save *her*. I gave you everything in return for that promise."

"And look what you've gotten!" Katiah opened her arms. "You were nothing. A wandering, wild thing. Without me, you would have been dead by now."

"I would have preferred it," Midas said. "Much preferred it to this daily curse of knowing I've failed."

"Failed?" She seemed surprised. "You are the most loved king in all the lands. Your territories have doubled since you came into power. You have wealth. Children."

"All of which I've poisoned because of this hole in my chest," Midas said.

Katiah blinked, appearing confused.

"And now you add this curse to it."

"What curse?"

He opened his mouth as if to explain. Then he walked over and touched the candle resting on the nightstand by the bed. It turned to gold.

"Impressive," Katiah said. "But I had nothing to do with that."

Midas narrowed his eyes. "I know you were here last night."

She gazed at him innocently.

"My advisors. They saw you with the goddess Denisia."

"They are an amusing group," Katiah said.

"I understand you have taken possession of Xander's soul," the king said.

"He offered it!"

"But that wasn't enough for you. You had to have my—" He choked. "My daughter too?"

"I don't know what you're talking about. I am helping Sargon, as your advisors surely told you. You can't expect any less, considering how disloyal you have been. But this . . ." She gestured toward the candle. "This is not my doing."

He waited, a large blue vein pulsing in his neck.

"Come." She walked over to the bed. "All this bickering. It's exhausting." She stretched out on the mattress and patted the covering beside her. "Let us be friends again, hm? I so enjoyed it when we were more friendly." She gave him a seductive smile.

He glowered at her. "And you *enjoyed* sowing distrust with my wife, too."

She shrugged and lay on her side. "It wasn't worth a little distrust?" She swirled one finger on the blanket. When he didn't answer, she pouted. "Besides, there would have been no need for distrust if you hadn't taken on the burden of a wife."

Midas turned a cold shoulder and walked to the end of the bed. "Reverse it," he said. "Bring my daughter back. I'll restore all the statues and paintings. I'll assign men to clean up the monument. I'll build you another one. Name it." His gaze dropped. "Please, Katiah. I'm begging you."

She smiled, tucking her chin. "Remember when you found me beautiful?" On her knees, she crawled to the edge where she could reach him, her fingertips finding his shoulder. He flinched under her touch. "I knew you could be a good king, a powerful king." Her hand drifted down his back, her breath on his neck. "Don't you remember how it was?" She pressed her lips against his skin.

In a blink, he whirled, grabbed her throat, and squeezed with all his might. She placed both hands on his wrists, but the magic was already taking hold, the gold flowing over her neck and onto her shoulders, threatening to move up into her jaw. With a mighty twist, she broke his grip, then hit him square in the chest. He flew back and slammed into the opposite wall. Katiah rubbed her throat, then got off the bed and straightened her gown. The gold drained off her like slick mud and disappeared at her feet.

"You dare treat me this way?" Her breath came quickly. "You shall pay for it, Karem, and pay many times over." She turned an angry gaze on him. "You think losing your sister, your wife, and your daughter gives you pain? You wait. You'll come to regret what you have done!"

Midas groaned and rolled onto his side. By the time he regained his footing, the goddess had vanished.

EMIR HAD HOPED for a bit of fresh air and some time to think. He was pushing it as far as his deadline to report to the barracks was concerned, but this opportunity would come only once. He'd saved the king's life. Surely that gave him a little leeway. Now he had an opportunity to elevate his position *if* he could figure out how to find water the king could drink. A witch's potion, perhaps? Gordium had to have a witch. If he saved Midas once more, he might escape the trap of being sucked into another king's army, where he'd be nothing more than another body with a sword.

It was near midday when he left the castle and took the main road into the city. He planned to hit the marketplace, thinking one of the traders would know if there was a witch nearby. If so, he would find her and ask about a spell, one that might at least diminish the power of Denisia's magic. The sun blazed high in the sky, casting everything in a brilliant yellow hue. Citizens busied themselves with the activities of living, some plucking bird feathers and skinning rabbits while others cooked meals, women sitting outside repairing clothing or watching young children. For a time, he was lost in his thoughts, his head down as his boots moved over the dry dirt. But then something compelled him to look up.

He started when he saw the two men. *No, no, no.* Not already. But they had spotted him. The Olgun brothers. How had they found him so quickly? He checked around for an escape route, but he hadn't reached the marketplace yet. Here there were only dwellings and narrow alleyways to duck into. *The boy,* he thought. *What will happen to the boy?*

The two men approached leisurely as if they had all the time in the world. The big one, Bain, was even more intimidating in person. Emir had heard stories, but the reality was more impressive. It was said Bain, a couple of heads taller than most men and thick with muscle, could squeeze the life out of a man with one hand. His brother, Baris, was the smart one, his leaner body calm as he observed his opponent.

"So it is the deserter," Baris said, slowing as they met in the middle of the road. His clothes were covered in dust, evidence of their long journey.

"One might say I was lucky to escape," Emir said.

"Not so lucky." Baris glared at him through small eyes, his tongue resting between parted lips. "Come with us peacefully, or I let my brother render you incapacitated."

Emir eyed Bain. The man's torso was thick with muscle, arms and legs like tree trunks. His head was square-shaped with a little hair at the top, his eyes large and set atop powerful cheekbones. Emir would never escape them both. Not without a distraction. "There are many opportunities in this city," he said. "Two skilled men such as yourselves could make your fortune here."

Baris cocked his head toward his brother. "He's stalling."

Bain chuckled in response, a deep-throated sound that resembled that of a large boar grunting.

"It would be wise to explore before you go running back to your king," Emir tried again. "Not every kingdom is the same."

Baris smiled, revealing a missing eyetooth. An athletic-looking man with a pinched nose, he was older than Bain and had little hair left. "You're a deserter," he said. "We don't intend to be like you. Now decide. Will you come willingly, or must we take you by force?"

Emir rested his hands on his hips. He struck the toe of his boot in the dirt, then launched himself left and ran down the alleyway between two rows of modest dwellings.

Baris flew after him. Emir had a head start, but it didn't last long. Baris pushed him from behind, knocking him down. Emir bounced back up on his feet and ran again, but he'd taken only a few steps when he felt a meaty hand on the back of his jacket. Helpless in the big man's hold, he was dragged back up the small alleyway. He lifted his arms and shed the jacket. Free again, he ran toward the road. Baris came at him from the right, pummeled his gut, and then smashed his cheek. Emir reeled, stumbled left, and tried to run again, but Baris was there with another blow to his other cheek and then across his back. Emir fell forward. Young children shouted behind him. As he scrambled to get up, two monster hands got hold of him and launched him through the air. He landed with a hard thud in the dirt. His head spinning, he forced himself to his feet. Baris hit him again in the gut, face, ribs, face. Emir grabbed his dagger, but Baris knocked it out of his hand. Emir darted to the left and ran straight into Bain. The giant drew back a long, straight arm. Emir felt the blow square in the throat. He fell flat, his breath knocked out of him.

"Think that did it?" Bain said.

"Let's get out of here," Baris said.

Bain grabbed Emir's wrist and dragged him across the dirt. Emir's boot heels sent up a cloud of dust. *No,* he thought. He wouldn't allow these thugs to ruin everything. His head swirled, his vision a gray blur. With a mighty effort, he managed a twist to the left, after which he fell still again. His body was leaving him, the day growing dark when he noticed a flash of light.

"My good sirs," a sweet voice said, "let's not be rude. Why don't you stay a while?"

Emir heard a groan and a thud, then he was released, his shoulders and head falling flat on the road.

"Hey." Bain's voice and nothing more.

CHAPTER
FOURTEEN

Anchurus entered the castle, intent on finding the king. He wanted to get to him as quickly as possible, but couldn't help noticing the changes that had occurred since he'd left only the day before. The stone floor gleamed. The entrance doors, some of the vases and flowers, all the sculptures, and much of the furniture had changed, too, all now emitting a golden sheen. At first, he took this to mean that his father was still well.

But then he walked into the strategy room.

King Midas sat slumped in his chair at the conference table. His skin had paled, his eyes sunk into his head, and his lips were chapped and dry. He held his mouth open as if he were having trouble breathing. His hands were covered in what appeared to be gold mitts, bulky and stiff, his royal robe rumpled over his shoulders. He brightened at the prince's entrance, his advisors glancing up from their position behind and to his left.

"Did you find her?" the king asked.

Anchurus shook his head. He'd been out all night, riding and praying, calling to the goddess as Xander had suggested. Denisia had not answered. A small cohort of men had been sent to the Isle of

Mount Nysa, but it would take them at least eight days to make the journey there and back. By then, it would be too late.

"Are you able to drink?" he asked.

"I'm learning the value of abstaining." With effort, King Midas sat up a little straighter and placed his hands on the table, the left over right. The mitts clanged together, so he separated them, but this proved too uncomfortable, so he let them fall back into his lap.

"You've had nothing since yesterday morning?" Anchurus looked frantically at the three advisors. Each wore a wool cap and held bowls of smoking liquid. The air was filling with a putrid scent, a mix of mildew and cooked mushroom.

"We are trying a new treatment, Your Highness," Fotis said.

"Will this one work?" the prince asked.

"We haven't tried it yet," Xander said.

"It's certain to work," Aster said.

Anchurus sat down opposite his father and gestured to them with an open hand. "By all means," he said.

"Must we?" King Midas asked.

"It will take only a few moments, Your Majesty," Fotis said.

"Time is not of the essence," Aster said.

Anchurus watched as the advisors stirred the liquids in their bowls. The smoking began anew. Someone started chanting in a low, nearly inaudible voice. He didn't know who it was at first, but then noticed Fotis' mouth moving. The old man uttered a rhythmic phrase in his pinched tone, the words spoken in a language Anchurus didn't understand. Aster added his voice next, a third lower, but chanting the same words, his tone rich and sonorous. They continued this way for a time.

Suddenly a high-pitched wail cut through, the kind a person might make if badly injured. Midas jerked his head to his left, where Xander stood. The young advisor was carrying on like a wounded animal. The other two accelerated their accompaniment, the drumbeat of their chant gaining momentum. King Midas stared, his eyebrows furrowed as Xander explored the full range of his vocal abilities, going up and down the scale in a slurring style and then back and forth over thirds and seconds, the nonsense words enough to make Anchurus laugh. But then it wasn't a laughing matter. The smoke thickened. King Midas coughed a couple of times. Xander renewed his wailing, gesturing to the others to keep stirring. Soon the king went into a full-blown coughing fit, at which point all the chanting and stirring stopped. The three men leaned forward expectantly. King Midas coughed and coughed. It seemed he might cough his innards out.

"Father?" Anchurus asked.

Gradually, the coughing eased. Xander offered the king a cup of water. Midas gazed at it warily, then sipped the smallest amount. Everyone waited, four faces surrounding the king in expectation. Anchurus imagined the relief that would release them from this horror, the celebration they might have. Then the king squinted, shook his head, and spat out a nugget of gold.

The advisors drooped in disappointment. Fotis produced a liquid vial from his pocket, and one by one, the advisors added a few drops to their bowls to extinguish the smoke.

"Open the door," Midas said. "Clear out the air."

Anchurus obeyed, then turned to the three advisors. "Do you have something else to try?"

"We'll keep looking," Fotis said.

"There are many options," Aster said.

"There are spells we haven't reviewed yet," Fotis said.

"Ingredients we haven't mixed." Xander said.

"I've sent messengers to Ancyra and Lydia," Fotis said, "to seek advice from the wise men there."

"I don't know if they'll know any more than we know," Xander said, only to receive a warning glare from Fotis.

"Wise men will have the solution," Aster said. "Wise men understand the world of the gods."

They all stared at him, knowing full well what he was really saying. At that moment, everything seemed hopeless. Anchurus glanced at his father. His eyes were heavy, his head drooping.

"Timon!" the prince bellowed. They all jumped. "Timon!" When the little man didn't come straight away, Anchurus moved out into the hallway. "Timooooon!"

They soon heard the steward's rushing steps. Timon appeared in the doorway. "Yes, my prince?"

"Get the king to his quarters immediately. Assign someone to be with him at all times. All times!"

"Yes, my prince." Timon bowed, then looked around the room. He was greeted with a strange spectacle of advisors in woolen caps holding smoldering bowls, the air thick with smoke, and King Midas slumped in his chair like he was already half asleep. "Your Majesty." Timon flew to the king's side.

Midas pushed himself to his feet. "Don't let me sleep long."

"Of course, Father," Anchurus said.

"It will be all right." Midas reached out to touch his son's shoulder and then stopped. He swayed in place, his gaze unfocused on the space in front of him. "It will be all right," he said again and followed Timon across the room.

When they'd disappeared through the door, the prince turned his attention to the advisors. They had removed their caps and stood looking down at the floor.

"He's not dead yet," Anchurus said.

Their eyes shifted, shame shading their faces.

"Aster's right," he continued. "We need the goddess' help. No more spells, potions, or chanting." He eyed Xander. "We must find Denisia."

"Locate the goddess?" Xander asked.

"Not locate her. Bring her here. Summon her. She needs to be here." Anchurus pointed to the floor beneath them. "*Now*. Tell me you can make that happen." He searched each of their faces in turn.

"Of course, Your Highness," Fotis said. "We'll put our minds to it."

"No nonsense," Anchurus said. "I want a solution."

Fotis rubbed his long beard. "I will consult our library. There are parchments on calling the gods, and there may be something in there about Denisia. We can try the standard summoning spells. We will need to gather the materials, but most of those we have. If we have to send out for something, that may take some time—"

"We don't *have* time!" Anchurus bellowed.

Fotis jumped, his one eye wide under a bushy eyebrow.

"There is no more time."

Xander watched the prince, his brown eyes full of pity. "She's not like the pretty one. She doesn't heed the calls of desperate men or desire to pad her home with human souls." He rubbed his upper arms. "She is of the Earth, tied to the green things."

"You think this helps," Anchurus said, "telling me what she *doesn't* respond to?"

The air was still smoky, the scent of mushrooms lingering. Xander shrugged, as if to say *I don't have any other ideas*, and looked to Fotis. Finally, it was Aster who spoke.

"There is no way," he said in his calm voice.

Anchurus faced him. "Tell me."

"Xander is incorrect. She does not love the green things. The trees. The plants. The crops. The flowers. She would not pine if these things were damaged." He paused. "Destroyed, perhaps."

"Destroyed?" Anchurus asked.

Xander's eyes widened. "The garden!" He turned to Aster. "The king's garden. That could do it. If we destroyed it."

"Destroy the gardens?" Fotis asked incredulously. "The king would have our heads!"

"The king can take heads from the grave," Aster said.

The truth fell upon them with new gravity. The king was going to die. Unimaginable, that someone so vibrant and strong the day before was now fading in front of their eyes. But it was a reality they could no longer deny. He would die if they didn't do something—and do it quickly.

Anchurus backed away from them. This couldn't be what he must do. But the more he thought about it, the more he knew this was exactly what he must do. He recalled how Denisia had made the flowers bloom in the guest room. The vines in her hair. The way she'd gripped the bush near the swing. She loved them all. Surely such a destruction as they were contemplating would get her attention.

He stared at the golden floor, his hands on his hips. The garden had always been there, since before he was born. When he was a boy, he remembered finding Midas walking the stone paths or sitting alone by the man-made creek. The year their mother had died, his father had spent more time in the garden than anywhere else. To desecrate it now . . . . It was unthinkable. He glanced at his father's chair. He could still see the king sitting there half asleep, his lips flaky and dry, his eyes sunken in. A nauseated feeling of guilt poured through him. He'd brought the goddess. He'd started all of this.

He tapped a finger on his belt and addressed the advisors. "How?"

Aster looked uncomfortable. "We wouldn't need the best way to send a message a goddess like Denisia wouldn't hear."

The others stared at him, confused. Finally, Xander covered his mouth. "Oh, no."

Anchurus turned to him.

Under the prince's stern gaze, Xander cleared his throat. "I'm afraid, Your Highness, that it must be . . . fire." He glanced at Aster, who shook his head in agreement. "Nature's greatest enemy," Xander went on. "The very thing the goddess of the earth would despise the most."

Anchurus looked as if he'd swallowed poison. "It will take time to prepare." After another moment, he turned and left the room. "Tonight," he said over his shoulder, and closed the door.

The room fell silent. Gradually the three advisors roused themselves. Fotis was first. Taking his bowl and cap in his hands, he walked toward the door. Aster followed, and finally Xander. They were silent all the way up the stairs and were nearing their room when suddenly Xander let out an "Oh!"

The other two stopped to look back.

"The figs," Xander said. "I shall so miss the figs."

King Sargon rode behind Elanur, his piebald unhappy at following her smaller, slower mount. The animal kept tossing his head and blowing snorts. Sargon couldn't blame him. He was impatient too, but he wasn't about to ruin his chance to get some answers.

They followed a narrow road that took them beyond the city's edge toward the northern hills. Two guards rode with them, one on either side of Elanur just in case she tried to flee, but so far, she'd made no effort to do so. She'd been leading them steadily on, the afternoon sun warm overhead, the horses' hooves kicking up clouds of dust. Sargon thought to call a halt to it, convinced she was playing with him. He'd kept her under watch her whole life. If she'd been going out to the hills to pray to a dark goddess, he would have known about it. But then he cast a sideways glance at one of the guards and wondered if his servants weren't as loyal as he believed. Katiah had suggested as much.

Which made him think of Emir, the deserter, Elanur's rebellious boy. He'd overhead people saying the child looked much like the king. He'd been able to see it himself in Emir's dark eyes, bold nose, and thick brow. And Emir was brave. Tales of his kills in battle were many. Sargon had heard them told among the men when they didn't know he was listening. He'd felt proud hearing them. Pride he'd quickly squelched. Elanur was a slave girl. She had not the standing to be anything more, and that meant her son could not be more, either.

Unless Emir had the help of a goddess.

The thought of Katiah assisting Emir, right under his nose, infuriated Sargon. He seethed in the saddle, his grip tightening on the reins to the point that the piebald nearly reared. Sargon exhaled and tried to relax, letting his gaze roam over Elanur's body. She sat light as a feather on her horse's back, her spine straight. He studied the nape of her neck, left bare under her hair, which she had wrapped into a messy knot.

They were climbing now. It had been some time since he'd ascended to a high enough elevation to look down on the city. Durukin appeared imposing in the afternoon sun. The dark castle stood elevated on the northern side, the winged bulls with his likeness on their heads guarding the gates. Seeing them from here, he wished he'd made them lions instead.

"Sire?" one of the guards said.

Sargon looked back to see Elanur had gained ground, turning a corner into the trees. One guard had stayed with her, the other waiting for the king. Sargon let the reins out, and his horse jumped forward, grateful for the chance to move a little faster, if only for a short distance.

Black pines became plentiful the higher they went, their branches packed densely enough to obscure the view. They blocked the sun, cooling the ground. Sargon narrowed his eyes, watching Elanur ride confidently on. She had led them onto what looked like a wildlife path worn soft over the years by ibex or chamois. It weaved between the trees, steadily climbing. The horses were growing winded. Sargon took a drink from his waterskin and had a flash of a memory. It was during the ride back from Elanur's village. She'd grown quiet, her little body slumped in the saddle, her dark hair matted and sweaty. So still had she become that he'd worried something had happened to her. He'd stopped his horse and leaned around to look into her face.

"Hey," he'd said to her. "You all right?"

She'd glared at him with those dark brown eyes, then hauled off with her little toddler hand and slapped his face. Normally such behavior would have earned her a sharp return slap from him, but the move had startled him so completely that he'd only stared at her. Then she'd pouted and started to cry again, so he'd opened his waterskin and placed it against her lips. She'd scowled before finally drinking great gulps that bulged down her small throat. Watching her, pity had gripped his heart, and he'd tucked a strand of her hair behind her ear. "It's all right," he'd told her. "It will be all right."

His horse shifted, shoulders pitched down. They were descending at a slight angle. Sargon sat up in his saddle, scanning. Elanur followed the path to the right, around a large boulder, then angled back left, pines and junipers bending toward her like protective spirits. Ahead lay the dark opening of a cave, the sun's light glaring from behind the rock, so there was no way to see inside. Elanur rode right up to it, halted her horse, and slid off. She had started to walk inside when the guard told her to stop.

"This is it?" Sargon asked as he dismounted.

She nodded, glanced at the guard, and walked on. Sargon motioned the guards to fall in line. In the darkness, he paused while his eyes adjusted. Elanur's face appeared in the glow of a torch. Holding it aloft, she led him through the tunnel.

It wasn't long before they entered a larger space. The air was a little warmer and smelled fresher, as if there were an opening somewhere. Elanur used her torch to light another on the wall, then proceeded to light several cressets positioned around the perimeter before coming back toward him. As the area glowed anew with yellow flame, Sargon realized he was in a very old cave. He wondered how he had not known of it before. In the center lay a cold fire pit, the ashes surrounded by black stones. The rest of the space was bare dirt and rock, though the ceiling was higher here than in the tunnel and covered with stalactites. Beyond, he thought he smelled water, but the light didn't extend far enough to see.

"You came here to pray to her," he said.

She nodded. "One night, she answered."

"When was that?"

"Over a full cycle of the moon ago."

About when Emir had disappeared. "How did it happen?"

"I was kneeling by the fire." She demonstrated. "My eyes were closed. When I opened them, she was there. Just there, where you're standing."

Katiah, here. Talking to Elanur! "And then?"

"She expressed sympathy for my suffering."

Her suffering! Sargon bit his tongue. She had no idea how much suffering she would have endured years ago had he not intervened.

"She told me she couldn't save me," Elanur continued, "but that she could save my son."

"In return for what?"

Elanur blinked. "She asked for nothing."

"Impossible. The gods always want something."

"What does she want from you?" Elanur asked.

Heat rushed to Sargon's cheeks. Indeed, the goddess had asked nothing of him. She had said only that she was there to make his dreams of defeating Midas come true. When she had seduced him, he'd assumed she'd come for his manliness. Now it appeared she might have desired Emir too?

"She set *our* son free," he said to Elanur, "and you didn't even think to ask her why?"

"I prayed to her for years," Elanur said. "On the day she answered, I was grateful. I had no reason to question her."

As he came upon her, she raised her chin. Looking into her defiant eyes, Sargon felt a familiar desire rush through his body. Yet, he made no aggressive moves. Instead, he studied her carefully, searching her expression. Despite his certainty that she was lying—why would the goddess talk to one such as her?—he could not find falsehood there.

With a deep inhale, he collected himself and walked back across the cave toward the tunnel. "Bring her," he barked to the guards.

THE FIRST SOUND Emir heard upon regaining consciousness was not a pleasant one—a beast, chewing and swallowing, inhaling air past bits of food between teeth, exhaling in low growls. More than one.

Perhaps three, considering the rise and fall of the rumbled warnings. He blinked open his eyes, careful not to move anything else. As his vision cleared, he found himself inside a modest dwelling. His back had been propped up against a wooden wall, a stout dining table in front of him. On its surface rested three candles, their yellow light providing some illumination in the dark room.

He thought back. How had he gotten here? The Olgun brothers had attacked him at midday. He checked the window against the far wall on his right. The shutters were closed, no light shining through them. The front door came next. Directly across from him, a low fire burned in the fireplace, the beasts between him and the flames. Hairy hips and angled hocks filled the space between the table legs, flag-like tails hanging low. His heart quickened. Wolves. But larger. He felt for his blade. His belt was empty. One of them, a jet-black beast, lifted its lip, showing sharp teeth as it bit into a thick piece of red meat. The other, a dark gray, held on fast, the two snarling until the meat split in two, allowing each to chew and swallow while the third, a cloud-like gray with white around its eyes, looked on.

"It's about time."

A woman appeared in another doorway beside him, so near the fabric of her gown brushed his upper arm. A blood-red crimson in a thin, almost transparent material, it gathered just under her breasts and flowed around her like storm clouds at sunset. She crossed the dining room to the wolves, clucking and cooing.

"Oh, my babies, look how hungry you were!" Emir saw one and then two tails wag as the thick paws surrounded her. She petted the upturned heads. "That's enough for now. We can't have you turning into gluttons. Go lie down."

The beasts searched for any remaining crumbs as they ambled over to the fireplace. The heavy *thunk* of their bones rumbled the floor under Emir's haunches. He kept a wary eye on them as he slowly got to his feet.

"You don't need to worry," the woman said. "I'm here to help you."

Emir stared at her, transfixed. She was a beautiful, pale-skinned woman with luscious dark hair and skin that emitted light like the moon. He'd heard stories of such a woman, one who traveled with three wolves. His mother had spoken of her often, told him tales of her powers. Katiah, the goddess of the underworld. Emir had thought it all made up, stories told to fascinate his imagination. But with the wolves and the dress and the way the hairs were standing up on his arms . . . "Katiah?"

"How delightful," she said. "You've heard of me."

Emir swallowed. A goddess! "Rumor is you are helping King Sargon."

She fixed him with her dark gaze. "I have a way you can help the king *you've* chosen to serve. Or, perhaps, replace?" She cocked an eyebrow at him.

"King Midas?"

"Sit down. Please."

He surrendered easily, walking toward the table. The wolves leapt to their feet.

"Leave him alone, darlings."

The beasts didn't attack, nor did they lie back down. Emir cautiously pulled the chair out and sat, keenly aware that his legs were now closer to the beasts' sharp fangs. "Why did you bring me here?"

"I saved you from them, didn't I?"

The Olgun brothers. "For all I know, you sent them after me."

"*He* sent them. You know how he is about deserters."

King Sargon. "How did you know about them?"

"Have you never heard stories of Katiah's powers?"

He paused. "You *are* the goddess Katiah, then?"

"Your mother sends her best wishes."

The room seemed to shrink, the air stale to breathe. "My mother wished for you to help me?"

Her features softened. "She is very loyal, your mother. I don't know as you deserve her. But her every thought is bent toward your safety."

Emir remembered how Sargon's guards had turned away just at the right moment, allowing him to slip out of the line unnoticed. How soon after, the boy had appeared out of nowhere to lead him out of the city. He'd thought it luck.

"How is the boy?" she asked, as if reading his mind. "Quite attached to you, it seems." When Emir said nothing, she went on. "Do as I say, and I can help your precious king to live a few more days."

"Only a few?" he managed to say.

"I'm a goddess, but I can't reverse the spell. That can only be done by the one who cast it."

Denisia. King Midas had called on her when the princess had turned to gold. "But it was cast under your influence."

"You *do* have your ear to the wall." She gave him a playful smile. "Each goddess has her gifts. In this case, Denisia proved useful."

"I thought you were the all-powerful one."

Her expression changed. She threw her arm in the air, and suddenly Emir was on the floor, unable to breathe. He tried to push himself back up, but an invisible force held him down, his face pressed against the wood, his throat closed. Blood rushed to his cheeks as he clawed at his neck. When his lungs burned, he raised his hand to her, begging for mercy. She released him. He sucked in air, inhaling great gasps until he could get up on all fours. It was many moments before he was able to return to his chair, the wolves watching every move.

"You say you have a way to help the king," he said in a raspy voice. "Why tell me?"

"You wish to help him."

"Many wish to help him."

She took a sip from a cup of tea that had appeared in front of her. "Do you know what this place is?"

Emir looked around. "A cabin."

"The cabin where your new king spent a good portion of his childhood."

Emir tried to imagine a young king Midas sitting here at this table or perhaps playing with a puzzle by the fire.

"He was one of the tribal people. One day, out of the blue, his village was decimated."

"I thought he was the son of King Gordius."

"That is the story he likes to tell, the one that makes it sound like he is the rightful heir. But that is not how it happened."

"How did it happen?"

She sat back in her chair and toyed with her cup. "After his village was destroyed, his people murdered, and his mother lying in a heap in the dirt, I saved him. I brought him here. The old couple who lived here was childless, but they'd always wished for children. They raised him until he was a young man."

"Where are they now?"

"Dead."

Emir wondered if she'd had anything to do with that.

"Oh, stop it!" she said. "They were sweet old people. I had no quarrel with them."

"But you do with Midas," he said.

"That's none of your business."

Emir glanced at the door, but the wolves were much too attentive for him to attempt any sort of escape. "How did he become king?"

"King Gordius had a very unhappy childless wife. So, when Midas started to mature, I introduced him. He was just what they'd prayed for. They took him in and raised him as the heir." She fingered a fold in her dress. "He was grateful for a time. But after he married *her*, everything changed." She stood up and turned toward the fireplace. "I have offered you something you want. You must give me your answer."

"Is this why you support King Sargon II?" he asked. "You wish him to defeat King Midas?"

"My plans are none of your concern."

"You have weakened him. It's the perfect time to strike. Why extend his life now?"

The black wolf nuzzled her hand. "You have a choice, Emir Alkan. Take what I have to offer. Or let him die."

"You care not which choice I make?"

"It's up to you. How much do you want your king to live?"

He didn't answer.

She turned toward the door. "About an hour north of here, there is a fresh spring that emerges from the rock above the creek that empties into the lake. The water is warm. Fill your waterskin with it and take it to the king. He will be able to drink." She waved her hand, and the teacup disappeared. "I will give you a head start, but you must leave now." She dropped her gaze to the wolves. "My darlings are aching for a hunt." The black one thumped his tail in response.

Emir's nerves pricked along the back of his neck. "If I don't wish to save the king?"

"There is a horse in the barn. Take it and return to the castle. Head southwest."

"King Midas' condition is dire. Might I take the horse to get the water?"

"Do that, and you will not find it." She looked at him pointedly. "You must earn your way, Emir Alkan. I know your ambition. Your desire to see Sargon pay."

Emir flinched.

She smiled at his reaction. "It's not so unusual. Sons often quarrel with their fathers."

"It is not a simple quarrel—"

She held up her hand, stopping him. "I have given you an opportunity. I wish to see what you will do with it."

"So this is a test?"

"Think of it as you like. Either way, my hospitality has come to an end." She twisted her finger, and the front door opened. The cool evening air flowed in, the darkness encroaching upon the cozy cabin interior. The wolves watched him, their gazes alert. He stood up and walked across the room, their attentiveness like tiny arrows all over his back. He cast a last look back at the goddess and then stepped outside, closing the door behind him.

Off to the left, the shadow of a barn rested in a clump of trees. The horse would be there. To the north, the dark outline of the hill rose into the sky. It would be a climb. Much easier to ride back to the castle. The king would die, and Prince Anchurus would take his place.

But now he knew that a goddess could turn a man into a king.

He checked his waterskin, searching his belt by habit. He found his dagger and sword returned. He had a fighting chance. Decided, he set off up the hill.

King Midas sat on his royal chair in the south room, his leopard skin shielding him against a chill that no one but him seemed to feel. The heavy gold mitts weighed on his hands, his clothing refreshed by a manservant since he couldn't touch the fabric himself. He wore a long tunic and sandals, a wide belt drawn around his waist. He wished Rastus would hurry. The commander of the king's guard had informed him of the capture of a couple of Sargon's spies caught just beyond the castle gates. Now Midas was to decide what to do with them. His first instinct was to order them beheaded immediately, but that was the dehydration talking.

He kept himself busy mulling over the confrontation with Katiah. She'd seemed to indicate that Elanur was alive. He cautioned himself about her trickery. Yet, he couldn't abandon the hope that he might still rescue his sister. After all these years, the thought of seeing her again tempted him greatly. He should gather the fighting men he had and leave now. But such a move would be foolish. More men were coming. More horses. He must wage a winning battle, a final battle. He would wait. But wait too long, and he wouldn't live to see his triumphant moment. *Rastus, where are you?*

He didn't notice when the child came in. He was just there, at the arm of the chair, as if he stood by the king's side every day. Midas thought he should send him away. But this was the boy his daughter had taken pity on, the ragged child she had dressed up in fine clothing and allowed to stay with her throughout her birthday festivities. The king's heart ached for his daughter. He'd visited her in the dining hall, telling her over and over that he would find a way to release her. He didn't know whether she could hear him, if somehow she was still alive inside the golden shell. If she was, he didn't want her to feel alone. So, he told her. He would fix it. She would be free again.

Now, with the strength leaving his body, he feared he would not be able to keep his promise to either his daughter or his sister, and the boy provided a welcome distraction. He was a beautiful boy with flawless golden skin and deep brown eyes that were comforting to look into. His smile, which came readily, was the sun rising over the hills, a little like Elanur's had been. So much did it soothe Midas' heart that he had made a game out of trying to get the boy to show his gleaming white teeth more often. His tongue thick in his mouth, he spoke to him. "Wouldn't you rather be outside playing?"

The boy pointed to the ground where he stood.

"You can't do anything for me now."

The boy made a series of gestures. The king had dismissed them before, but now he looked more closely. "Slow down," he said. "What's this?" He tapped the arm of the throne.

The boy formed a box shape between his hands and then drew them up high above him. The king copied the movements as best he could with his hands covered as they were. The boy showed him again, and Midas tried again. This time, the boy smiled. Anchurus used to smile like that when he was young. It had been so long ago. Now his son blamed himself for what had happened. Midas had to talk with him before the end came. The prince would make a good leader. A better one than his father had. He must not have any guilt hanging over his head when the time came.

"And this?" he said to the boy, tapping his belt. The boy stretched his hands out long, about the length a belt would be. Midas copied him. The boy grinned, and Midas smiled, his lips cracking with the effort. "Belt," he said and stretched his hands wide.

The boy nodded then pointed to the golden floor. Bending at the waist, he flattened both his hands and moved them back and forth as if he were feeling the smooth surface. He pointed again and repeated the gesture.

Midas lacked the strength to bend over, so he simply copied the motion. The boy said "throne" in his language and "floor," and Midas said, "The throne is on the floor."

The boy nodded enthusiastically, and Midas chuckled though it sounded like a wheeze. He coughed after that, and the boy came back to his side. When it passed, Midas reached out to pat him on the head then remembered and quickly withdrew his hand. Covered or not, he would not risk touching anything he didn't intend to change. "It's all right," he said.

He was just about to call for Timon when the double doors burst open. Rastus strode in wearing his royal jacket, which was similar to the soldiers' cream-colored uniforms except that it had maroon trim on the collar and cuffs to separate him as the leader of the king's guard.

Behind him walked two men with their hands tied behind their backs, one a hulk of a man and the other a muscular but wiry sort. Two guards followed with spears pointed at the prisoners' backs. The boy sobered and stood tall at the side of the throne. Midas thought of dismissing him—assessing spies was not an appropriate activity for a child—but he couldn't bring himself to do so. He did his best to straighten up in the royal chair and appear the king, if only for one more time.

EMIR FELL FORWARD, hitting his shoulder on a rock. He cursed out loud. It was taking him longer to reach the springs than he'd expected. The way was thick with forest overgrowth, fallen trees, and vines so tightly intertwined that they created a carpet of green nets eager to trap any human foot daring to pass by. He wrestled his boot out of the last one and ran again.

The night air was cool and growing colder by the minute. He'd brought no cloak for protection. He hadn't expected when he walked out of the castle that afternoon to find himself on a journey to the higher elevations. And Bain had pulled away his jacket.

He thought of the boy and wondered if he was worried. He considered abandoning this quest and returning to Gordium. He would retrieve the boy and disappear somewhere in the city—at least for a while. But Sargon's hunters would never stop. Not when they were searching for one of the king's *sons.* As long as he was in danger, he'd be putting the boy in danger too. His only hope was finding a position within King Midas' court. There, he would be protected and could extend his protection to the boy. With time, he might find a way to rescue his mother.

The incline leveled off. The sound of rushing water came from ahead and to the right. He picked his way around the trees and the overgrowth, trying to hurry. The king didn't have much time.

Soon a small lake appeared in the distance, just like Katiah had said, a strip of gentle waves reflecting the light of the moon. He could hear a waterfall—the source of the magic liquid he would return to the king, he guessed. It was on his side of the lake, up and around to the left. He'd just started that direction when the hairs stood up on the back of his neck. He drew his sword and whirled to face the beast.

The moonlight glinted off a pair of blue eyes. A rumbling growl vibrated the air. Katiah's dark gray wolf. So, this *was* a test. Emir glanced around, almost expecting the dark goddess to be perched on some higher rock to watch the show. But it was too dark to see very far. At the moment, it mattered not. The beast charged and hit him hard. Emir landed on his back, two thick paws on his chest and a set of sharp fangs coming at his neck. The sword was useless this close.

He dropped it and, bracing his arm against the beast's fangs, turned his body enough to throw it off balance. He grabbed the sword and ran up the trail, but a heavy weight hit him from behind, knocking the sword loose. Fangs bit into his skull. He rolled, reaching for his dagger, and collided with a boulder at the side of the trail. The weight lifted. He jumped to his feet, heart racing. The beast was gone.

He retrieved his sword, stuffed it into the scabbard, and gripping the dagger, climbed once again toward the waterfall. He managed nearly twenty steps before he was attacked again, this time from the side. He landed hard on his left shoulder, his palm splatting in a puddle of mud. The beast was on him in the next moment, paws heavy on his chest, the back legs between his own. Emir wrestled with it, his forearm the only thing keeping the beast's fangs from his throat. This wasn't the dark gray one but the lighter one with the white fur around its eyes. He tried to catch it with the dagger, but the wolf was too nimble. With a mighty shove, Emir cast it back onto the rocks. It yelped with the impact. Cradling his injured arm, Emir resumed his climb.

The land dropped away to his right, exposing a tall cliff. An attack here could send him falling to his death. He clenched his dagger and hurried forward. His breath came fast, his thighs burning with the effort of the climb. He had just allowed himself a moment to believe he might have gotten away when all three wolves appeared in front of him. Like ghosts of the night, they seemed to take form from nothing. Standing shoulder to shoulder, teeth bared, they blocked his path.

"Seems a shame to kill your pets, great goddess," he called into the night, "but if that's what you want." Shouting his war cry, he rushed the beasts.

They responded in kind, man and wolves running toward one another on the thin path to the waterfall, the drop to the lake below lengthening with every step. Emir got in the first blow, slicing at the dark gray wolf as it passed. He heard a whine, but, at the same time, the lighter wolf grabbed his left ankle. Caught in its grip, Emir turned and brought down the blade, stabbing the beast on its upper shoulder. It yipped and released him.

Emir limped forward. A heavy weight slammed into him from behind. He landed on his chest. The beast bit into the back of his neck. He groaned, twisted, and sliced through the air, catching something. A high-pitched whine answered. The weight lifted. A flash of black disappeared over the cliff. He waited, expecting a deadly thump and cry below, but there was nothing. He staggered to his feet and stumbled on.

Running water pounded his ears. Mist covered everything, making the rocks so slippery that he lost his footing twice. He regained his balance and continued the climb. His wounds throbbed, the back of his neck on fire. Finally, he reached the waterfall and plunged into the stream. It coated his skin, cleaning the gashes and bites. At first it stung so badly he shouted curses through the downpour, but soon the pain eased under the water's steady pressure. He opened his waterskin, allowed it to fill, and hung it from his belt.

Beyond, the lake looked peaceful and serene, the moon casting a striped glow down the middle of it. He wondered if there was another way back, but he could see none. Instead, the path continued on past the waterfall, headed the opposite direction from where he needed to go.

He would have to face the wolves again.

He double-checked the waterskin to assure himself it was secure. With a fresh grip on his dagger, he walked back down the hill. Senses alert, arms taut, he took step after painful step. Nothing happened. The night was quiet, the sound of the waterfall steadily fading behind him. No sign of Katiah's pets. When he reached level ground, he waited, certain they would ambush him at any moment. When he heard something approach, he crouched low, scanning. But it wasn't the beasts. There, near the edge of the forest, stood a solitary black horse. It was riderless, its reins dangling loosely from its mouth.

Emir checked around. He could see nothing else, but he sensed the goddess' hand at work. He walked cautiously forward. This was no old couple's workhorse left stranded in a barn. This was a pure-blood, a tall and well-proportioned animal with a thick chest and heavy hindquarters. Emir feared it would run away, but it stood calmly until he took hold of the reins.

"Did she send you?" he asked, patting the horse's neck. Apparently, he had passed the test. Taking the gift would put him even further in debt to the goddess, but speed was of the essence. He leapt up onto the saddle.

The horse whirled and galloped into the overgrown forest as if it knew the road to Gordium. Emir loosened the reins, and they flew through the trees, the moon lighting their way.

CHAPTER FIFTEEN

"You've lost your mind." Fotis stood by his desk staring at Xander, who'd just relayed his latest vision.

"I saw it!" Xander said. "We have to tell him now, before he burns the garden."

"The prince will be so happy for the news," Aster said. He was performing exercises by his bed. Currently, sit-ups, as evidenced by the low grunt he uttered after completing each one.

"She won't respond to the garden burning," Xander said. "I saw it. She won't come."

"So because you summoned the dark goddess, you are now the expert?" Fotis said.

"I'm telling you, it won't be enough!" Xander threw his hands up in exasperation. "The garden will be destroyed for nothing."

Fotis set aside the latest parchment he'd been reading. "You cannot go to the prince with this. I will not allow it. You'll have us all separated from our heads."

"Have you seen him lately?" Xander asked.

"The prince?" Fotis said.

"The king! He's pale as cream, and his eyes are sunken into his head. He can hardly stand upright." The young advisor was near tears. "He's our king. We have to hurry."

"But the prince is the heir to the throne," Fotis said. "King Midas would never have it."

"Do you think he'll be happy about the garden?" Xander said.

"I'm sure he'd much rather have his son burned alive," Aster said, following the comment with another grunt.

"He wouldn't have to know about it," Xander mumbled. When the other two gawked at him in surprise, he said, "The prince wants to save his father."

"And if it doesn't work?" Fotis said. "What then? The prince will be dead and the king near dead. Your plan would leave Gordium without a ruler. Are you prepared to face that?"

"To face what?"

They all jumped. Prince Anchurus stood inside the door. Aster leapt to his feet and gestured to the pouches on the table. "These are not ready, Your Highness."

Anchurus perused their work. "They will spread the fire?"

"With gusto," Fotis said, coming closer.

"Get them down there now," Anchurus ordered. "The trenches are near finished. We will be starting soon." He picked up one of the pouches and weighed it in his hand. "If you have anything else, tell me now. The king hasn't much time." He glanced at Xander.

"Nothing, Your Highness," Aster said, then squeezed his eyes shut.

"He means nothing," Fotis said. "We will bring the pouches down."

The prince lingered, studying one advisor and then the other. "Is this going to work?" When they didn't answer, he tossed the pouch back on the table and pointed his gaze at Xander. "You have something to say?"

Xander shook his head.

Anchurus glanced at the other two. "Tell me now. Whatever it is. You will not be punished."

Xander raised an eyebrow at the elder advisor.

"No," Fotis said.

"You're certain," Anchurus said.

"There is nothing to tell, Your Highness," Fotis said.

Anchurus appeared to consider that, then approached Xander. Xander took a step back, but the prince pursued him across the room until Xander ran up against the wall.

"The garden, Your Highness," Xander said breathlessly. "I'm afraid . . ." He paused, wringing his hands.

"Yes?" Anchurus said, leaning in close.

"It won't work," Xander said.

"Why not?"

"It won't be enough. For her to come."

"How do you know this?"

Xander hesitated. "A vision, Your Highness."

Anchurus turned to the other two advisors. "You weren't going to tell me?"

"There's no way to know for certain," Fotis said. "We will be burning what she loves, the green things. It seems a good idea."

"But you don't think it will work," Anchurus said.

"He thinks it will work," Aster said.

"Must I remind you what's at stake here?" The prince glared at them all. "The king is dying. If this plan is not going to work, tell me now."

"It won't be enough," Xander said meekly.

"Then what will be?"

Fotis examined his shelves full of parchments and slates. Aster stared at the front door. Xander scratched the back of his neck.

"Your duty is to the king," Anchurus said.

"The king." Xander rocked his weight from foot to foot. "Fire is the answer, Your Highness. It's just . . ." He glanced up at the prince's face. "Burning the plants and the trees . . ." He shook his head.

"Then what?" Anchurus asked.

Xander sought out his colleagues. They stared at him like

comrades on a sinking boat. “Something she loves more, Your Highness,” he said reluctantly. “We must burn you.”

Midas examined the painting of his wife on the far wall of the strategy room. She was gazing out the window with a faraway look, as if she longed to escape. Sitting for the artists had been an endurance exercise for her. This painting, in particular, had been difficult, as the artist had kept starting over, saying it wasn’t quite right. His struggle had forced her to sit for many days. Midas had threatened to dismiss him, but in the end, the stubborn man had succeeded in capturing the queen’s essence. It was Midas’ favorite likeness of her.

A fire crackled in the fireplace. Timon had built it for him. The little man now sat across from him at the conference table, writing on a parchment. He was balding, a patch of his scalp showing through on his crown. Strange that Midas hadn’t noticed it before.

“Everything must go to the children,” he said. “Pilar”—the head cook—“permanent protection for the rest of her life. Monthly allowance . . . determined by King Anchurus.” Saying the words made Midas swell with pride. His son, the king. He had imagined it often. He could see the golden crown on Anchurus’ head, his heroic face turned to the citizens of Gordium. He would rule well. Especially with Zoe’s counsel in his ear. *Zoe.* His chest muscles seized in a spasm. It was some time before he spoke again.

“Rastus, Bastian, yourself,” he said, indicating that these loyal subjects—the captain of the king’s guard, the gardener, and the minstrel, though Timon had become much more—should be secured for life.

“Your Majesty, I . . .” But Timon couldn’t finish his sentence. He went back to writing.

Midas continued, naming other people he wanted taken care of. Animals, too. Kanani, his stallion. Mabel, the goat. He thought of her funny face and smiled. She’d been the perfect companion for his anxious mount. Timon wrote furiously, scratching across the parchment. The king paused to give him time.

Water. His brain and body cried out for it. Trying to keep himself occupied, he contemplated Katiah's visit the day before. He remembered with disgust how she had lain on the bed trying to seduce him. How angry she'd been about his wife's decree to banish all likenesses of the goddess from the castle grounds. It occurred to him then that Katiah might have played a part in Demodica's death. The idea made a hollow in his chest. He looked again at his wife's likeness and a flush of shame heated his skin. *Not you too.*

Timon had stopped writing, his hand poised over the parchment. "Read it back," Midas whispered. The minstrel read carefully. The information was all thoroughly recorded. When he finished, Midas forced himself to say the word "Zoe."

Timon poised the reed pen to write.

"Must be cured. All castle resources . . ."

"Of course, sire." Timon wrote it down.

"You're responsible." Midas pointed at Timon. "Anchurus will have his hands full, and Rastus must keep the new king safe."

"Yes, sire," Timon said. "I won't rest until she is with us once again." He wrote something else down.

Midas surveyed the room. On the south wall hung paintings of his adoptive parents. His father—the former king—had been a quiet and honorable man, his mother beautiful and elegant to her dying day. Truly, they had been like real parents to him. But then he pictured his real mother, which made him think of his sister, and that brought back the rage that seemed to burn ever hot in his breast.

Elanur.

He was so lost in his reveries that he jumped, startled, when Timon appeared at his side with a napkin. The little man dabbed at his cheeks, then returned to his seat and pretended to write again. So. His body had enough water left to make tears.

He got up and walked over to the table map. Even now, he had men out buying more soldiers and horses. Soon his army would swell to twice its current size. He would finally have what he needed to march on Durukin and take Sargon's head. On the very verge of achieving his revenge, the life was going out of his body.

His anger flared. He swept all the figures off the table, uttering the loudest shout he could muster as they clattered to the floor. Next, he grabbed the edge of the table and tried to tip it over, but he lacked the strength. Suddenly, Timon appeared beside him. Together, they pushed it onto two legs and then let it go. It fell to the floor with a gratifying thud. King Midas panted, his arms shaking, his legs threatening to buckle. Timon rushed to get his chair, pushing it underneath him right before he fell back into it.

His chest on fire, Midas reviewed the scene before him, the fallen table with its legs helpless in the air and the figures scattered about like dead men. This illustrated his defeat, his complete and utter defeat. He allowed his head to drop back against the chair. Demodica, dead. His sister, a servant to a king. Zoe alone inside a prison of gold. He hit the arm of the chair with his covered fist.

"FAX," he told Timon. "FAX."

The little man ran out the door.

"FAX!" Midas called again, but it came out as a whisper, and no one heard.

Xander followed the prince around the king's garden, his hand over his nose as the smoke billowed into the night sky. "This isn't going to work, Your Highness," he shouted over the din of the flames. "She hasn't come. The king will be angry."

"The king will be dead," Anchurus barked. "Go!"

Xander started, assuming the prince was speaking to him, but Anchurus was pointing to one of his men. Another explosion tore through the surrounding space, the advisors' combustible pouches feeding energy into the fire. The flames spread to the next section of the labyrinth, their greedy tongues lapping up bushes, flowers, and tree branches, air pockets popping. Anchurus stormed into Bloom Square.

"But, Your Highness!" Xander ran after him. "We don't have much time."

Anchurus passed all the pretty plants with flowering blooms, their cheeriness only seeming to further sour his mood. As he exited the area, he gave the signal to the soldiers lining the perimeter. Xander covered his ears. *Bam, bang!* Something small hit him on the back of the head. He wriggled to shake it off, fearing whatever it was, it might be aflame. When he paused to check, only clods of dirt clung to his shoulders.

Across the garden grounds, flames reached into the sky, their appetites for green things not to be denied. Xander followed the prince as he advanced, shouting orders, lifting his hand to signal the release of the explosive pouches. They popped and banged in his wake, his presence like the spark launching the destruction of paradise. Up ahead, the fig orchard stood untouched by the fire, the trees surrounded in smoke.

"Please, Your Highness." Xander panted as he approached, sweat rolling down his face. "Consider the years your father has invested here!"

Anchurus gave the signal. Two more explosions. The flames alighted in the orchard and began crawling toward the delicious bark of the trees.

"Your Highness—"

"Stop heckling me!" Anchurus struck a nearby bench with his fist, breaking the backrest in two. The pieces fell, the ends clinging to the iron frame. He seized one of them, wrenched it away, and threw it. Before it landed, he grabbed the other one and did the same. With only the seat left intact, he raised his boot and dealt a strong strike in the center of it, repeating the action until it was smashed into several pointed shards. Again and again, he stomped on the wood, the pieces giving way underneath his fury, splinters raining about his boots. Next, he took to the frame, but it was driven firmly into the ground.

Eventually, he stopped and stood panting, his eyes like a trapped animal's.

Xander tried to come up with something comforting to say, but failed. Helpless and unnerved, he started walking away. At the last moment, he glanced back. The prince lingered by the bench. "We're near the entrance," Xander called to him. "In the clearing by the tall hedges. We will wait for you."

The prince made no acknowledgment, but Xander knew he had heard him. Knew it by the way the prince's shoulders dropped from around his neck. As Xander headed back to join his colleagues, he did so having seen two things he'd never seen before: the prince losing his temper, and the strong, brave son of the king whitewashed with terror.

Midas dragged himself down the hall. Rastus had offered to support him as he walked, but he didn't want to be viewed as a decrepit old man. *Water.* His craving for it had lessened somewhat, but the thought persisted while his muscles weakened. Each step was a battle between himself and the distance he had to cross. It was strange, this feeling of dying. Nothing like he might have expected. The sword through the heart on the battlefield. An assassin's knife in the back. A disease in his old age. These he had considered, even tried to prepare for. But this. This was demeaning. Humiliating. The headache banged against his forehead, an incessant pounding demon. His stomach raged with a hot pain. The rest of his body burned with a red fire. Even his mind was slowing down. The dehydration had weeded out most of his thoughts, with only one consistent worry: *Zoe.*

He'd called for FAX to meet him in the dining hall. When he arrived at the double doors, the guards did their best to hide their shock. But he saw their expressions. What a sight he must make. A fragile, shriveled-up king. They glanced at Rastus and then opened the doors. Midas passed between them. Upon catching sight of the golden figure, his heart plummeted in despair. She remained as he had made her: a lifeless statue.

How could he have been so careless? He swayed. Rastus offered an arm for support. Midas waved it away and walked forward. He stopped when he spotted the boy perched at the princess' feet. He sat cross-legged, his head low like a child who had lost his best friend. Regarding the king, he got slowly to his feet and bowed.

"She would be glad you're here," Midas whispered.

The boy signed something with his hands. It was more than Midas could follow. His legs were trembling. Rastus brought his chair. Midas wished for a cushion, but didn't want to bother asking. Instead, he focused on his daughter. He had envisioned what he was going to say, how he was going to express to her the significance she held for him and the city of Gordium, how she needed to go on making her inventions and suggesting her improvements. She must take her solutions to her brother and make him listen, as she had always made her father listen. He was going to tell her again how much she reminded him of her mother and how proud Demodica would be of her today.

But he spoke none of it. Instead, he asked Rastus to pull the chair closer. Then he removed the mitt from his right hand and took hold of Zoe's extended fingers. They were cold and hard like everything else now, but they were the same long fingers he knew. He held on to them, remembering all the times he had held her warm hand. He hoped that somewhere inside all that metal, perhaps she might feel him there.

As he stared at the folds of her dress, his emotions overcame him. He felt like he was crying, but there were no tears spilling from his eyes. They were gone now, too. Just as well. In the silence, he wept without weeping, Rastus and the boy his only company.

"Your Majesty! Your Majesty!"

Midas glanced toward the double doors. Timon burst in. Breathless, his hair standing wildly on his head, he ran across the room, stopping to bow. “Your Majesty, you must come. They’re burning the gardens!”

The dark horse breathed heavily, air bursting through its cavernous nostrils in powerful huffs. Emir let it walk for a spell. The night was getting on, but he hadn’t yet reached the castle. At least now he could see the glow of the city lamps in the distance. He glanced back, trying to retrace his steps. He must know how to return to the magical spring. One waterskin wouldn’t last the king for long.

The horse moved with the sluggish heaviness of fatigue, sweat dampening its hide. Emir longed to let it rest, but he kept imagining the king already dead. He had to hurry. The urgency possessed him, and he slapped the horse with the ends of his reins. It responded, and they were off again.

They crossed the wide hill, the horse’s hooves thudding hard into the dry ground. As they started to descend the other side, something caught Emir’s eye—a brilliant light blooming at the edge of the city. He squinted. A distant boom rolled toward him, like some type of explosion. A yellow-orange glow mushroomed outward, followed by a tower of smoke. Fire. But where? It seemed near where the castle might be, but he was too far away to be certain. He leaned back, extending the reins so the horse could have his head. When they reached level terrain, he urged the animal forward.

“Come on,” he said. “We’re almost there now.” Another distant boom, and then a high plume of light rose into the night sky. He checked the waterskin at his belt, something he’d done multiple times since leaving the spring. The horse’s lumbering gait jostled him about, the scent of smoke reaching his sinuses. As they drew near, it appeared a great fire was burning on the hill inside the castle grounds. Strange. His first thought was that Katiah was doing more of her mischief, but he couldn’t see the logic in that. Not that the goddess was logical.

He ran his fingers over his injured arm. Already it had started to heal, scabs forming over the gashes the wolves' fangs had left behind. His ribs, too, felt better, as did the back of his neck. It had to be the magical water. The goddess had tested him, but she had also provided a means to cure his wounds. He wished he'd had more than one waterskin to fill.

He urged the slowing horse forward, squeezing with his legs and speaking encouraging words in the animal's ears. Checking the waterskin again, he thought of the boy. Was he anywhere near the fire? He snapped the reins. "Come on. It's not far now."

KING MIDAS' guards carried him out of the castle on a flat platform, moving with the haste he could no longer accomplish on his own. Sitting upright, he scanned to the north, certain his eyes were deceiving him. They had to be, for it looked like the gardens were bathed in flames. The fire towered over even the tallest hedges as it leapt and danced into the night. He coughed, the smoke scratchy in his throat. Rastus directed the men to pause, but Midas motioned for them to continue. As they got closer, it became clear. The gardens were burning. The flames rose into the darkness like great tongues lapping at the stars, then sank again to consume their prey, the hedges cracking and popping as they shriveled into charred remains. Midas was reminded of his village so many years before, when it had been engulfed in the flames of a similar fire. Back then, the smoke had stung his eyes, the shouts of his people drowned out by the horses' hoofbeats. *Mama.* His throat tightened as he recalled the yellow blanket hiding her sweet face.

He spotted several of his men up ahead. They seemed to be surrounding the perimeter. The sight gave him hope. They would squelch the blaze. But then he saw that they were doing nothing of the sort. They stood with their shovels at their sides, waiting.

"Put it out!" he ordered, but no one heard. He gestured toward the fire, glaring at the men, but they weren't looking at him. They watched the flames instead, as if entranced. Gathering all his strength, the king shouted, "Stop!"

Rastus turned. Seeing the king's alarmed expression, he called the other guards to a halt. They all stopped and gradually set the platform down.

The king pointed toward the soldiers. "Out. Put it out."

Rastus ran to convey the order. He stopped near the first man and began talking to him. The soldier looked back and, upon seeing his king, immediately bowed low. Then he ran off as Rastus returned.

"Your Majesty," he said, "they are acting on the prince's command."

"Anchurus?" Midas whispered. *His son would have the gardens burned?* "Bring him."

Rastus ordered the other guards to watch over the king, then started toward the fire.

"Wait!" Midas called, but his commander was already out of earshot. Rastus ran in among the flames, his feet light on the path. *Stupid,* Midas thought. He shouldn't have ordered him into the fire.

"Follow him," he told the other guards. They lifted the platform and, ducking their heads, charged into the flames after their commander.

ANCHURUS PULLED on the ropes to make sure they held tight to the post. He stood with his back to it, his feet bound at the ankles, his hands crossed and tied behind him. Fotis, Aster, and Xander lingered next to him, all of them looking solemnly at their young prince.

"What are you waiting for?" Jaw clenched, Anchurus lifted his chin. "Get on with it."

"Is there anything you wish to say?" Fotis said.

"If it doesn't work, find a way to free Zoe. Is that clear?"

The three advisors nodded.

Anchurus gritted his teeth. "Very well."

Xander held the torch. He hesitated. He was about to burn King

Midas' only son alive. He looked at Fotis, but the old man offered no encouragement. Xander tried Aster, but the middle advisor had fixed his gaze on some unknown object in the distance.

"Now!" Anchurus bellowed.

Xander bent at the feet of the prince. Tears burned his vision. The prince. The proud prince. He might be wrong. What if he was wrong?

He lit the dried branches, moving gradually around the post. The flames quickly established themselves, forming a circle of fire. Anchurus hissed through his teeth. Aster grasped Xander's shoulders and pulled him back. Two rows of water buckets waited behind them—tools to douse the fire the instant the goddess showed herself.

Xander scanned the clearing. *Please come,* he thought. *Save him.*

Sweat streamed down the prince's face, but he remained silent. For a time, it was tolerable, standing with the other two in the heat and smoke, waiting for the goddess to arrive. Perhaps she would appear before too much harm was done. The prince could withstand a few surface burns.

The breeze blew overhead, but the air was stifling. Beyond, the men shouted as they kept the fire contained within the gardens, lines of them ready with water and shovels. Anchurus began to writhe against the post. The flames crawled closer, eagerly darting toward his trousers.

"It's not going to work," Xander whispered, wringing his hands.

"It will not work," Aster said.

"It had better work," Fotis said.

And then Anchurus screamed.

Xander rushed for the buckets, but Aster stopped him. The prince was burning, the flames now possessing his legs, his throat red and strained as he looked toward the sky in horror. Already he was pulling on the ropes, trying to get free. Xander desperately searched the area. No goddess.

"What in the gods' names are you doing?" Rastus appeared in front of them, fury on his face.

"We act on the prince's order," Fotis said.

Rastus ran for the water. He retrieved two buckets and was about to use them when Aster grabbed him from behind. Rastus lost his grip. The buckets dropped, water splashing onto the ground. Rastus twisted and barreled into the advisor. Aster stumbled back. Rastus scooped up a half-full bucket and hurried toward the prince, who was now staring at him with pleading eyes. But Aster was too quick. He grabbed Rastus again from behind. While the two struggled, the prince's screams grew louder, the flames eating into his legs and feet.

"You're killing him!" Rastus cried. "The king will have your heads!"

Xander hunted for the goddess, bending his every thought to her appearance. *Goddess Denisia. You must come. You must!*

"Do you see her?" Fotis asked from behind him.

Xander covered his ears. The prince's screams. They were too much.

"You're killing him!" Rastus cried again.

Where was she? Unable to stand it any longer, Xander darted for the buckets but paused when he saw four of Rastus' men approaching. They carried the king on a platform. At the edge of the clearing, they halted, the king suspended between them. Midas reached a desperate hand toward his son.

"Anchurus!"

The word died in his parched throat. The king dropped back, limp, the mitts hanging loosely from his wrists.

CHAPTER
SIXTEEN

Smoke seeped into the castle dungeon, crawling through the vent holes in the stone walls. As it thickened the air, the Olgun brothers grew more desperate. Bain beat himself black and blue slamming against the cell door, one shoulder and then the other taking the impacts as he sought to weaken the frame. Baris sat up against the wall, knees bent, trying to think of another way to escape. Both were calling for help when a woman's voice interrupted them.

Baris got to his feet. At first, he saw only a pale white light, as if the moon were shining from underground. Gradually, a figure took shape in the center of the cell. He recognized the goddess, the same one who had appeared before to stop them from taking Emir. She glowed, sparkles emanating from her deep-blue gown, her silky black hair falling in waves down her back. When her dark eyes found him, he could not move.

"Hello again," she said.

Behind the goddess, Bain had a stunned look on his face.

"I apologize for landing you here in the bowels of the king's castle," the goddess went on, "but you have to admit. They're better than some, hm?" When neither man answered, she moved to the back wall and ran her finger along the rock. "You see, I couldn't let you take the traitor. I have my own plans for him. I might have done much worse to you, but I took into consideration your ignorance of the situation. How much do you know about him, anyway?" She pinned her gaze on Baris.

The hunter shifted nervously. "He was a deserter."

"King Sargon sent us after him," Bain offered.

"And?"

"That is all," Baris said.

She stepped toward him. "You know nothing more?"

"The king wanted him back," Bain said.

"You retrieve people for him," Katiah said.

"We're hunters," Baris said.

"The best," Bain crowed.

"He sends us after deserters," Baris continued. "We capture them and return them."

"I see." The goddess smiled at each brother in turn. Perfect white teeth showed between her lush red lips. "That's wonderful. Because I need of a couple of men like you. I have someone I need captured. I think you two would be perfect for the job. The question is, can I trust you?"

"We serve King Sargon II," Baris said.

"Brother, she's a goddess!" Bain called out.

Katiah walked toward Baris, her dark eyes intensely staring into his own. She stopped only when she stood very close to him. "Forget King Sargon," she said in a sultry voice. "Do this for me, and I will be very,"—she drew out the word—"grateful."

Baris' cheeks flushed.

"Refuse," the goddess continued, "and I'm afraid you won't be serving King Sargon anymore. Or anyone else."

Baris took a step back. "Of course," he said.

"Excellent." Katiah's expression softened. "This will be fun!" She twisted her finger, and the heavy door keeping them in their cell swung back. Bain jumped, startled, and stared at the door as if he no longer trusted it. Katiah chuckled and sauntered out. Baris hesitated only a moment before following her, Bain on his heels.

Out in the corridor, Katiah pointed toward the exit. "You will escape the dungeon and make your way to the dining hall on the first level inside the castle. Second door on the right. There, you will find a golden sculpture of a young woman. You can't miss it—it stands alone near the table. You must capture it and get away without anyone seeing you. And don't worry. It looks as if it might be heavy, but there is magic about it. A goddess' magic." She leveled her gaze at one and then the other, as if to be sure her instructions were getting through. "Once you have it, you must get out of the city as quickly as you can."

"If we are caught?" Baris asked.

Katiah's spine stiffened. "You have a reputation for being King Sargon's best hunters. Is that correct?"

The brothers nodded together.

"This is an important task," Katiah said. "I trust you have the skills to complete it efficiently." She turned her back on them and started walking out. "Do not let me down, darlings. I'm counting on you." The surrounding light appeared to darken, and then she shimmered out of sight, the faint echo of a wolf's howl sounding in the distance.

On the Isle of Mount Nysa, Denisia ran down the hill from her dwelling, screaming in pain. Her whole body was on fire, her skin sizzling. She raced to the creek and plunged in, seeking relief in the cool water. It soothed her for a few moments, but then the pain returned, burning deep into her body. She felt as if her very blood were boiling. The three Nysiades called from a distance, their high-pitched chatter betraying their anxiety at hearing her screams. She answered them, longing for their comforting touch. Summoning her courage, she examined her skin, certain she'd find it burning off her bones. It looked the same as always, smooth and untouched.

The creek water no longer helped. She climbed out, moaning and crying as she headed for the trees. She grabbed hold of the first one, uttered a quick apology, and, clinging to the trunk, drained it of its healing moisture. Potent oils seeped inside her, leaving behind only a wooden shell, but it offered only momentary relief. She ran to the next tree and the next, flattening herself against them. None could absorb the fire inside her. She tore at her hair, eventually shedding the dress and running about in her underclothes. The Nysiades caught up and surrounded her, their lithe forms elevated off the ground as their ethereal voices filled the night, but none of it helped.

Driven near mad with fear and pain, Denisia dropped onto the forest ground and clutched the undergrowth into her fists. The Nysiades hovered over her, their singing intensified. Denisia closed her eyes and begged to be released from this torture. After a few moments of agonizing effort, she dropped deeper into the ground. The cool dirt surrounded her, absorbing the heat. The Nysiades' voices grew more distant. It was getting harder to breathe. She was trapped inside a moving cocoon and dared not open her eyes. Just when she was sure she was going to die, everything stilled.

The ground calmed. The pain faded. In her fists, she no longer clutched dirt, but grass. Smoke stung her nostrils. Coughing, she opened her eyes and saw fire. It was another moment before she realized she was in King Midas' garden. It was ablaze, the heat consuming everything. Through the smoke, she spotted a dark figure in the distance. It screamed. The blinding pain seized her body once more.

"Anchurus!"

He turned toward her, mouth open, neck straining upward. The flames ate at his feet and lower legs, now threatening his knees.

"No!" Pressing her hands against the grass, Denisia drew its moisture inside her. As it flowed into her body, her own pain subsided. When she felt full, she extended her arms toward the prince, sending the water through her palms. It gushed like a river and within moments, the flames disappeared, replaced by rising black curdles of smoke.

Anchurus sank against the post, his head low. Denisia dropped onto the now dry, brittle grass. The pain was gone. Blissfully gone. *Anchurus.*

THE DARK HORSE kept up its pace all the way to the castle entrance. Emir leapt off the saddle, shouting at the guards to open the gate. They refused. "I'm Emir Alkan," he told them, "the musician who won the king's contest. I have the cure for the king's illness. You must allow me in immediately!"

One of the guards came forward and, peering at Emir's face, recognized him. But he wouldn't open the gate.

"Do you wish the king to die?" Emir said. "I have the cure. His death will be on your hands."

The first guard considered this, then called for the tower guard to alert the commander to the situation. While they waited, Emir detached the waterskin from his belt. "This will save the king's life," he said. "You must let me through!" He gazed up into the watchtower, seeking someone who would listen, but no one responded.

Frustrated, he checked his arm. The bleeding had stopped. The throbbing in his ribs, too, had backed off to a dull pain, the magical spring water working quickly. He pleaded with the guard again. Finally, the gates opened, and another soldier walked through them. Emir rushed up to him and stopped abruptly when he recognized the man who had offered him the position with the king's army that morning.

"You missed your appointment," the soldier said, resting his hands on his belt.

"I've got water for the king," Emir said. "It's water he can drink. Let me through."

The man eyed him with the same mistrusting glare. "You missed your appointment," he said again.

"If you know anything," Emir said, "you know I saved the king's life this morning. Unless you wish him to die now, you'll allow me through to save it again."

The guard tucked his lips under and shifted his jaw, as if still tasting his dinner. He grunted, then stepped aside.

"Thank you," Emir said and ran past him.

"To the barracks tomorrow," the soldier said, "or these gates will be permanently closed to you!"

Emir kept running. Smoke burned his eyes, the flames casting such a bright light it seemed much like day. The king would be inside, he was sure, away from danger. He burst through the unguarded front doors. He was about to call out when he paused.

It was strangely dark, with only two lanterns lit. He jogged forward, searching for someone, anyone. The castle was too quiet. There were no servants rushing about. He imagined they had all gone out to tend to the fire, which was to be expected, but his skin prickled in the smoky air. Stepping cautiously into the hallway, he stopped to listen. There. Voices. They seemed to come from the dining hall. Yet there was no light.

"We can't carry a sculpture out of here in plain sight."

Baris! Emir recognized the hunter's voice. His muscles stiffened.

"Everyone's gone," Bain whispered. "No one will notice."

"All right," Baris said. "You grab that end."

They were stealing something. Emir couldn't take them both at once, and the king still desperately needed water. Whatever they were pilfering was probably of little consequence.

"What do you think she wants this for?" Bain said.

"Go!" Baris ordered.

Footsteps approached. Emir was about to hide himself when it dawned on him what they were taking. They were in the dining hall.

They'd mentioned a sculpture. And that a "she" wanted it. *She. Katiah.* Of course. The perfect prize for King Sargon. Princess Zoe!

He looked left and right. There was no one to offer assistance. He could close the doors, but he had no way to lock them. The footsteps grew nearer. His only advantage was surprise. He gripped the hilt of his sword and readied himself.

"It's heavy," Bain said.

"Be quiet," Baris said.

Bain was on the left. Emir bent his knees. The men came through the double doors. Emir swung his sword. Bain howled. The sculpture fell with a thud. Emir sliced again, unsure in the darkness where his blade was going. Bain punched wildly. He missed Emir, but Baris was more accurate. The brother thumped Emir hard on the back of the neck. Emir turned toward his attacker, but Baris dealt another blow to his cheek. He fell to the ground, his sword clattering onto the golden stones. Baris pounced on his belly and punched one side of his face and then the other.

"Stop," Emir said. "She's alive."

"It's Alkan!" Baris said.

"Get his legs," Bain said. "I'll take his arms."

"But the sculpture."

Emir tasted blood. He groaned and tried to get up.

"We have to take him back to the king," Bain said.

"But we have to take her first," Baris said.

"Can't we take them both?"

"We'd never make it out of here."

"But the king's orders!"

"Would you rather the king's wrath or that of the goddess?"

Emir was losing consciousness, the men receding down a dark tunnel.

"Come on," Baris said. "We'll come back for him later."

The men grunted with the weight of the sculpture, their footsteps retreating. Emir tried to get onto his hands and knees. His limbs failed him. He choked on his own blood. Zoe.

They were taking Princess Zoe.

SARGON STOOD in the doorway of the dining hall. Elanur's back was to him, her hair freshly washed, combed, and pinned with a luxurious red barrette at the side of her head. The borrowed dress covered her shoulders in a rich red fabric, a cream-colored shawl draped lightly around her neck. She sat with her hands in her lap, her gaze directed to the empty plate in front of her. Sargon inhaled and, resting his thumbs on his leather belt, strode into the room.

She stiffened at the sound of his footsteps. He took his chair at the head of the table, putting her on his left. Once he was settled, he motioned to the servants, and they began serving dinner: lamb, parsnips in gravy, peas, and warm bread. Sargon started eating immediately. After a time, Elanur followed his lead. They ate together in silence, the servants standing by to refill their cups with water and wine. When they finished, dessert was a vanilla custard with cinnamon. Sargon cast a glance at Elanur when she took her first bite, noting the delight she tried to hide.

After the meal, the servants cleared the table. "I trust you enjoyed it," Sargon said.

Elanur didn't respond. She had folded her hands in her lap again.

"Tell me how you called the goddess, and I will show mercy to Emir."

She lifted her gaze. "What sort of mercy?"

"I will not kill him."

"You must not torture him."

"He is a deserter."

"He must not be an example."

"You wish me to pardon him?"

"I wish you to make him heir to your throne."

The statement was so shocking it took Sargon a moment to absorb it. Then he laughed. "Heir to my throne?" He stared at her in disbelief. "You think I should let a deserter become king?"

"It is a fair exchange," she said. "I help you summon the goddess who visits your nightmares. You defeat Midas. You take his kingdom. You get everything you want. Making Emir your heir is the only way I get what I want."

"For your son to be king?" Sargon asked.

"For my son to be safe. Only if he is heir will he be protected."

"From me, you mean."

She closed her mouth, her lips a deeper red in the candlelight.

"My wife and I have two sons," Sargon reminded her.

"Your wife is dead," she said.

His wife—the daughter of a wealthy man in Babylonia—had lived ten years after they'd married. The marriage had been a strategic and productive one. Raima had born him two children—Senna and Riba—before dying during childbirth with the third, who hadn't survived. "My sons are alive," Sargon said.

"They are not the men Emir is," Elanur said. "You know it."

Sargon rested his forearm on the table. "You wish me to believe that your concern is for the kingdom?"

"My concern is for my son."

"Yet you would argue he is more suited to be king than either of my sons."

"Emir is your son, too."

Preposterous. An unthinkable idea. He wondered how Elanur had come up with it. The hairs stood up on the back of his neck. "Did *she* tell you to ask me this?"

"Katiah?" Elanur frowned. "She doesn't care who sits on the throne."

He detected no deception in her gaze. "You ignorant woman. She's playing us both." He pushed his chair back from the table.

Her gaze followed him. "What would a goddess care about such things?"

"Why did she help me in the first place if she's so divorced from the world of men?" he asked. "Why did she help you?"

"I prayed to her for years. I was loyal."

Sargon laughed. "You think that's all it takes to get a goddess to visit you? Come, Elanur. You're not stupid."

She glared at him, insulted, but didn't look as confident as before.

"Katiah is the goddess of the underworld," Sargon said. "She is not some benevolent being who appears to make you feel better."

"That's just what she did for me," Elanur said.

Sargon walked over to where hung a painting of his brother, the king before him. He'd thought to have it removed once Shal had been killed, but changed his mind. It was an homage to the man, most people thought. But to Sargon, it was a reminder of what happened to weak leaders.

"I have my hunters out searching for Emir. They will bring him back to me soon. If you don't do as I ask, I will do to him what I've done to so many other deserters like him. His fate is up to you." Sargon turned and headed out. "Take her to the guest room for the night," he ordered the guard by the door, "and tell my advisor to meet me in my study."

The guard bowed low.

"Your Majesty," Elanur said.

Sargon turned back. He could see her profile only, the rest of her hidden inside the tall-backed chair.

"We summon Katiah together," she said. "Discover what her true intentions are."

"And then?"

"You call your hunters off Emir's trail."

"Just let him go?"

"If he never returns, he's not here to embarrass you. Or to take your throne."

"You would give up this wish?"

"For his safety, yes."

Sargon crossed his hands in front of him. "What if they have already found him and are on their way back as we speak?"

"*If* they bring him back," she said, "I want your word you will let him go."

His word. He might give it and then break it. But he wouldn't. Not with her. He knew himself well enough to know that, and she knew it too. He considered a moment more, then started out of the room once again. "Tell the guard what you will need," he told her. "We will summon her tomorrow."

CHAPTER
SEVENTEEN

Xander's ears throbbed as if inflamed with the prince's torturous wounds. Anchurus hung limp on the post, smoke smoldering around his feet. Denisia lay on the brittle grass beyond, King Midas prone on the royal platform.

The sounds returned one by one. First, the fire. The rest of the gardens were still burning, the flames crackling and roaring as they consumed flowers and trees and bushes and vines. Second, the voices. The soldiers continued to manage the blaze, shouting back and forth at one another as they maneuvered their shovels and buckets. Xander turned to see Fotis and Aster behind him. Rastus remained in Aster's hold. All of them looked as stunned as he felt.

"They should stop the fire," Xander said. It came out a mumble.

Aster blinked as if awakened and released Rastus. The commander of the king's guard cut the prince's ropes. Anchurus folded at the waist, falling. Rastus grabbed him under the arms. Aster appeared on the other side and together, they lowered the prince to the ground. Rastus rushed away to check on the king.

"Get her to help," Fotis said to Xander and then followed Rastus.

The goddess was still on her stomach, the dead grass forming a brown circle around her. Xander approached carefully. His plan had worked. She had come. But now what? He turned back to see Fotis kneeling by the king, but Midas hadn't moved.

"Denisia?" he called. She didn't respond. "Goddess Denisia, are you all right?" He rolled her over and slapped her on the cheek, twice. Finally, she stirred and opened her eyes.

"Anchurus?" She pushed herself up and looked around. "Is he . . .?"

"They're tending to him now." Xander stood and extended his hand. "The king is over here. Is there anything else you need?"

On her feet, she searched the clearing. "Anchurus!" She bolted across the grass.

"But the king," Xander said. "Wait!"

Anchurus lay flat on his back near the post, his pants burned up to his knees, his legs a patchwork of charred black skin and weepy red mash. Parts of his shirt were burned as well, the bottom an uneven blackened rag, his belly inflamed. The cloth remained intact over his chest, his neck and arms bright red with heat.

"We must get to the river." Denisia pointed toward the king. "That," she commanded, referring to the platform. "Use that."

"But the king needs your help!" Xander caught up, breathless.

"His son will die!" she said. "Bring it now."

Xander looked from the prince to the king. Finally, he jogged over and told Rastus what the goddess had requested. Rastus cast a look back at the prince, then directed three of the five guards to do as Xander asked.

When they returned with the king's platform, they found Denisia crying by the prince's side.

"He wished for you to save the king," Xander said. "We thought that if someone you loved . . ." He couldn't finish the sentence.

"*You* did this?" She glared at him, her eyes rimmed with tears.

"He called, but you didn't come," Xander said. "He asked us to find a way."

Footsteps approached. Xander turned to see Aster jogging into the clearing. "They are not putting out the fire," he said and observed the goddess. "You are helping the king?"

Denisia's face reddened with anger. "How dare you do this?"

"Anchurus didn't call for you," Aster said. "He didn't ask for your help."

"You had no right," she said.

"You seek to kill kings and leave princes behind to manage their grief?" Aster said.

Anchurus stirred and uttered a low moan.

"Help me," Denisia ordered. Together, the guards eased the prince's charred body onto the platform. They lifted him and, keeping step with one another, started toward the river, Denisia leading the way.

"He did this so you would save the king," Xander called after her. "He will have suffered for nothing!"

Denisia ignored him.

"Please," Xander said, but it was no use. She hurried on, disappearing into the night.

Emir was dreaming of his mother. She'd cooked his favorite meat pie with lamb and cheese. It was a rare thing for them to have meat, and he wondered where she had gotten it. He feared she'd been hurt, for it was usually from powerful men that they managed the nicer things. These thoughts bothered him even as he heard his mother humming over the fire. When she called him to eat, he jumped up and ran to the table. She turned around. Two bruises marred her face at the cheek and chin. She set the pie down in front of him and, standing back, gave him a crooked smile.

"Go on. Taste it," she said.

"Who did this to you? Mother, who did this?"

He awoke to his own shouts. Pain radiated through his back, up into his neck, and across his shoulder. He blinked but saw only darkness, one eyelid swollen nearly shut.

Princess Zoe. The Olgun brothers.

He crawled over to the wall. Sitting up against it, he took a moment to catch his breath. They'd worked him over good, but they hadn't killed him. King Sargon wanted him alive. A blessing for now. He remembered his errand and touched the waterskin at his belt. He had to get to King Midas.

Small fingers tapped his shoulder. A flood of joy washed over him. "What took you so long?" he asked.

The boy knelt by his side. Emir wrapped his arm around his neck, drawing him near. The boy motioned with his hands, but it was dark and Emir's vision was blurry.

"Later," he said. "I need you to do something." He removed the waterskin from his belt. "Take this to the king. Do you know where he is?"

The boy pointed.

"Don't go into the flames," Emir said. "Understand? Be smart. But find the king. Have him drink." He handed over the waterskin. The boy frowned. "I know," Emir said. "But he'll be able to drink this. Go. Hurry."

The boy took the waterskin but didn't leave. With one hand, he made the symbol for *princess*.

"I couldn't stop them," Emir said.

Where? the boy signed.

"I don't know," Emir said. "We'll find her." He gripped the boy's shoulder. "Go save the king. Can you do that?"

The boy stood up, then hesitated.

"Go on. I'll see you in my room later."

The boy dashed off. Emir sagged against the wall and closed his eyes. A few moments of rest. Then he would have to tell the king. If the boy succeeded in saving him. Which he would. He would. Then Emir would have to relay what had happened.

The thought filled him with dread. How was one to tell a king that his daughter was gone?

. . .

THE FLAMES BEGAN TO SUBSIDE, the roar dimming to a gnawing crackle. Every breath stung of dust and smoke, but the heat had backed off, moving from a skin-eating bite to a dull ache. The soldiers worked to calm the fire, passing buckets from man to man, their faces dirty with ash.

Xander had returned to sit by the burning post, his gaze unfocused on the space in front of him. The king lay still on the grass near the entrance, Rastus standing beside him. The commander's two remaining guards lingered nearby, awaiting his orders, the other three still attending the prince. Fotis was with the king, too, having positioned himself at Midas' right with his nose pointed toward the night sky. Aster had left.

The evergreen hedges that had once formed the perimeter of the clearing stood distorted versions of their former selves, the flames having shaped them into gnarled and bony skeletons with blackened centers and edges. The garden was a graveyard, and it was all Xander's fault. His idea to bring the fire. His idea to burn the prince. It should have worked. The goddess had come, but he'd never guessed she would refuse to help the king. Flat-out refused.

"Self-pity is so attractive," Aster said, appearing in front of him.

"Go away," Xander said.

"Your loyalty to the king is not admirable," Aster said. "You didn't try to save him to the end."

"And look what happened," Xander said. "Failure. Utter failure."

"You wanted the goddess to come," Aster said. "She did not come. Obviously, you are a fraud. The king should have you beheaded."

"I never thought that she'd refuse to help him," Xander said. "We're supposed to consider all factors, Fotis says."

"Of course, you can control what a goddess does," Aster said.

"I should have considered it."

"Considered she might refuse," Aster said, "and, in considering it, refrained from trying to bring her here? Allow the king to die without effort? A sound solution."

"But what have I done?" Xander said. "The king's gardens are ruined. The prince is hurt. Badly." He blinked back tears. "He may die, along with the . . ." He glanced back at the king.

"He's dead," Aster said.

The words startled Xander at first, but then he remembered whom he was talking to. The king lived, but it wouldn't be long now. Xander lowered his gaze and saw Aster's open hand.

"The advisors do not belong at the king's side," Aster said.

Xander looked away. To take the hand would mean to admit defeat. To concede that the king was lost and there was nothing more they could do. He thought it over again, searching for some hidden solution, but came up with nothing. The hand remained steady and sure. Finally, he took it, and Aster helped him up. They stood together for a moment, then slowly walked over to where Fotis was standing. They took their positions next to him and turned their backs to the solitary line of hedges that had been left unharmed, their faces toward the wreckage beyond. None of them dared glance down at the king. Instead, they regarded a vague spot in the distance, somewhere between the burned hedges and the smoke. The soldiers continued their shouting, splashing buckets and clanking shovels until the light began to fade, the flames losing life.

Finally, Xander could stand it no longer. He looked down at the king and was startled to see Midas' eyes open and gazing back at him. "Your Majesty!" Xander dropped to his side.

"Anchurus?" Midas whispered.

"He's with Denisia," Xander said. "She will heal him."

The king's features relaxed.

"I'm sorry," Xander said. "We wanted to save you. The prince wanted to save you. But we've failed."

The king didn't respond. He'd gone too still.

"Your Majesty?"

The king's eyes were closed.

Xander shook Midas' shoulder. "Your Majesty!"

The other two advisors squatted beside him, Rastus watching it all with a somber expression. "We have to do something!" Xander looked desperately around. "Your Majesty?" The king was like a rag doll in his grip.

A firm hand took hold of Xander's upper arm. "Shaking him will surely save him," Aster said.

"He's not dead!" Xander said. "He can't be dead. Your Majesty!" Xander scooted forward and placed the king's head on his robed thigh. "He needs help breathing. It's too smoky. We need to get him out of here. Find something to move him," he barked at Rastus. "Find something!"

Rastus cast his gaze about, then walked away, his two guards following.

Xander patted the king's shoulder. "It's all right. We're going to help you." He was crying now, shaking his head. "How could we do this, Fotis? How could we fail him so?"

Fotis looked down at his king. His wooden eye fell out. He caught it in his palm but didn't replace it. On the other side, Aster laced his fingers in his lap. The three sat that way, Xander crying in muffled sobs, their backs to the entrance. Suddenly, from behind and to the left, the child appeared. He paused a moment, as if getting his bearings. Then he rushed forward and dropped by the king's side.

The advisors all leaned back in surprise. The child opened his mouth and then pointed to the king, repeating the pattern with desperate movements. He pulled off the waterskin cap and scrutinized the three men. They all exchanged glances. Finally, Xander pushed his knee farther under the king's neck, propping his head, and pulled the royal chin down. The boy positioned the waterskin and poured. Much of the spring water missed its target, flowing in thin streams down the sides of Midas' neck and into the grass. Some settled onto his tongue and trickled down his throat. The boy paused and waited. The advisors stared sadly at the king and then the child. Nothing happened.

The boy gestured for Xander to open the king's mouth again. Xander complied. The boy poured. After another pause, he tried a third time. When the king still didn't move, he capped the waterskin, set it aside, and tapped on the king's chest. *Tap tap tap* changed to *thud thud thud.* Lines creased around the boy's face, his mouth in a grimace.

"It's all right," Xander said. "We tried. It's all right."

The boy slumped onto his bottom. Rastus returned, he and his men carrying a plank between them. They brought it up next to the king and positioned it on the ground alongside. Rastus gave the advisors a questioning look. Fotis shook his head, all of them gazing upon the king in sorrow.

Suddenly, Midas choked and sputtered. Water spewed onto his cheeks. He opened his eyes.

"Your Majesty?" Xander exclaimed.

The king eyed his youngest advisor. "Xander?" He surveyed the rest of them. "Where is my son?"

Anchurus was almost fully immersed in the cool river water, but it had not soothed his pain. He was awake now, his face taut with agony. The guards were holding him as gently as they could without causing further anguish, but when he cried out, they were so startled they let him go, plank and all. He might have fallen under had they not recovered fast enough to stabilize him again.

"All right, take him out," Denisia said.

The guards eased him onto the bank. There they held him while Denisia packed cool mud onto his wounds. Every touch hurt, each pain a stab in her own flesh, the whole task a torturous experience. Denisia kept working, finishing his legs and then moving to his stomach and arms, hiding the reddened skin with the slick brown mixture. His chest continued to rise and fall with quick breaths, but gradually, he stopped his writhing movements.

"Don't let it dry," she told the guards. "Do you understand me? Keep it moist. You." She pointed to the third guard. "Find a container and pack more of this mud in it. Take it to the castle so it may be used again later."

The guard left to do as he was told. Denisia touched the prince's cheeks with her cool, wet hands. "What were you thinking?" she asked him.

When he turned to look at her, his eyes were red and wet. "Did you cure Father? Did you lift the curse?"

"I am treating you," she said.

"He's dying." Anchurus tried to get up.

Denisia placed a muddy hand on his chest. "You must stay still."

"I called you to help him." He searched her face. "Are you refusing?"

Her mouth went dry. She withdrew her hand.

Anchurus looked confused. Then his expression changed. "You are helping *her.*"

"That's not it," Denisia said.

"You have cursed him!" A raw coughing sound escaped his damaged throat. "He can no longer eat or drink. He will die."

"It was his wish," was all she managed to say.

A shadow descended over the prince's hazel eyes. He turned to the guards. "Take me back!" he shouted. "Now."

"Anchurus," Denisia pleaded, "listen to me. Your burns need the mud to heal. You must remain here a little longer."

"Get me away from her," he demanded. "Now!"

The two remaining guards lifted the platform and started to walk away. Anchurus' mouth twisted as they moved him, but he kept his jaw closed, his gaze focused on the night sky.

"Anchurus." Denisia watched them go, a fierce heat cutting through her chest. She wanted to follow, try to explain, but how could he understand her choosing her grandfather over the king? Or her desire to keep Anchurus safe from Katiah? *As if that's going well.* The mud would help, but he needed more. A burn remedy. Lavender flowers and rose water. Calendula and St. John's wort. She knew of an herbalist in the city.

She walked back toward the castle gate, the smell of smoke thick in the air, the burned grasses dissolving into ash under her feet.

"Where is Anchurus?" Midas demanded as he lifted himself on his elbows.

The boy offered more water while Xander stumbled over his words. "Denisia. She took him to the river, Your Majesty. To heal his wounds."

"How badly is he hurt?"

"We don't know yet, Your Majesty." Fotis leaned forward. Aster and Rastus came closer too, every one of them looking at the king with the same shocked expression.

"What are you all staring at?" he asked.

"We thought you were . . ." Rastus began.

"You appeared to have expired," Fotis finished for him.

"The boy had nothing to do with it," Aster said.

They all turned to the child.

"Tell us where you found the water," Rastus said.

The boy answered, but they didn't understand his gestures.

Midas motioned to the waterskin. The boy helped him to a long drink. "The curse has lifted?" Midas asked.

They all looked about uncomfortably. Finally, Fotis spoke: "I'm afraid this is no ordinary water, Your Majesty." He motioned to Rastus, who offered a little of his own water. The king sputtered and coughed out a coil of gold.

"You must show us where you got it," Rastus said to the boy.

"We'll go with him," Midas said.

They all watched in astonishment as their king started to get to his feet. Rastus stepped up to help. Midas panted with the effort, his form still emaciated and weak. His back to the charred remains of his gardens, he directed the boy to go ahead.

The child led them all onto the path that would take them to the castle doors. They proceeded slowly, keeping pace with the king, and had just reached the stone walkway when the two soldiers carrying the prince came up behind them.

"Father?" Anchurus struggled to raise his head.

"Anchurus!" Midas turned. "What is this?" He gestured toward his son's wounds.

"The only way to get her attention," Anchurus said.

"Who?" Midas asked.

"The goddess Denisia, sire," Fotis said.

Midas looked around. "Where is she?"

"At the river," Anchurus said in between another series of hoarse coughs. "Did she do this?" He pointed to Midas, glancing at Fotis.

"This was her doing," Aster said.

"She refused," Xander said.

"The child brought special water," Fotis said, "enough for your father to recover. *Temporarily*." He raised an eyebrow.

Anchurus looked at the boy, then lowered himself back down onto the platform. "She didn't help us."

"You expected her to?" Midas asked.

"It's why we did this." Xander watched the prince with sad eyes.

"*We*?" Midas glared at his youngest advisor.

Xander ducked behind Fotis.

"It was my idea," Anchurus said, but he was mumbling now.

Midas bade the guards to take his son inside. "He must not be left alone. Call the medicine woman immediately."

The guards marched up the path, carrying the prince between them. Fotis and Xander fell in line behind them. Midas nodded to the child, who once again took the lead. Aster stayed with Rastus, both of them flanking the king. The group continued to the main castle stairs. The king and his company waited as the guards carried the prince inside, Fotis and Xander following. Rastus and Aster were just about to start up with Midas when the heavy doors opened again and a man came stumbling out.

"Your Majesty." Emir stopped and bowed. "I must speak with you." He staggered down the steps.

"Alkan?" Midas said.

"You must go after them."

"Who?"

"The Olgun brothers."

"They're in the dungeon."

"They escaped." Emir panted as he came to a halt in front of them, his hair mussed on his head, blood and bruises all over his face. "They came into the castle. I tried to stop them." The child hurried to Emir's side and tried to brace him up. Emir patted the boy's shoulder. "Your Majesty, they've taken Zoe."

Midas stared at the musician. "Zoe is trapped in gold."

"They took her," Emir said. "I tried to stop them, but I failed. You must send men after them."

"Show me," Midas said.

Limping, Emir led them all inside the castle and down to the dining hall. Rastus lit the lamps at the entrance. Once they could see well enough, they made their way through to where Zoe's sculpture had stood. There was nothing there but a bare piece of golden floor.

"Send men after them, Your Majesty," Emir said again. "They haven't been gone long. We can still catch them."

Midas walked forward, his arms out as if by beseeching the air he might make his daughter reappear.

"I saw them," Emir repeated. "They took her."

Midas rotated, scanning the room until he'd turned full circle. He let his hands fall to his sides. The gold mitts clattered to the floor. Rastus ran to pick them up, but when he offered them, Midas ignored him. After two audible breaths, he turned and walked straight up to Emir. "Why didn't you come to me immediately?"

"I tried, Your Highness."

"I will go," Rastus said. "I will find her." He handed Aster the mitts and started out of the room.

"I will not assist him," Aster said, speaking for the first time since they'd entered the dining hall. "I do not know the road to the east. We cannot leave tonight."

"Wait," Midas said. "Rastus. Wait."

Rastus paused, Aster at his shoulder.

Midas leveled his gaze on Emir. "They escaped?" he asked.

"I encountered them here. As they were leaving."

Midas held him in an uncomfortable stare. "You used to fight for Sargon II."

"Yes."

"You are a deserter."

"Yes."

"And those hunters came here for you."

Emir hesitated. "Yes."

"Let me go, sire," Rastus said. "I will find her."

"It would not be wise for us to move immediately," Aster said. "The dark goddess will not deliver the princess to King Sargon II to use against us."

Midas shook his head. "We march to war tomorrow. Rastus, I need you here. Aster, you are an advisor, not a soldier."

Aster rested his hands on his hips and began to circle the room.

Midas kept his attention on Emir. "You say they will take her to Sargon. You must find them before they get to him." He addressed Rastus. "Send two of our best men with him."

"Yes, Your Majesty."

"Do not send me, Your Majesty," Aster said. "If they do not have to deal with the goddess, an advisor may not be helpful."

"Do you have a weapon to use against her?" Midas asked.

Aster exhaled in frustration.

"Alkan will go." Midas looked around for the boy. "Where did you get the water, son?"

The boy pointed to Emir.

"A warm spring to the northeast, Your Majesty," Emir said, a bit too eagerly. "In the mountains."

"*You* brought it?"

Emir looked from the boy to the king and nodded.

"How did you find it?"

Emir hesitated. "I had heard stories as a child," he said, "of a magical spring. I thought . . ."

Midas narrowed his eyes. The musician dropped his gaze. "Tell Aster where to find it," Midas said, "then go."

Emir bowed his head. Aster led him out, the boy hot on their heels. The king waited until they were gone, then turned to Rastus. "The armory," he said. "Now."

RASTUS LIT a torch on the wall, pulled a key from his pocket, and slid it into the tall wooden cupboard that stood in the corner of the armory. Holding the flame aloft, he stepped back, revealing the sword hanging inside.

Midas remembered the day Katiah had given it to him—the day she'd presented him to King Gordius and his wife, Queen Rhea. He was to appear a confident warrior, she'd told him, so he must have a weapon. He had worn it proudly when kneeling before his new parents. It had hung heavy and ungainly on his skinny waist, but he had learned to wield it. For years, he'd used it in battle. It had seen many a kill. Even after he'd become king, he'd used it, often riding out to fight with his commanders. The sword had served him well, and he'd viewed it as a protective talisman. It was only when Anchurus had reached maturity that Midas took a step back. He'd wanted to give his son enough room to develop his own reputation. He'd still worn the sword occasionally, but then Demodica had ordered all traces of Katiah removed. She hadn't been aware that his sword had come from the goddess, too, but Midas couldn't use it in good conscience after that, so he had locked it away.

Now, he looked upon it anew. When Katiah had presented it to him, she'd pointed out the gold inlays in the sword handle and suggested he call himself "the future King Midas." An heir to the throne could not be called Karem Savas, she'd explained. That was a lowly tribal name. *Midas* was the Greek word for "the touch of gold," an elevated name suitable for a king. He'd accepted it with pride back then. Ironic, he thought now.

"Bring it," he told Rastus. "When we ride to war, I will need it."

Rastus bowed his head. He hesitated before touching the sword, then tucked it under his cloak and locked the cupboard.

"One more thing," Midas said. "When you assign the men to go with Emir Alkan, instruct them to kill him at their discretion."

Rastus looked surprised.

"He is a traitor and a liar," Midas said. "If not for him, Zoe . . ." He stopped. "He is working for Katiah. Allow them to search in case they may overcome the thieves, but if the princess comes into Sargon's possession, they are to carry out their mission. Understood?"

Midas strode out the door, leaving Rastus to close it behind him.

CHAPTER
EIGHTEEN

Sargon rested his back against the stone wall that framed the lion's enclosure. He watched while Elanur and the two guards he'd assigned her arranged the elements. The fire pit came first, surrounded by a circle of rocks. One of the guards lit the kindling, and soon the flames were blazing. Elanur scented the air with herbs that gave off a spicy sweet aroma. She had changed into a heavy sand-colored robe tied at the waist, a crown of wildflowers twisted into her hair. She danced around the fire, making graceful, waving movements with her hands and chanting words Sargon didn't understand. The old dog she'd requested lay nearby. A necessary sacrifice, she'd insisted. With gray hairs around its eyes, it gazed at her with halfhearted interest.

Sargon glanced into the lion pen. Tai was there, lying under the shade of his tree, his gaze on Elanur as if he, too, thought her entrancing. Sargon smirked. The lion had good taste. He turned back to Elanur, wanted to ask how long this summoning spell would take, but she had a look of intense concentration on her face, her skin glowing by the light of the fire, so he let her be.

What would he say should the goddess appear? The last time

he'd seen her, she had admitted to helping Emir escape. She had also given him the sharpest pain he'd felt in years, then offered her help in defeating Midas. Interesting that she referred to it as the "final" battle. He tried to deduce what she was up to, but he couldn't figure it out. What prize awaited the goddess who helped him attain victory over the king to the west?

Elanur continued to chant, scattering herbs and beseeching the skies to bring the goddess to her. Bent at the waist, she moved her hands into the fire, lifted them with the smoke, then pushed them back down, making wind waves over the flames. She was like a snake in the water the way she swirled and straightened, and he found her fascinating. He could watch her dance all day if he wasn't so eager for the result.

The beast's breath whispered through the bars. "You can't have her, Tai," he murmured. "Behave yourself, and I'll feed you the dog when it's over."

The lion grunted and settled his heavy body on the ground. Sargon smiled to himself. The male had chosen to sit right behind him. Its presence there made Sargon feel stronger. With that strength, he realized what he must do: charm the goddess. Only by disarming her did he have any hope of getting the answers he needed.

Tai jerked. Sargon heard them too—the sound of heavy footsteps. Candana, his advisor. There was no less graceful a man in the kingdom.

"Your Majesty." Candana breathed heavily as he bowed low.

"What have you discovered?" Sargon asked.

"Little," Candana said, perspiration glistening on his upper lip. "She seems . . . omniscient."

Sargon's gaze rested on the flames. Elanur still danced around them, chanting, the old dog panting across from her, oblivious to its scheduled fate. "A weapon?" Sargon asked.

"No weapon will harm her, Your Majesty. At least, none that I could find a record of."

"Very well." Sargon waved his hand, eager to be rid of the man. Candana bowed again and lumbered away. Never had the king been so powerless against an enemy. Surely, the goddess had some sort of weakness. He was about to interrupt Elanur with the question when she paused and went to the dog. The animal wagged its tail. Elanur scratched it behind the ears, then glanced back at the guards. The taller one stepped up with a knife. He squatted down and took hold of the dog's neck.

"That will be quite enough."

The knife clattered onto the stones, and the guard ducked his head in submission. The dog wagged its tail and whined. Elanur dropped to her knees. Katiah had appeared, hovering over the middle of the fire like a spirit. She observed them all, then turned her gaze to Sargon. "Hello, darling. It seems you've missed me."

Denisia stood outside of Prince Anchurus' room, her arms full of herbs, roots, and jars of dried blossoms. The guards had denied her entrance. She gave them a whiff of the intoxicating aroma she'd applied to her fingers, and they became much more cooperative. The medicine woman had come and gone, they said, and now the prince was resting. She smiled seductively, offered them both a drink of wine, and then slipped past them.

A window against the far wall let in the early morning sunlight, the smell of smoke still in the air. Denisia shut the door behind her, then tiptoed across the room and set everything down on the bedside table. She needed to mix the ingredients into a poultice and cover his wounds. Anchurus lay on his back, wearing only a tunic that left his legs bare from the knee down, bandages covering the skin. Taking water from the nearby basin, Denisia went to work as quietly as she could. She had been at it only a short while when she sensed the prince's gaze on her.

"Father?" he croaked.

"He's alive," she said. His brown eyes looked mucky, his skin ghastly white. She stirred the powders, roots, and leaves together.

"You?" he asked.

She shook her head. "The boy brought water the king could drink."

Anchurus shifted his weight and winced, arching his spine.

"Be still," she said. "This will help."

He peered at the wooden bowl. "You can go." When she ignored him, he tried to sit up.

"You must rest," she said.

He sat up anyway, crying out at one point. Frustrated, he glared at his bandages as if pondering how he might beat them into submission. After another few breaths, he swung his legs off the bed.

"Are you trying to kill yourself?" she asked.

"My boots," he demanded.

Denisia set the completed mixture down on the nightstand. "They were burned."

"Bring me boots!" he shouted at the door. Footsteps hustled away down the hall. "I don't need your . . ." He glanced at the mixture. "Concoctions. If you still refuse to help Father, then go."

"Anchurus, please," she said. "It was his wish. Besides, if I cure him, I will lose Silenus."

"What does your grandfather have to do with it?"

"He's better now. Like he was."

"I don't know what you're talking about."

She glanced down at her hands. She didn't want to admit she'd made a deal with Katiah. "If I help the king, Grandfather will be sick again. As sick as he was the night of the party, or worse."

"What does . . .?" Anchurus searched her face. "Why would . . .?" He stopped, his breath coming fast with the pain.

"The king's wish and my grandfather's health," she said. "They are connected."

He narrowed his eyes. "You *did* make a deal with the dark goddess. That's why she was there. Not just to *meet* you."

"It was the first time I met her!" Denisia stirred the mixture.

"You failed to tell me the rest of the story."

"You don't understand."

Anchurus exhaled heavily. "It matters not. He is the king."

"So, what, he's more valuable?"

"Yes!" When she didn't agree, he looked around again and spotted another pair of boots across the room by his trunk. Slowly, he pushed himself toward the edge of the bed.

"What are you doing?" she asked.

The balls of his feet settled on the stone. He squinted, his eyes weeping. "Get out."

"I can't do what you want me to do. Please understand."

"Then get out!" He glared at her, his neck turning red.

Overcome, she left the bowl on the nightstand, wrapped her cloak around her, and exited the room. As she hurried down the hall, a sob escaped her throat. She covered her mouth and willed the tears to stay in her eyes. Near the stairwell, she spotted a servant coming up with another basin of steaming water.

"There is a mixture on the prince's nightstand," she said, touching the girl's arm. "Apply it with clean fingers. Add more water if you need to. Then wrap new bandages. Do it immediately. Do you understand?"

She feared the young woman wouldn't accept her authority, but she nodded as if she did. Denisia stepped aside to let her pass, then flew down the stairs. When she reached the first level, she ran into an old woman carrying a tray of food. It was the head cook, Pilar. Denisia remembered her from the birthday festivities.

"Where is the king?" Denisia asked.

Pilar looked her over, her small gray eyes discerning. "So you're still here."

Denisia blinked. "The king?"

"He's gathering his army."

"For what?"

"To go after that fiend, of course!"

"Who?"

"King Sargon." Pilar leaned closer. "Will you help him?"

"He's going now?" Denisia asked.

"Haven't you heard? They've taken the princess."

"Taken her? What do you mean?"

"Sargon's hunters." Pilar walked past her and started up the stairs. "Did it during the fire."

"Zoe's gone?"

"As if it weren't bad enough the poor thing was turned to gold."

Turned to gold! Denisia placed her hand against the wall. No wonder the prince was so angry.

"The king will get her back," Pilar said. "If he can last that long." She continued on up.

"The king," Denisia called.

"In his strategy room," Pilar answered. "He doesn't like to be disturbed there."

Denisia reversed direction, her feet gliding under her dress. She didn't stop to think how Midas would feel seeing her again. She simply climbed up the stairs to the third level and ran down the hall. At the door to the strategy room, she was generous with her wine, wiggling her scented fingers under the guards' noses. They stood by sleepily while she charged inside.

The king was at his battle table, his commanders surrounding him, all of them poring over the plans he had laid out. Denisia was so struck by the change in him she remained near the doorway, speechless. His face looked drawn, his cloak sagging on his shoulders. His skin was pale and dull on his cheeks, yet his eyes flashed when they found her.

"Seize her!" he said in a weak voice.

The door guards, jerked awake by their king's order, stepped in and took hold of Denisia's arms. She fought against them, but they held fast, their thick fingers digging into her flesh.

"How dare you come here now?" the king said, his glare etched in fury.

"Your Majesty," she said, "I came to stop the prince."

"You were too late."

"He's still alive."

"Barely!" Midas turned back to his battle figures.

"You can't let him go with you."

"He's not going."

"He was asking for his boots."

The king moved a figure on the table. "You will not lift the curse?"

"I can't."

He set the figure down with a decisive slap.

"Your Majesty," she said, "once you made the wish—"

"Take her," Midas interrupted. "To the dungeon."

"Your Majesty," she said, "I may be able to assist you—"

Midas turned his back on her.

The guards pulled her out of the room.

"Your Majesty! Wait!"

They took her back down the stairs, through a narrow breezeway, and into another stairwell, this one narrow and steep. The air smelled of dirt, fire, and human waste. Blackness surrounded her until she reached the last step, where two oil lamps glowed in a dark area beyond. They pulled her in, then dragged her all the way to the back and dumped her into a dark cell, securing the heavy wooden door behind her. She waited until their footsteps receded, then curled into the corner and wept.

"Will you stop that infernal noise?" Fotis lay flat on his bed. "I'm trying to rest."

Xander sang a little louder, belting out an old drinking song while mixing a new concoction at his table. "The army fought the battle long, and all believed them done and gone," he crooned, "but then the king rose from the dark, and oh, he lives! Aliiiiiive!" Xander thrust his fist high. "Aliiive he is, the soldiers cried, and on they fought o'er those who'd died, but proud the king he rode ahead, and called the charge. Attaaaaack!"

Fotis groaned and rolled toward the wall. "It is barely dawn. You could have waited."

"We don't have time to wait," Xander said.

"We just got to bed," Fotis said.

"The king is alive! He returns to claim his land, and time waits not for any man."

"Oh, shut up," Fotis said.

Under his blankets, Aster hadn't budged.

"He rides to war, you know," Xander said.

Fotis opened his one eye. "He what?"

"They went straight from fighting the fire to readying for battle."

Fotis sat up on one elbow. "Today?"

"Look for yourself." Xander gestured toward the window.

Fotis heaved a great sigh and got out of bed. Wearing only a long nightshirt, he shuffled to the window. Below, soldiers mingled over the castle grounds. Some of them engaged in practice fighting, while others stuffed their saddle packs with supplies. Servants darted in and out, their arms full of packed food that they distributed among the men. The entire scene was rushed activity, as if everyone were already behind.

"But the king is still weak," Fotis said.

"They took his daughter," Xander said. "So we go to war." He sprinkled something else into his bowl.

Fotis returned to his corner of the room to get dressed. Aster staggered to the water basin to wash.

"What are you making, anyway?" Fotis said.

"It's for the prince," Xander said, peering over the parchment that lay on the table beside him.

"The prince?" Fotis laughed. "He's not going anywhere."

"The king posted guards outside his room," Xander said.

Fotis pulled a long tunic over his head and tied it with a belt at his waist. "Good." He set about moisturizing and placing his wooden eye. When he had gotten it securely into the socket, a slow frown crossed his face. "What are you up to?"

Xander poured brown goo from a bottle into his mixture and stirred some more.

"I hope not another disaster like last night," Fotis said.

Xander stopped stirring. Aster stopped washing. The room filled with silence. Several moments passed before Xander started stirring again.

"I apologize," Fotis said. "But you must learn—"

"She came," Xander said, interrupting him.

"The goddess failed to come," Aster said at nearly the same time.

"So she came." Fotis ladled himself a cup of fresh water. "But she did nothing. She intends to do nothing. It was the musician who saved the king. Calling the goddess did nothing but create ruin and nearly kill our prince."

Xander's face turned red. He retrieved a wide cup from the shelves under the table and poured his thick muddy concoction into it.

"Just because you can do a thing doesn't mean you should," Fotis said.

"You knew she would remain unmoved," Aster said.

"I gathered she would," Fotis said. "We heard her make the deal, remember? Her grandfather is too important to her."

"She loves the prince," Xander grumbled.

"She's a goddess. They play with men all the time." Fotis swallowed the last of the water. "She's no better than Katiah. They're all the same. I hope *that* has nothing to do with her." He pointed to Xander's cup of goo.

Aster dug into his trunk for clean clothes.

"I told you," Xander said. "It's for the prince."

"I still don't see why you had to wake us all up for it."

Xander finished scraping the bowl. The cup was now full of the brown mix. He started putting everything else away. When his table was clear again, he lifted his gaze to Fotis. "We have to stop the king. If he sets out on this path, it will not turn out well."

Fotis exhaled in frustration. "Defeating Sargon seems to be the key to everything. I don't see why—"

"He hasn't had another vision." Aster stepped forward in pants and a long-sleeved linen shirt, his hair combed and damp, his beard glistening with water drops.

"Is that it?" Fotis asked.

Xander walked to his corner of the room.

"Well?" Fotis said.

Xander started making his bed.

"You're being a child."

Xander finished and straightened the items on his nightstand. Once everything was in order, he took his messy apron off, hung it from the hook on the wall, and changed his shirt. Refreshed, he raked his fingers through his fine brown hair, patted his cheeks, and walked toward the door, picking up the prince's cup on the way.

"Where are you going?" Fotis said.

"To the prince."

"Did you have a vision or not?"

"Obviously you don't want to hear about it."

"Oh, for the sake of the gods." Fotis rolled his one eye. "Tell me."

"I think not. It will be one more thing for you to berate me with."

"Berate? I have done no berating!"

"I agree," Aster said, "you never berate."

Fotis nodded his acknowledgment, then realized Aster wasn't supporting him. He huffed and followed Xander to the door. "I merely point out that you must be more cautious. You get something in your head and you fly off a cliff."

"I'm a constant disappointment." Xander opened the door.

"I didn't say that."

Xander strode into the hall.

"Xander, get back here!" Fotis said.

Aster strapped his dagger to his belt and followed the young advisor out.

"You too?" Fotis threw up his hands. Soon he remained in the room all by himself. "Vision smision," he muttered. "If the king wants to go to war, he'll go to war." He sighed heavily, then relented, following the other two. He didn't get far. They had stopped in the hallway. The prince stood in front of them, sweat pouring down the sides of his temples.

"Something for the pain," he said through gritted teeth. "Now, please."

Emir slapped himself across the cheek. It was past dawn, and his eyelids were heavy, his body sagging in the saddle. They'd been riding all night, having left soon after he'd spoken to the king. Two men he didn't know rode with him: Selim and Arda. Selim was the sterner of the two, with dark hair and thick eyebrows that made him look like he was always frowning. Arda was the more innocent, his gaze taking everything in but following Selim's lead. They were both trim, fit soldiers and would probably be helpful in a pinch, though Emir doubted they could best the Olgun brothers should they come upon them. He was still nursing his wounds from the last time. Besides, he thought, the men were probably more like chaperones. What they had planned for him wasn't hard to guess from the way the king had reacted. Emir might have fared better if he'd told the truth—that Katiah had led him to the water. Either way, he was doomed no matter which king he served.

He could try to escape, but there were two of them, and they rode swifter horses than his. Something they'd arranged on purpose, he was certain. So here he was, traveling back toward Sargon, the very direction he'd vowed never to go again, with two men intent on killing him whenever they thought it convenient.

His only way out, at least at the moment, was to find the princess. He urged his heavyset horse into a canter. The other two followed suit. They traveled up a long sloping hill, dust billowing out behind them. Upon reaching the top, they paused to take in the view. There was the road below, twisting and turning as it flowed down the hill, moved to the right to skirt another rise, and extended straight on into the distance. In the gray light of morning, it was just visible between the grassy flats and rocky outcroppings, a stretch of earth a little darker than the rest.

"What's that?" Arda asked, pointing.

"Your mother," Selim said. "She's making you dinner."

Arda dropped his hand, then raised it again. "There. See?"

Emir followed the young man's line of sight. He could make out nothing but the path at first, but then he spotted it, the small cloud of dust. "That's them. Come on!"

The three thundered abreast down the hill. Emir hadn't considered that the sculpture would slow the Olgun brothers down, but of course, it had. He touched the hilt of his sword, his heartbeat quickening. He might rescue Zoe after all and return her to the king. Silly, the joy this thought gave him. Stupid to imagine that he could regain the king's favor, especially now that he'd lied to him. Perhaps, though, he could be redeemed. The boy would like that.

"Katiah." Sargon opened his arms wide. "I'm glad you came."

Katiah glanced at Elanur, then knelt by the dog and petted its head. "I don't understand why people insist on killing them in my name."

"But I thought—" Elanur began.

"I know." Katiah rubbed the animal's ears. "Go on now," she said, pointing down the pathway. "Go home." The dog obeyed, lumbering its way out of the animal enclosure. Katiah stood up and observed Elanur. "You wished to see me?"

Elanur turned to Sargon.

"Oh," Katiah said. "Well. Perhaps you should leave us."

Elanur hesitated.

"Don't worry," Katiah said. "He'll behave."

Elanur walked past, giving the king a wide berth. Once she was clear, she looked back at Katiah. The goddess gave her a sweet smile, so she kept walking, one of Sargon's guards following her. When they had disappeared onto the pathway beyond, Katiah's smile faded. "You have changed your mind?"

"Changed?" Sargon glanced after Elanur. "Perhaps." He took a breath. "You helped my son escape, and now you're protecting his mother. I'd simply like to understand these things before going to war."

"So you will ride to battle as we planned?" Katiah waved her hand over the fire. It blazed and receded according to the direction of her palm. "That is wise, for Midas rides out to meet you tonight."

Sargon's eyebrow shot up. It was all the surprise he would allow.

"He's managed to gather some assistance," Katiah said. "Doubled his numbers, though I'm not sure how skilled they are."

Another surprise. "We should have moved earlier."

She stopped playing with the fire and walked toward him. For a time, the flames seemed to follow, licking at the hem of her dress before receding again into the pit. "All will be well," she said. "Despite your former rudeness, I am bringing you a gift." She sauntered closer, a soft glow emanating from her skin. "The hunters you sent to capture Emir? They are making their way back to you now."

"The Olgun brothers?" Sargon turned his body as she approached, his left shoulder toward her. "They got him?"

"They got something much better."

"I ordered them to—"

"King Midas' daughter." She watched the surprise he couldn't hide spread across his face.

"The princess?"

"You will use her as a bargaining chip."

"The king's only daughter." Sargon thought about that. "And Emir?"

She looked at Tai, who lay at the edge of his enclosure, licking his foreleg. "We all have to make sacrifices."

"I don't like the idea of sacrificing my son."

"You're getting the kingdom of Gordium with the princess as a bonus. I think that's enough, don't you?" She reached through the bars. Tai sniffed her flesh. A low growl sounded from her right. She jerked her head. Zehra had made a stealthy approach.

Sargon battled with himself. He would not give up his son. Still, it would do no good to say that out loud. "Will you join us when we ride?" he asked instead.

"I will come when it's time." She stroked Tai's nose. Zehra uttered another low growl. "I want you to bring her."

Sargon cast a dubious look at the lioness.

Katiah rolled her eyes and withdrew her hand. "Elanur. She must go with you to battle."

"She is a slave!"

"Don't be so shocked, darling. You've ridden with her before."

Sargon's throat tightened. Once again, he was a young man, the image of the dark goddess' terrifying face flashing in front of his eyes.

"I've seen how you look at her." Katiah walked back toward the fire. It had calmed, the smaller flames offering a peaceful light. "It's what you want, for her to witness your great triumph. You see, darling, I'm making all your dreams come true."

It took him some time to recover. "She is nothing compared to you," he said.

Katiah acknowledged that with a lift of one shoulder. "When you ride out, head toward Karama, and bring Elanur with you. And, darling"—she paused, her back to him—"it's not wise to attempt to deceive a god. It never turns out well." She took a few steps and then disappeared into a swirling fog.

CHAPTER NINETEEN

The king's advisors stared at the prince. He was standing in the hallway outside of their room, his face shiny with perspiration. Xander handed over his mug of muddy goo. Anchurus swallowed it in three gulps and pressed his forearm to his lips as if to keep the stuff from coming back up.

"What will that do?" he said, returning the mug.

"Numb the pain, Your Highness, but only for a limited time. You will need more."

"Make more," Anchurus said. "Enough for several days. Pack it for travel."

"Several days?" Xander asked. "But that will take time, Your Highness. We need more raw materials—"

"How much time?"

"A day at least?"

"That will not do." The prince's shoulders rose with his breath. "Make as much as you can and deliver it to me by nightfall."

"But—"

Anchurus cast him a curt glare.

"Of course, Your Highness." Xander bowed his head.

The advisors watched as their prince walked away. His body jerked with every step, the pain riding an invisible line from his heels up through his spine and into his shoulders.

Xander strode back inside and set up his table once more. The other two followed, Fotis closing the door behind him. He and Aster stood by as Xander retrieved all the ingredients he'd just put away. Then he flattened the parchment and turned to Fotis.

"It's a simple recipe," he said. "Might you get it started? I'll be back soon."

"Where are you going?" Fotis asked.

"He's not going to talk to the king," Aster said.

"What about?" Fotis said.

Xander dusted off his hands and hurried out of the room without answering.

"He's going to get himself into trouble," Fotis grumbled. "Get *us* into trouble."

"Much better for the king to go to war." Aster ambled over and picked up the parchment.

"He will go to war anyway," Fotis grumbled. "We can't stop that."

"And we shouldn't try," Aster said.

"What good does it do to try?" Fotis plopped down on the edge of Aster's mattress while Aster started to measure ingredients into the bowl. "Who knows how much time he has left, but however much that is, he's going to spend it chasing after his enemy."

Aster stirred and consulted the parchment again.

"You can't make enough to last him through all this," Fotis said.

"It's amazing what I can do all by myself," Aster said.

Fotis stroked his long beard. "You think Xander can stop him?"

"Like we can stop the rain," Aster said.

"Then why in the name of the gods didn't you say anything?"

"We are not advisors," Aster said. "We are not to advise the king."

Fotis thought about that for a minute. "But if we know he's going to ignore that advice—"

"We are not advisors," Aster interrupted. "That is not our job." He added a little water to the mixture and stirred again.

Fotis scratched his temple. A long sigh escaped his lips. Finally, he stood up and crossed the room. From the opposite wall, he pulled a smaller table and set it up next to Xander's where Aster was working. He consulted the parchment, then got his own big bowl and began measuring ingredients into it. Aster lifted his gaze to his friend's.

"Pass me the willow bark, please," Fotis asked.

Aster handed over the leather satchel. Fotis took it and, without a word, removed one piece of bark and crushed it into his bowl.

DENISIA SAT in the corner of the dungeon cell, her shoulder pressed against the stone wall. Now and then she heard a distant thump overhead or a soldier's call drifting down from the castle grounds. But mostly it was silent, that deep sort of silence that comes when one is burrowed low into the rock, hidden away from the rest of the world.

She hadn't tried to escape. After shedding her tears, she'd retreated into the corner and allowed the stone and dirt to hold her, her body sinking into it as if she were a fungal parasite happily existing in the dark and dank, the silence like a balm in her ears. Strange, perhaps, that she was comfortable in the dungeon, happy to be hidden away.

So it was that Katiah found her. Denisia was so lost inside herself that she hardly noticed her sister at first, registering only the white glow that briefly illuminated the cell, leaving the dark goddess in its wake.

"Oh, my dear Denisia." Katiah clucked her tongue. "What has our king done to you now? And you had such faith in him."

Denisia avoided her gaze.

"And did you *see* what they did to his magnificent garden?" Katiah gasped. "I didn't think until this moment how that must have affected you." She stepped back and leaned against the wall. "Who would destroy such beauty? Surely no one who knows you. They would understand how much pain it would cause you, you being the goddess of the natural world. I can't begin to imagine who might have taken such a dastardly action."

Denisia lazily turned her head. "What do you want, Katiah?"

"Only to see how my sister is doing."

"*Half*-sister."

Katiah blinked innocently.

"You've come to help me out of here?" Denisia asked.

"Oh, I wouldn't dare underestimate you," Katiah said. "If you wanted out, you'd be out. What's more intriguing is why you've stayed in." She turned to examine the surrounding walls. "I can only imagine it has something to do with that handsome prince of yours."

"He's not mine," Denisia said.

"Do you mean to say he's fair game?"

"Stay away from him!" Denisia cast her a warning glare. "He's endured enough without your meddling."

"Endured? What did the poor boy endure?"

Denisia pulled herself to her feet. "If you're not here to help, then leave."

"I wondered how you're getting along is all." Katiah finger-combed a lock of her hair. "If maybe you might be feeling a little better about our deal."

"Better?" Denisia asked, incredulous.

"You didn't believe I would help your grandfather. And then you were so worried about what the wish might do to the mighty King Midas, and, of course, his son. From what I've seen so far, they've only benefited from it."

"Benefited? The king nearly died. And the prince nearly died trying to save him!"

"So *that's* why he threw you in here," Katiah said.

"He didn't *throw* me," Denisia said.

Katiah smirked. "So they burned the gardens to get you to lift the spell. Is that right? But you said the prince endured something. What was that?"

Denisia didn't answer.

"Let me think," Katiah said. "Did he burn himself too? My, what a man will do to get your attention."

Denisia grimaced, squeezing her eyes shut.

"You got here in time to save him," Katiah said, "but still you refused to save the king." She shook her head. "He must have been so disappointed. I have to admire you, Sister. You're a woman of your word."

"My actions are for Silenus," Denisia said.

Katiah raised her hands in surrender. "As long as you hold firm to our deal, your grandfather will remain in only the best of health."

"While the king dies." Denisia examined the walls, wondering how she might make her exit. "You will do nothing to end his torture?"

"It is not my spell he's under," Katiah said.

Denisia rolled her eyes. "As if that matters."

"Of course it does," Katiah said. "I don't have the powers you do."

Denisia crossed her arms over her chest, unconvinced.

"I did ease it a bit," Katiah said. "Surely you didn't think the child saved him?"

"You will take credit for saving his life?" Denisia asked.

"For the moment," Katiah said.

"Why not for good?"

Katiah laughed again. "Can you be so naive? It is *your* curse. I have no power over the elements. Gold. Silver. Iron. You are the goddess of the earthly things."

"Yet you hold me hostage to this deal," Denisia said. "You could let me out of it, allow Silenus to live well."

Katiah smoothed an eyebrow. "I don't know why you're so worried about it. It was the king's wish, not yours."

"You care not that he goes to war?" Denisia asked.

"It's what his heart desires," Katiah said. "Thanks to your gift, he now has the means to make his one dream come true, the one he's longed for ever since he was a boy. Of course, back then I thought I'd be the one to help him, but no matter. He'll get to see the consequences of his decisions."

"Is that what this is about?" Denisia asked, dropping her arms. "You're *jealous?*"

"Don't flatter yourself," Katiah said. "This isn't about you. It's about loyalty and gratitude, characteristics the great King Midas failed to develop despite my best intentions."

"*Your* intentions?" Denisia asked.

Katiah's eyes flashed. "If not for me, he'd have been dead long ago!"

The room darkened. Startled, Denisia looked around, then turned back to her sister. Katiah's cheeks had reddened, showing a startling contrast to the rest of her fair skin. The light that had emanated from her had dimmed as well, accentuating the blackness of her eyes. She scowled at Denisia before stepping back to compose herself. Pulling a napkin from her bosom, she patted her brow. "You'll watch after the handsome prince," she said, "despite everything?"

"There is no need," Denisia said, eyeing the goddess warily.

"Oh?" Katiah asked.

"He won't be going to war."

"Come, come." Katiah chuckled. "You really must stop being so naive. Your handsome prince seeks remedies even now to help him manage the pain."

Denisia looked doubtful.

"Go see for yourself," Katiah said. "Then tell me how wonderful King Midas is, that his only son believes he must approach death's door for him. As if nearly giving his life on the burning post wasn't enough." She smoothed her hair back from her face. "It is too bad sweet Zoe got caught up in all this. She's the only one of the lot who's worth anything."

After a long parting gaze, Katiah moved to the door. Her dress shimmered, and then her body transformed into a fog that disappeared into the wood.

Denisia thought over her sister's words. Anchurus, trying to go to war? She must check on him. She surveyed the cell for something she might use to force the door open, but there was nothing. She was trapped. Panic licked at the edges of her mind until she remembered that she had moved through the earth from Mount Nysa to Gordium. Surely, she could escape from a simple dungeon.

She closed her eyes and calmed her breathing. When she felt centered again, she walked over and leaned against the door. Cut from thick pine, the wood was old, stiff, and lacking any living essence, but she could still feel the fibers within it. She clung to them as she fought her way through, her shoulder gradually melting into it, then her ribs and hip. As her cheek came near, she squinted her eyes shut. It was nauseating, as if she were coming apart from the center out, so she forced her mind to focus on the other side of the door where freedom lay.

When the guard came to deliver her evening meal, he found an empty cell.

A SHORT TIME LATER, Denisia hurried down the road from the castle to the city of Gordium covered in the same dark cloak she'd worn before, the hood pulled low over her forehead. It was warm for the afternoon, but she was glad to be disguised. She could move faster that way.

Her feet kicked up dust as she turned into the third alleyway between the dwellings. Laurel leaf and sage. A dense bush. A cat. These reminders she kept at the forefront of her thoughts. It wasn't long before the hair stood up on her arms. She stopped and looked left. There. The same bush, though the blooms she'd created had already wilted.

The dwelling looked lifeless. She took a deep breath and knocked three times. No answer. The same as before. She tried again. Nothing.

Following a hunch, she walked around to the back side. There, she found a narrow opening just wide enough to slip through. Turning sideways, she shuffled along, the stone and dried mud pressing against her. Ahead, she spotted what she was looking for. Another door, this one much slimmer than the first. She knocked. "Lady Verna, it's Denisia. I must speak with you. Please." She paused, but heard nothing on the other side. "It's Denisia. Silenus' granddaughter. I need your help."

The door creaked opened. Small blue eyes peered out.

"Lady Verna?" Denisia asked.

The woman retreated inside, leaving the door open.

"I'm sorry to bother you again," Denisia said.

"It is time." The old woman's voice was thin, the words tremulous in her throat. She walked with a stooped posture, the candle flame flickering precariously.

Denisia followed until she stood in what appeared to be the main room of the dwelling. There was the familiar scent of sage, though she detected a trace of bergamot too, a pleasant addition. There were no windows and only two candles burning—the one Lady Verna had set on the table in front of her and another by the wall on Denisia's right.

"You've grown up," the old woman said, taking her seat.

"You knew me before?"

"You were a wilted sapling," Lady Verna said. "'Twas all I could do to keep your heart beating."

"What do you mean?" Denisia sat down at the table across from her.

"He brought you here," Lady Verna said. "Begged me to save your life."

"Who did?" Denisia asked.

"Your grandfather. Who else? You don't remember?"

Denisia's gaze darted about. Silenus had brought her here?

"And now you've come back," Lady Verna said, "because you've messed it up."

"Messed what up?" Denisia asked.

"You were an innocent child." Lady Verna swept the table as if dusting off crumbs. Her face was haggard and thin, with only a few faded hairs left in her eyebrows. "You were in pain. Hot with fever. I suppose it's no surprise you can't remember." She lifted her hand and traced Denisia's face in the air. "A shame. Children rarely remember their parents' sacrifices." She cocked her head. "Or their grandparents'."

"Sacrifices?" Denisia asked.

Lady Verna reached into a small cabinet that sat against the wall. "Smell this."

Denisia brought it to her nose. Laurel leaf.

"Close your eyes." Lady Verna drew her hands down through the air and started humming, a wavering sound that fought its way over tired vocal cords. "Poor little child is so sick," she crooned. "Grandfather wants her well, but nothing comes for free. Extract it from me, he said. And so it was."

Denisia was lying on a flat surface, animal fur soft against her back. A younger Lady Verna sat on one side of her, Silenus on the other. The two of them were holding her hands. Her body was hot and sweating, her head hurt, and she was having trouble breathing. She saw the worry in Silenus' eyes. He looked from her face to the witch, and there it was, a slight nod. *Yes.* Lady Verna took his offered hand and began to chant.

"And so it has been," Lady Verna said, interrupting her thoughts, "until now."

Denisia opened her eyes. The dark dwelling surrounded her once again. The vision had been so real! "What did he sacrifice?" she asked.

Lady Verna looked surprised at the question. "How many immortals do you know who suffer from soft mind?"

"*You* did that? You did that to him?"

The witch's expression hardened. "He wanted to save your life.

One doesn't conjure life out of the air. There must be an energy source."

Denisia's body felt hot again, her breath trapped in her chest.

"If he hadn't brought you to me, you wouldn't have survived." Lady Verna looked down at the table. "Perhaps that would have been better."

"Better than what you did to him," Denisia said.

"I did nothing but what he wanted," Lady Verna snapped. "I was the conduit. That was all. And I delayed the effects of the spell. That's why you had time to get to know him as he was." She pointed a long finger. "I didn't have to do that."

Denisia turned away. She couldn't feel gratitude for the woman who had stolen her grandfather's mind, no matter what the reason.

"He should have reminded you of what occurred," Lady Verna said. "Then maybe you wouldn't have gone and made a mess of it."

"You keep saying that," Denisia said. "Why?"

"You've interfered with the dark forces." The witch glared at her. "Disturbed the sacrifice. Now you expect *me* to fix it for you. A goddess—even a *half* goddess—should know better." She got up from her chair. Taking the candle with her, she shuffled across the room to a heavy wooden desk tucked away in the far corner. "Now where did I put it?" she muttered.

Denisia perused her surroundings, letting her gaze roam over the dilapidated couch against the wall, the waist-high wolf carving next to it, the dead potted tree on her right, and the shelves full of ceramic jars and bowls opposite her. So long had she wondered how Silenus could have become ill. *Soft mind.* Immortals didn't fall victim to such things. Now she knew. The weight of his sacrifice settled heavily onto her shoulders.

Lady Verna returned to the table with a small wooden box. She placed it between them. "This is what you came here for. To fix your mess. It's the best I can do."

The box was made of polished hazel wood with strange markings on the top, dark symbols that had been burned into the surface. "But how will this help?" Denisia asked.

"You've used the dark forces to take your grandfather's sacrifice away," Lady Verna said. "In doing so, you've adhered those forces to you. They now feed on the misery of those you love. Everything that has gone wrong since then can be traced to your action. If you want to change it, listen carefully."

Denisia sobered. Everything, her fault. The king's failing health. The burning gardens. Anchurus' wounds, Zoe's imprisonment and kidnapping, and the war to come. All because she had granted one wish. One wish Katiah had encouraged her to grant.

"Gather them all together," Lady Verna said. "Everyone who has a part to play in this mess you've created. Once they're all present, open the box and speak the words."

Denisia started to ask what words, but Lady Verna held up her hand.

"Once the words are spoken, the box will open a cavern. Into it must go what is most precious to the one you have cursed. When the cavern is satisfied, the curse will be broken, and all will return to as it was."

"It wasn't a curse," Denisia said. "It was a wish."

Lady Verna stared at her with a flat expression.

"I can take the wish back myself," Denisia said.

"So why haven't you?"

"Because Silenus will suffer again."

Lady Verna sat back in her chair. "Then why are you here? You've already made up your mind."

"But Anchurus . . ." Denisia started.

Lady Verna arched an eyebrow. "Lift the curse and the king lives," she said. "Surely the prince would be pleased?"

"But he may still . . . I'm afraid he's going to die."

Lady Verna shook her head. "As long as the dark forces cling to you, more will die. This is your chance to right your wrongs. To return things to the way they were."

"I can't." Denisia stood up. "Grandfather is well now. He's like he was before. He's . . ."

The old woman reached into the sleeve of her dress and withdrew a rolled parchment secured with a red ribbon. "When the time comes, open that," she said, handing it over. "The pronunciation will become clear to you."

Denisia stared at the parchment. When she didn't take it, Lady Verna set it on the table and picked up the candle.

"I trust you can find your way out." With a low hum in her throat, she walked across the room.

"Wait," Denisia said. "There must be another way?"

The old woman retreated into a dark space, pulling a drape closed behind her. "You showed so much promise as a girl," she said sadly.

Silence fell, the remaining flame flickering against the wall. Denisia waited for a while, but the witch did not return. Finally, she snatched up the box and the parchment, stashed them both inside her cloak, and made her way out of the dwelling. At the old bush, she paused and looked down. The sculpture was there, the cat as lifeless as the stone.

CHAPTER TWENTY

King Midas exited his strategy room and started down the hallway. Hearing footsteps, he glanced up to see his son emerging from the stairwell. The king paused and observed as Anchurus walked toward him, pain visibly radiating through his body with every heel strike. It was like watching a dog pick its way over hot stones.

"What are you doing?" Midas asked.

Anchurus stopped and stared at his father, perspiration shining on his forehead. "Are you all right?"

"How in the name of the gods are you walking around?" Midas looked at his son's legs, his burned feet concealed within his boots.

"They've been tended to," Anchurus said, reading his gaze.

"No." Midas shook his head. "You're not going. We need you here. The kingdom needs its prince."

"Since when do you fight the battles and I stay in the castle?"

"Come." Midas led the prince back to the strategy room. Inside, he took his seat at the conference table. Anchurus lowered himself down opposite him, his jaw clenched, the tendons taut in his neck.

"Listen to me." Midas leaned forward. "They found water I can drink, but that is all. I still cannot eat. It's given me, at best, a few more days."

"Where was the water from?" Anchurus asked. "Perhaps we can find food—"

"This is a curse from a goddess," Midas interrupted. "Only the goddess can lift it. There is no other remedy."

Anchurus pursed his lips. "We will force her. Entrap her."

Midas shook his head. "You can't force a goddess to do anything. Listen, I'm going to move forward with the plan. I will defeat Sargon. You and Zoe . . ." He paused. "You will rule over the new peaceful kingdom of Phrygia. There will be no more wars. You can have a family. Children."

"So that's it, then." Anchurus threw up one hand. "You're going off to die in battle. What about Zoe?"

"The hunters are taking her to Sargon," Midas said. "Once he is defeated, we will get her back."

"But she'll still be as she was."

"I've tasked Timon and the advisors with that." Midas tried to lace his fingers but couldn't. They were still covered in the mitts. "Perhaps when I'm gone—"

"The curse will be lifted?" Anchurus interrupted. "Everything will go back to normal? I doubt that's how it works. We must find leverage against her now. A way to compel her to comply with our wishes. Her grandfather is her weakness."

Midas leaned back in his chair. "Silenus is a kind old man. But if the curse lingers after I'm gone, you must do what's necessary." He considered his son. "It's why I need you here. You are not the man to lead this army. Not now."

Anchurus bristled. "And you are? You're going to ride out there and what, rally the men two seconds before Sargon's arrow takes you?"

"I've asked Baran to lead."

The prince tapped a finger on the armrest. "Very well. Send Baran. You stay here with me."

"I can't do that," Midas said.

"If I'm not up for battle, then neither are you."

"You have many years in front of you. I have days."

"You would choose to spend them on the battlefield?"

"I would choose to look my enemy in the eye. See him fall. I would choose one more chance to see if my—" He stopped.

Anchurus waited, but his father said no more. "If you have only days to live," the prince asked, "then why Sargon? This isn't just about territory."

The old memory flashed in Midas' mind, the young soldier glaring down at him from atop his magnificent stallion, Elanur trapped in front of him. "He took something from me," he said. "I want him to pay for it."

"What?" Anchurus asked. "What did he take?"

His last moments with his son. He should be honest. But he'd buried the secret so deep inside him it was difficult to unearth. He glanced at the last chair at the end of the table. He'd found Anchurus there when he was only five years old, playing a wooden flute. Even at that age, the boy had made beautiful music with it. "It was all a very long time ago," he said. "I don't want to talk about it now."

"Why not let it go?" Anchurus said. "Say a proper goodbye to the people. Live out the rest of your life with us in the castle where you belong."

It was the closest his son would ever come to pleading with him. The gesture touched Midas deeply. He wanted to tell him so. Instead, he stood up and set his chair back in its place. "I have to see this through."

Anchurus watched him, as if hoping Midas would change his mind. When he didn't, a wall came down in front of the prince's gaze. "As you wish," he said coolly, and stood up.

What Midas wished was to breach the barrier he'd just erected between himself and his son, but he didn't know how. He retreated to his strategy table. "I must meet with the commanders. We are going over the battle plans. You don't need to attend."

His son flinched as if Midas had struck him.

"You're in pain," Midas said. "Go rest."

Anchurus walked stiffly to the door. He had just started to open it when a knock came from the other side.

"The advisor, Your Majesty," the guard announced.

The prince lifted the latch.

"Your Highness," Xander said, bowing his head.

"What is it?" Midas called.

"I must speak with you, Your Majesty."

"Come," Midas said.

Anchurus exited the room, but not before giving Xander a long, probing look. Midas wondered what that was about. He motioned for Xander to take a seat.

"Is he doing any better?" Xander asked.

"I don't know how he's walking around at all," Midas said, "unless you had something to do with that?"

Xander tilted his head. "A few herbs."

"Is that what you came to tell me?"

"No." Xander twisted the tie on his robe. "It's that . . . well. As you are aware, I get visions from time to time." He pulled a napkin from his pocket and patted his brow. "This battle, Your Majesty. You've waited a long time. Now you have all these extra soldiers. You might expect a great victory, but . . ." He tucked the napkin away. "I fear you will not be pleased with the result."

Midas narrowed his eyes. "You foresee defeat?"

"I see nothing about the battle," Xander said. "It's something else. Something dark and frightening." He peered at the king. "It involves you, sire. And the prince, and Zoe, I think."

"Your vision included Zoe?" Midas came toward him.

"Please, sire. I beg of you. Don't go."

Midas studied his face. "Was it you who told Anchurus to burn himself?"

Xander blinked several times. "The goddess needed something more compelling than a burned garden to respond."

"And wasn't that you and the other two advisors standing there doing nothing while my son burned nearly to death?"

"We wanted to save him," Xander said, "but—"

"You wanted to see if your idea would work," Midas interrupted.

"Your Majesty, you were dying."

"So it was all right if my son died too?" The king glared at his advisor. "After all these years, I would have thought you of all people would understand this. But you are young, so I will spell it out for you. Nothing is more important than my children. That means nothing is more important to *you* than my children. Not even me. Do you understand that?"

"But, Your Majesty, you are the king and—"

"Anchurus is the prince," Midas interrupted again. "Zoe is the princess. Without them, there is no one to rule the city of Gordium or the kingdom of Phrygia. If I die, they are still here. But if they are gone, the whole balance of power sways. Anyone can come in and take over. Even Sargon. A king lives forever only through his children. The children come first. Is that clear?"

Xander nodded and wiped his sweaty palms on his robe.

"One more thing." Midas leaned close. "If you *ever* allow something like that to happen to one of them again, I will have your head."

The young advisor trembled.

Midas waited for his message to sink in, then backed away. "Pass that along to your cohorts."

"Yes, Your Majesty." Xander bowed his head, but didn't get up.

"Is there something else?" Midas asked.

"Only a thought. I might advise that you not allow Anchurus to go with you."

"We've already settled that," Midas said.

"Forgive me, sire, but are you certain?"

"Do you know something I don't?"

"Only that the prince ordered more of the . . . um, herbs."

"He deserves as much pain relief as you can give him."

"But I think he's preparing to go with you."

"He knows we need him here. Now my commanders are on their way. If there's nothing else?"

Xander followed the king's gesture to the door.

"Oh, and, Xander."

Xander paused.

"When my men return with the princess, find a way to release her from the gold. Understood?"

"Yes, Your Majesty." Xander hurried out of the room.

EMIR and his two companions had climbed steadily through the afternoon and into the evening. Now, as the sun set on the horizon, a pine forest rose on their right. These hills had pines only at the higher elevations, where the air was cooler and the wet season longer. Tall and pointed, they hovered at the edge of Emir's vision like ghosts, shadowed and nebulous in their vigil. He kept on for another little while, but soon felt the hair sticking up on the back of his neck. He swiveled his head, scanning the surrounding area.

"What is it?" Selim asked.

"Listen." Emir halted his horse. Selim paused a few steps ahead, Arda behind them both. The animals shifted, the change too sudden for them to hold still. When they heard nothing, Emir nudged his mount into a slow walk while the other two settled in on either side of him. A figure took shape in the middle of the road ahead. Emir grasped the hilt of his sword as they proceeded, straining to see through the fading light. They found the figure covered in a dark cloak. Arda dismounted and yanked it off. There rested the Zoe sculpture, the body bent at the waist in the pose the princess had taken to help her father.

"To arms!" Emir shouted.

Arda leapt back on his horse, and the three men clumped together, weapons drawn. Nothing happened.

"Have they gone?" Selim whispered.

"Wait," Emir said. The horses settled, their breathing quieter. Arda shifted in his saddle, the leather creaking. Emir studied the trees. This had to be a trap. "Stay alert," he said.

The words had just escaped his lips when Arda's horse leapt forward, galloping off in a panic. Bain sprung from behind him, having hid himself in a trench. He pulled his sword and charged. Selim responded, urging his horse into a gallop straight toward the hunter. The big man danced out of the way, then grabbed Selim's leg and jerked him out of his saddle. The young soldier landed with a thud and rolled to his feet, sword drawn. Emir searched for Baris and, failing to find him, rode past Bain and sliced at his back. He caught only air.

"Arda!" he called, but there was no answer. He turned to see Selim putting up a valiant resistance, both hands on his sword as he adjusted his stance. Emir thundered by and got in a slice to Bain's upper arm. The monster hardly flinched.

"Baris, you coward," Emir called. "Show yourself!" No one appeared. Selim cried out in pain. Emir rushed back in time to see Bain lifting his sword for a killing strike. A whizzing sound rushed by, and Bain staggered back, an arrow lodged in his upper chest. Arda emerged from the darkness and shot another arrow. It hit between the monster's ribs.

"Keep at him!" Emir turned his horse. "Baris!"

Arda fired again, hitting Bain in the torso as he passed. Selim regained his feet and advanced, sword aloft. He'd taken only three steps toward the faltering Bain when the big man pulled an ax from his belt and thew it. Selim grunted, teetered, and fell, the ax jutting out of his chest.

"Baris!" Emir called, but the brother remained hidden. Cursing, he rode back toward the others, but he was too late. Selim was down. Arda charged, all the while firing more arrows at Bain. The giant grabbed the horse's reins, wrenched the animal around, latched a meaty hand onto Arda's belt and yanked him off. Arda was on the ground only a moment before Bain stepped on his throat, breaking his neck.

Emir pulled his dagger and threw it hard. The giant ducked. The weapon landed harmlessly in the dirt behind him. Emir gripped his sword and, when the big man charged, urged his horse forward to meet him. But Bain didn't come for him. At the last moment, he wrapped his arms around the horse's neck and, using his own weight, drew the animal down. Emir leapt off just before the horse fell.

He had little time to recover. Bain laughed as he came on, Arda's arrows still clinging to his chest, his heavy footsteps pummeling the ground. Emir got in a few cuts on the man's upper leg and side, but it was like slicing at a tree. Bain knocked the sword out of Emir's hand, leaving him defenseless. Emir's heels hit Selim's body, arresting his retreat. Bain grinned and barreled forward. Emir waited until the last minute, then dropped, yanked the ax from Selim's chest, and brought it around as hard as he could. The blade found its mark in the big man's abdomen. A groan escaped his throat.

"No!" Baris shouted from nearby. Emir dashed away, found his sword, and waited, crouched and ready. The stealth brother approached from behind him. Emir might have met his doom in that moment if Baris' grief hadn't betrayed him. As it was, the brother cried out as he attacked, giving Emir just enough of a warning to avoid a fatal strike. The blade slashed the back of his arm.

"Bain!" Baris dropped to his brother's side.

"Get it out," Bain murmured.

Baris grasped the ax handle, then hesitated. Already, there was a puddle of blood surrounding his brother's body. He let go.

"Take it out!" Bain said.

"This is it, Brother." Baris covered the wound as best he could with his jacket, patting it down around the blade.

"I can handle it. Do it!"

Baris shook his head.

"No." Bain stared at Baris with pleading eyes.

Emir stood nearby. "Take him and go," he said. "I won't follow."

But no man could survive that wound, not even a giant like Bain. Baris was clearly reluctant to leave him. Emir glanced back at the sculpture. He wouldn't get far dragging it along behind him, but neither did he want to return without it. He had to make his stand, and now was the time. Grasping his sword, he crept up behind Baris.

"Jaklin," Bain whispered.

"I'll take care of her," Baris said. "I promise."

Bain lifted a meaty hand. Baris grasped it and gripped hard. Just as Emir drew back to strike, Baris whirled to meet him, sword to sword.

The next few moments passed in a blur, Baris fighting, enraged, while Emir did his best to match him. They danced away from the sculpture, Baris a flitting shadow. He sliced Emir's leg and then his side, at one point pushing him down from behind. Emir hastily regained his footing just in time to get punched in the face. He leaned his left shoulder in, intending to knock the other man down, but Baris was too quick, leaving Emir to stumble over his own feet. He fell onto his arm, rolled, and got back up.

Baris tackled him again, and they both staggered to the ground. The hunter's hands wrapped around his throat. Emir wriggled and punched, three times catching Baris in the gut. The hands came off, and Baris punched him back. Emir's vision swirled. He tasted blood.

"You will die, traitor," Baris said, choking him again. "I will avenge Bain!"

White lights flashed in front of Emir's eyes. He felt himself receding from the scene, lifting above it as if he'd been caught by a bird. *No.* He couldn't go out this way. Not after everything.

"That's quite enough, Baris."

A sultry voice. *Katiah.* A swell of relief passed through Emir's body.

"Let him go," Katiah said. A deep and threatening growl accompanied her words. The pressure on Emir's neck lifted. In the next moment, he was restored to his body as if thrown into it. Gasping for air, he looked left to see Baris's arm clenched between the black wolf's teeth.

"Welcome back," Katiah said. She was smiling down at him, her moon's glow illuminating her face, a tight-fitting jacket and pants making her appear even taller than usual. She tossed her head and sauntered over to Baris.

"You've done well," she said. "I'm inclined to let you go, but you must promise to release the traitor for now."

"I must avenge my brother," Baris said.

Katiah glided over to where Bain lay in the dirt, though she took care not to step in the blood. "He was strong. But you were always the smart one."

"He deserves to die!" Baris pointed at Emir.

"If you insist on that now," Katiah said, "I'm afraid it's you who will be dying." The wolf pulled him a few more steps back, its teeth getting a good grip on Baris' arm. The hunter grimaced. "Decide." Katiah waited, her hands on her hips.

"Very well." Baris sagged in the wolf's hold.

Katiah lifted a finger. The wolf released him and trotted over to her side. "Take your horse and go," she said.

The brother's horse appeared a few steps away. Baris lingered near Bain's body, then mounted and rode off down the road, headed toward Sargon's kingdom.

Katiah sauntered over to the sculpture. "It really is a shame she ended up like this."

"Can you release her?" Emir stood up and looked around, spotting his own horse a short distance away.

"Only the one who cursed the king can lift the effects of that curse," Katiah said.

"You mean the goddess Denisia?"

"Of course. Or haven't you learned that she's the villain in all this?" Katiah smiled at him. "Come. We still have a long way to go. And bring her." She pointed to the statue.

"Where are we taking her?" Emir asked.

"To King Sargon, of course."

"She belongs in Gordium."

"That's not part of the plan."

Emir picked up his sword and slid it back into its scabbard. "I'm not taking her to King Sargon."

Katiah mounted a horse that had appeared beside her, a dark one with a long, luxurious mane and tail. It was much like the one that had taken Emir from the magical spring back to the castle. "Your choice, of course," she said. "Return to your King Midas. But you will go empty-handed. The princess is traveling with me."

"I show my face in Sargon's kingdom, and he has me killed," Emir said.

"Are you so sure?"

"He sent them after me, didn't he?"

"Yes, darling, but he's under my influence now. And besides." Katiah bent her gaze toward him. "Your mother would love to see you."

Emir considered that as he retrieved his horse. "Is she why you're helping me?" he asked, taking the horse's reins. "Or do you want something else from me?"

The goddess gave him a mischievous smile. "I'm still thinking about that. But it's been fun, these little meetings of ours. Wouldn't you agree?"

Emir was unsure how to respond to that.

"Make your choice," Katiah said. "Tell King Midas you failed and his daughter is in King Sargon's hands. Or come with me and show your mother some appreciation."

"And then?"

Katiah rode away without answering him.

Emir hesitated. To ride back to Gordium empty-handed was no choice. Midas would have his head. Indeed, his fate was the same in either direction, except with one choice, he would have the goddess' protection. And she'd already saved his life twice.

Or was it three times?

He found rope still on the sculpture's arms. The trees weren't far. He'd use a few branches to make a tram. Then he would direct his horse toward the one place he didn't want to go.

"Katiah," he called. "Wait."

XANDER BURST INTO THE ADVISORS' room, allowing the door to smash against the wall.

"What in the gods' names—" Fotis began.

"We are cooked," Xander said. "Cooked! I give us three days, tops." He shut the door behind him. "Of course, it comes with the job. A king's advisor might be executed at any time. One wrong prediction and off with his head. But King Midas. He's different, we said. Kinder, more understanding. But what king could understand this? It was too much. Too much to expect of anyone, say nothing of a king. A father." He approached the other two advisors who were still mixing herbs at their tables. "What does a king's advisor do in his last days? I could run away. But they'd come after me. Of course they would, and then I'd be a traitor, and you know what they do with traitors—"

"Xander!" Fotis barked. "What is it you're going on about?"

"They execute them is what they do." Xander continued, as if he hadn't heard. "But not the simple chop-the-head-off way. No. With a traitor, you're burned alive. Burned alive! It's justice, isn't it? I let the prince burn, and now I'm going to burn." He snatched the water bowl, which was almost empty, and went to the water bucket in the corner. "I can't be burned alive! I'm not the prince! I'm not brave! I can't stand there and watch the flames eating away at my flesh. My gods, what on earth did I do?" He scooped water into the bowl. "What did we do? Why didn't you talk me out of it?" He directed the question at Fotis. "The goddess came, but she didn't save the king. Why can't I see the end goal? I get wrapped up in what I think needs to happen. And I'm right. All the time I'm right. But I miss the end goal." He took the bowl back to them and set it on the table.

"Why didn't you remind me? We were to save the king. Save the king, you idiot!" He hit himself in the head. "The goal was to bring Denisia here, yes, but so she could save the king. And she wasn't going to save the king. That should have been clear. But no, I plowed ahead anyway, and what happened? She didn't save the king. She barely saved the prince. Now he's going to be a cripple the rest of his life or even die, and for what? Because I knew that to bring her here, his life had to be in danger. I was right. I was right." He leaned on Fotis' table. "It didn't matter, did it? Why didn't you tell me?"

"We tried to tell you." Fotis pulled the bowl toward him.

"You didn't try hard enough!" Xander wailed. "And now he's going to behead us. I know he will, because there's no solution. There's no way to bring Princess Zoe back. We've examined every possibility, haven't we? We've scoured all the parchments and talked to all the advisors of old—the few that are still alive, that is, and that's not many considering how many were *beheaded!"* He shouted the last word. "Or burned alive. Which way would you prefer to go?"

"You're making a lot of sense," Aster said, still mixing away.

"He's going to execute us!" Xander said.

"He's not going to execute us," Fotis said.

"Haven't you been listening?" Xander threw up his hands. "We didn't save Zoe. We didn't save the king. We allowed his flowers to burn, and then we burned the prince near to death. It's a wonder we're still alive at this very moment."

Fotis packed the last of the herbs he had mixed for the prince in a pouch, set it aside, and started sweeping off the table's surface.

"You're cleaning?" Xander asked. "That's what you're going to do with your last days? Clean?" He stared at the older advisor. "Shall I get the broom for you? The bucket? A dust cloth? Will you go to your death proud that you've left a sparkling room for the next advisor?"

"Oh, stop it," Fotis said. "The king is not going to execute us."

"You didn't see him!" Xander said.

"I didn't have to." Fotis dusted off his hands and checked Aster's work. The second advisor was now packing his last pouch, so Fotis started gathering up the remaining materials.

"You're not listening to me!" Xander pounded the table with his fists.

Aster tucked the finished pouch into a nearly full leather bag while Fotis wiped down the emptied wooden bowls and placed them back on the shelves.

"Hello?" Xander waved at them. "You're not paying attention!"

"You're giving us such a good reason to," Aster said. He stacked the cleared tables against the far wall, restoring the usual space in the middle of the room.

"He wants us to find a way to free Zoe," Xander said.

"We knew that." Fotis headed for the water basin.

"He plans to save her in battle," Xander said, following him. "Then he expects us to make her well again."

"We can't do that." Fotis stooped over to wash his hands. "He knows that."

"Then why did he just tell me that's what he expects?"

"What did you go to see him for, anyway?" Fotis asked. "Oh, yes. You were going to convince him not to go to war. Sounds like that went well."

"It's going to be a disaster." Xander stared up at the ceiling. "He's riding off thinking he's going to some victorious last battle. But it won't end well. And Anchurus is going with him."

"We already knew that too," Fotis said, drying off.

"The king doesn't," Xander said. "Anchurus assured him he will stay here to watch over the kingdom. And King Midas believed him. He believed him! I know the prince better than that. He isn't going to sit here while his father rides off and fights the one war he's been fighting his whole life. The prince is going. But the king thinks he's staying. What do you think he's going to do when he finds out?"

Fotis and Aster exchanged glances, Aster now the one washing. "He won't blame us," Fotis said. "You're just riled up the way you get sometimes."

Xander retreated to his side of the room. "Yes, that's it. No need to worry yourself. It's just Xander flying off in his usual fit. His visions mean nothing. Nonsense, all of them."

Fotis sighed, sitting down in his chair. "What do you expect us to do?"

"I'd love to hear all about the vision again," Aster said, drying off and crossing the room to his small desk.

Xander sat down on his chair against the wall. "I see a large black hole. Everyone is there. King Midas, King Sargon, Zoe, Anchurus, even the goddesses."

"Denisia?" Fotis asked.

Xander nodded. "And Katiah. And the musician. Or spy." He eyed Fotis. "A huge hole opens up in the middle of them, wind swirling around like a whirligig." He moved his hands in a fast circle. "Powerful winds, like in a storm. Strong enough to take them all down into the blackness. Everyone moves back, but then someone charges forward." Xander drew his hand across the air in front of him, simulating someone moving.

"Who?" Fotis asked.

"I can't see it." Xander shook his head. "The king will have our heads."

"It won't be our fault!" Fotis sputtered. "There's nothing we can do."

Aster rested his hands on his hips and turned toward the window. It was nearly dark outside. "We must not go."

"Go?" Fotis said. "Go where?" When Aster gave him a blank stare, Fotis said, "Surely you don't mean to battle?"

"We have many other choices," Aster said.

"Of course we do," Fotis said. "We stay here. We wait. We deal with whatever happens when they get back. That's what advisors do. They don't run off to war. We can't do anything out there. What would we do? And besides, the king would forbid it."

"And the king would have to know," Aster said.

"Are you suggesting we disobey him?" Fotis asked.

"He has ordered us not to go to battle," Aster said.

"Well, not specifically, but . . ." Fotis scratched his head. "It's not as if we're not recognizable."

"You can't go in disguise," Aster said.

"I won't go in disguise," Fotis said. "I am the king's advisor! I don't disguise myself and go off to war with soldiers. Why would I do that? And I refuse to get on one of those infernal animals ever again."

"You don't mean a horse?" Aster asked.

Fotis pointed at his wooden eye. "The last time I rode one, I ended up with this!"

"Truly?" Aster asked. "I wasn't aware of the story."

Fotis harrumphed and dismissed the tease with a lift of his shoulder.

But Xander had bent an ear to Aster's suggestion. He stood up suddenly. "If we're there, we may be able to make a difference."

Fotis stomped his foot. "We are *not* going off to war. At least I'm not. You two want to do something foolish, very well. It's your heads at risk, not mine."

"I could get us some soldiers' uniforms," Xander said. "And horses. Most of them are easy to ride in formation." He raised his voice for Fotis to hear. "You simply sit on the saddle and hold on."

"I'm not doing any such thing," Fotis said. "Imagine. Advisors going off to war. Without the king's order!"

"We slip into the ranks." Xander continued. "We should take some things with us. Explosives, the stinky weed, and the sleeping herbs."

Aster checked around the room. Soon the two of them were alight with activity, scouring the cupboards for what they needed, then packing those things into the bags they pulled from behind their beds. It was rare for them, as advisors, to travel, but they had a time or two when the king had visited other kingdoms. They knew how to prepare, so they packed while Fotis sat by watching them. It didn't take long before they each had a full bag sitting by the door.

"Anything else?" Xander said.

Aster shook his head. They scooped up the bags, Aster nabbing the prince's sack of herbs in his other hand. "I'm not going to arrange for our mounts," he said.

"Good," Xander said. "I'll get our uniforms." They were both out in the hall when they paused and looked back. Fotis had floated to the middle of the room to watch them, but when their questioning gazes turned to him, he pointed his nose up and retired to his bed.

CHAPTER
TWENTY-ONE

"All is ready, Your Majesty." Sargon's top commander bowed his head. He'd ridden up holding a torch, all but a tuft of his brown hair hidden underneath his helmet.

Sargon took the news with feigned disinterest, his gaze sweeping over the men he'd gathered at the edge of the city. Soldiers stood together in multiple rows in either direction, their commanders holding torches like beacons in the oncoming night. The sun glowed orange on the horizon, the air filled with the subdued sounds of hooves in the dirt, leather saddles creaking, flags rippling, and the distant calls of men. That the goddess hadn't shown herself made him nervous. Trusting his army to her word was uncomfortable at best. Particularly with Elanur nearby, a slave woman mounted and positioned at the king's side. The men knew better than to say anything. But he had seen their sideways glances, their confused expressions.

"How may I serve?" The commander spoke again, apparently believing his presence had been forgotten.

"To your post," Sargon said. "We depart shortly."

The man urged his horse into a trot and disappeared down the row to take his place among the soldiers, the flame like a flag behind him. He was one of thirty commanders leading a force of about four thousand. Sargon would overpower his rival to the west, expanding his territory so far that the ocean would be within reach. Only the kingdom of Lydia would remain, and conquering it would not be difficult once he'd established himself in Gordium.

The horses were growing restless. Victory depended on meeting King Midas soon, preferably at the three-day mark. He scanned the shadowed faces behind him, about half on horseback, the rest on foot or with supply wagons. He was tempted to ask Elanur if the goddess was coming, but the men would find that strange.

"Shall we ride?"

Senna sat beside him. Skinny and angular, the young man was impatient as always. Sargon refused to acknowledge him. Had his son kept silent, he'd have given the command, but now he was forced to wait. The boy needed to learn to keep his place. Riba was younger still and injured from the last battle, so he was in the back somewhere, commanding the supply units. Sargon hoped he'd be able to handle that much. A flighty young man, he wasn't known for his strategic thinking. Elanur was right about Emir besting both of his legitimate sons, something he hated to admit, even to himself.

He sighed quietly and thought of his lions. He'd visited them at feeding time, a last look just in case the worst happened. It was his habit. Being in the presence of their power and strength reminded him of his own, preparing him for what was to come. He and his men would descend upon Midas without mercy. They would end this feud once and for all.

More moments of painful waiting. Katiah had made it sound urgent that he ride out. But he couldn't shake the feeling that he was being played. That they all were.

Finally, he drew his sword and pointed it at the sky. The commander of the king's guard raised the kingdom's blue flag in response, signaling everyone to stand ready. Sargon waited until he had the army's full attention, then lowered the sword until it pointed directly west, loosening the reins at the same time. His piebald leapt forward, and the king felt the breeze of momentum on his face. A second later, he was rewarded by the thundering of hundreds of hooves behind him, his men filling the air with their deafening war cries. A smile creased his lips. This was his chance to crush his rival, and goddess or no goddess, no one was going to take it from him.

THOUSANDS OF GORDIUM SOLDIERS, riding four abreast, paraded out of King Midas' castle grounds at sunset. They took the main road into the city, the citizens showering them with wildflowers to bless their path. It was a momentous occasion, as there were more men than ever before, more horses tossing their heads and flicking their tails, and more supply wagons filled with food and water. After five lines passed, the king himself came, flanked by Rastus on his right, Baran on his left. He rode his stallion, Kanani, his hands covered in the mitts and disguised by the long sleeves of his cloak. It was difficult to rein, but he managed, having looped the tied leather over one wrist. Despite the awkwardness, he was happy to be moving with the power and energy of his mount underneath him.

The people murmured at the absence of the prince, whispering among themselves about his rumored injuries, but still they cheered their king, bowing low as he passed and shouting a new chant: "Long live the golden king! Long live the golden king!"

Once they had left the city gates behind and crossed the bridge, Midas pulled Kanani over to the side of the road. He motioned Baran and the other commanders on, but Rastus joined him. Together, they stood on a small mound looking back while the soldiers filed by row after row, calm and focused as they rode out under the blood red blaze of the kingdom's flags. Midas ached for the presence of his son, but his heart was calm knowing that Anchurus would be safe here at home. If only Zoe were the same, he could take his last ride in peace.

"We will return victorious, Your Majesty," Rastus said.

Midas acknowledged the statement with a slight tuck of his chin.

They had a long journey ahead of them. He wanted a drink, but he couldn't hold the waterskin with his mitts on. He would have to wait. At the back of the troops, the men were bringing along a wagon full of the spring water Emir had discovered. Midas doubted he would use it all. His strength was quickly leaving him. Now, he wished only to make it through the battle.

"Is there something we forgot, Your Majesty?" Rastus asked.

Kanani danced impatiently underneath him. "There are moments in one's life that must be savored," Midas said.

Rastus remained silent after that. The two of them watched as the soldiers crossed the bridge and rode by. All of them bowed their heads at the sight of the king. Horses. So many horses! Midas had always wanted more horses, and now he had them. Many he'd purchased from nearby Ancyra, but most were on loan from the kingdom farmers, some traded by citizens in return for gold objects. He turned back to the city, comparing how it looked now to how it had appeared when he'd first arrived with Katiah all those years before. Most prominent was the castle on the hill, the way it gleamed in the peachy light. It had seemed glorious before, elevated as it was, but now it shined like a beacon for all to see, and Midas couldn't help but be proud of that. The curse would kill him, but it had also enhanced the kingdom he was leaving behind. That was something, anyway.

The feeling lasted only as long as it took him to remember his daughter's entrapment. An old rage rose powerfully within him, and he whirled Kanani around. Sargon would not determine Zoe's fate as he had Elanur's. He urged the stallion into a gallop, and, pointing his covered fist to the sky, called out from the depths of his being, "Sargon!"

The soldiers turned, surprised to see their weakened king suddenly charging at a full gallop beside them. The horses lifted their heads and perked their ears. As Midas swept down the line, they all began to follow. Soon the entire army had moved into a gallop, a great dust cloud rising behind them. The ground rumbled with their thunder, wild animals darting away to hide, even the birds of prey banking to avoid the oncoming flood of men. Midas called out again, and the soldiers echoed him, thousands of voices shouting Sargon's name. Midas rode high in the saddle, tears streaming down his cheeks.

HIDDEN in the tenth row behind the king, Prince Anchurus gritted his teeth. He'd managed the ride quite well at a walk, but now that his father had rallied the troops into an all-out gallop, his wounds burned with a new ferocity. He feared he would pass out, so he pulled Ambrose back into a gentle canter. As the horse shifted its gait, the pain eased a little. Anchurus took a breath, then reached into his breast pocket and pulled out one of the satchels the advisors had given him. Tipping his head back, he squeezed the mud-like contents into his mouth, then tossed the bag and grabbed his water-skin, washing it down with a quick swig. He'd consumed one pouch of the herbal mixture already, but it was clear he was going to need all the help he could get.

At least his bandages remained intact. The castle healer had done a good job of it, applying the goddess' muddy gel before rewrapping his legs. A younger healing woman, she'd blanched when taking the old wrapping off. Some of the dead skin had lifted away, the wounds yellow with pus and weeping anew. She'd gathered herself quickly, her hands even gentler than those of the experienced woman who had tended him that morning. But he could tell by the look on her face that he hadn't seen the worst of these injuries yet.

He'd asked her then what his chances were of regaining his health. She'd given him several assurances that with time and care, he could expect to heal, but her eyes had betrayed the truth, the way they refused to look into his own. After cooling his forehead once more, she'd left, gently closing the door behind her. He'd made his decision then. He would see this through with his father, and it would be the last thing he did.

The herbs were working their magic. His body felt lighter, and though the fever still burned, the pain in his legs had backed off to a more manageable level. He held to the front of the saddle. He'd been reluctant to do so initially, but then remembered he was dressed like all the other soldiers, no longer the prince, but one of thousands of men going off to battle. A thicker bridle hid Ambrose's telltale star, one with an extra decorative piece that covered the middle of the horse's face. Anchurus was surprised at how easy it was to fool everyone. He had to admit there was a bit of mischievous fun to shedding his princely persona even for a short time.

Ahead, the king rode with his fist thrust into the air. A swell of pride rushed over Anchurus' chest. No, he wouldn't miss this for anything.

"He's right up there!" Xander adjusted his helmet for the hundredth time as he bounced clumsily on his horse. The squatty white mare had an abrasive trot, one that punished her rider's bottom unmercifully. "That's Ambrose. I don't know why no one else has noticed it."

"People always pay close attention." Aster rode beside him, a much more graceful rider aboard a plain sorrel gelding. "And he's wearing a prince's royal uniform."

"I suppose," Xander said. "I do wish they'd slow down." His words were accompanied by the percussion of his lungs being jostled inside him. "We have a long way to go."

"The king's obsession remains dormant."

"I've never seen him like this, and he's gone days without food."

"We don't ride to find his daughter."

"I think his hate for Sargon trumps even that."

Aster fell silent.

Xander tried again to adjust his helmet. It was far too big for him while the uniform was too small, his flesh bulging against the breast plate and pant legs. "He just took another one of the herbal pouches. Did you see?"

"No doubt the galloping is easy for him."

"He's taking too much," Xander said. "His heart is going to give out."

"He's very weak."

Xander looked behind him again. He wouldn't admit to Aster what he was looking for, but he figured his companion knew, anyway. He felt a pang of sorrow when he didn't see the old man. Whatever words the two had exchanged, he relied on Fotis for strength and felt unsteady without him nearby.

"He would know how to fix this," Aster said.

"But he might say something to make me feel better. Or at least make me laugh." Xander pushed his helmet back from his eyes. "Fotis was right. This is stupid."

"It's always stupid to try to help," Aster said.

"But what are we going to do? We can't do anything."

"The future is known to you."

Xander's mare started to slow, losing her place in line. He kicked his heels, urging her forward again. "Even she knows this is stupid."

"Horses never sense a rider's intention," Aster said.

"So it's my fault." Xander sighed and looked around. Long stretches of flatland spread out before them, interrupted with periodic swells of hills. Everything was falling into shadow with the coming night. The air was pleasant, though. Not too warm or cold. He tried to take a drink from his waterskin, but he was bouncing so severely that it spilled all over his chin.

"Using one's legs while riding doesn't help," Aster said.

"Oh, use your own legs." Xander replaced the waterskin, then did his best to follow his friend's advice, eyeing Aster's graceful seat in the saddle. "How do you do that?"

"Grip with your hips," Aster said.

Xander frowned. "What do you mean?"

"Your hips," Aster said and moved his knees back and forth.

"Oh, your knees." It took Xander a few attempts, but he finally managed to reduce the bouncing. "Oh! I think I've got it." He rode that way for a time, but then his legs tired, and soon he was back to bouncing along.

"Weakness is a virtue," Aster said.

"Oh, hush," Xander said. "We should be thinking about a way to free Zoe."

"Thinking will help."

"What else are we going to do? This is boring."

"The king lives to amuse you."

"Are you saying you have no ideas at all?" Xander asked.

"It wouldn't do to ask the goddess Denisia."

"We could ask her if she were here!" Xander rolled his eyes.

Aster said nothing.

Xander peered at him. "Is she?" When Aster didn't respond, Xander whirled around. With the dimming light, it was getting more difficult to make out individual faces. "Are you teasing me?"

"It's unusual for a goddess to be disguised," Aster said.

"Like what? A soldier?"

"There are many other options right now."

"She could be a horse." Xander laughed at his own joke, then quickly sobered. "She couldn't do that, could she?"

Aster glared at him.

"So she's here!" He turned his gaze forward. "Do you know what that means? She wants to help us."

"A goddess is always most interested in what men are doing," Aster said.

"Not *men.* One man."

Aster shrugged.

"Why didn't you tell me?" Xander asked. "You've let me fret all this time."

"You're fretting is not amusing."

"So glad I can entertain you." Xander drew out the phrase in a sarcastic tone.

Aster smiled.

"You're so aggravating!" Xander threw his arms out, spooking the mare, who swerved to the left, throwing him off balance. He grabbed for the saddle and managed to hang on until she straightened again. "Touchy, aren't you?" he asked her. The mare flicked her ears as he steered her back in line. Xander turned to Aster. "Where is she?"

"She wouldn't be five rows behind us," Aster said.

The troops slowed to a walk, but still, Xander couldn't find the goddess. "When should we talk to her?"

"It's uncommon to stop for rest on long treks like these."

"Of course. When we stop to rest." Xander pressed his lips together. "What a stroke of good luck. The goddess is here. She'll help us." He turned to Aster. "I'm so glad we came." When Aster only raised an eyebrow, Xander added, "Aren't you?"

"Trusting a goddess is always a good idea," Aster said.

"She's here for him. I'm sure of it." He smiled to himself. It was a good sign. Denisia was here to help. There was no other reason for her to be there. Was there? Xander wished again that he could ask Fotis for his opinion.

FIVE ROWS back from the advisors, Denisia sneezed, then purposely lowered her voice to clear her throat. She waited to see if the soldiers had noticed the high-pitched sound, but they seemed lost in their own thoughts, the endless marching of horses' hooves deadening their ears. She pressed her hand over her mouth. The air was so horribly dusty. She wondered why that surprised her. She'd observed enough of these marches. One would have thought she would know what they were like, but only now, riding in the midst of it, did she truly understand what Anchurus had lived through much of his life.

She moved her sprightly little bay over to the left, seeking clearer air. The soldier next to her thankfully kept his gaze forward. She took a drink from her waterskin and another from her wine bag. Up ahead, she could see Ambrose. No other horse had such a gait, so flashy and energetic, his feet like springs and his tail held proudly aloft. Anchurus had come as she'd expected, though she'd hoped he wouldn't. He sat a proud soldier, back straight, armor on. She'd seen him throw the pouch away after tilting his head back and knew he was taking herbs for the pain. Too many for his own good, she guessed, but the fever was likely getting worse. This had to end. All of it. It had to end.

She touched her breast pocket to feel the small box there inside her leather vest. Before infiltrating the castle barracks, she had read the words silently several times. Another few run-throughs and she'd have them committed to memory. She hoped she was pronouncing them correctly. Of course, she hadn't uttered anything out loud. She didn't dare trigger the magic before it was time. But she had whispered them in her head, formed her lips and tongue around them.

With every rehearsal, she thought of Silenus and nearly changed her mind. She'd wished she'd been able to talk to him before leaving Gordium, but he was traveling with Chetin. He would have told her whether Lady Verna's story was true—whether he had given up his memory in exchange for Denisia's life. He could still tell her, but once the spell was cast? If everything truly returned to as it was, as the witch had said it would, Silenus could once again be plagued with soft mind. It was this thought that threatened her resolve over and over again. Despite everything, it was helpful that Anchurus was there. Only the prince's suffering kept her moving forward.

She gently nudged her horse to the left, hoping to limit the dust coming at her. This was why kings rode at the front. She'd always thought it rather foolhardy, taking a risk like that. A single arrow could bring one down. But no king would want to suffer the whole journey back here. He'd be covered in dust and grime by the time they reached their destination and probably unable to speak without coughing. How inspiring would such a king be?

Denisia wondered what her face looked like now. Anchurus probably wouldn't recognize her, which was just as well. She glanced ahead to mark him with her gaze. She had brought her own herbs and mud along with some fresh bandages, but she didn't know when she might find the courage to approach him. Watching him now, her heart felt heavy. He would never look at her the same way again. So why was she doing this? She could return home, live out her life with a lucid Silenus and the loving Nysiades, removed from the world of men. But the thought left her feeling like a shell—a discarded chrysalis. And she was no butterfly.

A raven's caw came from overhead. Denisia spotted it a little to the left, its black form outlined against the gray clouds, its flight a parallel line to the king's march. She checked the ground below it but saw nothing there. Still, she knew—ravens often followed wolves, hoping to share in the spoils of their hunts. She couldn't be certain, but she suspected this raven might be following Katiah's wolves. She imagined the beasts keeping their eyes on Midas' progress. If they were, Sargon would not only be expecting them, but would have a good idea of when the two armies would meet, giving him a clear advantage.

She considered alerting King Midas, but then thought better of it. Even if he knew, he wouldn't change course. Best to keep her presence secret as long as possible.

She sneezed again. This time, the soldier to her right glanced over, but she ignored him and took a drink, doing what she could to appear tough in the saddle. Straight back. Strong legs. Firm arms. It was exhausting.

Far back in the middle of Midas' army, a weathered soldier named Halen drove a supply wagon pulled by four stout workhorses. Stacked high with barrels full of food, weapons, and the king's water, it creaked and moaned as it rolled over the mounds and through the pits in the road. Halen was doing his best to avoid hitting any rocks that might break one of his fragile wooden wheels, but it was proving difficult as they moved out of the plains and toward the base of the rocky hills beyond. He'd stocked extra wheels in the back, but still it was a measure of pride not to have to use them. Halen had already survived eight battles without a single wheel lost. That fact had gained him a reputation he wanted to keep. If he weren't the wagon driver, he'd be on foot, trailing along behind the riders for league after league until his feet were covered in blisters.

He turned to check his cargo. The barrels vibrated with the movement of the wagon, jostling against one another, but they were all upright and intact. Halen saw nothing out of order, so he focused on the path ahead. He was fortunate to have his original team with him this time—Black, Blacker, Night, and Mountain. On the march to the last battle, Mountain had been lame. Halen had replaced him with a brown gelding that had appeared stout enough, but his team had had to drag the beast along the whole time. Halen couldn't remember his name, so he'd taken to calling him "Dead" after just a few miles because of his lack of energy.

This time, Mountain was back and trotting along at his usual bouncy pace. Halen was grateful. With the four dark beasts pulling the wagon, all signs pointed to a successful march, which would give him one more to add to his reputation. Indeed, on this quiet night marching across the dry brown lands of Phrygia, Halen thought that the gods had blessed him, for it seemed with such a mighty force around him, nothing could go wrong. Midas would emerge victorious, and they would return to Gordium as heroes.

And so Halen drove proudly, oblivious to the small child tucked away inside his wagon. Quiet as a bug, the boy wore a ragged lambskin cloak and carried a waterskin at his belt, easily pressing himself flat behind a barrel where a soldier was unlikely to look. Now and then he popped up to observe his surroundings, but then quickly ducked back down, his features etched with worry, his mouth open to breathe through the dusty air.

CHAPTER TWENTY-TWO

Emir started to slip off his horse. He caught himself at the last moment, mistakenly jerking the reins as he regained his balance. The animal flicked an ear back, as if irritated. Behind him, the Zoe sculpture rode along, still nestled safely within the makeshift tram. It consisted of two tree branches with the soldiers' jackets tied between them, the statue resting on top and secured with rope. Emir was surprised it had remained in place this long, pulled along by his horse as it was, but then it was possessed by magic. He didn't know if it was Katiah's or Denisia's magic, or if it had something to do with the fact that a real human being existed inside it. But if it were a normal solid gold sculpture, neither he nor the Olgun brothers would ever have been able to transport it so easily.

On the horizon, the sky had lightened with a slight tinge of gray. Dawn would soon be upon them. He and the goddess had ridden together all night, but the landscape spread tediously on, the dusty road interrupted only occasionally by a hill to cross. The only way he could tell they'd traveled any distance at all was to look behind them. There, he saw nothing but a flat stretch of prairie, the forests they'd traversed the night before no longer visible.

Ahead, it looked the same, the road ceaseless in its tyranny. It reminded him of the journey he'd taken when he'd fled from Sargon, the long and arduous nature of it. The boy had been his only respite, his childish enthusiasm infectious. Emir had thought then that he'd never come this way again, and now here he was. At least the boy was safe in Gordium. Emir hoped to see him again, partly because he wanted to ask if he knew the goddess Katiah, if perhaps a beautiful woman with lustrous, dark hair had instructed him to help Emir escape. Katiah had said as much, but he'd prefer hearing it from the boy.

He took a small sip of water. He'd pilfered the soldiers' supplies before leaving, poured their water into his waterskin, hung Arda's remaining arrows over his shoulder and secured his bow to the saddle. Afterwards, he'd placed their swords on their chests and their hands over the hilts, closed their eyes and turned their faces to the sky. He'd lingered a moment in reverence, a profound sense of guilt enveloping him. If it weren't for him, the two men would still be alive.

"Brood any louder and I won't be able to hear myself think," Katiah said.

Emir inhaled the light floral scent emanating from her skin. She'd stayed with him all night, a chaperone to keep him from taking the Zoe sculpture back the other direction. "You're leading me to Sargon," he said. "You can't expect me not to be concerned about that."

"Sorry to disappoint you, darling, but this isn't about you."

"You'll let me go, if I wish it?"

She gestured to the road. "No one is holding you."

Emir shifted his gaze to the sculpture. He should leave it. He'd never be able to wrench it away from Katiah's grasp.

"This is boring," she said with a yawn. "Why don't we liven it up a bit?" She stopped her horse and lifted both hands to the sky. The sunlight faded. When Emir looked up, a cloud had settled directly overhead. His mount grew nervous, flicking its ears back and forth as it sidestepped, the tram straining behind it. Emir held the reins taut. The goddess uttered three short words and dropped her arms. The cloud disappeared.

"Hello?" a new voice said.

Emir gaped at the sculpture.

"Hello? Is anyone there?"

Katiah grinned and nudged her horse forward.

"Father?"

It was the princess. The thought of her *in there* horrified Emir. It was bad enough, her being trapped, but much worse now that she was aware of her circumstances.

Katiah cocked an eyebrow at him, as if curious to see what he might do.

"Father?" Zoe asked again.

"This is Emir Alkan," Emir said finally. "The musician."

"Oh good," Zoe said. "Emir, I seem to have gotten myself locked up inside a dark room. Can you get me out?"

Emir glanced at Katiah, who only smiled. How was one to inform a princess she was now a sculpture?

"Emir?" Zoe said.

"We're working on it," he blurted.

"Is Father all right?"

"He is . . . worried about you."

"Tell him I'm well. It is dark, though, and I seem to be really hungry."

Emir glared at Katiah, but she ignored him. "I'll ask Pilar to bring something," Emir said. *Stupid!* Pilar couldn't bring anything. "Are you sure you're all right?"

"Perfectly, except I don't remember how I got in here? Or where here is?"

"We were . . . attacked." Emir felt like he was making things worse. "Two hunters came after me."

"Hunters?"

"Sargon's men. He doesn't take kindly to deserters." He paused. "Like me."

"I see," Zoe said.

"Your father put them away. But they got out."

"Out of the dungeon?"

"They may have had help."

Katiah smiled at him.

"Our guards are loyal to the king," Zoe said.

"I don't believe it was the guards," Emir said with a wry look at the goddess.

"Then who?"

Emir glanced again at Katiah, but she seemed not to care what he told the princess. "Perhaps if you think back to breakfast."

"Father was choking. You saved him." Zoe paused a beat. "Is he truly all right?"

"He found some clear water to drink," Emir said.

"Oh! That's wonderful news." He heard the smile in her voice. "And food?"

"Nothing to suit his palate."

Another pause. "How long has it been since breakfast?"

Emir hesitated. "Three days."

Zoe fell silent until they reached a bend in the road, traversed it, and put it far behind them. "No wonder I feel hungry," she said.

Emir smiled. The princess was showing her trademark resilience.

"And Anchurus?" she asked. "He's all right too?"

Emir winced. "He's doing his duty."

"I have the strange sensation I'm moving," Zoe said. "Must be the hunger talking."

"Oh, buck up, child," Katiah said. Emir's gaze jerked toward her. "I thought you were smarter than this."

"Emir, who is with you?" Zoe asked.

Emir watched the goddess.

"Katiah, is that you?" Zoe said.

"I expected you to figure that out much sooner," Katiah said. "They said you were smart."

"Emir, what's going on?"

"He's trying to blame me, Princess," Katiah said, "but your father's greed is what got you into this pickle. You might as well face that now."

Zoe was quiet.

"Oh, come, come," Katiah said. "Don't you remember what happened? It wasn't that long ago."

"The golden touch," Zoe said.

"Your father's greed," Katiah corrected. "He cared more about the gold than you. Painful to imagine, but we all have to deal with our disappointments."

"Emir. Emir, am I . . .?"

Emir groaned inwardly. Here it was. The truth, whether she was ready for it or not. "When you went to help your father," he said, glaring at the goddess. "He touched you. By accident."

"Yes." The horses' hooves clomped steadily along as Zoe examined her memory. "Oh . . ." Her voice trailed off at the end of the word.

"Of course he did." Katiah raised one hand in a dismissive fashion. "He was focused on himself, as always."

"He didn't mean to," Zoe said.

"He had only his selfish desires in mind. As if I haven't given him enough."

"You? What have you given my father?"

Katiah shook her head. "No surprise he never told you."

"Told me what?"

"He was an unknown waif, the victim of a village raid by Sargon's father. Without me, he never would have been anything. But King Gordius' wife was as barren as the dry land around us. She prayed to me every day to relieve her of her suffering. So I rescued your father and took him to them. They accepted him as their own and raised him to be king. If not for that, you'd be wandering the plains cooking deer meat and sleeping in tents!"

Thunder rumbled in the distance. Emir glanced toward the horizon, but there were no clouds in sight.

"Your father was grateful for a time," Katiah continued, "but then everything changed. Your mother started it. Demanding your father banish me from Gordium." They rode up a hill, the horses digging in for the climb.

"My mother died," Zoe said.

"A tragedy, for sure," Katiah said.

The hairs stood up on the back of Emir's neck.

"A sickness," Zoe said.

"Unfortunate."

Emir was certain Zoe was thinking the same thing he was. But how could one ask if a goddess had killed her mother?

"My father worshipped you long ago," Zoe said.

"I saved his life," Katiah said. "He owed me."

Emir shifted in his saddle. He should go. Katiah had given him permission. But without him, who would watch over the princess? Who would know where she was should an opportunity arise to get a message to the king?

They rode in silence for another little while before Zoe spoke again. "Emir? Are we going to war?"

"You should be happy," Katiah said. "It's what your father has always wanted. Revenge against Sargon. I guess he never told you that story either. No matter. There will be war. And it will be deadly. But don't worry. You're wearing the best armor there is."

They crested the top of the hill and rode across it, the tram bouncing along on the rocks. "Must you torture her?" Emir asked in a low voice, hoping the princess wouldn't pick up on it.

Katiah gave him a chilly glare. "I'm allowing her to be present at a key moment in her father's life. It's a gift." She narrowed her eyes. "Is that why you're still here? You believe you can protect her somehow?"

Emir pointed his face into the morning breeze. "She is blameless in this." He sensed the goddess' gaze on him, intense in its disapproval.

"She has a part to play," Katiah said.

"Do I?" He gripped his reins more tightly.

"That remains to be seen. But now it's clear I have coddled you long enough." She pulled her horse to a halt and made a slight wave with her hand.

Emir felt a sudden sting in his shoulder. An arrow! He jerked in the saddle, scanning. From the south, a rider galloped toward him.

"Protector of King Midas' daughter, hm?" Katiah tossed her head. "You should rethink your loyalties." She flicked her hand again, then rode away. The princess—suddenly elevated, tram and all—floated along behind her.

Emir jerked the crude arrow out of his skin and clenched his knees to his mount. He intended to go after the goddess, but a sharp sting in the side of his leg stopped him. From the left, Baris came, bow reloaded. Emir turned his horse toward his enemy.

There was no choice now. He would have to defeat the hunter. Only then could he decide what to do next.

EARLY AFTERNOON on the second day of their journey, Midas allowed the men to stop for a rest. They found a grassy rise that offered a wide view, and Rastus gave the signal, all the commanders following suit. One by one, the companies came to a halt. The soldiers gratefully dismounted, most stretching their tight muscles before taking up the task of building a short-term camp.

"Easy, Ambrose." Anchurus found an open spot by a lonely larch tree that looked perfect for a rest. Gripping the saddle with both hands, he slid down the side of the stallion, letting his feet settle slowly on the ground. Knives stabbed at his heels and cut into his calves. He clenched his teeth, his shirt soaked in sweat. He pretended to organize his supplies, putting a little more weight on one foot and then the other and doing his best to keep his expression still. He was so focused on managing it all that he jumped when he heard the small voice in his ear.

"Take these."

Denisia hovered near his shoulder. She wore a soldier's uniform, her hair hidden inside a helmet. From a distance, he wouldn't have recognized her, but up close her brown eyes could not be mistaken. She pressed several mushrooms into his hand. "One at a time." She held his gaze, then left.

It was all he could do not to call her back, for her presence had been comforting, but the soldiers were mingling about now. He would draw attention to himself. Besides, she was the reason he suffered. He opened his fingers and saw the innocent-looking mushrooms sitting there, spongy fungi covered in mottled brown. They didn't look appetizing at all, but the pain was great. He popped one into his mouth, chewed and swallowed, tucked the rest into his pocket, and set to loosening the strap on Ambrose's saddle. He worried someone might recognize the horse, but Ambrose had attracted his share of dust with the march. Anchurus pulled the saddle off. The horse gave a grateful shudder, dirt clinging to the sweaty spots. Convenient camouflage.

It didn't take long for the mushroom to kick in. When it did, the pain backed off considerably. Anchurus stacked his gear, tied Ambrose to keep him near, and pulled some hard bread and cheese from his bag. There was a spot of shade under the tree. Holding his spine straight, he sidestepped into it. All around him, soldiers ate, talked, and rested, their numbers scattered across the rise. It was a strangely peaceful sight, considering they were off to battle.

Moving carefully, he lay down flat and stared up at the sky. Relief flowed over him. Closing his eyes, he saw Denisia's face. He began to wonder if he had really seen her or if his mind was playing tricks on him. The mushroom was real enough, its medicine pouring through his limbs like warm honey. So much had he suffered that he surrendered wholeheartedly to it, letting a sweet slumber take him deep underground where there was no more war and no more fire, only the soft, cool earth accepting him into its welcoming embrace.

DENISIA WATCHED the prince from a distance. She had wanted to return to him when he'd lain down to rest, but she remained where she was, sitting on a flat stone, her horse tethered to a stout bush behind her. From her elevated position at the edge of the camp, she could easily gaze down on him and all the other soldiers stretched out across the wild grasses.

She pulled the box from inside her vest. Staring at its wooden surface, she saw Silenus' face and prayed the spell would leave him untouched. Lady Verna had told her everything would return to as it was. As it was before the curse, Denisia assumed. But how long before?

"Madame Goddess, I beg your pardon."

Denisia jumped at the sound of the stranger's voice. She tucked the box away before whirling around.

"Xander, one of the king's advisors." Xander bowed his head.

"I know who you are."

"I used the utmost discretion approaching you," he said. "I won't reveal your identity."

She glared at him, worried about just that, but he wore a uniform like hers, apparently desiring the same anonymity. "What do you want?" she asked, getting to her feet.

"To tell you I'm happy you're here. For our prince's sake. We were concerned until we spotted you."

"We?"

"Aster is with me."

Denisia removed her wine bag and took a drink. "I have nothing to say to you. It is your fault he is as he is."

Xander clenched his hands together, but didn't go away.

"I do not wish to speak to you!" Denisia said.

"Then perhaps, great goddess, will you listen?"

She longed to wrap him up in a tightly wound cage of grass and abandon him to his fate. But such a move would reveal her presence. "Be quick about it."

Xander took a hesitant step toward her. "I must warn you. You may be making a mistake."

"You warn me? Who do you think you are?"

The advisor opened his hands. "Forgive me. I get visions sometimes. And usually, they're correct." He paused, his gaze darting about. "I've seen a black hole with everyone around it. The king, the prince, the princess, Sargon, you, Katiah. I know your intentions are good. But might there be another way?"

"Another way for what?"

"To solve this problem."

She longed to dismiss him, but he'd come close to envisioning a scene that sounded remarkably like the one Lady Verna had described. An open cavern. Everyone of importance around it. Except she hadn't planned on Katiah being there.

"You might lift the curse from the king," he continued. "It wouldn't save the prince, but it would make him happy. And he doesn't have much time left."

"I cannot."

"Your grandfather. Yes."

She glanced at him. "You understand, so leave me alone."

"But if you proceed, great goddess." Xander reached toward her, pleading. "I fear it may bring about an even greater tragedy than the one that is already playing out."

"I am a goddess!" she said.

"But I'm the reason he suffers. I knew his pain would compel you to come, but you were too late, and he—"

She grabbed a fistful of dirt and flung it at him. It wasn't enough. She uncorked her wine bag and dumped that over his head. As it absorbed into his hair, the excess dripping down the sides of his face, she threw more dirt. Xander sputtered and ducked, wiping his cheeks with his fingers. Suddenly, she paused and looked around.

She would draw attention to herself. Seething, she turned her back on him. "You should leave now or I'm not sure what I'll do next."

Xander peered out from between his arms, red wine clinging to his lashes. "Great goddess. I apologize. It's just . . ." He seemed near tears. "I've seen it. It wasn't clear at first, but the closer we get, the more vivid it becomes." He gazed at her, imploring. "Someone dies. I know you don't want that and—"

She had him by the uniform collar, her face a breath away from his. "*Who* dies?"

He blinked, his mouth curling.

"What do you mean?" she asked again.

"When the black hole opens," he stammered. "If you open the black hole, he . . ." He paused, as if unable to get the next word out.

Heat flowed through her body. He hadn't said it, but she knew whom he meant. She felt it in her racing heartbeat, the sweat tickling her scalp. "You know nothing," she breathed.

"Great goddess, lift the curse. It will make him happy. He will love you again."

She shoved him aside and turned her back. She had already made up her mind. She knew what she was going to do.

Xander brushed himself off. He stayed a moment, as if he might say more, but then she heard his footsteps walking away. When he had disappeared down the incline, she heaved a sigh of relief and checked on Anchurus. At first, she couldn't see him. Panicked, she rushed forward. After a few nervous moments, she found him lying exactly where he'd been before. Was he breathing? She hurried down the hill. Lowering her head by his nose, she listened. His soft exhale warmed her cheek. Relief poured over her shoulders, hot tears burning her eyes. She pulled back and gazed upon his face. For the first time in many days, he seemed peaceful. She could remove his boots. Redress the wrappings. But she knew what she would find. The burns had been too severe. He was already hot with fever.

"It will be as it was before," she whispered. "You will be well again." She touched her forehead to his, then checked around.

Certain no one was looking, she placed a quick kiss on his cheek and returned to her stone on the hill.

The camp had settled into a quiet rest when the boy dared creep closer to the king's tent. Two soldiers guarded the entrance, so he sneaked to the back and ducked underneath, wriggling his little body like a snake until he stood on the inside.

"What are you doing here?" Midas sat propped up against a trunk, his covered hands in his lap.

The child sat down near him.

"You're quite the sneaky one, aren't you?"

The boy gave him a shy smile.

"We're going to war. It's no place for a boy."

The child made some hand motions, but the king shook his head, so the boy drew a picture in the dirt. It resembled a man.

"Who?" Midas asked.

The boy placed his hands in the position one would use to play the oud and pretended to strum, bobbing his head and swaying from side to side.

"The musician!" Midas said.

The boy nodded.

"He's gone after the princess."

The boy let loose with a flurry of hand gestures.

"I don't know. Why would you wonder about him?"

The boy stared at the drawing he'd made in the dirt, then drew a smaller figure next to it.

"You know him?" Midas asked.

The boy nodded.

Midas narrowed his eyes, then rested against the pillow. "It doesn't matter. You must go back."

The child shook his head and pointed to the drawings.

"This is no place for a child," Midas said.

The boy puffed up his chest and gripped his hands into fists.

"I know. You're strong." Midas glanced toward the tent flaps. "Rastus!"

The commander of the king's guard appeared. "Your Majesty," he said, a surprised gaze on the boy.

"Get him something to eat," Midas said. "Then bring him back. He stays in here for now."

"Yes, Your Majesty."

Midas turned to the boy. "Go on. He'll get you something."

The boy followed Rastus out. The king's guards shared their meal with him, some cold beans and dried meat. When he finished, he returned to the tent to find the king asleep, his head against the pillow behind him, his covered hands still in his lap. Rastus laid a blanket down on the opposite side. The boy sat there until the commander had gone. Then he dragged the blanket over next to the king, lay down with his head on his arm, and fell asleep.

When Katiah caught sight of Sargon's army late in the afternoon, she was surprised to see how far they had come. She had expected to travel the entire day before finding them, but then she'd noticed dust clouds in the distance. She slowed her pace, allowing the tram to settle in the dirt, following at her leisure until they stopped for a rest. Sargon's scouts found her soon after that. She let them approach and went willingly as they escorted her to the king.

She rode into camp like a vision, her hair gleaming in the sun, her clothes clinging to her body. When the men's eyes left her, they shifted to the cargo she carried, the golden sculpture now bouncing along on the tram behind. She enjoyed all the attention, but when she spotted the king, her breath caught in her throat. He was dressed all in black, his thick hair falling in waves over his head, his chiseled brow hiding his dark eyes in shadow. Her legs melted in the saddle. She would have him that night, she decided. She would allow herself one last pleasure before everything changed.

By the time she stopped her horse in front of him, she was her regal self again. "I hope I'm not disturbing your rest, Your Majesty."

Sargon bowed his head. "Great goddess." He glanced behind the horse. "You have brought me something?"

"You may want to keep me on your good side," she said.

Sargon gestured for his men to release the sculpture. When they had cut it free from the tram and stood it up, he walked leisurely around it. At one point, he tried to lift it, grasping it under the arms. With a little effort, he succeeded, then set it back down. "What is this?" he asked the goddess.

"You don't know?"

"A golden sculpture would be valuable," he said, "though it would belong in a castle, not an army camp. But this is no sculpture of gold. It's too light."

"It is gold," Katiah said, dismounting, "but it is magical gold. And the sculpture is quite unique. Why don't you tell him, my dear?" When the sculpture didn't respond, Katiah raised her hand to the sky. Dark clouds gathered overhead, and a wolf howled in the distance.

"Ow!" Zoe said. "All right, I'm here!"

Katiah lowered her hand. "It would be better if you cooperated, princess. This is King Sargon II. He deserves your respect." She turned to find Sargon smirking, his dark eyes dancing in the gleam of the gold. "Tell him who you are," Katiah commanded.

"I'm Princess Zoe, daughter of King Midas. The king who will soundly defeat you."

Sargon stared at the sculpture. For many moments, he said nothing. Suddenly, he burst out laughing. Katiah glared at him. He raised his hands in self-defense. "I didn't realize you had a sense of humor!" he said.

"This is the king's daughter, you imbecile!" Katiah hissed. "The king has the touch of gold, a magical gift from the goddess Denisia. His attempt to even the odds between you. He has touched the princess as he's touched everything else in the city of Gordium. He now comes to you with a larger fighting force than you expect, more horses, and better weapons."

Sargon's laughter faded. He looked from Katiah to Zoe and back. "This is real?" he asked.

"I told you I was bringing her," Katiah said.

Properly chastened, the king sobered. "Princess Zoe," he said. "I've heard much about you."

"Your goddess hopes to use me as a weapon against my father," Zoe said. "But it won't work."

Sargon raised an eyebrow. "It was your father who trapped you. I would think you would be angry with him."

"I'm angry with the one who's responsible," Zoe said, "and she's standing next to you."

"Denisia offered your father anything he might wish for," Katiah said. "I had little to do with it."

"He could have wished for anything?" Sargon cast Katiah a glance. "Lifelong safety for you and your brother. Peace for your lands. Great bounties of crops for your people. Yet he chose to wish for gold so that he could fight me, and now here you are. You forgive him all that?"

"He wished for the means to stop your tyranny," Zoe said. "And he will."

"Our soldiers number in the thousands," Sargon said.

"He will conquer your kingdom," Zoe said. "Then all the lands will be at peace."

Sargon crossed his arms over his chest. "Did he ever explain this obsession with me? Did you ask him about it?"

Zoe didn't answer.

"He attacked me first, you know. Many years ago."

"He heard of your cruelty to your people," Zoe said.

"What he deems cruel, I see as proper management."

"Define it however you like. The people will welcome King Midas as their new leader."

Sargon cocked his head at Katiah. "Leverage," he said. "You have my gratitude. What do you wish in return?"

"I trust you brought Elanur?" Katiah said.

Sargon gestured toward a smaller tent nearby.

"You won't mind if I see for myself?" the goddess asked.

"Be my guest."

Katiah glanced at Zoe. "After your rest," she told Sargon, "you will head for Karama. You will find your rival there." She winked at him, then left the two behind and walked toward the smaller tent.

XANDER HAD no idea how long he'd been asleep, but now he was awake. He'd heard something. He listened, senses alert. There. A snap. He froze, then slowly turned his head.

"Xander, you nincompoop!"

"Fotis?" Xander rose up on one elbow. "Is that you?"

"Is it safe?" Fotis asked.

Xander spotted a long nose peeking out from behind a nearby tree. "It is you!"

"Is it safe?" Fotis hissed.

"Safe to what?"

"Come over there!"

Xander glanced around. "Unless you think it isn't?"

"Well, is it or isn't it?" Fotis asked.

"Do you think it is?" Xander asked.

"What do *you* think?"

"I think so?"

The old man crept toward him with his nose pointed to the sky. He'd found a soldier's uniform, though it was too short for his height, the legs showing his bare ankles.

"Hide me," Fotis said.

"Where?" Xander asked.

"I don't care! They can't see me."

"You're disguised."

"Don't you have somewhere to hide?"

"This is it." Xander gestured to the ground.

Aster, who had been resting nearby, now turned toward them. "Armies always bring deluxe accommodations."

Fotis grunted and circled a few times like a dog seeking a comfortable spot. Finally, he lowered his tall frame into the dirt. A few moments later, he lay down and draped his arm over his forehead.

Xander watched him, a small smile playing on his lips. Fotis had come. Despite his misgivings, he had come.

"If this turns out to be a mistake, I will have your head," the old man said.

Xander smiled again. "At least you still have your other eye."

Fotis *harrumphed.* "This horse was much better behaved."

"Where is it?"

"Just over the rise. It found some wildflowers with an appealing flavor."

Xander lay back down and laced his fingers over his belly. "Denisia is here."

The old man lifted his head. "Here?"

"Disguised," Xander said. "Like us. In the army."

"What is this, a party?" Fotis asked.

"She's watching over the prince," Xander said. When Fotis let his head plop back down, Xander lifted up on his elbow. "You know what that means, don't you?"

"I dare not try to fathom."

"She wants to reverse the spell."

"Don't see that it matters now."

"How can you say that?"

"The battle is nigh," Fotis said. "There will be blood. The king and his son are weak and vulnerable, and the princess is lost."

"I spoke to her about it," Xander said.

"Did that do a lot of good?"

"I asked her to reconsider."

"Reconsider what?"

"Her plans."

"Why do that if she wants to help?"

"The way she's going to do it," Xander said. "I don't think it will work. It would be better if she would lift the curse." He paused. "I told her so. I think she listened to me."

"Of course she did," Aster interjected. "A goddess would be ignorant not to be supremely interested in your wisdom."

"Indeed," Fotis said. "The goddess is changing course as we speak all because of your advice."

Xander looked up at the sky, the sun almost directly above him. He was too happy for them to bother him this time. "No matter," he said. "It's going to be all right now."

"And how is that?" Fotis asked.

"You're here," Xander said and closed his eyes.

CHAPTER
TWENTY-THREE

It was late afternoon on the third full day of travel when King Midas' army began the climb that would lead them to Karama. The soldiers were tired, dusty, and sweaty, but they knew that the battle was nigh and so had begun to shift restlessly in their saddles, those on foot stepping up their pace.

Midas didn't know for sure that Sargon would meet him there, but he sensed Katiah watching with her vengeful eye. She would remember what the valley of the tower rocks meant to him. He'd told her once about an old memory, his last of his father. He'd been young and afraid and a disappointment then. This was his chance to prove himself, his final opportunity for victory.

They approached from the northwest. Once over the bench hills, they'd be able to see the enemy coming from the east. Before then, they would be blind, relying on the scouts for eyes. This was the treacherous part of the journey. If Sargon caught them there, they'd have a difficult time defending themselves. Midas had pushed his men hard with the goal of arriving first. He hoped it had worked.

The soldiers proceeded in an orderly fashion, two men abreast on the road. They kept their pace even, the scouts regularly going up and back. Three hills they climbed, hauling up, marching across, and descending the other side. When they finally crested the last one and looked out on the valley below, the sun had begun its descent toward the horizon.

Midas called a halt. Thousands paused behind him. Once the dust had settled, he scanned eastward and with a sigh of relief, confirmed Sargon had not yet arrived. The sun's rays drenched the land in a honey-like glaze, the ground a mix of pale sand and sandstone covered in sagebrush and wild grasses. But it was the rock formations what made this valley unlike any other. Consisting of basalt, tuff, and hardened lava, they erupted like fingers from unseen hands, many with acorn-shaped tips, others with fatter bases that lifted to pointed tops. Some resembled mushrooms sprouting from the earth like parasites feasting on subterranean stone. Ghost streams and rivers weaved between them like aged veins, their beds long gone dry, though a few still clung to shallow waters stagnant and filled with biting bugs. Known for its many graveyards of men, the varied landscape of Karama was perfect for surprise attacks and hidden assassins.

Midas' body felt weak in the heat, his limbs worn ragged by the journey. He glanced at Rastus, who helped him drink some of the spring water. Another scout approached from below, his horse digging in for the climb. Midas watched him come, wishing he might slow time. In the next few moments, everything would change, and thus would begin his end. He was in no rush to greet it. He took another drink, savoring the taste on his tongue. The scout was nearly upon them when Midas felt the glimmer at the edge of his vision, a shadow on the horizon like the reflection formed after staring into the sun too long.

"They're here, Your Majesty," the scout said. He was out of breath, his horse's lungs bellowing through cavernous nostrils.

Midas' heartbeat quickened. Already! He had managed only a brief respite.

"Some may have split off to the south," the scout said. "I saw tracks." He pointed, indicating the bench hills on the opposite side of the valley, the ones that now provided a backdrop for the finger rocks.

Rastus dismissed him and turned his gaze to Midas. It was time for action.

The king resisted. In this moment, he could savor his victory, sense the power in the army he had built. He could imagine striking Sargon down. Rescuing his daughter. Reuniting with his sister. It was all there for the taking. Once he moved forward, everything would become less certain.

"Rastus," he said. "There is a woman named Elanur. When this is over and Sargon is defeated, you must ask about her."

"Someone you knew, Your Majesty?" Rastus asked.

Elanur's chubby face appeared in Midas' mind, her little arms extended in excitement. She wouldn't look like that anymore, but it was how he remembered her. He let the vision wash over him, savoring it, hoping that somehow, despite everything, he might see her again. "She is a slave," he said. "One that Sargon took from the outlying villages. Someone in his inner circle may know what happened to her."

"Slaves are often forgotten," Rastus said.

Midas looked west, his gaze following the long road they had traveled. "Elanur," he said again. "If you find her, take her to the castle. Make sure she's well cared for."

"Yes, Your Majesty."

Midas turned back to the east. On the horizon, the shadow was taking shape, long and dark like a poisonous snake. Another scout raced toward them on a small black horse. "Your Majesty," he said, "they come in three groups. They mean to surround us."

The light had changed in the sky, going from a bright yellow to a softer gold. It was time to move. Midas felt the urge to pat Kanani's neck, to encourage the stallion as he'd always done before riding into battle, but the mitts prevented it. Disappointing. He directed his gaze over the valley once more, observing the finger rocks, bench hills, and dark nooks and crannies from which any soldier might emerge. He thought of the boy, wondering where he had gotten off to. He hadn't seen him since he'd welcomed him into his tent for the night. He trusted the child's instincts would keep him safe. After a long inhale, he turned around to face his men.

"They have come," he said, his voice not as commanding as he'd hoped. He cleared his throat. "This is our time. History will remember this day as the day King Sargon II was defeated once and for all. We are strong. We will be victorious."

Once the cheering had subsided, Rastus called the commanders to the front for a conference. Soon smaller units were breaking off from the main one, some traveling back west and some east, while more darted downhill, seeking hiding places among the rocks and ravines. Midas motioned the rest to follow him into the valley. There was a clearing there. He would meet his enemy and make his stand.

"To victory," he said to Rastus, and didn't look back.

DENISIA HAD all she could do not to break rank and chase after the prince. Anchurus charged down the steepest part of the hill on Ambrose's back, leading one of the smaller companies away from the main army. He was far enough behind that the king wouldn't see him, a group of at least twenty with him. She could have easily blended in with them, but it was too risky. She held her place in line. She had a different task to complete.

Xander's warning echoed in her head. Someone would die if she unleashed the magic. But it was clear to her now that Anchurus would not survive his injuries. His only hope was the spell. And what did the pudgy advisor know? Lady Verna had said all would return to as it was. Before the curse. Before the prince was burned. Before he'd grown to hate her. Before everything between them had fallen apart. As it was. She would make it as it was. Silenus had trusted the old witch. Denisia hoped she could, too.

The bulk of the army followed the king toward the clearing. She rode along, knowing she would have to break away soon. If all went well, the two kings would follow standard battle practice and meet together before the fighting started. Sometimes kings sent emissaries rather than meet themselves, but Denisia suspected King Midas would demand to see his enemy face to face.

She hoped she was right. It would make things a lot easier.

WHEN SARGON first spotted his enemy, he thought about climbing one of the bench hills to the south to gain a superior vantage point. But some of his commanders had already gone that direction. Better to face King Midas himself.

He turned to the men behind him, two of them carrying the golden princess suspended between them with ropes. Every time he saw the sculpture, he had to reconvince himself that there was a person inside. He shifted his gaze to Elanur, who was also behind him and to his right. He realized with surprise that the two were not unalike. Indeed, there were similarities in the hands and the eyes, as well as the slope from the cheek to the chin.

"Stay back," he ordered the men. "They are not to be seen until I say so."

The guards responded, the one leading Elanur's horse drawing her closer while the ones with the princess tightened their hold.

"He won't fall for it," Zoe said.

Sargon was relieved to hear her speak. She hadn't said a word since they'd left camp long before, leaving him to wonder if the whole charade had been one of Katiah's tricks. But the princess was still in there, which meant he maintained leverage over King Midas.

"You can't deny it will be difficult for him to see you in my custody," Sargon said.

"He is planning a rescue even as we speak," Zoe said.

"My troops spread across these lands like the clouds across the sky," Sargon said. "My commanders lead smaller companies that will soon surround your father's men. There is no chance King Midas will be able to steal you without getting killed."

"You don't know my father or his allies."

"I doubt he has a better ally than I do."

"If the goddess is so devout," Zoe said, "where is she?"

It was true—Katiah had disappeared after visiting Elanur and hadn't shown herself again. "She is here," he said, scanning the surrounding rocks. "We will defeat your father and then we will have all of his riches for ourselves."

"Father!" Zoe yelled. "I'm here, Father!"

"Silence her!" Sargon ordered. One of the men covered her mouth with his hand, but of course it did no good.

"Father, he means to surround you!"

They were still much too far out for Midas to hear, but Sargon was irritated. He thought about sending her farther back, but he didn't like the idea of having her out of his sight. He needed her nearby to use against King Midas when he was ready. For a time, they proceeded with her shouting warnings, one after the other. At one point, he turned his sword on her fair head, but the metal only clanged against the gold.

"What's the matter, great king?" Zoe said. "Am I bothering you?"

Sargon frowned, then turned back toward Midas' approaching army. "Shout all you want, Princess," he said, "for this is the day your father dies."

KATIAH STROKED her black wolf between its tall ears. "Patience, my dear. Soon you will have all the prey you could wish for."

The beast looked up at her with eager eyes. They stood inside one of the squatty rock formations in a cave hollowed out by natives ages before. It featured a view of the clearing through a hand-carved slit in the rock—the perfect lookout. From her southern position, Sargon was on her right, Midas on her left. It was surreal to see them coming on at almost the exact same moment. She had seen the smaller units breaking off from Midas' group. Shortly after, similar units from Sargon's army had taken up their positions. They would all end up fighting in the various nooks and crannies that formed this land, murders hidden in dark draws, bodies dragged into caves. Each would surprise the other at times, for there were plenty of hiding places. All would be equal, which was just what she'd wanted.

She smiled to herself. She had predicted Karem would choose this place. He'd told her about it six moons after his village burned. They'd been walking by the river near the cabin when he'd described the battle here among the rocks of Karama. His father had led the men. Young Karem had been impressed with his bravery but disappointed in his own cowardice. He'd hidden in one of the caves when the fighting had begun. A simple memory, but meaningful. Katiah knew all men returned to thoughts of their fathers when they sensed death gaining ground behind them.

She still wore her warrior's tunic, dark pants, and black boots, but her tan cloak would camouflage her nicely in this valley. She'd tied her hair in a braid, the early evening breeze playing with a few strands about her ears. She smoothed them back and checked the armies' progress once more. The two would come together shortly before sunset. She couldn't have planned it better. Her stomach tightened in anticipation. There would be blood, death, and then she would be . . . what?

Avenged. Restored. The man who had betrayed her would be dead, his army decimated, his kingdom left for the taking. She could start over, put someone new on the throne. She'd hoped Emir would be right for the job, but he'd angered her with his excessive concern for Princess Zoe. After all she'd done for him. Why didn't any human male remain loyal? Part of her regretted leaving him to contend with the hunter on his own. If he survived, perhaps she would reconsider him. But no matter. The battle was nigh, and she was eager for it. Let them all kill each other. It was what they deserved.

With nothing to do but wait, she lay back inside the cave and closed her eyes, her wolf keeping an eye on the entrance. She would rest, conserve her strength. Breathing deeply, she ignored the quivers in her stomach as the image of Midas' face appeared behind her eyes.

He deserved everything he had coming. Everything.

EMIR HID near the top of a dune-shaped mound, taking a moment's rest while watching Sargon approach. Baris' horse stood behind him, weary from the fast trek. They'd left the hunter's body dead in the dirt a day's journey out. After a long fight, Emir had finally disarmed him with a lucky kick to the groin, then swiftly broken his neck. The horse Katiah had granted the hunter carried two saddle bags full of supplies. Emir had found enough to eat to sustain him, along with some extra water. He'd thought about returning to Gordium for the boy, but, despite his better judgment, had followed the dark goddess' path straight into battle.

Now he was rewarded by the sight of the princess suspended between two riders just behind King Sargon, who appeared tall and strong on his piebald warhorse. Emir imagined slashing the man's thick neck and watching the blood gush out as the king struggled to breathe. It would be delicious, particularly after all the years they'd suffered, he and his mother. But he had to focus on his mission, King Midas' orders echoing in his ears. He was running scenarios in his head when he spotted the rider on the king's right.

He stopped. Looked again.

Mother?

What was she doing there? He stared, confused at first and then angry. The bastard. Sargon had brought his mother to battle? So typical of him. Emir nearly called out to her, but stopped just in time. He would only get himself captured. As it was, she seemed well enough. She sat erect in the saddle, a thin scarf over her head, her hands unbound. He glared at the king, his arrogant father riding to a mighty victory. He would get her killed. For nothing.

Emir chewed on the inside of his cheek as the men marched by. His mother. Here. Katiah had mentioned her, but he'd never imagined King Sargon would allow a slave woman to ride with him. Whatever was going on, Emir had to answer only one question: What now? He was unprepared. One man alone against thousands. He would have to wait for the right opportunity. Or find a way to create one. Either way, his rescue mission had changed.

He waited while Sargon's men passed him by, headed for a clearing not far ahead. A good place for old rivals to meet before ordering their men into battle. Midas' army approached from the opposite direction. There wasn't a lot of time.

Below, he spotted a narrow path he could follow while finding cover behind sagebrush and boulders. He'd have to leave the horse. He grabbed his sword and an extra dagger from the saddle, then crouched low and darted off.

"You shouldn't give up so easily." Xander turned to the other two advisors. They'd managed to break off from the main group and now stood huddled with a group of about fifteen soldiers in a ravine near the clearing. Both armies marched toward each other, the kings proudly leading, their flags waving in the evening breeze. Xander tried to see the princess, but they were too far away. "He must have her with him," he whispered.

"It would be logical," Fotis said.

"She isn't his prized possession," Aster agreed.

"So we go ahead with our plan, then?" Xander asked.

"It's not a good day to die," Aster said.

Fotis grunted. "The king's advisors, off to save the princess. A stellar idea."

"There are many others here to help her," Aster said.

"We are not soldiers," Fotis said.

"We don't look like soldiers," Aster said.

"Appearance will not save us when the time comes," Fotis said.

"I hope we can time it right," Xander said.

"It's a poor plan," Fotis said. "We'll never get close enough to—"

Aster pulled a bow from behind his back, stopping Fotis mid-sentence.

"We attach the explosive to the arrow." Xander demonstrated the plan to Fotis. "Aster shoots it into the enemy's ranks. It explodes. The soldiers are confused. We rescue the princess. Ta-da!"

Fotis rolled his eyes.

Aster reached into his pocket, pulled out ten pouches, and showed them to the old advisor. Xander pulled out ten more.

"These are toys," Fotis said. "Sargon's men will kill us after the first one blows."

"It's wonderful to be so optimistic." Aster tucked his pouches back into his pocket.

"Do you have a better plan?" Xander asked, but Fotis only grumbled.

The armies were moving quickly. Xander glanced at the rest of the soldiers. They were mice in the ravine, silent and hidden. "We're going to have to leave before they do," he whispered.

"How are we going to do that?" Fotis asked.

"They will be interested in stopping us," Aster said.

"You're saying we should just walk out?" Fotis asked.

"He's right," Xander said. "They won't want to give themselves away."

"Won't *we* be giving *them* away?" Fotis asked.

Xander didn't know what to say to that. He looked around for Denisia. The last he'd seen her, she'd still been with the army. He prayed to the gods that she had reconsidered. Perhaps she would lift the curse and forego her other plan. Either way, it was out of their hands now. All they could do was try to rescue the princess before the battle began.

"Now?" Xander asked.

"Not now," Aster said, his keen gaze intense on the converging armies beyond.

"Let's do take our time," Fotis said, rubbing his knee. "This ravine is quite comfortable."

CHAPTER TWENTY-FOUR

The armies marched toward one another, the Karama Valley braced for the oncoming battle. Tower rocks reached for the fading sun's rays, beseeching them to linger a bit longer for fear of what horrors the dark might bring. The evening breeze fluttered the kings' flags, warning all who would see them that it was time to leave or be prepared to fight. A steady rumble of hoof-beats accompanied the scene, pieces of armor catching the last of the light in random flashes.

The rules of engagement dictated there would be no attack until the leaders had spoken, but rules had been broken before. Gazes sharp, weapons at the ready, they all came to a halt near the clearing, leaving sufficient space between them for an open forum. For a long while, the men stared across the expanse at one another. Finally, two lone riders broke away from each group. Their exchange was brief, after which they both raced back to their respective rulers. Another long pause took place, the kings seeking their rivals amidst the thousands of figures spread before them.

Midas was the first to step out. With Rastus on one side and Baran on the other, he directed Kanani forward, his gaze on the figure he believed to be Sargon. Remaining upright in the saddle had become a challenge, but he could not falter now. He kept Kanani to a slow walk, his position becoming more precarious with each stride. Soon he began to wonder if Sargon had the courage to meet him, but finally three riders broke free of the mass beyond.

Come, you coward, he thought. *I want to see your face once more.*

Sargon rode between the other two men, his horse a monstrous black and white piebald. Midas knew it was him, for he held the same cocky posture, his thick arms the very ones that had trapped little Elanur against him all those years ago. Midas saw her face as clear as he'd seen it that day, the tears glistening on her chubby cheeks, and the old rage burned in his belly. By the time the two groups came together, his anger had replaced his weakness, leaving him seething in the saddle.

"King Midas," Sargon said, coming to a stop a short distance away.

"Sargon," Midas answered.

His enemy noted the insult of the missing title with a cocked eyebrow. "There is something you wish to say?"

Midas studied the man, surprised to find him so much older. In his thoughts, his rival had always been the strapping youngster staring down at him from his perch on the powerful sorrel stallion. Now he was more mature, with wrinkles on his brow and around his eyes, and Midas was no longer the orphan beneath his feet.

"Perhaps you wish to surrender," Sargon said. "Save your men."

"Why would I bring my men this far to surrender?" Midas asked.

Sargon waited a beat. "Because I have your daughter."

Midas controlled his features, his hands clenched inside the mitts. This he had expected. Still, it wasn't easy to hear. "My daughter is gone."

"Indeed?" Sargon said. "Then who is the golden girl I have in my possession? A speaking sculpture, of all things." He watched Midas with his dark eyes. "She says her father will defeat me handily. You have to give her credit for her loyalty."

Zoe speaking? It had to be a trick. "The gods are playing with you."

"If that is so, I welcome it." Sargon patted his horse's thick neck. "We did defeat you, and we will defeat you again."

Midas watched the way Sargon's full lips remained parted even after he stopped talking. "You don't remember me, do you?"

"If I met you in battle, you were unremarkable."

"Before that. I was a boy."

Sargon chuckled. "The boys I knew were powerful warriors. I doubt you were one of them."

"I was never part of your father's army." Midas observed his enemy's face. Sargon did not know. Midas had thought of little else but Sargon since the day Elanur had been kidnapped, but it seemed Sargon had thought nothing of him. "Before you were king. When you were doing your father's dirty work. You slaughtered a village. Set all the tents on fire. Stole the children. One little girl. A toddler." He pointed at Sargon's left leg. "I stabbed you."

Sargon's hand went to his thigh. A cloud passed over his features.

"You tried to kill me that day," Midas said. "But you failed. I think we both know why."

Sargon glanced back at his men. The piebald danced underneath him. He pulled the reins taut, then squared his shoulders and returned his attention to Midas. "I will give your daughter your best wishes." He whirled his horse and retreated, his commanders flanking him.

"It was Katiah," Midas shouted after him. "She helped me become king. Me, the tribal waif! But you, the warrior, she sent home to your father to scrape your way to the top. Do you truly believe she means well for you now?"

Sargon continued for several more steps before pulling the piebald to a stop. His men paused beside him. "That was you?" he said, turning around.

Midas kept his gaze steady, his posture erect.

"You were the boy." He gazed upon Midas as if seeing him for the first time. "The donkey boy. I wounded you."

Midas pulled his cloak back to reveal the old scar.

Sargon urged his horse forward. When he got close enough, he eyed the mark, tracing its path from Midas' neck down until it disappeared under the thick fabric of his cloak. "That's why," he murmured. "That's it." His gaze returned to Midas' face. "Now it all makes sense." He studied his rival for another moment, then signaled his men. Midas' commanders came to attention. "I want to show you something," Sargon said. "That is all."

Midas nodded his assent. Sargon gestured once more. Two more riders started forward, the horses approaching at a smart trot. As they drew near, Midas noticed that one of them was a woman.

"As I recall, I gave you a chance to join us that day." Sargon angled the piebald so that it stood perpendicular to Midas, giving him a clear view of both the woman approaching and his enemy's reaction. "Do you remember?"

Midas didn't answer, his gaze trained on the woman. Thick hair covered her head, slim shoulders balanced over the saddle, legs tight to the girth. She wore a blue cloak that circled her waist and swept around her arms in layers, the last trailing behind her back. The guard held a rope tethered to her mount.

"Now I understand why you've been so relentless in your pursuit," Sargon said. "Always attacking. I thought you were mad. But now. Now I see." The guard came up alongside Sargon's commander, the woman next to him. "King Midas," Sargon said, "I advise you again to surrender. I have your daughter. And if what you say is true, it seems I have your sister as well." The soldier led the woman's horse forward. "Elanur," Sargon said, "meet King Midas."

Elanur! She bowed her head. Midas' heart raced.

"He says that he is your brother," Sargon said to the woman. "Does he speak the truth?"

Elanur lifted her gaze. For a long while, she studied Midas' face. At one point, she urged her horse forward. The animal took only two steps before the guard pulled it to a halt. Elanur sat stone-still, her gaze never wavering from King Midas.

"Karem? Is that you?"

Denisia crept a little closer, tucking herself behind a nearby rock. The two kings had met in the clearing as she'd expected. As they conversed, small groups of soldiers stole away into the shadows, cutting off exit points. Brief battles raged even as the valley seemed to hold its breath. It was as if the hills were alive with creeping, crawling soldiers fighting over nooks and crannies, spreading like rodents into every ravine and draw.

She turned her attention to the slave woman Sargon had brought forward, wondering what she had to do with the dark king's plan. She seemed intent on Midas, her gaze never leaving his face. Midas, in turn, looked distressed. Partly from a lack of nourishment, Denisia was sure, but there was something more. His gaze darted from Sargon to the woman and back as if he feared what the woman might say.

Denisia searched the area, seeking Anchurus, but he remained out of sight. She pulled the box from her breast pocket, closed her eyes, and said a small prayer to the gods for her grandfather. Tucking it away, she peered around the rock. She would have to get closer for the spell to work. She eyed her path to the next mushroom-shaped formation, then ducked low and dashed out.

Midas stared at the woman across from him. In his mind, Elanur was a toddler, little more than a baby with her chubby cheeks and swirly hair. Yet here sat a mature woman, her cheeks drawn and her black hair wild about her head.

"Mother," he whispered, but it wasn't her. He urged Kanani a few steps forward. The woman watched him with dark eyes. She looked unfamiliar, yet he knew her. He stared, battling with himself until he caught Sargon's sneering expression. He drew Kanani to a halt, suddenly on guard, but couldn't resist the woman's face. How many times had he imagined seeing her again? Everything in him longed to take hold of her mount's rein and lead her back to the safety of his own troops.

"Are you all right?" he asked.

"Is it really you?" the woman said. "You are the king?"

"I am Karem." The name sounded strange on his tongue. He saw her as a toddler sitting on Sargon's horse, her hands reaching toward him. "Do you remember your doll? The one Mother made you?"

She looked down. Slowly, a smile whispered on her face. "Sunshine."

Needles poked at Midas' eyes. It was her. His sister! No one else would have known that. A lump rose in his throat. "I wanted to come earlier. I tried to come."

"Did Emir find you?" she asked.

"Emir?"

"Enough!" Sargon waved his hand. The escort pulled Elanur's horse back. A gap opened between the siblings.

"Wait!" Midas glanced from his sister's face to Sargon's, but the other king's features had hardened.

"I have news, woman," Sargon said to Elanur. "I've recaptured our son."

Son? Elanur and Sargon?

Hoofbeats sounded off to the right. A group of horsemen rose out of a ravine. Behind them trailed a man on foot, hands bound with ropes. When the riders shifted into a gallop, the prisoner fell and was dragged along the ground. Elanur screamed. Midas looked at her stricken face, then back at the oncoming soldiers.

"You should have trusted me," Sargon said to Elanur. "I always keep my word."

The soldiers hauled the prisoner into the clearing, positioning him near their king. He got up, his clothes covered in dirt and dust, blood on his temple and cheek. Midas stared at him. This was the gifted musician, the one who had brought the hunters, the reason Zoe had been kidnapped. This man was Elanur's son?

"You promised!" Elanur said to Sargon.

"It's all right, Mother," Emir called through a scratchy throat. "It's all right."

Midas looked from Elanur to the musician and back. *His nephew?*

"You've joined our family reunion, son," Sargon said. "Say 'hello' to your uncle over there."

The musician's gaze found Midas, then jerked to his mother's face in surprise.

"Sargon," Elanur said with a warning glance, "she is watching."

Sargon laughed. "Do you think I am afraid of her? Let her come!" He pulled his sword from its scabbard and thrust it toward Emir's throat. "He's a traitor!"

"No!" Elanur leapt off her horse and ran to her son. He stood poised between the guards, his ropes drawn tight, defiant before Sargon just as Midas had been defiant all those years ago.

"You will release them!" Midas blurted.

Sargon turned to him. "Why would I do that?"

Midas looked back at his sister, his mind racing. His men were prepared, waiting for his signal. It was the chance he had so long hoped for. But one wrong move and Sargon would kill Emir, his nephew. Perhaps even Elanur. And Zoe was still in the dark king's possession. Midas could defeat him in a battle, but if his family were decimated, what would victory matter? He surveyed the area, the setting sun casting the rocks in a pale orange light. These were the last actions of his life, his next move the one that would most affect his children.

"King Sargon." The title tasted vile in his mouth. "Let us both save our men and preserve our resources. Let us come to an agreement. I will offer you—"

"No, no, no, my darling." A voice echoed from above. "There will be no peace agreement today."

Everyone looked up, soldiers in both armies shifting to see where the voice was coming from. Katiah stood on top of a stout rock formation, her dark pants and black boots shadowed against the sky.

"Great Katiah, please," Elanur pleaded. "Save my son!"

"Don't listen to her, Mother." Emir struggled against the ropes. "She doesn't care about you."

"She helped you escape," Elanur said.

"Then why," Sargon said, dropping his sword from Emir's throat, "is he once again in my custody?"

Elanur shifted her gaze from Sargon to Emir and back. "Great goddess," she said, looking upward, "please. I have always worshipped you."

"Which is flattering, my dear." Katiah stepped toward the edge of the formation. "It's too bad your son and brother don't share your loyal nature."

"It wasn't the goddess who brought them to you!" Sargon circled around behind Elanur. "I have them both at my mercy." He gestured to each in turn. "You are worshipping the wrong person."

Elanur backed toward Emir, placing her body between the king and her son.

"King Sargon." Midas directed Kanani forward, but didn't get far before his rival's guards blocked his way. "The goddess is playing with us."

"It is not *us* she wishes to play with." Sargon turned to his enemy. "Surely you can see it now? This is all for you." He stretched his arms out, taking in the entirety of the scene. "The boy she saved. The boy she made king." He shook his head, clucking his tongue. "What did you do to make her so angry?"

Midas seethed inside his cloak. If only he could draw his sword across the man's neck. "You are caught in the goddess' web just as surely as I am. Do you wish to continue playing out this game for her?"

"She was the one who told me to bring your sister." Sargon dismounted and dropped the piebald's reins. "She wanted to savor this moment when you would be reunited." He approached Elanur, who stood rooted in place, her hands out to shield her son. "If it were up to me, she'd be safe in my city where she has been all this time. But now I see the brilliance of the goddess' plan. The look on your face!" Reaching Elanur, he took her roughly by the upper arm. Emir pulled against the ropes. "She is mine," Sargon said to Midas. "My slave. My mistress. And that is our son." He pointed to Emir. "And back there is your daughter." He gestured into the depths of his troops, then shoved Elanur away from him. "They will all be going back with me. I offer you now the choice I offered you then. Swear allegiance to me, *Karem*, and they will remain unharmed."

Midas released the reins. Kanani charged forward, thundering across the clearing. Midas dove off just in time to drive his sword into Sargon's chest. Pulled it out. Drove it down again. The fiend! But the victory was only in his imagination. In reality, he remained rooted in his saddle, every muscle in his body aching from being held taut for so long. The last of his strength was leaving him. And now everything was falling apart. He glanced back at his men. His brave men who now numbered in the thousands. It was a sight he had waited all his life to see. But what good would it do now? He'd been a fool.

He addressed Sargon. "Let my men go," he said. "Let Elanur and Zoe go. Leave Gordium alone, and I will return with you."

Sargon laughed. "You think yourself such a prize?"

"I wanted my sister back," Midas said. "Now here she is. Release her, and I shall be content to bow to your rule. The great king of Gordium at your mercy."

"My men are here to seize your kingdom." Sargon took a step toward him. "Your only choice is to fight or surrender. It's up to you how many will die."

"If we fight, we will both lose men," Midas said.

"Such is war," Sargon said with a shrug. "But I have the goddess on my side."

Midas clenched his teeth and glanced up at Katiah. He could no longer make out her features. The sky had faded to gray. Soon, night would be upon them.

"Your Majesty," Rastus said under his breath. "We came to fight."

Sargon, as if sensing a change, remounted his horse. A heavy anticipation settled over the clearing. Midas waited, Kanani shifting nervously underneath him.

"Your Majesty?" Rastus said.

"Father, don't let him win!"

Midas' head shot up. The voice came out of the depths of the opposing army, distant but clear. *Zoe?*

"He must not win. Father," the princess called. "For the people!"

Midas searched but couldn't see her.

"Don't let him win!"

There was no doubt. It was her voice. Iron poured down Midas' spine. He pulled Kanani's reins tight and glanced once more at Elanur. If he fought, he might lose her again. But he could not let his daughter down, or his entire kingdom. With a quick glance at Rastus, he raised his arm. Rastus lifted his in turn, signaling the men.

"No!" Katiah dropped into the clearing. "You will *not* seize victory on this day, Karem!" She turned toward Elanur, raised both hands to the sky, and began to chant. Dark clouds collected above her, and then a dazzling white light burst forth. Katiah caught it, and in one swift motion, redirected it toward Elanur. The slave woman stood stunned, unable to move fast enough, but Emir, who had watched it all, lurched forward, pulling Sargon's men off their horses as he surged with all his strength, diving in front of his mother just as the white light came. His body absorbed its power and fell hard to the ground.

THE THREE ADVISORS crouched behind a nearby table-shaped rock formation, two of them wearing Sargon's uniforms. They had found two dead soldiers in a draw, victims of one of Midas' guerrilla groups. It had been Aster's idea to take their clothing. Xander thought it distasteful, but had to acknowledge the wisdom in it. Now they stood in tunics too big or too small, their own pants retained underneath, the perfect disguise for penetrating Sargon's army. Only Fotis remained in King Midas' uniform.

Beyond, the golden princess hung suspended between two soldiers at the edge of the fourth row back. When Sargon's men had dragged Emir down into the clearing, the advisors had taken advantage of the distraction to shuffle closer. Aster led them through another ravine and down behind a cluster of rocks. It was as close as they dared to go without the soldiers spotting them. There, they waited until Katiah announced her presence.

"Not now," Aster said.

With a last glance back at the elder advisor, Xander followed his friend, walking toward the enemy soldiers while trying his best to appear as if he were one of them. Some of Sargon's men turned as the two advisors approached, but with Aster in the lead looking very soldier-like, they paid them no mind. Aster took position behind a tall sagebrush, set fire to a pouch, stabbed an arrow through it, and shot it into the troops. Once the confusion started, he repeated the action three times, then dropped the bow. He and Xander hurried to the next row and threw more flaming pouches.

"There she is!" Xander said, referring to the princess.

They made their way toward the targeted fourth row. Aster tossed another pouch. Then Xander. Each burned a small flame on the ground. More of the soldiers looked down, their horses sidestepping nervously as the smoke thickened. From the clearing behind them came a bone-chilling shriek. The soldiers craned their heads to see more clearly. The advisors had soon tossed twenty of the flaming pouches among them. When Aster signaled that the last had been thrown, they ran back toward the rocks.

"You there," one of Sargon's soldiers called. "Halt!"

His words were muted by the mini explosion underneath him. It was only the first. One after another, the pouches released the pent-up energy they had stored, spewing bits of herbs, dust, and gases through the ranks. Ear-splitting booms and pops assaulted the air, flames alighting on arms and legs and coming to rest on horses' blankets and hides. The animals reared and whirled, some of them galloping off in the opposite direction, others charging up into the hills. Red, green, and gray smoke polluted the air, obscuring vision. Spicy smells overwhelmed the soldiers' sinuses, sending many into sneezing fits.

"Stop!" Aster said, charging forward.

Both advisors ran toward the fourth row. Aster reached the princess first. Only one guard held her, the other having lost his hold of the rope in the confusion. Aster drew his dagger and tried to cut the remaining tie, but the guard's horse was backing away in fear, tossing its head and rearing as the soldier struggled to regain control.

"Who's there?" a voice said. "Is someone there?"

"It's us, Princess!" Xander rushed to her side. "We're rescuing you!"

"Xander?" Zoe asked.

"Hang on!"

Aster sawed the dagger back and forth, skipping about to keep pace with the jerking movements of the horse. "The princess is not released!" he shouted as the rope slithered off of the sculpture. The princess fell down into the dirt.

"Aster?" Zoe called.

Aster grabbed her arm and started to pull her off the road. The soldier came after him, his sword poised to strike.

"Don't!" Xander whirled around, his hands up. The soldier sliced downward, his blade grazing Xander's chest. The young advisor froze and stared down at himself while the soldier rode on toward Aster, preparing another strike. Aster ducked out of range just in time.

"I don't need your help!" he beckoned to Xander.

The young advisor stood trembling, his eyes staring vacantly ahead of him.

"Xander. The princess. Not now!"

Xander was too slow. The explosions had stopped. The smoke was clearing. Aster tried to pull the princess away on his own, but he didn't get far before more soldiers surrounded him. He yelled nonsense words and flailed his hands, but they stood their ground. He looked back to see Xander's gaze on him, his face as pale as the moon.

MIDAS STARED AT EMIR ALKAN, the man he had welcomed into his castle. He had impressed the citizens with his sensitive musicality. Saved Midas from choking. But it was because of him the men had stolen the princess. He'd brought the life-giving water, but lied about how he'd found it. Lied about working with Katiah. A traitor without honor. Midas had ordered Rastus to have him killed.

And now Emir lay dead in the dirt. Struck by the very goddess he'd seemed to work for. Katiah's white flame had seared a wound the size of a man's fist in his chest.

His nephew.

"Your Majesty," Rastus said. "The order?"

Midas watched Elanur crying over her son's body. Popping sounds distracted him, minor explosions across the clearing. Blue, gray, and red smoke rose above a clump of soldiers beyond.

"FAX?" he mumbled under his breath.

Sargon looked down at Emir, his face strangely twisted in shock and grief. Elanur wailed, rocking back and forth. Katiah approached from the right. She was walking toward Emir, her hands out, face stricken. Midas watched as her gaze shifted from Emir's body to Elanur and back. Might she complete her original intent and kill his sister? Gritting his teeth, Midas lifted his arm. "Attack. Attack!"

The army moved. A colossal caterpillar, it came toward him, troops racing through the valley like a million legs, more men streaming down from the bench tops where they'd been hiding, others emerging from the ravines like scorpions, all of them shouting their war cries. Across the way, Sargon's men responded, thundering from the east while break-off units charged from the south. For a few moments, it was glorious. Midas felt time slow, the men flowing toward him like a river while he twirled Kanani around in the middle of the stream. When they caught up to him, he turned back to face his enemy. "Attack!" he called again. Rastus and Baran echoed the order, Sargon's men answering from the other side.

The Karama Valley erupted into chaos. Thousands of soldiers charged toward one another in a passion for murder. Battle cries echoed off the flat rocks, horses' hooves rumbling the ground underneath, the sound soon accompanied by painful wails as hundreds of swords and arrows found their marks.

A small figure darted out from the right, catching Midas' eye. The boy? The child ran toward the musician, his mouth open, face strained with anguish. Midas slowed Kanani, his men giving way around him as they charged the enemy. The boy fell into the dirt beside Emir and began rocking back and forth, his small hands on the musician's leg and then over his torso and head. Elanur looked up at him, her own face carved in grief. The boy grabbed Emir's shirt, his mouth opening and closing like a fish pulled from the water, the tendons in his throat straining against the uncooperative voice. He pounded Emir's chest, desperately demanding he return to life.

The scene transported Midas back to his own grief at his dead mother's side. He didn't remember the sound of his voice, only that he had said her name over and over. The scene in front of him was grotesque in its cruelty, the boy unable to release anything from his dead throat. He took Emir's hand in his and, clutching it to him, rocked back and forth with his mouth still opening and closing in useless attempts to cry.

All around him men were fighting, but Midas' gaze was riveted to the child. Suddenly, the boy leapt to his feet and turned on Katiah. Horror spread across her face as he advanced, his hands in a flurry of activity, his mouth shouting words no one could hear. The goddess took a step back, shaking her head as if in apology. The boy picked up a handful of dirt and threw it at her, then another and another. She ducked, her hand shielding her face, wincing as the boy shouted his silent rage over and over again. He finished with a flurry of hand motions, ending with a shove toward her as if pushing her out of his world. He fiercely wiped his cheeks and darted back to the dead man, dropping to his side once more.

Midas watched it all, his breath in his throat. He glanced several times at Katiah, worried she would strike the boy, but she remained where she was, staring at him like a mother after a lost son.

"Take him!" Sargon shouted.

Midas raised his head with a start. Sargon was pointing at the boy. The two soldiers who had captured Emir went after the child.

"No!" Midas shouted. "You will *not!*" With his men in the thick of battle around him, he charged the dark king.

CHAPTER
TWENTY-FIVE

Denisia scurried out of the ravine and headed toward the clearing, grateful for the helmet that was still on her head as she ducked and weaved to avoid getting hit by a stray sword or swinging ax. She gripped the small box in her hand, the corner poking into her palm. A slick film of sweat covered her skin. Beyond, thousands of men battled, iron and bronze weapons clashing together. In the middle of it all, Sargon sat poised on his piebald, his sword drawn as Midas came at him.

"No!" A new rider galloped down from the hill adjacent to the clearing. "I challenge you, King Sargon!"

Denisia stopped in her tracks. It was Anchurus on Ambrose.

Sargon whirled to face his new enemy, the dark king now suspended between father and son.

"*Oh, no,*" Denisia whispered.

The prince charged, but Sargon blocked, their horses skittering underneath. Midas hesitated on the periphery, his gaze riveted to his son. Sargon spun around, a new grin on his lips. Anchurus sat poised for battle, though Denisia saw the way he gripped his legs unnaturally to avoid pressing his wounds against Ambrose's girth. Around them, the men battled, the stench of sweat and blood rising into the air as the valley filled with the painful cries of injured soldiers. The prince charged again and, with a swipe of his sword, sliced Sargon's thigh as he passed. Sargon didn't even check the wound. He only grimaced and whirled his horse, the reins tight and short. Anchurus attacked again, urging Ambrose toward the piebald. They collided, and both men fell.

Midas tied Kanani's reins together and dropped them on the animal's neck. He leaned forward and, gripping the sword between his mitted hands, signaled the stallion to advance. They would run down the dark king, it seemed, but when they passed by, Sargon ducked and sliced an easy cut across Kanani's foreleg. The animal stumbled, sending Midas over the top of his head. The king slammed onto the ground and skidded to a stop on his belly.

Denisia arrived just as Anchurus, his face red with rage, lunged at King Sargon. The two resumed their battle on foot, dead and injured men piling up around them, soldiers climbing over bodies to fight new enemies on the other side. Sargon blocked the prince's every blow and returned them in kind. *Clang clang clang,* the metal clashed. Anchurus pursued. Sargon retreated. Then Sargon attacked and Anchurus fell back. All around them, hundreds upon hundreds pressed together, pulsing and inflamed, their weapons darting and flying, yet they left space for the king and the prince to fight, their respect for their leaders overcoming every other instinct.

Denisia stood riveted, watching it all. Midas was struggling to get to his feet. Anchurus attacked again, his strokes wild. Sargon waited for him, seemingly content to allow the wavering prince to expend himself. Near the rock tower where Katiah had stood hung the boy in the guards' grip, Emir's dead body abandoned in the dirt.

Denisia removed her helmet. She couldn't afford to wait any longer.

SARGON WAS GOING TO KILL MIDAS' son.

Midas could see it coming. Anchurus was going after the dark king with everything he had, but his face poured sweat and his strikes were wildly off their mark. Sargon bled from the minor wound in his leg, but he seemed not to notice, waltzing around the clearing and fending off each of the prince's attacks with ease.

Midas got to his feet, his hands still covered in the gold mitts. Why hadn't his son obeyed him? Anchurus was supposed to be back in Gordium, safely ensconced within the walls of the castle. But the young advisor had been right—the prince didn't want to miss his father's final battle. No matter. Anchurus would not die here. Retrieving his sword and clenching it between both mitts, Midas strode confidently forward. He would hit Sargon from behind, and together, he and his son would wreak the revenge he had so long desired.

After only two steps, his legs buckled. He dropped to the ground. Anchurus turned, distracted. In that moment, Sargon's sword found the prince's upper arm, cutting a long slice across it. The prince grunted and shuffled away, his gaze still on his father, warm blood dripping off his elbow. Midas struggled and failed to get up. He found his son's eyes and saw the fear in them.

"Behind you!" Midas said.

Anchurus leapt out of the way just as Sargon struck. Now on the edge of the clearing, the prince swayed, panting heavily. Sargon, in contrast, looked as if he were just getting started.

But then Sargon wasn't covered in burns.

Midas tried again to get up.

The no-good bastard of a king was going to kill his son.

Fotis wavered from his position behind the rock tower. He'd followed the other two as closely as he could while remaining undetected. He'd witnessed their failure to rescue the princess and their subsequent capture. Now they stood between two of Sargon's meatiest soldiers, their wrists bound in front of them. Aster's gaze darted about—seeking a way to escape, Fotis was sure. Xander, his tunic stained with a stripe of blood, stared into the distance as if he were still stunned.

When Sargon released his army to attack, the men flowed like a river toward Midas' side of the clearing. Soon, only two guards remained to detain the advisors, two more clinging to Zoe. Fotis breathed a little easier, as the soldiers now focused on fighting their enemy rather than on detaining any stragglers. If he was to help free his colleagues, this was the time, but he had no extra materials with him. All the pouches were gone. Unable to dream up any other viable idea, he resigned himself to the role of observer.

Beyond, the fighting was fierce, men shouting and crying out in pain, dust rising above the clearing where the bodies undulated like a bubbling mass set to boil over a fire. Fotis had hope at first, guessing the armies were well matched. But as the evening progressed and the musician was killed, the boy captured, and the injured prince caught up in a losing battle with Sargon, his hope dissipated. It seemed inevitable that Sargon would emerge victorious.

Xander swayed as if weakened by his wound, though Fotis didn't think he had lost that much blood. Aster had managed to move a little closer to him. Fotis took a few deep breaths, then slowly stood up, shaking the kinks out of his legs. It was folly, what he was about to do, but he couldn't sit and watch anymore. Smoothing his uniform—the one marking him as being from King Midas' side—he started toward the guards.

They paid him no mind at first, their gazes riveted to the battle beyond. Fotis was surprised at how close he got before the nearest one—a chunky, clean-shaven man with a wide backside—finally noticed him and drew his sword.

"Stay back!" he ordered.

Fotis kept walking, Aster's keen gaze upon him. Xander had fallen to his knees.

"I surrender." Fotis raised his hands above his head.

The two guards exchanged glances.

"I'm one of Midas' soldiers," Fotis said. "I am here to be your prisoner."

The chunky guard looked askance at his companion, then shoved the old man with his foot, sending him to the ground in a heap of limbs. "Who is this Midas that his soldiers surrender like cowards?"

"He's not a coward," Xander said in a small voice.

"Shut up." The other soldier, a tall young man with a short beard, pointed his sword at Xander's neck. Xander flinched and ducked his head.

Fotis got back up on his feet. His wooden eye was gone. He scanned the dirt and, failing to find it, addressed the men once more. "Would it not be wiser to let us all go? Then you could join your fellows in the fight."

"Sargon doesn't release prisoners," the chunky guard said.

"Xander?" Zoe called from behind. "Is Father all right?"

"He's fighting, Your Highness." Xander twisted his neck away from the sword's tip.

"Shut her up!" Xander's guard demanded.

"We can't!" one of Zoe's guards said.

"Fighting?" Zoe asked. "Who is he fighting?"

"King Sargon, Your Highness," Xander said. "The prince is trying to help."

"Anchurus!" Zoe exclaimed.

"I said shut her up!" Xander's guard bellowed, poking Xander in the neck.

Zoe's two guards backed their horses a few steps away, pulling the princess with them.

"Xander?" Zoe called. "Are you still there?"

"You shut up," Xander's guard said, pressing the sword far enough into the skin that a thin trail of blood trickled down Xander's neck.

Aster bristled. Fotis squared his shoulders and raised one finger.

"Perhaps we might make a trade," he said. "The sculpture for

King Midas' eldest and most experienced advisor. Which is me." Fotis gestured toward himself. "Imagine which your king would prefer. A golden statue or one who has advised his enemy for years? I have many secrets to reveal. If you think about the situation we find ourselves in, I believe you will agree that this is the best course of action—"

Xander's bearded guard slid off his horse, startling Fotis.

"I apologize if I said something offensive," Fotis said. "I was only making a suggestion."

"I'm tired of your voice," the bearded guard said, storming toward him.

Fotis retreated. "Understandable. Completely understandable. I've been told in the past that my voice can be rather annoying, particularly after a while, and we have been conversing for some time . . ."

Fotis babbled on while the bearded guard pursued him, the remaining guard chuckling at the scene. Aster took advantage of the moment and vaulted into the empty saddle. Using his fingers, he pulled the dagger from his belt and, with a swift motion, threw it into the chunky guard's back. The man drooped forward and fell off his horse.

"Not now, Xander," Aster said. "Get off!"

Xander gazed about, dumbfounded.

"Don't hurry!" Aster said. He searched for another blade and found one tied to the saddle, but there wasn't time to cut the ropes that bound his wrists. Beyond, Zoe's guards were getting away. Aster gripped the reins in his fingers and urged the horse after them.

"Aster!" Fotis called.

Aster looped the reins over his neck and leaned forward, encouraging his mount to move faster as he wriggled the dagger free of its ties. When he got close enough, he flipped it into the back of Zoe's right guard. The man arched, then slumped forward. His horse ran wide, stretching Zoe in between until the rope pulled through the right guard's listless hand. The left guard continued gamely on, the sculpture bouncing along after him. Aster pursued.

They flew down the road between the bench rocks. Hoofbeats rumbled behind him. Aster glanced back to see Xander, a rag doll on the panicked horse's back.

"Don't hang on!" he yelled.

Ahead, the left guard slowed, Zoe's bouncing making his escape difficult. Aster caught up and leapt aboard, abandoning his own horse. He looped his roped wrists around the man's throat, choking him before throwing him off. On the ground, the guard lost hold of the rope, and Zoe fell to the ground. Aster pulled the horse up and went back after the princess.

"We haven't got you, Your Highness," he said as he jumped off and approached. "We're not going to get you out of here."

"Aster?" Zoe asked.

"No," Aster said. He steadied the princess on her feet, then readied himself to lunge. When Xander's horse came near, he used both hands to grab one of the loose reins. The horse pivoted around to face him, Xander bewildered on its back. Using the dagger on Xander's saddle, Aster cut his and Xander's ropes, then gave Xander the line to the princess. "You must not protect her!" he shouted, then leapt back up onto his horse. With a hearty "yah!" he raced the opposite direction, praying to the gods that Fotis was still all right.

He slowed as he approached the area where they'd been detained. He couldn't see the guard or Fotis. Beyond, the hills were only shadows. He eased his horse forward, scanning, listening. He was getting close to the fighting when he noticed the uneven shapes resting a short distance beyond. He pulled the horse to a halt. He didn't want to know. He waited until Xander came up beside him, pulling Zoe along by the rope.

"Fotis?" Xander asked.

Midas' soldiers fought on, shadowed figures dancing in the gray light of dusk, their swords clashing, their groaning cries merging to create a spine-chilling chorus. Aster heaved a heavy sigh, then gently nudged his horse forward, approaching the still lumps in the dirt. The first was the bearded soldier, a small blade no bigger than one's hand sticking out of his neck. The second one . . . Aster squinted his eyes shut.

"I didn't know he carried a blade," Xander said.

Fotis appeared to be looking up at the sky, but when Aster knelt by his side, he found that the old advisor had no more breath coming out of him. He gently closed the one eye, then let his palm rest against the old man's cheek. Behind him, Xander wept.

GET UP, Denisia thought. *Come on, get up!* But King Midas remained in the dirt, crawling forward on his belly toward the fighting men. It was valiant, but it made Denisia angry. He was distracting rather than helping his son, and Anchurus had already suffered another wound because of it. How the prince was managing to stay upright, she didn't know, but Sargon was circling with his tongue resting on his lower lip, playing his game with all the delight of a wild cat.

She fingered the box. What if she did nothing? Sargon would kill the prince. Midas would die. Sargon's army would emerge victorious and take the Zoe sculpture back with them, condemning the princess to live out her life in a golden cage, and the boy would be a slave in Sargon's castle. Gordium would fall, and she would retire to the Isle of Mount Nysa with Silenus, who would remain alert and in possession of all his mental faculties.

If she lifted the curse? But it was too late, and King Midas was too weak. Prince Anchurus would still die, and Silenus would descend back into soft mind.

Rastus helped Midas to his feet and guided him toward the sidelines. Behind them, the boy was still wriggling between his captors, trying to break free, the musician lying dead with his mother mourning over him. The swords clashed again, and Anchurus fell to his knees. Sargon rested his hands on his hips and laughed.

"This is your revenge, mighty Midas?" he asked. "This is what you've planned your whole life?"

Anchurus tried to get up, but when he put weight on his left foot, it buckled and he fell down again. Sargon tossed his sword from one hand to the other. He walked around the prince, readying himself for the kill.

Denisia darted to the right of Midas, set the box on the ground in front of her, and began to chant. As she spoke, she pulled the paper from her breast pocket, but she didn't need it. She'd practiced the words so many times they'd become familiar, odd sounds emanating easily from her throat.

Sargon ignored her at first, but soon she felt his dark gaze upon her. She elevated her voice and continued on. It was almost like she was singing, but there was no tune, only words spoken in rhythm as in a poem, harsh and forceful words she had to push past her teeth, words that required her full breath with each phrase. She reached the end of the second stanza and inhaled. The ground started to tremble.

Anchurus propped himself up, leaning heavily on his sword. Denisia launched into her third stanza. The shaking grew so violent she had to brace herself, bending her knees to avoid toppling over. Sargon took a few steps back toward his men while beyond, the armies continued fighting as if nothing had changed.

The rumbling deepened. Denisia raised her voice. Soon she was shouting over the din of the quake, the earth shifting, debris flying down from the tower behind her. A long crack formed in the ground from north to south. Upon Denisia's last word, it split and separated, the two sides pulling away from one another in a chaotic storm of rocks, thunder, dust, and a deep growl, implying something ominous beneath.

Denisia stumbled back, barely escaping the abyss to land on its west side. Midas was there too, Rastus supporting him. Sargon had moved away to the east. Denisia spotted Anchurus there too, his gait a painful and ungainly one as he disappeared into the throng of enemy soldiers.

The rumbling persisted, the chasm expanding. Men from both sides lost their footing and fell in, screaming, to their deaths. The rest pushed back, trying to save themselves, but many more were sucked into the darkness, some taking advantage of the new situation to force the enemy's men in. The air filled with their cries as they dropped into the unknowable depths, hundreds feeding the new void, its open belly hungry for more with every bit of space it claimed. The horror continued for some time, chaos erupting among the ranks as the men sought refuge in the crowds. Finally, the trembling stopped. Everything went quiet. Her limbs wobbly, Denisia waited and, when nothing happened, remembered there was one more step to take.

She crept toward the canyon's edge, her gaze on Midas. He was supposed to throw his most precious possession into the newly made hole, but he had nothing with him but his sword. Nevertheless, everything Lady Verna had predicted so far had come true. Denisia had to complete the spell. She paused and prepared to read the last paragraphs on the paper.

"King Midas," Katiah shouted.

Denisia jerked her head to see the dark goddess emerge from a nearby rock on Midas' side. She gestured Denisia's direction.

"Thanks to my glorious sister, your day of reckoning has come!"

CHAPTER TWENTY-SIX

Anchurus saw Rastus pull his father to safety. Sargon had moved a few steps away, his attention on the strange chasm forming beyond. Denisia was there, chanting words Anchurus didn't recognize. A magical spell. For what purpose he couldn't tell, but it gave him an opportunity.

He forced himself to stand. It took all his strength not to cry out at the searing pain, his feet wet from the weeping wounds inside his boots. He pulled the last mushroom from his pocket, swallowed it, and struggled to clear his vision. A dark void formed between the armies, widening each time Denisia raised her voice. She stood on the other side of it, near Midas and Rastus. Anchurus searched behind him, trying to find Zoe, but he couldn't see her. Torment overwhelmed his lower body as he walked forward, pushing past Sargon's men. Most had paused their fighting, confused about how to proceed with the earth coming apart only a few steps away. Anchurus looked back, his sense of alarm growing as the chasm expanded, more and more black space opening up between him and his father.

When the rumbling finally stopped, Anchurus saw Katiah

descend on the king. *Now what would she do?* He had to get over there somehow. He cast his gaze around and spotted Ambrose only a few steps away. A river of relief poured through him. He uttered a low-pitched whistle, the one he'd always used to call the horse. Sharp ears pricked forward.

"That's it," Anchurus whispered. "Come on." He approached carefully, his foot strikes sending so much pain through his legs it made him sick to his stomach. He whistled again, a short two-toned call. Ambrose was clearly nervous, his head up as the ground cracked and shifted beyond, rocks and trees tumbling into the chasm. Anchurus kept walking, all the while talking in a soothing voice. When he reached the stallion, he gathered the reins and leaned gratefully against the animal's neck, patting and stroking the smooth hide.

"Good boy, Ambrose. Good boy." He rested a moment, inhaling Ambrose's musky scent. Katiah was saying something, but he couldn't quite make out all her words. He had to get off his feet. He took hold of the saddle's edges and began to lift himself up. The world spun around him, his body a sizzling fire. He squeezed his eyes shut. When he reopened them, he was aboard. He settled himself on the stallion's back and pulled taut the reins.

Across the clearing to the north, he spotted movement. Two figures on horseback lingered beyond Sargon's men. He squinted. It appeared Zoe's sculpture was suspended between them. Both of them wore the enemy's uniform, but they had removed their helmets. The chubby one resembled Xander. Xander, in the midst of battle! The other looked like Aster, though it was impossible to be certain from this distance. He watched them, wondering if the advisors had reclaimed the princess. It would be a miracle. Yet they, like him, were trapped on the wrong side of the abyss.

Across the divide, Midas was on his feet. Denisia hesitated, as if uncertain what to do next. The prince felt a moment's pity for her. He didn't know how creating a canyon between the two armies would help, but at least it had paused the fighting and given him a little more time. Without the interruption, he imagined Sargon would have killed him by now, leaving Midas to suffer the dark king's fury. He regarded the enemy's soldiers. Those at the front of the lines had fallen back, their gazes on their king, awaiting his order. On King Midas' side, it was much the same.

Anchurus looked longingly toward the princess. He wished he might speak to her once more. *They will figure out a way*, he wanted to tell her. *They will save you.* He watched her guards' faces. He thought the one who resembled Xander was shaking his head. Strange, but he felt the advisor's message was for him. No matter. He returned his attention to the clearing and eased Ambrose forward.

His chance would come. He had to be ready.

WITH RASTUS' help, Midas clumsily maneuvered his sword into its scabbard and then turned to see Denisia watching him. Her red hair had fallen loose, the soldier's uniform too big for her small frame. Her gaze darted across the chasm, then back to a parchment she held in her hands, then across the chasm once more.

Katiah stood next to her, glaring at Midas with a haughty expression. She appeared to be enjoying it all, her dark eyes alight with eagerness.

The king remained on his feet only because Rastus supported him, but it didn't matter now. He'd left his pride behind and stood the frail and broken man he was before the being who had saved him so many years before. For a moment, he remembered her as she had been then, his heroine. His safe harbor.

"I still remember the first time you appeared to me," he said. "I thought I'd gone to the afterworld. But you delivered me to the kind old people in the mountains. Told me I had a great destiny." He looked into her dark eyes. "You saved my life."

She lifted her chin, angling her face away as if nothing he said affected her.

"I'm sorry, Katiah. I should have treated you better. It is because of you that I am who I am today."

Beyond the sounds of fighting resumed, the chasm having left some of Midas' men on Sargon's side and vice versa. Soldiers got into small skirmishes, more falling into the depths, their cries a dismal accompaniment to the scene playing out in the clearing.

"Your destiny awaits you," Katiah said. She gestured toward her sister. Denisia returned her gaze to her parchment, her hands trembling. As the earth cracked and moaned, she stepped forward and began to read, elevating her voice so that those around her could hear.

"The chasm as opened stands ready to receive
Your sins all forgiven, your woes to relieve
Into its long mouth the sinner must throw
His most precious thing come from now, long ago
And should he mistake his true feelings and free
A possession not qualified as what it must be
The chasm will grow till the sinner relents
And into the dark throws the thing that was meant.
Only three tries will he have to succeed,
And if on the third try seeks to deceive,
All that he loves shall be sucked down below
Never again for the wide world to know."

Lightning struck the center of the canyon. They all jumped back, retreating until the sky calmed. Denisia tucked the paper inside her jacket.

"Your most precious possession," Katiah said with a smirk on her lips. "You must produce it, and all will be well."

The king turned to the other goddess.

"Throw your most precious possession into the chasm," Denisia said, "and everything will return to as it was. Before."

"You could have lifted the curse," Midas said.

"It would not have restored everything to as it was," Denisia said.

"As it was?"

"Before." Denisia emphasized the word with a hinting glance across the chasm.

"You have to give it up, Karem." Katiah twisted her finger, and his crown appeared on his head.

Midas took it off and held it in his mitts.

"You wouldn't have it without me," Katiah said. "You should have been grateful."

Midas glanced at Denisia. "As it was."

"Before," she said.

With Rastus' help, Midas walked toward the chasm. The goddesses fell in behind him, all of them cautiously approaching the cliff's edge. Across the blackness, Midas saw his son atop his horse. His heart filled with hope. *Everything as it was.* He looked but couldn't see Zoe. Finally, he grasped the crown in one hand and tossed it in.

At first nothing happened, but then the earth shook again. The deep rock cracked open, new winds circling and diving around them, the space expanding in between. Rows of men vanished as the canyon widened at an even faster pace.

Rastus pulled the king to safety, Katiah and Denisia quickly retreating. Across the way, the boy had broken free of his captors and now sat with Elanur near Emir, the two having drawn his body away from the abyss. Sargon strode up and down the line, trying to reorganize his men.

"Hm," Katiah said. "I guess that wasn't it." She rubbed her chin. "My sister says you have two more tries. Your most precious possession. It wasn't your kingdom. Perhaps . . ." She eyed Sargon across the way. "Your desire for revenge. It has fueled everything, hasn't it?"

Midas contemplated his enemy. Even now, looking at the man, he wanted nothing more than to kill him.

"What would he throw into the chasm for that?" Denisia asked.

"How does one give up the desire for revenge?" Katiah walked back toward the cliff. At first, no one followed her, so she turned and addressed Rastus. "Be a dear and bring the king along," she said to him. Then she called out to Sargon while lifting her hands to the sky. "Darling, care for a brief chat?"

With a wild wind, Sargon was lifted up and over the chasm, then dropped onto Midas' side. He leapt to his feet, bewildered, his hand on his sword.

"Uh-uh-uh," Katiah said, shaking her head. "We need you peaceful for a moment." She twisted her fingers, and Sargon's hands were bound behind his back with a black rope. He struggled but failed to free them. When Midas, Rastus, and Denisia arrived, Katiah once again beseeched the sky.

"Great darkness," she said. "The golden King Midas offers you his desire for revenge." She turned to Midas. "You must say the words."

Midas clenched his fists inside the mitts, longing to press his fingers into his enemy's throat. How delicious it would be to watch the gold flow over him, trapping him forever in an inescapable prison! He walked up to him and for many moments looked into his dark eyes. On the other side of the abyss, Elanur stood, watching. His mother. Murdered. His sister's life. Taken. Her son's life. Wasted. He wanted revenge. He deserved justice! Instead, he forced himself to look at his son lingering in the shadows beyond.

"I release my desire for revenge," he said. "I seek only peace." He turned and nodded to Rastus, who cut the ties that bound Sargon's hands. The dark king rubbed his wrists, his glare fierce upon Midas.

"That's your cue to go, darling." With another twist of her finger, Katiah sent Sargon flying back to the other side. Midas watched him recover there, feeling a new heaviness in his heart. But there was no time to reflect. The earth cracked and moaned, the wind kicked up, and they all had to run back again to avoid falling into the darkness. It wasn't enough. The chasm expanded once more, chasing after them like a demon from the deep, the wind determined to suck them down. It consumed soldiers on both sides, row after row as the canyon grew, insatiable in its appetite. Elanur and the boy tried again to pull Emir's dead body along with them, but they were weary and it was heavy. At the last moment, the chasm snatched it, drawing it into the void. The two scrambled to safety, Elanur clinging to the child. For another many moments, the cries of lost men filled the night until at last, the lightning flashed twice, the thunder cracking deep. Then everything fell silent once more.

Midas dropped to his knees. Rastus went to lift him up, but Midas waved him away. The moans of the men droned on in his ears. He checked to see if Anchurus was still all right, but he could no longer see him among Sargon's men. He turned a dark gaze on Denisia. "This is a trick," he said to her. "There is no absolution. It will take all I have. And then I will die."

Denisia looked nervously from the king's face to the chasm beyond, then pulled out the paper and silently read through it again. Finding no answers, she glanced up at Katiah.

"It isn't working," Katiah said, raising her voice, "because the king is trying to deceive it." She strode forward, hands on her hips, and addressed them all, the kings and soldiers, the prince and princess, bathing in their attention. "The 'golden king' thinks he can escape his punishment. He thinks he can ignore and betray and take all the glory when he's done nothing to deserve it. But dark magic will not be deceived." She turned back to Midas. "You have one more chance to right everything that has gone wrong. Throw into the chasm that which means the most to you. Should you fail, all you have will be lost."

"Which would make you happy, wouldn't it?" Midas spat. "You have desired only to see me suffer."

"Come, Karem," Katiah said. "Will you give up so easily? So many people are counting on you." She gave him a pouting look. "You do have one more chance. What is it you're not telling us?"

Midas hung his head. There was only one thing left, and there was no way he was throwing it into the chasm. He couldn't, anyway. She was on the other side.

Suddenly, a mighty wind erupted around them. Dust flew into his eyes. A powerful blast rocked his body and then quickly passed. He looked up.

Xander and Aster appeared windblown and frightened astride their horses, the Zoe sculpture held suspended between them.

"Father?" the sculpture said.

Midas glared at Katiah.

The dark goddess smiled. "Does this help?"

Midas pushed himself to his feet. When Rastus stepped up to assist him, the king whispered into his ear. Rastus tucked his chin in acknowledgment. Standing close, he received the king's sword and slipped it under his cloak. Midas loosened the mitts, undoing the latches on his wrists, then whirled and strode toward Katiah. Around him, the soldiers had stilled, the fighting halted. With the sun now gone over the horizon, darkness was taking over. Katiah's outfit, with its ever-present moonlit glow, attracted everyone's attention to her.

"This is not happening," the king said to her.

"Father?" Zoe said.

"Do you hear me?" Midas stopped in front of the dark goddess. She smirked in return. Behind her, Denisia still held the paper in her hands, her head twitching like a bird's as she took in her surroundings, her features etched with worry.

"I will go in," Midas said. "Me. That's it. Nothing else!" He glared at the dark goddess and Denisia in turn, then clenched his fists and stormed toward the abyss.

"Your Majesty," Rastus said. "Wait."

"Father," Zoe called. "Xander, what's going on?"

"Your father is walking toward the chasm," Xander said.

"Get me up there!" Zoe commanded. "He will not accomplish anything by throwing himself in."

"She's right, you know," Katiah called. "Your death will change nothing."

Midas kept walking, Rastus close behind him. "Your Majesty, please reconsider," the commander said loudly enough for the others to hear. "This cannot be the right decision."

"You don't know what the right damn decision is," Midas said.

"I know you are not the most precious thing to you, Your Majesty," Rastus shouted. "This won't work."

"It's the only way to get *her* to back off!" Midas pointed an accusing mitt at Katiah.

"Xander, hurry!" Zoe urged. "I demand it!"

The two advisors rode forward with the princess suspended between them.

"You are not doing this." Midas whirled and glared at them. "Where is Fotis? He'll listen to sense."

Neither advisor met his gaze.

"Where is he?"

"He did not give up his life for the princess, Your Majesty," Aster said.

A scowl formed on Midas' face, the skin wrinkling around his eyes. He scanned the area as if imagining the old man would pop up and surprise them all. But where there had been three advisors before, now there were only two.

"What's the matter, darling?" Katiah said, catching up. "A little frustrated?"

"Xander, what's happening?" Zoe asked.

"Get her back," Midas ordered.

"I don't want to live like this," Zoe said. "Father, if I can lift this curse, you must let me."

"She's right, Your Majesty," Denisia said, coming up behind Katiah. "Generations will be affected. Think of your people."

"You're lecturing me?" Midas shouted at her. Denisia stepped back, a startled look on her face. "I was kind to you," Midas said. "To your grandfather. This is how you repay me?" His eyes were wet, his cheeks red with rage.

"It was your wish," Denisia said quietly.

Midas' shoulders tensed. He raised his hand to strike her.

"Father," Zoe said. "Please. It will secure Gordium. Keep our people safe. Let my existence mean something."

"Mean something?" Midas turned to the golden sculpture that

was his daughter, his expression melting as he lowered his hand. "My girl, you mean everything. You are the heart of Gordium. You bring light to all the people's lives. The city would be nothing without you."

"I can't go back like this."

"You can! You have your voice. You have your good heart. You will find your way."

The breeze sounded a whistle from low in the chasm, the darkness deepening with every passing moment, the air growing colder around them. "Xander," Zoe said, "I order you to push me in."

"Take her anywhere near that cliff and you will go in with her," Midas said with a stony glare.

"It's the only way, Father."

Xander sat with drooped shoulders, dried blood on his tunic, tears flowing down his chubby cheeks. He looked at Denisia, but the goddess had cast her attention elsewhere. From across the chasm, a horse's footsteps approached. Xander turned his head. A look of horror passed over his face.

"*No,*" he whispered.

King Midas followed his gaze. On the other side of the canyon, Anchurus trotted forward.

"No no no." Midas ran for the cliff's edge.

The animal shifted into an easy canter, the prince at home on its back. The two floated toward the chasm, a flame-like glow emanating from the earth as it anticipated their approach. Anchurus' face came into focus in the new light, his jaw set.

"For Zoe, Father!" he said. "For Gordium."

"No!" Midas shouted. "Stop!"

Denisia ran forward. "Anchurus!"

The horse kept coming. Midas reached the edge of the cliff and searched for some way across or around, but of course, there was none. He turned back to Katiah. "Stop him!" he cried.

Katiah met his gaze, but took no action. Rastus laid a hand on his cloak. The horse wasn't going to stop.

"Anchurus!" With Rastus clinging to him, Midas ran south. If he got closer, perhaps. "Anchurus, no. Stop!" He raised one hand into the air and shouted as loud as he could. "Halt!" The wind blew his words back into his face. "Halt! By the command of your king! Anchurus. Stop!"

The prince did not pause. At the final moment, he thrust both hands forward onto the horse's neck, giving it the last bit of encouragement it needed. The ground gave way beneath Ambrose's feet. Airborne, Anchurus looked across the chasm at his father, raised his hand in salute, and then bowed his head. Midas saw him frozen in time, he and the horse held suspended in the air. Then they both fell, the chasm greedily swallowing them until it seemed they had never been there at all.

Denisia screamed.

"No!" Midas reached out, Rastus the only thing keeping him from tumbling forward after his son.

"Father?" Zoe asked. "Xander? What's going on?"

Midas struggled against Rastus' hold, but the commander was too strong and his own body too weak. The king dropped at the chasm's edge, his forehead against the dirt, great sobs wracking his emaciated body as the dark goddess looked on, her own expression a mixture of triumph and grief.

ONCE AGAIN, the ground rumbled and roared, the depths shifting and heaving with new movement from below. Rocks loosened and fell, trees cracking and collapsing as new dust filled the air. Then, with a mighty surge, the earth began to move. The soldiers shuffled backward, anticipating another widening of the chasm. Xander and Aster just managed to hang on to Zoe in their retreat. Rastus grabbed the king and pulled him back, Katiah moving with them. Denisia stood numb at the edge of the cliff, allowing the tremors to toss her where they would. Eventually, she lost her footing and fell, and there she stayed, her legs splayed in front of her. More rocks tumbled down, trees bending, their branches snapping as the two sides of the canyon lumbered toward one another.

In the midst of the chaos, Midas stood up and, with his back to Katiah, pulled the mitts from his hands. He gave Rastus a curt nod. The commander took the mitts in exchange for the sword. Midas clenched the hilt against his palms and watched as the golden color swept over the blade like butter.

"Look at that," Katiah said. "You did it."

She was coming up behind him, her voice sounding closer over the rumbles in the earth.

"Well, in truth, your son did it for you. But you can be proud."

Midas turned, gripping the sword behind his back. It grew heavier as it changed, pulling on his shoulders. In front of him stood the beautiful woman who had saved him on the flatlands, the one who had comforted him when no one else could. Despite the uncertain ground at her feet, she moved gracefully, her steps confident even as the wind tried to push her into retreat. Her gaze was haughty and distant, but as she got closer, her expression softened.

Midas' stomach twisted. Katiah, his savior. He felt a moment's regret. Then, gripping the sword with both hands, he used the last of his strength to stab the dark goddess through the belly.

A powerful vibration came back through his arms. Unable to hold on, he let go. The sword remained embedded in Katiah's stomach, the tip extending out her back. She stared at the golden blade. Tenderly, she cupped her hands around the hilt.

"You kept it," she whispered. "The one I gave you when you went to King Gordius the first time. You kept it." She lifted her gaze to him, her eyes searching his face.

Midas breathed heavily, swaying on unsteady feet as the chasm behind him continued to close. A thunderous roar bellowed from below and blasted out with a gust of wind that nearly blew him over. Dust swirled about as the gold spread from Katiah's abdomen to her flanks and hips. She gaped at her own body, her expression morphing to one of fear. At one point, she grabbed the sword and tried to pull it out, but it remained embedded in her body, the gold now flowing over her breasts and onto her thighs.

"No." She looked down in horror, then up at the king, her black eyes pleading. "What have you done? Karem?" Like a flooding river, the gold covered her neck and face and drained down into her feet, hiding the living person in a metal prison. In a blink, it was over, the sculpture standing rigid with the sword through the middle, the eyes staring at the king with grief-stricken surprise.

With a mighty crack and boom, the ground collided with itself, a last swell of wind pushing past them in a gale, the very sky seeming to suck it up and out until it disappeared above the clouds. Amidst a finishing storm of falling rocks and dirt, the earth settled once again into a single entity, leaving behind only a long, dark scar to indicate that anything had ever happened. Midas blinked dust out of his eyes and stared at the goddess. He waited for her to wake up and strike him with some death-giving blow. But as the valley quieted down, it became clear that the gold had embraced her. She lay quiet, encased in its glimmering shell, as if she'd become the monument she had always desired he build for her.

"Father!"

Midas turned, then realized with a start that he was holding on to Rastus. But Rastus hadn't turned into a sculpture. Instead, he stood looking somewhere beyond, not even realizing the danger he was in. Midas followed his gaze. Someone was coming toward him in the distance, a slight figure with long blonde hair.

"Father!"

She ran into his arms and embraced him, her small head pressed against his neck. He inhaled her nearness, her sweet scent returned. Trembling, he began to cautiously return the embrace, tears flowing down his face as he searched the land between what remained of the two armies. He dared to wish perhaps there might be more, but the chasm had sealed shut, Denisia sprawled nearby like a discarded doll, the crack in the earth a silent grave.

CHAPTER TWENTY-SEVEN

Three moon cycles after the great Battle of Karama, Denisia walked through the city of Gordium with her head down, a linen scarf covering her hair, a dark cloak obscuring her figure. She treaded the same roads she'd taken when she'd come searching for her grandfather. It seemed long ago. Back then, she'd been on her way to the castle. This time, she had a different destination in mind.

Silenus was still on the island. She thought of him with a twinge of anxiety, but she had left him in good hands. Five of his followers, along with a changing guard of Nysiades, had committed to his constant care, creating a schedule so he would never be alone. Already he had voiced his complaints loud and long, but she had only nodded and smiled. Yes, the young girl could be irritating. And the chubby boy smelled like body sweat and lamb fat. She listened to it all and then told him it was the way it must be. She told him this again and again, but every night she lay in bed unable to sleep because of her seething rage.

Everything had gone wrong. So very wrong. Silenus' illness had resurfaced with a vengeance. He was worse than before. Anchurus had not been healed, but instead had been killed. Things had not returned to "as they were."

And that meant someone had lied.

She picked up her pace, sensing that she was getting closer. No one paid her any mind, the cover of darkness aiding in her desire to remain anonymous. She was a solitary figure walking down the road, eyeing the families gathered near their dwellings, children helping their mothers, fathers telling stories around crackling fireplaces. One mother called her three sons in. They ran across in front of Denisia, shouting and laughing as they went. Might she and the prince have had children? It wasn't something she had thought about before. She did now. One more thing she had been robbed of. One more reason she deserved justice.

She turned down a side road and slowed, fingering the dagger at her belt. It had a stout blade with a staghorn handle. Chetin had made it at her request, though he'd been unable to hide his concern when he'd presented it to her. She didn't owe him an explanation. She was a goddess. He, a mere mortal.

Another turn and she slowed again. Yes. At the end of this narrow alleyway. She saw the bush, but not the cat. The home was dark, but she'd been through this game before. She knocked three times. When no one answered, she pressed her palm flat against the wooden door. Closing her eyes, she inhaled and pulled the energy from the fibers. Within moments, they aged, turned brittle, and contracted. When she opened her eyes again, the door was thin and fragile. She leaned her weight against it. It easily gave way.

Inside, it was near black. She retrieved a candle from under her cloak, along with a tinderbox. When she lit it, she saw the witch staring at her from the other side of the room.

"Lady Verna," she said. "It's rude not to open the door when a goddess comes calling."

The old woman sat in a small chair. She wore a simple brown robe. Her feet were bare.

"Nor is it polite not to speak to a guest," Denisia said.

The witch said nothing.

Setting the candle on the table where Lady Verna had given her the box, Denisia looked around. Soon she spotted other candles, so she used hers to light those until the room glowed yellow. Lady Verna watched with hollow eyes.

"You saved my life once," Denisia said. "But you said a price had to be paid. That price was my grandfather's mind." She put her original candle back on the table and glared at the woman. "What is the price for a life that is lost? Answer me!"

The woman met her gaze but didn't speak.

"Do you think your silence will save you?" When the woman still didn't answer, Denisia withdrew her dagger. "Speak, or I will use it."

"You're going to use it anyway," Lady Verna said.

"You have no desire to convince me not to?"

"You will not be convinced."

Denisia had expected an argument. Wanted a fight. Not this passive surrender. "You said everything would go back to how it was. You lied."

"You asked for a way to make things right," Lady Verna said. "I gave you one."

"It didn't make things right," Denisia said. "He died!"

"The king survived," Lady Verna said. "He rules Gordium once again with the princess, alive and well, by his side. There is peace between the two kingdoms, an outcome that might please anyone, particularly a prince."

"None of that matters," Denisia said with a toss of her head. "He was the one I wanted to save, and now he's dead."

Lady Verna opened her hands in front of her. "How was I to know what was most precious to the king? You are better acquainted with him than I am. You might think you would have thought of it."

The truth of those words sparked pain in Denisia's breast. "It was *your* magic!"

"Magic belongs to no one," Lady Verna said. "It simply is."

Denisia's arm was shaking, the dagger trembling in her hold.

"You were the one who allowed the dark magic to make your grandfather well," Lady Verna said. "You came asking for help releasing it. I gave it to you."

"You didn't think to be clear about what would happen?" Denisia asked.

"I was as clear as I could be," Lady Verna said. "You know as well as I that the consequences of our spells are not always predictable."

Denisia's face felt hot. The room seemed to close in around her. It was too small, with too many objects cluttered about. Something thunked. She turned to see the cat duck under the drape.

"I should never have saved you," Lady Verna said. "Had I let you die, none of this would have happened. But I took pity on you and Silenus. I will have to pay the price."

Her face seemed a spirit's glowing in the yellow candlelight, her body nothing but bones. Denisia lunged, and, with a scream, plunged the blade into the old woman's chest. It slid in with little effort, thin skin and muscle easily giving way. The woman tensed, then her body released. She slumped in the chair, her head lolling to one side with a gentle exhale.

Denisia let go of the dagger and stood back. She waited for the woman to wake, but Lady Verna was dead. Her body looked frail, the dagger sticking straight out of it, a little blood seeping into the robe. Denisia shook all over, her skin cold. She hurried out of the dwelling, then ran back up the road and out toward the city gates, never stopping until she came near the guards at the archway. When they let her out, she saw Chetin waiting for her not far away. He helped her up on her horse, and together they galloped back the way they had come, Denisia pushing her mount to its fastest pace.

They had left the city far behind when she heard the wolves. She turned toward the sound, tracing the outline of the forests to the north. *Come to me,* she thought. *You will be mine now.* Sensing their growing nearness, she closed her eyes. A new view opened in front of her, the pines gliding by on either side, her companions galloping on a parallel trek, their dark tails streaming out behind them.

. . .

GORDIUM AWOKE to a beautiful spring day, the sun glimmering over the eastern hills. Down in the market, the traders set up their tables while out in the pastures, the sheepherders moved their stock. Children ran up and down the streets playing and laughing, and out by the Sangarius River, women washed clothes and hauled them back in baskets. Through the air came the smell of fresh bread and cooked meat. Over it all floated the sound of a happy flute playing a tune.

Up in King Midas' castle, Xander smoothed his new robe. It felt soft on his skin, the rich maroon color dazzling. Never had he possessed a garment of such quality and beauty, made by the head seamstress. Aster wore a similar glorious robe, only his had gold threads in the ties and around the collar to designate his new status as lead advisor. The third robe, a white one with gold trim, hung over the chair in the corner waiting to be buried with Fotis' other belongings in the tomb of the advisors. After the goddess' spell, they'd never recovered his body, but his spirit would join those who had served King Gordius and the kings before him, his sacrifice garnering him a place of honor among the kingdom's most elevated defenders.

"It would not have looked good on him," Aster said.

Xander turned to see his friend also admiring the white robe. "He would have appeared a king himself," Xander said.

Aster shook his head in agreement.

"Well." Xander sighed. "We should be going. The ceremony begins shortly."

They walked out of the room together, Aster in the lead, the space in front a hollow emptiness. Fitting, as they were headed to the courtyard where the unveiling of Prince Anchurus' statue would occur. The sculpture would hold a place of honor where everyone who approached would see it. Suitable and appropriate, Fotis might have said. With many of the citizens of Gordium invited, it was bound to be a great celebration. But as Xander descended the stairs behind his friend, a heaviness settled over his chest. The princess was restored and Midas cured, but along with all the soldiers who had sacrificed their lives, there were two very important men missing, their absence a persistent void.

When they reached the first level, Zoe came toward them. She wore a cream-colored gown with delicate folds that caressed her collarbones, gold threads sewn in patterns about her waist and wrists. She walked with three of the new workers in the castle, instructing them, pointing, and then sending them on their way. As she stepped into the lobby, the sun caught the waves in her hair, highlighting the radiant golden hues.

"Good morning!" She grasped Aster's hands first and squeezed, clinging to them longer than usual, her smile warm. Then she turned to Xander. "This is a glorious day for our kingdom."

Xander bowed his head, unable to hold her gaze for long. She had forgiven him for his part in the chaos. Indeed, it seemed she had never blamed him, but he couldn't help but blame himself.

"Father is in the garden," she said. "He wants to see us all."

They followed her out the front doors. Beyond, the great new sculpture towered above them, its base sitting on a mighty platform the workers had used to transport it to the castle, the rest covered in fabrics so the art would remain hidden until the unveiling. Xander squinted as he looked up at it, judging it to be three times the height of a man. How the artists had built it so quickly he didn't know, and he had to admit that part of him was eager to see it. The other part made him turn his gaze away and focus on Aster's shoulder blades instead.

They walked in silence, servants running and chattering all around them. The tables were filling with platters full of food, meats and cheeses and fruits and parsnips and carrots and sweet peas and onions, so much food as to surpass even that which had been prepared for the princess' birthday. Xander remembered that day with a pang of nostalgia. It hadn't been that long ago and yet it seemed like many years. The prince had been so handsome then, but Xander couldn't think of that without remembering the dreadful scene when Anchurus had charged into the dark chasm to be lost forever.

"Don't keep up!" Aster said.

Xander jolted back to the present. He was standing on the path to the garden, the gap between him and the others growing. He hurried forward and returned to his place in line.

Soon the grand hedges rose up beside them, another of the great blessings that the magic had wrought: The gardens had been restored. The air cooled around him as the evergreens soaked up the heat, the dirt soft and giving under his feet. He directed himself to breathe more deeply. He wanted to enjoy every scent as they passed through Blossom Square, the colors dazzling in the bright daylight. They moved past the path that led to the hazelnut orchard, crossed the small bridge, and turned right to make their way toward Rose Field. Beyond, the fig trees seemed to smile from their orderly rows, their fruits little green pouches on the branches. Xander saw a flash of the blackened skeletons they had been, the flames devouring them from the ground up. His breath caught in his throat, but then he saw again their youthful leaves and sighed in relief.

Haluk opened the gate, his presence another reminder that, for the most part, things had returned to normal. Inside, many of the roses were in full bloom, the scents so heady that Xander could almost taste the petals. Beyond, the king sat on the bench wearing his most elegant maroon and gold royal robe. The blush had come back to his cheeks and his body had filled out again, but there were more lines around his eyes than there had been before.

"My advisors," he said, opening his hands to them and then resting his forearms on his knees. "I've brought you here because I have an important task for you."

Zoe moved to the king's side, the advisors bowing and then standing in front of him.

"The kingdom is secure," Midas said. "Our soldiers have begun again to train. They will be ready should Sargon decide to attack, though I believe his interests lie elsewhere now." He steepled his fingers. “Baran is preparing a new group of elite soldiers equipped to carry out secret operations.”

“Like rescuing Aunt Elanur,” Zoe said.

A shadow passed over Midas’ face. The king’s sister was assumed back in Sargon’s hands as she had been before the curse. After everything, she still remained a prisoner.

“Princess Zoe will have a group of engineers at her disposal,” the king continued, “to create new weapons, armor, and other tools with which to maintain our superior defenses. In these ways and more, we will ensure the safety of our kingdom. But there remains one concern.”

“The great king defeated the dark goddess,” Xander said, assuming the king’s meaning. “She is locked in the tomb underground.”

“She is not encased in gold,” Aster added, referring to the one piece of magic that had remained after the curse had been broken, an anomaly attributed to the unique way a goddess’ powers may affect another goddess.

“Yes,” King Midas said, “but we must not doubt her influence on her followers. She has servants who, at this very moment, are likely planning to secure her release.”

The dark goddess. Returned. Xander shuddered at the thought. He had escaped with his soul. He didn’t wish to imagine it at risk again.

“And there is the situation with Katiah’s sister,” Midas said.

“But Denisia would have no reason to wish us harm, would she?” Xander asked.

Midas glanced at Zoe.

“It is rumored that the dark goddess’ beasts now answer to Denisia,” she said.

“The wolves?” Xander asked. When Zoe nodded, he shuddered again.

“Whatever happens, we must not be caught unprepared,” King Midas said. “Find a way to ensure that Katiah does not escape. Then come up with something we can use against Denisia, should we need to."

The advisors exchanged glances.

"The sea is not deep," Aster said.

Xander shook his head. "We throw Katiah out to sea and we'd make it easier for her followers to raise her." He crossed his arms over his chest. "I summoned her with a spell. Perhaps there is one that would block anyone else from summoning her?"

"We'll need as many safeguards as possible," Midas said. "What about Denisia?"

Aster raised his eyebrows. "We are well prepared to discuss potential defenses against her powers."

"Do you really think she'd attack us?" Xander said.

"She didn't get what she wanted," Midas said. "That means she's an unhappy goddess. And unhappy goddesses tend to turn their desires for revenge upon men."

"Not again." Xander rubbed his forehead.

"Indeed." Midas stood up. "It is as it is. Our obligation is to the people. The kingdom of Phrygia must remain safe." He paused, lost in his thoughts for a moment. "I'll expect a better proposal on both fronts in three days." He looked them up and down. "You certainly *appear* to be capable," he said, referring to their new robes. He gave them a mischievous smirk, then walked past them. Zoe took his arm, and they both headed back toward the gate.

Xander's mind raced with worries. Denisia with the wolves? The last time he'd seen her, she'd been sitting at the edge of the closing chasm, slumped and defeated in the dirt. He didn't know what had happened to her after that. No one knew what had happened after that. Everything had gone dark, and then they'd all awoken back in Gordium as if nothing unusual had occurred at all. Except Fotis was gone, and Prince Anchurus was gone, and none of the soldiers who had perished had returned.

"Xander?" Aster stood at the gate.

Xander hurried to join him, then settled in beside his friend as they walked back to the castle. "We tried this before," he said. "You can't defeat a goddess."

"The king did not defeat one," Aster said.

Xander replayed the scene when King Midas had stabbed Katiah with his sword. "The king no longer has the touch of gold."

"The gods are not numerous," Aster said.

"That didn't work out so well last time," Xander said.

"It is not possible there are other solutions. And we must not come up with something in three days."

"Yes, or we will lose our heads," Xander said in a mocking tone. "Aster, do you think there will ever come a time when we won't have to worry about being executed?"

"Of course not," Aster said.

"When will that be?" Xander said.

"Not after we are executed," Aster said with a wry smile.

Xander sighed. "Very funny."

Sargon rode through the castle gates and out into the city of Durukin. The sun shined warmly on the eastern horizon, the air alive with birdsong. It was early, but the sound of iron clanging against stone drummed a steady beat as the workers made progress on his monuments. He thought again about how he didn't need to go. This was a job his guards could handle on their own. It was demeaning, perhaps, for him to accompany them. But he couldn't help it. He had to see her face one more time.

He squinted in the light as they took the main road down the hill. Only a few people traversed it this early, mostly young men carrying the rewards of their morning hunts back to their dwellings. They bowed as the king passed and hurried on, none too eager to receive any of his attention. On either side of the road rested the homes built for the highest servants of the king, stone and wood shelters of significantly better quality than most of the rest in the city. Certainly better than the servants' quarters in Kalhu, where his father had reigned. Sargon and his men didn't have far to go to reach the one that was hers, the one he'd granted her after the Battle of Karama.

He pulled his piebald to a stop and waited. One of the two guards, a tall one with two missing front teeth, dismounted and banged his fist on the door. It rattled under the force. When Elanur opened it, she was dressed in the same poor clothes she always wore, her hair done up in a sloppy bun and covered with a scarf. She gazed upon them without fear and bowed to the king.

"By decree of the great King Sargon II," the toothless guard said, "you are free to go. You have one day to leave this place."

Elanur centered her gaze on Sargon. He waited, wondering what she would do, all the while memorizing her face, her eyes, and the curve of her chin.

"The great King Sargon II decrees you should take this with you." The guard handed her something wrapped in red deer hide.

Elanur stared at it, then glanced at Sargon once again.

"It was Emir's," he said. "He left it in his quarters when he . . ." He almost said *deserted*, but then thought better of it.

He expected she would respond, acknowledge his graciousness. Instead, she took the package, stepped inside the door, cast her gaze about, then snatched a bag she had already packed. Stepping out once more, she pulled the door closed behind her, then hurried down the walk toward the road. Sargon watched her back, certain she would turn to lay eyes on him once more, but she did not. Heat pulsed up his neck. He could run her down. Demand she open the package. Then kill her right there. That would teach her to be so defiant. But he waited until her figure had grown too small to follow, then turned his horse around and headed back to the castle. It would soon be feeding time for the lions. And from what the caretakers had told him, Zehra was pregnant. Something to celebrate.

The guards followed him up the hill. At the castle gates, he paused to glance back. His monuments were taking shape. He could see from where he stood that they'd almost completed the face on the right. Katiah had been correct. He did have a strong nose. They'd positioned him gazing west, toward his enemy, a design he had approved when he'd planned victory over Gordium. Now he wished he could turn it around so that it gazed south and east, for his future kingdom would take shape in that direction. But it was too late. Too much wasted time and materials. He would leave it as it was, his likeness staring across the lands at his old enemy. A reminder of what had been, perhaps. The persistent nightmares, the dashed dreams of love, the sweet victory snatched, the death of his son. Now that he'd released Elanur, all of it was over. He wished to be rid of it. It was time to move on.

He rode through the gates, his piebald tossing his head. The guards bowed low. He barked at them to move. They rushed to close the gate behind him. He continued toward his castle, thinking about the sculpture up in the tower. Perhaps he would finish it now. He'd memorized her features well enough. He saw himself carving the details into the stone, capturing the curve of her neck and the plush flesh in her lips. Her gaze would be cast upward as it always was when she'd looked at him. But as he dismounted and handed the reins to the stable boy, he knew he would never step foot near the sculpture again. It would remain unfinished, forever awaiting his return.

When King Midas emerged from the gardens, Rastus was waiting with five other members of the king's guard. They all fell in step around Midas, officially escorting him and the princess back to the unveiling. Beyond had gathered a great crowd, the citizens who had been allowed through the gates now clustering about the hidden sculpture, their faces upturned in excited anticipation. A horn sounded and everyone came together: the king, the princess, his advisors, Rastus, Baran and all the commanders, Pilar and her kitchen workers, and Timon and his company, all of them surrounded by soldiers and castle servants. The king stepped onto the pedestal by the veiled sculpture and held up his hands, silencing the crowd. When they had stilled, he looked out at them all, his gaze reaching far into the back and beyond, toward the city.

"People of Gordium," he said in his biggest voice. "We have gathered to pay tribute not only to one man but to all of you who have sacrificed to make this city the heart of Phrygia that it is. We gather to celebrate what we have accomplished and to mourn those we have lost. And I announce to you today one other very important thing: there will be no more unnecessary wars."

The crowd broke into robust applause, clapping and cheering so loudly that the king had to wait until they had calmed down to speak again. "From now on," he continued, "we fight to defend our kingdom. We fight when the threat to our borders grows great. But we no longer ride out seeking battle." He saw the image of his son flash before his eyes, Prince Anchurus sitting proudly atop Ambrose as he led the men out of the castle grounds and beyond. How many times had he sent him out, and for what? His throat swelled. He waited until he could swallow again. "We will not look to war to seek glory, but to our people and our accomplishments within. Our citizens will be safe, but no longer sacrificed."

More clapping and cheering. Midas used the time to steel himself. He had to stay strong for just a few more moments. The people calmed once again. He spotted a young child in the front, a boy. It wasn't *the boy*, but the sight gave him a start. He felt anew the pain at the boy's disappearance. "And now," he went on, "I'm pleased to present what you all have been so eager to see. Our artists have been working day and night. We acknowledge their dedication." He gestured to his right where stood the seven men who had worked together on the sculpture, along with the many servants who had transported it to the castle. The crowd responded with a polite applause.

"People of Gordium," Midas said, "I give to you with pride our homage to our prince, the leader of our fighting force, the man who . . ." He had to stop. His voice was trembling. He exhaled and tried again. "Over the years, this man expanded our kingdom far beyond what we could have dreamed it would be." He stopped again. He was going to say more, recount his son's glorious deeds, his bravery and courage, his talent at the harp and any other musical instrument he chose to play. He was going to tell them how the boy's thoughtful nature had come from the queen and his stout heart from his grandmother, but his throat had pinched tight and would not relax. Realizing this was one battle he would not win, he surrendered. "Today, we honor my son, Prince Anchurus."

The seven artists surrounded the sculpture, their hands on the ropes. At the king's gesture, they all pulled together. The coverings fell in fluttering waves. In their place stood the bronze form of Prince Anchurus atop the mighty Ambrose. He was dressed in full uniform and riding out to battle, his back straight, his gaze pointed toward the horizon. Ambrose's front foot lifted high with an energetic step, his neck bowed to his master's hand, his long tail lashing to the left. Prince Anchurus held the reins between two fingers as he always had, his features strikingly correct, even his eyes somehow emanating the gentle authority he'd always carried.

The crowd gasped and moaned, and after the surprise had lifted, they clapped and cheered, but Midas barely heard them. Towering above him rose his son as he should have been, elevated, celebrated, and honored, the ruler Gordium should have been able to look forward to. Midas dropped his gaze, his eyes stinging, his chest tight. He hadn't expected it to be this good. It seemed as if Anchurus would come to life, look down on him and speak in the direct way he always had. Midas clenched his teeth, a swell of emotion threatening to possess him in its wave.

A warm hand slid inside his. He turned to see Zoe's eyes also glazed in tears. He put his arm around her waist, and they stood together for a long time, the sun beaming warm on their skin. A reverent silence consumed the courtyard, everyone sensing the gravity of the moment. Some of the citizens wiped their faces, their tears showing the love they'd felt for the prince. The soldiers stood at attention, gazing upward toward the likeness of their leader.

The whole valley seemed to still, even the birds respecting the moment.

Finally, King Midas glanced at Rastus. The commander turned to the crowd, extended his hands, and announced it was time to eat. The people dispersed, all of them drifting off to one table or another. The quiet lingered for a few moments, but gradually conversations began again, the air filling with the buzz of human voices.

Midas and the princess made their way to the royal table beyond. Zoe welcomed the people who came to greet them, the wealthy lords and ladies, peasants and farmers, and even the servants. Beyond, several children played a game with a ball, while under the shade of the four royal trees, a small band of musicians performed light-hearted tunes that inspired some couples to dance. Above it all, Prince Anchurus gazed toward the horizon, a proud sentinel destined to represent forevermore the courage and pride of Phrygia.

Xander and Aster remained on the walkway in front of the castle stairs. Xander kept his gaze down, his guilt preventing him from admiring the sculpture for long. "I miss Fotis."

"I do not," Aster said.

"What are we ever going to do without him?"

"We will not serve the king," Aster said.

Xander spotted Midas in the crowd. He was following his daughter, his demeanor unusually reserved for such an event. "Do you suppose he will find a new third advisor?"

"A king does not require good advice," Aster said.

"Good advice that we didn't give him."

"Bad advisors are not executed."

Xander rubbed the back of his neck. "We do still have our heads. But now we must find a way to make sure Katiah doesn't escape."

"The easier task will be Denisia," Aster said.

"Denisia with wolves!" A cold chill passed over Xander's shoulders.

"It is a tragedy you no longer have to fear Katiah taking possession of your soul," Aster said.

"Thank the gods," Xander said. "Our king saved me from that."

The two watched King Midas as he and the princess took their seats at the royal table. The servants presented each with a meal. When the king started eating, the advisors made their way toward the food tables themselves. They filled their bowls, meandered to an open patch of grass, and sat on one of the rugs that had been laid out.

"I guess there's no need worrying about it now," Xander said, crossing his legs. "We have a glorious day in front of us."

"And not enough food to eat." Aster dove into his roasted leg of lamb.

Around them, everyone was eating and chatting, the air filled with the happy joy of people gathered together in harmony. Soon, the children had lured the princess away from her meal and convinced her to play a game of catch. Their faces reminded Xander of the boy. No one had seen him since the battle. Some believed Sargon had taken him as a slave. Others feared he may have been killed in the scuffle. Whatever his fate, it seemed they might never know if he had lived or died in all the chaos.

He did his best to put it out of his mind, but after they had eaten their fill and returned to the castle, he couldn't shake the feeling that Prince Anchurus, Fotis, Emir Alkan, and the soldiers hadn't been the only ones lost to the dark magic. As Aster used a slate and rock to ponder the question of Katiah in her tomb, Xander toyed with his herbs and powders, contemplating new combinations. He dared glance at Fotis' area only once, the white robe still resting over the chair as if the old man might come out at any moment and slip it on. Xander imagined him standing there with it draped over his tall body. He could almost hear what Fotis might say.

Quit staring, Xander. I'm not a painting. Get back to work. The king is counting on us.

"And what will *you* do?" Xander mistakenly said it out loud.

Aster looked up, eyebrows raised. He watched Xander's face, then glanced over to Fotis' corner. "I will not consult my parchments," he said in his best Fotis voice. "You could help, you know."

Xander broke out laughing. Soon Aster joined him, the two snickering while outside the window, the sun bathed the castle in golden light, the last of its rays coming to rest on Prince Anchurus' face. As the citizens returned to their homes in the city and the surrounding farms, and the servants performed the last of their duties, from somewhere in the distance came the haunting tones of the harp. Some lifted their heads, hearing the faintest melody, but then it drifted on, as if the song had been stolen from the clouds and now longed to return to their soft embrace, its remnants carried over the air by the wind and then across the waves of the Sangarius River to where the gods dwelled in the great beyond.

EPILOGUE

With weary eyes, Elanur watched the sunset. She sat on a flat rock at the edge of the city of Durukin, her bag with all her possessions at her side. Ten days had passed since Sargon had released her. Ten long days with little food to eat. She'd looked for a way through his guarded perimeter, but every time she got close, one of the soldiers would glare at her and she'd walk on. She'd fully expected Sargon to come after her, but now it seemed he'd let her go. He'd truly let her go.

She wanted to leave Durukin, but she had no horse and no supplies. Gordium was a long journey away. She'd never make it without help. Her only friends were other slaves like herself who possessed no more than she did, often less. She had no one to ask, and no money to pay for transport. Sometimes, the way the soldiers looked at her, she wondered if they would bargain her release for a price, but that was something she couldn't bring herself to do. Now that she was free, she couldn't imagine ever again being a slave to a man. Even for just one night.

The hide-wrapped item bulged in her pocket. She'd examined it tens of times already. That Sargon had thought to give it to her still touched her in a way she didn't understand. Her captor. Her tormentor for all these years. He'd seemed to care nothing for Emir. But when their son had died, she'd noticed his stricken expression. And now there was this.

She set the item in her lap and unfolded the edges to lay bare the small whistle. It was about the size of her thumb. Unfinished, the surface of the oak felt rough to her finger. She traced the lines the carving knife had made, imagining her son bent over and concentrating, his face like stone. He'd hollowed out the center and bored two holes about halfway down. She guessed he'd planned a third but hadn't gotten to it, as there was still room for it. Nor had he completed the mouthpiece, though marks in the wood indicated where it would go. He'd probably planned to come back for it, but then he'd escaped. She'd never gotten the chance to ask him how he'd done it. She glanced at the guard standing about ten steps away and wished she had.

The whistle fit perfectly in the square piece of hide. One her son had made, or had Sargon packaged it? She would never know. Folding the edges over the instrument, she struggled against the lump in her throat, her eyes stinging with more tears.

Someone was coming. She tucked the whistle away and ducked behind a nearby dwelling, peering out. Slaves walked home after a day of work on the king's monument, at least fifty of them. When they had passed, she slid toward the hills to the south, wondering how she might ration her last piece of bread. She didn't get far before having to stop. A line of guards marked the southern perimeter of the city, their dark armor and broad shoulders intimidating, particularly in the fading light of evening. She sighed. There had to be a way out. Katiah had helped her son, it seemed. But at the thought of her, Elanur felt a wave of anger and, right after it, a swell of guilt. What if she had never prayed to the dark goddess? Might her son still be alive?

A single beech tree stood not far away. She walked over to it, dropped her small bag at its base, and sat down, her back against the trunk. The orange colors of the sunset coated the western sky in a sweet syrup. Her brother was somewhere over there in the distance. Like her, he had lost a son. Both of them, grieving. But he had his daughter, his men, and his kingdom. She was alone.

She closed her eyes and had almost fallen asleep when sensed she was being watched. She peered out to see a child staring back at her. Clothed in shabby garments, the dress torn at the hem, she wore a rough remnant of rabbit fur over her shoulders. Thick dark hair covered her head, dry and dirty. Some had been shorn off as if with a dull blade as it appeared in multiple lengths about her ears. Elanur stared, certain she knew this child. This was the boy, the one who had grieved over her son's death. But it wasn't. This wasn't a boy. Was it?

"Child?" she asked. "Is it you?"

The girl pointed west. Elanur looked, but didn't understand. The girl came a step closer and pointed again. No words. Just like the boy.

"You were there?" she asked again.

The girl gestured with more urgency. Gestures like the boy's. Elanur followed her gaze. "Do you want to go that way?" The girl nodded and motioned for Elanur to come. "What is your name?" Elanur asked, but then realized she'd never learned the boy's name.

The girl drew in the dirt what appeared to be a bird.

"Bird?" Elanur asked. The girl cupped her hands as if holding something small. "Small bird?" Elanur asked again. The girl seemed to consider that, then brushed away the drawing and once more pointed west.

"Wasn't it you who was there?" Elanur asked. "At the battle?"

The girl's features softened, her brown eyes intense on Elanur's. After another moment, she took Elanur's hand. The touch was shocking, the small hand against hers. How long since Emir had been that small? Elanur looked into the dark eyes, tracing down to the little nose and chapped lips. The girl tugged on her hand until she stood up.

"All right. I'm coming." Pulling her bag over her shoulder, Elanur straightened her dress and followed. Together, they walked back into the city, the girl moving more quickly now so that Elanur had to nearly run to keep up.

When they reached the more populated areas, she smelled meat cooking. Her stomach stirred. She had eaten only one piece of fruit that day. She longed to stop and savor the scent, but the girl moved at a relentless pace. They traveled across city streets one after the other, passing like shadows between dwellings. The light was growing dim, but the oil lamps were taking over in most locations, so it was still easy to pick their way through. They were within sight of the perimeter guards when the girl suddenly turned right and maneuvered south. Elanur stayed with her, constantly checking to be sure no one was following them.

Her legs had grown weary when they came to a small pen of goats. Some of the animals came over to nibble on the girl's fingers. Elanur approached cautiously, scanning the area but seeing no guards or anyone else. The girl opened the gate and stepped inside. She'd brought her all this way to show her some goats? Elanur kept her bag high to prevent the animals from chewing on it. They moved to the wooden shelter in the back, the goats close behind. One began chewing on the back of Elanur's dress. She whirled around. It stood back, blinking its almond-shaped eyes. Elanur grasped the fabric and hurried after the girl, who was already in the shelter waiting for her. The goats followed. As soon as Elanur entered, the girl shut them out.

Elanur tensed, certain she'd been fooled, but there were no guards. Instead, the girl fiddled with something on a corner table and returned with a lit oil lamp. She set it down nearby, then, with her bare hands, cleared away dirt, manure, and dried grass until she'd revealed a square piece of wood with a round handle. She tried to pull it up, but it was clearly heavy. Elanur stepped up to help her. Between the two of them, they managed to lift it and set it aside.

The opening revealed a deep hole. Elanur peered down and realized she was looking into a tunnel. The girl released the latch on the shelter door, then hurried back and jumped into the hole. Elanur yelped, but when she looked down, the girl was perfectly fine and gesturing wildly for her to follow. One persistent goat pushed the door open with its nose. Elanur had an exciting thought: Had her brother arranged for her escape?

The girl pointed to the side. She meant for the board to be replaced. Of course. They couldn't leave the hole open for someone to discover or for the poor goats to fall through. Elanur handed the lamp down, then grabbed her bag and lowered herself into the opening just as the curious goat came inside. Reaching up, she pulled the board back into place, and then turned to see the girl already walking on, the flame lighting their way.

The space easily accommodated a child, but Elanur had to stoop to avoid hitting her head. The tunnel smelled of damp earth and burned oil. It had been created with care, wooden supports placed at intervals to prevent a cave-in. They traveled for a good while. West, if Elanur sensed correctly. She wondered if Emir had come this way. Had the child shown him as well? She still wasn't certain it was the same child, though she couldn't believe this girl could be anyone else but the boy she had held while they both mourned Emir's loss.

They marked a steady pace until they finally reached a dead end. By the glow of the lamp, Elanur saw a rope ladder hanging down against the wall. The girl handed her the lamp, then climbed up. At the top, she appeared to turn a latch and then pushed. The cover gave way to the deep blue of night above.

Elanur blew out the flame, set the lamp on the ground, then climbed until she once more felt the night air on her face. She paused and looked around. At first, she saw only the shadows of the hills beyond, but then she turned and saw the lights of Durukin. With a jump in her heart, she realized she was right: the girl had gotten her out.

"Did you help my son this way?" she asked as they replaced the tunnel cover. "Emir Alkan? A few moons ago? The one who . . . was killed?"

The girl slapped her hands together, brushing off dirt, then looked away into the night. A somber expression took over her features, her eyes shadows in the deepening dark. At one point, she wiped her cheek with the back of her arm. Then she started walking.

"Wait," Elanur said. "Where are you going?"

The girl pointed west.

"To Gordium?" Elanur asked. "Do you know the way?"

The girl motioned for Elanur to follow. Elanur gazed out at the vast oncoming darkness before her. The journey would be long. She had only the clothes in her bag, along with the one piece of bread and a small amount of water. She could end up starving out there or dying of thirst. "We need supplies!" she called.

But the girl was already far ahead of her. Elanur looked back at the familiar yellow glow of the city. There lived Sargon and his guards. But there, too, was shelter and the comfort of others. In front of her lay darkness and the unknown. But somewhere out there waited King Midas and his beautiful city of Gordium. And the child—for surely it was the same child?—had been there before. With her son.

"Wait!" she called and ran to catch up. *Little Bird. Wait for me.*

THE END

THANK YOU

Thank you for reading *The Curse of King Midas!*

It took me two years to finish this story, from draft one to draft twenty something! I was thrilled to see it in its final form, and even more thrilled that you've read it all the way to the end. :)

Reviews are (ahem) gold to authors. If you've enjoyed reading about King Midas and his world, please consider rating and reviewing the book on Amazon.com, Goodreads.com, or wherever you regularly purchase your books. The review doesn't have to be complicated—just share your honest thoughts about the story. I'd be grateful!

Stay tuned for Book II in The Midas Legacy, coming soon!

Get the scoop on future releases, discounts, deals, and behind-the-scenes insights at www.colleenmstory/newsletter.

ACKNOWLEDGMENTS

I want to thank my friend and colleague, Roger Evans, for saying something to me about writing the story of King Midas. I never would have thought to try it without your suggestion, and it turned out to be one of the most enjoyable stories I've written. Thank you for the idea and for your support of my endeavors.

Next, thank you to all of my beta readers—your feedback was critical to the process of streamlining the plot and characters. Special thanks to Deborah Ludlam, who is an amazing reader, Elizabeth Bauer, Keeya Zieler, and Abigail Smith. Many thanks to my editor, Laura Josephsen, for catching those things I missed.

Damonza design, the cover blew me away. Thank you for knowing how to nail it so well! And I've never had a map before, so thank you to BMR Williams for your speedy and efficient work.

Sending love to my first reader, my mom. I'm so glad you enjoyed this story as it gave me wings to carry it forward. My gratitude to those first readers who graciously gave of their time to read the book and send early reviews. I know how busy you are and I'm so appreciative! Thanks also to friends who jumped in to read early and support the launch. It means a lot to me.

Thank you to my newsletter subscribers—I enjoy sharing this journey with you. Thank you to every reader who's read one of my books and taken the time to leave a review.

Finally, my gratitude to my family and to the source of all that is. I am lucky beyond belief!

ABOUT THE AUTHOR

Photo by Ellibean Photography

Colleen M. Story is a novelist and freelance writer with over 25 years in the creative writing industry. *The Curse of King Midas* is her latest novel and was recognized as a top-ten finalist for the Claymore Award prior to publication. Her previous novels include *The Beached Ones* and *Loreena's Gift*, which was a Foreword Reviews' INDIES Book of the Year Awards winner.

Colleen's series of popular success guides for writers—*Your Writing Matters, Writer Get Noticed!* and *Overwhelmed Writer Rescue*—have all been recognized for their distinction. She frequently serves as a motivational speaker, where she helps attendees remove mental and emotional blocks and tap into their unique creative powers.

A lifelong musician, Colleen plays the French horn in her local symphony and pit orchestras. When not writing, she's exploring the beautiful Pacific Northwest and making up more challenging games for her smart German Shepherd to play.

Find more at colleenmstory.com and writingandwellness.com.

amazon.com/stores/Colleen-M.-Story/author/B016CMG616
x.com/colleen_m_story
linkedin.com/in/colleen-m-story-81408034
instagram.com/colleenmstory
youtube.com/ColleenMStoryteller

CONSIDER THESE OTHER TITLES BY COLLEEN M. STORY

THE BEACHED ONES: Daniel and his younger brother grew up in an abusive home. Daniel escaped. Now an established stunt rider, he intends to go back to rescue his brother. But then one jump goes horribly wrong . . .

"A poignant tale of forgiveness and redemption that reaches beyond the grave. Story deftly weaves the paranormal into this touching and heart-wrenching novel that will have you staying up late to accompany Daniel on his journey to the end."

~Melissa Payne, bestselling author of *The Secrets of Lost Stones* and *A Light in the Forest*

LOREENA'S GIFT: A blind girl's terrifying "gift" allows her to regain her eyesight—but only as she ferries the recently deceased into the afterlife.

"This book sucked me in and I could turn the pages fast enough to see what was going to happen to Loreena next. I really liked how although Loreena is blind she didn't let that defeat her . . . . I absolutely loved this story and I will be on the lookout for future books from Story."

~JBronderBookReviews

OVERWHELMED WRITER RESCUE: Stop drowning in your to-do list and start living a more joyful creative life!

"If you read only one self help book this year – grab this one! It is not just for writers. This book is very motivating and so easy to read quickly."

~Laura's Reading

WRITER GET NOTICED!: Stop feeling invisible and start attracting the attention you deserve!

"[A] Five Star must have in your library . . . . I found her information and self-discovery processes applicable in other aspects of my life as well!"

~Susan Violante, Reader Views

YOUR WRITING MATTERS: You start to wonder if you're wasting your time. Does your writing even matter?

"I wish I'd been able to read this book when I was a beginning writer. . . . It would have helped me vanquish my self-doubts, ignore naysayers, and encouraged me to develop the craft of writing."

~Joe Wisinski for Readers' Favorite

Made in the USA
Monee, IL
21 May 2024

9d5622f0-f979-431f-be74-dd52c9da34c0R01